Some women would kill for it...
Lucinda just wants to lose hers!

"SMART, SASSY, AND SEXY...
ELIZABETH BEVARLY DELIVERS
ROMANTIC COMEDY AT
ITS SPARKLING BEST!"
Teresa Medeiros

"ELIZABETH BEVARLY
KNOWS HOW TO SHOW
READERS A GOOD TIME."
Oakland Press

"BEVARLY'S VIBRANT
CHARACTERS AND PLAYFUL
LANGUAGE MAKE HER...
AN EXCEPTIONALLY
ENGAGING READ."
Publishers Weekly

Whoa, baby.

That face. That incredibly handsome face. The face, when it finally appeared, was, without question, the most arresting face she'd ever seen. Max's mouth was full and sculpted, as if he were in a constant state of readiness to devour a woman alive. And his eyes . . .

Oh, his *eyes*.

His eyes were the smokiest, most turbulent shade of gray she'd ever seen in her life. The moment her gaze connected with his, a hot crackle of something reckless and sharp bolted through Lucy's entire body, and every last scrap of decent thought fled her brain.

Good thing she was speechless, she realized.

Rosemary, however, suffered from no such condition. "Lucy French," she said with a smile, "meet Max Hogan. Looks like you two are going to be roommates for a bit. I hope you can get along."

ELIZABETH BEVARLY

The Ring on Her Finger

AVON BOOKS

An Imprint of HarperCollinsPublishers

This is a work of fiction. Names, characters, places, and incidents are products of the author's imagination or are used fictitiously and are not to be construed as real. Any resemblance to actual events, locales, organizations, or persons, living or dead, is entirely coincidental.

AVON BOOKS
An Imprint of HarperCollins*Publishers*
10 East 53rd Street
New York, New York 10022-5299

First Avon Books paperback printing: January 2003

Avon Trademark Reg. U.S. Pat. Off. and in Other Countries, Marca Registrada, Hecho en U.S.A.
HarperCollins ® is a registered trademark of HarperCollins Publishers Inc.

Printed in the U.S.A.

10 9 8 7 6 5 4 3 2 1

For Jane and Steve McKinley
(and David and Lauren and Chris, too),
who are the epitome of "the good neighbors."
Thanks so much for all the nice things you do.

Acknowledgments

As is always necessary, I must first thank my editor, Lucia Macro, for the astonishing amount of patience and tolerance she has for me. Thanks must also go out to all of the wonderful people who answered questions for me on this book. Thanks to Dennis Ryan for being a scholar and a gentleman, and Irish to boot. (And while I'm at it, thanks for turning me on to UB40 when we were in college, too. I owe you big for that.) Thanks to Jan Scarbrough and Barrett Shaw for being scholars and gentlewomen, and knowledgeable about horses to boot. Thanks to Jim(my) Bevarly for being a scholar and my brother, and knowledgeable about Formula One racing to boot. Any mistakes that may appear in the book are entirely my own and result from my general state of befuddlement.

Thanks, as always, too, to my writing posse—Teresa Hill, Barbara Samuel, and Christie Ridgway—for all the usual things, not the least of which is helping me maintain my sanity. Thanks to Teresa Medeiros for always answering her phone when it's me, even though she has caller-ID and really should know better. And more thanks—and love—to David and Eli, who daily amaze me with their ability to endure all of my odd, writerlike behavior and still not have me committed. All of you mean the world to me. I couldn't get by without any of you. Thanks.

Chapter 1

One might have supposed that the sight of four police cars roaring up to the Wemberley estate, their lights tumbling and sirens wailing, might have captured Lucinda Hollander's attention. Especially since, when it happened, she was gazing out the window, wishing something exciting would happen at Babs and Barclay Wemberley's annual Endsummer Night's Dream masque. So not only did the sight capture her attention, she was grateful for it. The former because of the wish fulfillment angle—certainly it gave her pause to think about what she might wish for in the future—and the latter because it gave her something to focus on besides the conversation going on around her, something she preferred not to focus on, quite frankly, because that conversation focused on, well, her.

What captured even more of Lucinda's attention—and gratitude—was when lots police officers armed with lots of guns began to pour out of those four police cars. Because let's face it: A hundred and fifty adult people dressed as enchanted woodland creatures had nothing on real police officers wielding real guns.

Naturally, the first thing she did upon seeing said police officers—not to mention said guns—was to turn away from the massive Palladian window in the Wemberley ballroom to remark upon the new development to her mother and older sister, who, as they always did at functions like this one, had affixed themselves to Lucinda's sides. This practice was common for Francesca and Antoinetta Hollander, because they always feared that Lucinda might say or do something that would embarrass (read: defame, dishonor, and/or disgrace) the Hollander name throughout Newport, Rhode Island. Not that Lucinda ever *had* said or done anything that would embarrass (read: defame, dishonor, and/or disgrace) the Hollander name throughout Newport, Rhode Island, mind you. But Francesca and Antoinetta—and Lucinda's father and older brother, for that matter—always wanted to make sure, just in case. Affixing themselves to the general vicinity of Lucinda's sides whenever possible—even Richard and Emory Hollander weren't more than a half dozen steps away from her at the moment—seemed the most effective way to do that.

But whatever remark Lucinda had been ready to utter about police officers and guns was halted when she saw that Francesca and Antoinetta were busily chatting with the fourth member of their little conversational party—Mimi Van Meter, also known as Mrs. Wentworth Van Meter. Mr. Van Meter was the newest of Richard Hollander's executive vice presidents at First Union Bank, where he himself was president and CEO. So Lucinda hesitated before speaking up. After all, she didn't want to be rude.

But then she heard what her mother and Antoinetta were busily chatting about with Mrs. Van Meter, and couldn't quite help wondering how she might indeed interrupt—politely, of course—barring whacking one or the other of her family members upside the head with a blunt object. Because they were chatting about their favorite topic under the sun: Why Lucinda Hollander Is an Underachiever. One would think that since they considered her something of an embarrassment (read: defamer, dishonorer, and/or disgracer) to the family, they would discuss anything *except* Why Lucinda Hollander Is an Underachiever. But nooooo. . . . Instead, they always had to be sure everyone in Newport understood that they were aware of the fact that Lucinda Hollander Is an Underachiever, but that the Hollanders, of course, were Not to Blame.

"Well, it's only because she has a different learning pattern, you see," her mother was telling Mrs. Van Meter. "Her teachers never bothered to make allowances for the fact that she simply learned differently from the other children. And, of course, Lucinda would never apply herself to learn new things on her own. She's not the kind to take any sort of initiative. I suppose she is a bit lazy in that regard. She never made good grades at school, but it *wasn't* because she was stupid. Hollanders simply are *not* stupid."

"Hollanders aren't lazy, either," Antoinetta was quick to point out, "at least, the rest of us aren't. Lucinda must have gotten some rogue gene that Emory and I thankfully escaped."

And she'd also gotten the best costume of the three of them this evening, too, Lucinda couldn't help adding to herself, feeling a bit smug in that—mainly because she couldn't feel smug about anything else when it came to family matters. Emory was the academic star, with his Ph.D. in microbiology and his research grant from Johns Hopkins. And Antoinetta was the social standout, with her golden good looks, her sterling personality, and her endless supply of suitors and invitations. But *Lucinda* was dressed most appropriately for the party's theme of "Centaurs and Satyrs and Elves, Oh My," having opted for a wood nymph motif, complete with wispy, white diaphanous gown and flowers woven into her waist-length blond braid and silvery shadow adorning her blue eyes. All modesty aside, it put Richard's clunky gargoyle suit (and Lucinda had politely refrained from pointing out that gargoyles did *not* qualify as woodland creatures, seeing as how they were more urban in nature), and Antoinetta's much-too-revealing fairy costume (or, at least, it would have been revealing, had Antoinetta had something to reveal in that regard) to shame.

So there.

"Oh, don't be silly, Antoinetta," Lucinda's mother was saying now. "There are no rogue genes in the Hollander DNA. The Hollander DNA is extremely well established, not to mention flawless. Lucinda has a different learning pattern, that's all. And she never takes the initiative."

Antoinetta nodded after realizing her gaffe. "Different learning pattern," she repeated dutifully. "That's what she has. Though, honestly, try convincing some people of that. Did you know," she told Mrs. Van Meter, "that we once had a teacher suggest to us that Lucinda might be dyslexic?" She emitted a sound that was part gasp, part chuckle. "Dyslexic! A Hollander! Can you imagine?"

Francesca squeezed her eyes shut tight and shuddered visibly. "And I'm sure I don't have to tell you what Mr. Hollander had to say about *that*," she told the other woman. "Because, of course, Hollanders simply are not dyslexic. No one else in the family has ever been dyslexic. There's no way Lucinda could be. She just has a different learning pattern. She never takes the initiative." With an eloquent roll of her eyes, she concluded—lest Mrs. Van Meter had missed it the first time— "Lucinda couldn't be dyslexic. She's a Hollander."

Lucinda sighed to herself and did her best to tune out the complaints of her mother and sister—they were, after all, the same sort of comments she had heard her entire life, and were therefore easy to tune out. She knew, of course, that she wasn't dyslexic. She was, after all, a Hollander. But she wasn't lazy, either, even if she didn't ever take the initiative. If she'd had trouble at school while she was growing up, it was only because . . . because . . . because . . .

Well, because she hadn't found it interesting, that was all. Learning had bored her silly. She would much rather have been painting or sketching instead of being cooped up in a classroom, required to learn things that didn't appeal to her and learn them in a way that worked for other students, but not for her. Lucinda enjoyed the visible aspects of the world. She liked pictures. She enjoyed learning from pictures— she'd been a whiz at absorbing knowledge with visual aids. And she especially liked creating her own pictures. The written word just didn't intrigue her, that was all. She was a picture person, not a word person. She wasn't dyslexic. She simply had a different learning pattern.

And since her mother and sister were far too busy hammering that fact home to a total stranger to learn about police officers and guns, Lucinda decided to search for her escort for the evening, Archie Conlon. Archie, she was certain, would be interested in the goings-on outside. He enjoyed visuals as much as Lucinda did. And *he* wasn't dyslexic.

So there.

She was particularly proud of Archie, because he was a *real* suitor, one she had found all by herself, and not one arranged by her father with one of the obsequious sons of one of his obsequious VPs at the bank. In fact, Archie Conlon had been Lucinda Hollander's bona fide beau for almost six months *in a row*, ever since she had run into him—quite literally, because they had both ended up liberally spattered with hummus in the buffet line—at the fund-raiser her mother had arranged for the Independent Dance Group of Inner Toledo, or IDGIT, as it was more familiarly known. And even if Lucinda and Archie hadn't quite generated an incendiary bonfire of passion together—or even a little Cub Scout stick fire of zest, for that matter—she had high hopes that the two of them would ignite a spark of, um . . . something, ah . . . substantial together. Soon.

But as she searched for Archie in the Wemberley ballroom, she realized that he was nowhere to be found. Which was more remarkable than the police officers and guns outside, because where Lucinda had dressed appropriately for the party's theme—as she had *told* Archie she would be dressing—he had, for some unfathomable reason, opted for a perfectly re-created Bozo the Clown, right down to the mammoth red shoes and colossal orange hair that, honestly, could put a person's eye out if he wasn't more careful.

She still wasn't sure how he had come to associate Bozo with woodland creatures, and it was probably better not to ask. There was such a thing as too much knowledge, after all.

Of course, that wasn't something anyone in Newport, Rhode Island, would ever accuse Lucinda Hollander of having, was it? No, people in Newport, she knew, had two opinions where she was concerned: Some thought her an idle, conceited, standoffish (and not particularly bright) heiress, while others considered her to be an idle, timid, unobtrusive (and not particularly bright) heiress. All because she simply had a different learning pattern and would never take the initiative.

Some people, Lucinda thought, were just too judgmental.

When she couldn't find Archie, and when her mother and sister showed no indication of stopping for breath anytime soon, Lucinda turned her attention back to the disturbance outside, which now seemed to be moving inside. Good heavens, what had Barclay Wemberley done *now?* she wondered. She thought he'd gotten that insider trading business straightened out ages ago.

"Lucinda, thank God I finally found you."

She swung her gaze away from the window to find Bozo—or, rather, Archie—striding toward her over the glossy hardwood floor of the ballroom, the crystalline light of the overhead chandeliers bouncing garishly off of his white rubber pate.

"Darling," he said as he came to a stop before her and dropped onto one knee—a gesture that couldn't have been easy, Lucinda thought, seeing as how the length of his shoe nearly surpassed that of his lower leg. Then, from somewhere amid the drape of his big, blue Bozo suit, he whipped out a small black box. "Marry me," he said without preamble, opening the box to reveal . . .

Well, there was no way she could get around it. The ring inside was absolutely hideous, despite the gargantuan diamond at its center. In fact, it was the gargantuan diamond that was most offensive, cloudy and yellowish, and of a shape that most closely resembled . . . Hmmm . . . The state of Montana came to mind. A generous person might have said the gem was *nestled amid*—but Lucinda couldn't help thinking it was instead *beaten into*—dozens of lesser stones of indeterminate origin, though they may have come from the planet Pluto, as they seemed to have been burned to a crisp as they entered the Earth's orbit.

"Oh," she said upon seeing the ring. "Oh, my. Oh, my goodness. Oh, my goodness gracious. It's, ah . . . it's, um . . . It . . . it . . . It's remarkable," she finally concluded, congratulating herself for both her discretion and her honesty.

"It's perfect for you," Archie said, tugging the ring from its velvet housing. "Because you, my darling, are remarkable, as well."

As Lucinda was wondering if she should take his comment as a compliment—oh, surely, she should, she told herself—and before she had a chance to react, he seized her left hand in his, and, with no small effort, shoved the ring down over her fourth finger. The action brought tears to her eyes, though not because she was so touched by his ardent proposal. Actually, it was because the ring was much too small, and it hurt like hell as it scraped over her knuckle.

"Ouch!" she cried, as Archie completed the gesture. She snatched back her hand and immediately, instinctively, tried to remove the ring. But it wouldn't budge. Although she could twist it from front to back—barely—Lucinda was completely unable to raise it over her knuckle. "Archie, what do you think you're doing?" she demanded.

She glanced over at her mother and sister to see that they were as startled by his proposal as Lucinda was. After further consideration, however, she decided their astonishment wasn't such a bad thing. Because it had shut them up faster than a blunt object would have.

When she returned her attention to Archie, it was to find that he was still on bent knee, but he was gazing at her now with dumbfoundedness. At least, Lucinda *thought* he was dumbfounded, though, truly, he may have been something altogether different—it was hard to tell with the big red perpetually happy Bozo smile and the skinny black, perpetually surprised Bozo eyebrows painted on.

"What am I doing?" he echoed incredulously. "I'm pro-

posing. I want you to be my wife, Lucinda. This can't come
as a surprise to you."

"Well, of course not," she assured him. Because, in truth, it
was more of a shock than anything else. "But, Archie, I
just . . . I don't know what to say. We've never discussed
marriage before. We've never even—"

She stopped herself before she blurted out that business
about the Cub Scout stick fire of zest, not wanting to offend
him—or, for that matter, to illustrate for her mother and sister what the nature of her relationship with Archie might be,
though they probably had their suspicions now, seeing as
how he was proposing marriage to her. That, she thought,
was a rather revealing factor. And Lucinda tried very hard to
take Archie's proposal seriously. Truly, she did. But it was
just a tad difficult, what with all the flaming orange hair en-
circling his white rubber head. Maybe if she asked him to get
rid of the squeaky nose . . .

"Archie," she began again, more softly this time, striving
for gravity in the face of that squeaky nose. She ceased grappling with the ring, telling herself she'd remove it later, when
she was alone. Alone with a really big can of Crisco. "Honestly, I don't know what to say," she told him. "This is so sudden, and—"

"Please, Lucinda," he pleaded. "Promise me that you'll
marry me. Promise me that you won't take the ring off."

"But, Archie—"

"Promise me," he repeated more urgently.

As if I could *take the beastly thing off*, Lucinda thought,
giving the ring another unobtrusive—but unproductive—
tug. In spite of the stuck ring, however—not to mention
Archie's earnestness—she couldn't quite bring herself to
make such a promise to him. And she didn't want to think
about why she was so hesitant to do so, especially since she
had just been trying to convince herself that they would
someday be substantial to each other.

Before anyone in the small group could utter another
word, however, the *thumpthumpthump* of rapid foot stamp-

ing alerted them all to a quartet of uniformed police officers, who raced into the ballroom just then. And although everyone was clearly surprised by this new development, it was Archie who reacted the most strangely—by hurtling to his feet and running straight for the nearest window. And then, as Lucinda—and everyone else in the room, including the quartet of uniformed police officers—watched in amazement, Archie threw himself toward the window as if he were Steven Seagal. Or, more accurately, as if he were Steven Seagal's stunt double. Or, most accurately of all, as if he were Steven Seagal's stunt double dressed as Bozo the Clown.

In any case, it was quite extraordinary, watching Bozo go crashing through a Palladian window that way. It was even more extraordinary, Lucinda thought as she—and everyone else in the room, including the quartet of uniformed police officers—ran to the now shattered window, to see Bozo jump up from where he had landed in the rhododendrons amid a shower of glass, and go scampering off into the darkness with a different quartet of police officers—and a handful of German shepherds, too, she noted—hot on his trail.

What odd behavior, she thought. Even for Archie. It was certainly something else to consider before giving him a reply on his proposal.

When his fleeing figure dissolved into the darkness at the edge of the Wemberley yard, Lucinda spun back around to find that the quartet of police officers had dwindled to a duo. Presumably the other two had joined their brothers and sisters—and arms—and had lit out after Archie. Both of the remaining officers, however, were gazing directly at Lucinda.

"Are you Lucinda Hollander?" one of the men asked.

She smiled brightly and tossed her long, beflowered, blond braid over one shoulder, striking what she hoped was an inviting pose. "Why, yes, I am," she said amicably. "Have we met? Wait, don't tell me," she quickly halted him when he opened his mouth to speak. "Let me guess. It must have been at Nonni and Forrest Caldicott's fund-raiser for the Police Officers' Scholarship Fund last Christmas, yes?"

"Ah, no," the man told her as he began to make a cautious approach. "We've never met, Miss Hollander. But you're under arrest for the murder of George Jacobs."

Lucinda gaped at him, certain she must have misunderstood. "I-I-I beg your pardon?" she stammered.

The policeman took another step forward and began to reach for her hand, and, instinctively, she shoved both of her hands behind her back and took a step in retreat. "But I don't even know a George Jacobs," she objected. She expelled a single, anxious chuckle. "This is some kind of joke, isn't it?"

She scanned the crowd until she found Babs Wemberley dressed as a shimmering butterfly—though one of the hostess's silvery antennae had been bent to an upside-down L during the mayhem—and demanded silent confirmation that this was just part of the evening's, admittedly rather tasteless, entertainment. But Babs only looked horrified by the turn of events, and, eyes wide, she slowly shook her head.

Lucinda turned to her mother and Antoinetta, then to her father and Emory. All, however, were clearly as stunned as she by the policeman's announcement. Because none of them could seem to think of anything to say, either.

"But . . ." she began again, turning her gaze back toward the—once again approaching—policeman. "But . . . but . . . but . . ." Unfortunately no other words except for that one, not especially polite one, came to her rescue.

"And when we get down to the station, Miss Hollander," the policeman said as reached for her again, "there are a couple of people from the FBI who'd like to talk to you, too."

"The FBI?" Lucinda repeated. For one scant, delirious moment, she was almost able to convince herself that he was talking about the Future Beauticians of Idaho. But then she realized that there was no reason why future beauticians from any state beginning with an *I*—or any other letter of the alphabet, for that matter—would want to talk to her. Not that she could think of any reason why the Federal Bureau of Investigation would want to speak to her, either . . .

And then, suddenly, she understood. It was *Archie* who

she had just seen throwing himself through a window in a panic-stricken frenzy, *Archie* who had clearly been the primary target of the police. Obviously, *Archie* had done something illegal—though there was no way Lucinda would ever believe he had murdered someone—and she, evidently, was considered guilty by association.

See? Visual aids really did enhance her learning ability.

"Come on, Miss Hollander," the policeman said again. "Let's go peaceful-like, okay? No reason to cause any more problems than we already have for Mr. and Mrs. Wemberley."

Something hot and manic splashed through her midsection, and she searched frantically again for anyone who might come to her aid. But everyone in the ballroom—even her own family—seemed to have been struck dumb, and all were watching the goings-on as if riveted to their television sets.

Gosh, evidently reality TV still had nothing on reality itself, she thought inanely. The critics going to be so happy about that.

The rational thing to do, she told herself, would be to allow the police to arrest her, go rationally down to the station, and explain in a rational manner that she had nothing to do with whatever they suspected her of doing. That would be the rational thing to do.

What she *actually* did, though, without thinking—never mind being rational—was take a step backward. When she did, her foot landed on something hard and flat that made the ballet slipper she was wearing skid back farther than she intended. She halted and glanced down to see a small shard of broken glass appear beneath her lifted foot. Then she glanced back up, behind her this time, and saw the gaping window, its sheer drapes drifting inward on an errant wisp of warm, damp air. A craggy spike of lightning rent in half the dark night beyond in a way that was quite theatrical, really. It was punctuated by a restless grumble of thunder, something Lucinda couldn't help thinking must be a sign.

What happened next seemed almost unreal, and was utterly without planning. One minute Lucinda was staring at the policeman, who reached for her again. And the next minute . . .

Well, the next minute, she was picking herself up out of the rhododendrons outside and running into the darkness in the opposite direction from the one in which Archie had fled only moments ago.

She didn't stop running until she reached the oceanfront condominium of her best friend since childhood, Phoebe Bloom, though she did run long enough—and far enough out of her way—to somehow elude the authorities. She supposed she'd had the element of surprise on her side. It was only natural that everyone would take a moment to watch a fleeing wood nymph who hurled herself through a window previously shattered by Bozo the Clown before collecting themselves enough to go after her. But she hadn't had very good equipment for running a marathon, something that had hindered what might have been better progress under other circumstances.

Diaphanous gowns, she learned the hard way that evening, did not mix well with thunderstorms. Nor were ballet slippers the most effective footwear one might choose for escaping snarling German shepherds.

As a result, it was past midnight when Phoebe opened her front door to Lucinda's frantic knocking. But their friendship was such that they shot first and asked questions later, so the moment Phoebe saw Lucinda's wet dryad costume, she hustled her friend inside and rushed to the bathroom, returning moments later with a beach towel.

Phoebe was quite clearly in for the night, though that was scarcely surprising seeing as how she had, by choice, no social life to speak of. Her short, dark hair was slicked back from her forehead, still wet from a recent shower, and she'd removed her contacts in favor of tiny, oval, black-framed glasses. She sported huge, hot pink cotton pajamas spattered

with images of European landmarks, which oddly comple-
mented the electric blue nail polish on her toes.

After handing off the towel to Lucinda, she padded across
the room to turn down the stereo, and the Dean Martin music
that had blared from the speakers—his signature "That's
Amore," which Lucinda absolutely *adored*—softened to a
mere melodic buzz. Then, without even asking—it must have
been obvious, after all—Phoebe wove her way through the
clutter of Danish Modern furniture to the bar on the other side
of the room, where she immediately began to prepare a
pitcher of martinis.

"What the hell is going on?" she demanded as she shook in
several dashes of chartreuse for color—and that little extra
buzz—and stirred the now-green concoction. She nodded toward Lucinda's ruined costume, adding, "I know the Wemberleys are supposed to be known for their creative party
themes, but Babs just doesn't seem the type to go for a Mud
Wrestling Smackdown motif. What gives, Lucy?"

Only Phoebe called Lucinda "Lucy." Not because Lucinda
didn't like being called that—on the contrary, she actually
preferred "Lucy" to "Lucinda"—but because no one else had
ever seemed to think of her in such a way. The name "Lucy"
evoked an image of someone who was spontaneous and un-
worried, someone who had a jaunty disposition and a clever
way with words. "Lucinda," on the other hand, suggested
someone who was sedate, sententious, and gloomy. Not that
Lucinda was any of those things, either, but that just showed
how misunderstood she was by others.

Yet from the first day twenty-two years ago that Lucinda
and Phoebe had made each other's acquaintances at the ages
of six and seven, respectively— when Phoebe's mother came
to work for the Hollanders as their housekeeper—Lucinda
had become Lucy. Looking back now, she realized that one
of the things that had bonded her to Phoebe so readily was
the fact that the other girl saw something in Lucinda that others had overlooked. Even today, Phoebe Bloom was the only

person who knew Lucinda backward and forward, inside and out. And she was, without question, the only person Lucinda trusted. Add to that the fact that she was a Dean Martin fan, too, and, well, it was just serendipity, that was what it was. To Lucinda's way of thinking, there just wasn't a performer working today who could touch that man—nosirree.

"Lucy?" Phoebe asked again, her voice growing anxious in light of her friend's silence. "What's wrong? What's happened?"

Lucinda sighed heavily. "Oh, Phoebe, *every*thing is wrong. The oddest thing just happened."

Phoebe gave the pitcher of martinis one final stir, then poured a generous serving for each of them. "Maybe you should start from the beginning," she said as she crossed the room again. She handed one angular glass with zigzagged stem to Lucinda, then took the seat next to her on the red, kidney-bean-shaped couch. "We'll work from there."

After carefully picking one last wilted flower from her now thoroughly knotted and bedraggled braid, Lucinda gratefully took the glass and enjoyed a healthy taste. Oh, Phoebe did make the nicest martinis. As the mellow spirits warmed her belly with a radiance that spread leisurely throughout her midsection, she described the episode that had unfolded at the Wemberleys' party, along with her absolute mystification over what it could all be about.

But of all the bewildering, bizarre details Lucinda revealed about the evening's events, Phoebe latched most readily on to the one she considered most important: "He actually came dressed as Bozo for an enchanted woodlands theme?"

Lucinda nodded. "I'm afraid so."

Phoebe shook her head in disbelief. "What a moron."

Tactfully, Lucinda refrained from comment, and instead halfheartedly defended Archie by saying, "He has a good job with the government, with excellent job security and wonderful benefits."

Phoebe shook her head at her friend with much disappointment. "Excellent job security and wonderful benefits do not a dream man make," she pointed out. "He may be a G-man, but has he found your G-spot?"

"Phoebe!"

"Well, has he?"

"We've only been dating a little while . . ." Lucinda said, knowing it was a lame defense. After all, earlier that very evening, she herself had been wondering about, if not the actual location of her G-spot, certainly Archie's willingness— or lack thereof—to look for it.

"And this ring!" Phoebe added, jerking up Lucinda's hand. "It's horrific! What was the man thinking?" Grimacing, she dropped Lucinda's hand as if it were covered with slugs. "He is *such* a moron."

For several moments, Phoebe said nothing, only gazed at Lucinda with her dark brows arrowed downward, obvious concern clouding her whiskey brown eyes. Then, very softly, she said, "I told you so."

"Told me what?" Lucinda asked.

"I told you Archie Conlon was trouble."

Lucinda expelled a soft sound of disbelief. "You never said he was trouble. You said he was a moron," she countered. "And you said he has the personality of a piece of lettuce. And you said he dances like a rabid pig. And that he's as interesting as a hard-boiled egg. And that he smells like cheese. And you also told me that his head is shaped like an avocado. You know, come to think of it, Phoebe, you could have just called him a Cobb salad and been done with it. But you never said anything about him being trouble."

"You don't think a man who reminds a woman of a Cobb salad isn't trouble?" Phoebe shot back.

Lucinda sighed. "I think what happened tonight certainly qualifies as trouble. But, Phoebe," she continued before her friend had a chance to interrupt, "I can't believe Archie would be involved in anyone's murder. I can believe he'd be in the wrong place at the wrong time, and maybe even doing *some*thing he shouldn't, but you'll *never* convince me he could hurt someone."

Phoebe blew out an exasperated breath. "True," she conceded. "Archie's too big a moron to be a murderer. Still, he's obviously tied up in something he shouldn't be. And he's dragged you into it with him by association." Then another, obviously alarming thought struck her, because she hastily covered her mouth, and her eyes went as round as Mardi Gras coins. "Omigod," she said from behind her splayed fingers. "I'm harboring a fugitive from justice in my house!"

Lucinda jumped up from the sofa, horrified by the realization that she'd put her friend in such a position without realizing. "Oh, no," she said. "I didn't even think about that. Oh, Phoebe, I'll leave right now. Pretend you never saw me."

Phoebe tugged her back down to the sofa. "Are you kidding? This is great! I've never harbored a fugitive from justice before. I can't wait to tell somebody!"

Lucinda bit her bottom lip anxiously.

"Well, not until after you're gone," Phoebe assured her. "Speaking of which, you should probably be gone soon. If what I see on TV is true, and, hey, it goes without saying that everything I see on TV is true," she added wryly, "then the coppers ought to be pounding down my door with a battering ram any minute. So whatever we do, we have to do it fast." She gazed at Lucinda expectantly. "So. What *are* we going to do?"

Lucinda swallowed the lump that rose in her throat, squeezing her eyes shut tight to hold back the tears she felt threatening. "I don't know," she said. "But I'm afraid to talk to the police. They must have something incriminating they can use against me. I mean, they had enough evidence of something to arrest me. And innocent people go to jail all the time," she continued, feeling hysteria bubbling up, unable to do anything to stop it. "Sometimes for years. Sometimes they even *execute* innocent people. I've seen it on TV."

"Now, Lucy," Phoebe interjected in a placating voice, "let's not get carried away." She cupped a hand on Lucy's shoulder firmly. "Think a minute, sweetie," she said solemnly. "WWDD?"

WWDD? Lucinda echoed to herself. It was the philosoph-ical tenet that she and Phoebe held sacred, the question they asked themselves whenever they were in a bind. *What Would Dino Do?* "Well," she began, "he'd probably fix a drink, then call up Sinatra and the boys, then go into hiding, then sing 'You're Nobody 'Til Somebody Loves You.'"

"Exactly," Phoebe said.

"And the cops would break down his door and take him away in cuffs before Sinatra and the boys got there," Lucinda cried. "Phoebe, that's not going to work for me, not this time. I have to hurry or I'm going to wind up on death row."

"Lucy—"

"But what if it happens?" Lucinda interjected. "At the very least, I could go to jail. For years!" Her panic full-blown now, she dropped back down to the sofa and gripped Phoebe's pajama shirt by the lapels. "Hide me, Phoebe," she said desperately. "You've got to hide me!"

"What? Like in those Bugs Bunny cartoons?" Phoebe asked. "You want me to stuff you in my oven, and then, when Officer O'Malley shows up, turn on the gas and throw in a match to prove you're not there?"

Lucinda blinked in response. "Well, no, but . . . But there must be something you can do. You're the brains of this oper-ation, Phoebe. Think. Tell me what to do."

"First off, Lucy," Phoebe said, her patience clearly taxed, as it always seemed to be whenever Lucinda brought up the topic of their comparative smarts—or lack thereof—"I'm not any smarter than you are. I don't know why you've always thought you weren't very bright. Just because you always had trouble in school and didn't make great grades, that doesn't mean you're not bright. People have different learn-ing patterns, you know. Yours are obviously unconventional, and your teachers just never figured them out, that's all. Be-cause you're plenty smart."

Lucinda mentally brushed off her friend's comments. She knew it made Phoebe mad whenever she disparaged her own intelligence—or lack thereof. But, hey, Lucinda wasn't the only one who felt that her IQ could use some magnification. Lots of people thought she wasn't very bright. Which, now that she thought about it, might go a long way toward explaining why she didn't think she was very bright.

"And second off," Phoebe said, scattering Lucinda's thoughts, "how am I supposed to know how to elude the police? I've never had to."

"No, but if you did," Lucinda said, "I bet you'd be really good at it."

"True," Phoebe agreed absently, her mind obviously wandering over what Lucinda's alternatives might be. "What would I do if I were in your situation?" she murmured slowly, the wheels of her brain still turning. "Hmmm . . . If I were in your situation, I'd probably . . ."

She smiled suddenly and sat up straighter, setting her martini on the coffee table before them. She studied Lucinda thoughtfully for a moment, then nodded slowly. "You know," she said, "it just might work."

"What might work?" Lucinda asked.

But instead of answering the question, Phoebe jumped up from the couch and dashed out of the room. Lucinda caught up with her friend just in time to see her flee into her office and seat herself before her computer, where she began tabbing through screen after screen.

"What are you doing?" Lucinda asked.

"Finding you a hideout," Phoebe answered. "And while I'm at it, I'll find you a job, too. It's two-for-one day here at Dust Bunnies."

After graduating from Brown University with her MBA, Phoebe had followed in her mother's footsteps and had gone into the housekeeping profession—except that she had done so on a much larger scale. She'd started her own housekeeping service, calling it Dust Bunnies, and with the advent of the Internet, she had gone national with it. Big-time. Nowadays, Dust Bunnies supplied some of the country's wealthiest and most distinguished families with all manner of good housekeeping staff. In fact, the company had grown by such leaps and bounds that Phoebe's wealth rivaled that of many of her clients.

Lucinda studied her friend's actions curiously, but did her best not to look at the computer itself. She really hated computers. Instead, she turned her back on the PC and focused her attention on Phoebe, watching the scrolling images on the computer screen reflected in the other woman's glasses. "What are you talking about?" she asked. "I don't need a job. I have a job."

Phoebe waved a hand negligently at her friend. "You don't have a real job," she said. "You raise money for the Junior League."

"That's a real job," Lucinda objected.

"Oh, sure, driving cookbooks all over town," Phoebe said. "You call that a fulfilling occupation?"

What Lucinda called it, Phoebe didn't want to know. Maybe it wasn't the most noble occupation in the world, but it was a useful one. Hey, *In the Kitchen with Bitsy and Friends* made a wonderful Christmas gift, she reminded herself. And some of those recipes—especially Coco Jorgensen's Oyster Stuffing—had become holiday traditions for many Newport families.

"Ah-hah," Phoebe said when the rolling images came to a halt in her glasses. She read something she'd found and smiled again. "Perfect," she added, punctuating the statement with a satisfied sigh.

"What?" Lucinda demanded. "Phoebe, tell me."

Her friend glanced away from the screen and grinned at Lucinda. "Ever been to Kentucky?" she asked.

Lucinda shook her head, unsure where this was leading.

"Have any objection to cutting and coloring your hair?"

Lucinda felt a pang of reluctance, but said, "I guess not."

"Mind lying about your age?" Phoebe asked.

"Of course not."

"Changing your name?"

"Well . . ."

"How about Lucy French?" Phoebe suggested. "That's kind of a nice play on your name. Still sort of geographic."

"Phoebe, you're giving me a headache. What's all this about?"

"You asked me to hide you," her friend reminded her. "So I'm going to hide you."

"In your oven?" Lucinda asked warily.

Phoebe shook her head, her grin growing broader. "Nope. Not in my oven," she said. "I'm going to hide you in my computer."

 Chapter 2

Lucinda—or, rather, *Lucy*, as she was to be from here on out—at least while she was a fugitive from justice—halted outside the elaborate, wrought-iron security gate of the massive estate belonging to Justin and Alexis Cove of Glenview, Kentucky, and found herself wishing she'd asked the cabbie to hang around for a few minutes, just in case she had the wrong address. Or else, just in case the local police, acting on an anonymous tip, had preceded her here and were waiting just beyond that gate to grab her, wrestle her to the ground, and lead her away in shackles to meet her doom.

Ultimately, she decided to stay put. Mostly because she had nowhere else to go. Strangely, though, for the first time in days, Lucinda—or, rather, *Lucy*—felt something resembling a sense of being safe. She had no idea *why*, seeing as how she was about to embark on a false identity and undertake an unfamiliar profession in a place she'd never visited before, but there it was all the same. Something about her current situation made her feel oddly exhilarated. As if she were starting her life all over again, with a clean slate, with no expectations, and with the opportunity to do and be whatever she wanted to do or be.

Four days had passed since she'd snuck away from Phoebe's condo at dawn, her hair newly shorn and dyed pale brown, dressed in one of her friend's funky outfits and carrying two suitcases packed with some of Phoebe's less-outrageous clothing. Phoebe had also given her a thousand dollars in cash, since neither knew how long Lucy would be required to keep up appearances.

And, true to her word, Phoebe had found the ideal place for Lucy to hide: with Justin and Alexis Cove of Glenview, who needed a temporary housekeeper while their regular housekeeper was away for a few months to tend to a convalescing parent. Phoebe had assured the Coves via e-mail and a follow-up phone call that their new, temporary housekeeper would arrive on the appointed day, and would be in keeping with Dust Bunnies' flawless reputation of employing reliable college students in various cities who needed work in exchange for room and board and a small salary.

When Lucy had reminded her friend that she was twenty-eight years old, and had been booted out of college eight years earlier because of her poor performance, Phoebe had told her she could easily pass for someone five years younger, and that, hey, here was her chance to go back for her degree. So, while she was at the computer, creating Lucy French's bogus personnel file for Dust Bunnies, Phoebe had also taken it upon herself to go on-line and hack into the computers of the University of Louisville, and had enrolled Lucy in the English department's graduate studies program, because Phoebe had always wished she had minored in English, and gosh, this was the next best thing.

Currently, Lucy French was halfway through her MA in literature, with a focus on metaphysical poetry, and she was maintaining an admirable 3.5 average, so what was the problem anyway, Phoebe would like to know. Lucy had replied that the problem was that Lucinda Hollander had majored in art and had struggled mercilessly to maintain a D average before flunking out completely, and knew absolutely nothing about metaphysical poetry. Phoebe had in turn replied, "Two words: John Donne," and that had been the end of that. Then she had driven Lucy as far south as Newark and put her on a bus to Louisville.

Four nights ago, this hadn't seemed like a bad idea. Then again, four nights ago, she'd been under the influence of four

green martinis and more panic and terror than any human being had a right to feel.

Now, as she studied the palatial Tudor home of the Coves
from a distance, Lucy was having second thoughts about this
whole ludicrous scheme. And third thoughts. And sixteenth
thoughts, too.

It was housekeeping, she reminded herself halfheartedly.
How hard could it be? Dusting, vacuuming, setting the table.
That should be a piece of cake for her, seeing as how she had
been around housekeepers all her life. And she had done her
fair share of entertaining over the years, too, not to mention
having *been* entertained a time or two herself, thank you very
much. Besides which there was a whole chapter on silver-
ware placement in *In the Kitchen with Bitsy and Friends*,
complete with visual aids. All Lucy French would be required to do for the Coves was clean rooms—two or three
thousand of them, judging by the size of the place—and keep
track of a few party preparations . . . at the very height of the
holiday season. Still, even Lucinda Hollander should be able
to do that, right?

Pushing aside all her doubts—for all of five seconds—she
inhaled a deep, fortifying breath and told herself everything
would be fine. Evidently, the Coves were wealthy enough to
keep an entire fleet of servants on hand, so if Lucy needed to
ask anyone a question or two—hundred—there would
doubtless be someone around who could answer them. And
really, the Cove home wasn't all *that* much more grand or
prepossessing than the house where she'd grown up. Sorta.
So why should she be so terrified of entering it?

Gosh, she immediately answered herself, could it be because she was about to enter it under false pretenses? Could
it be because she was about to intentionally misrepresent
herself? Could it be because she had authorities of the federal
persuasion looking for her, and she had no idea why? Could
it be because she was going to have to look up metaphysical
poetry the first chance she got? Could it be because she *still*
had that moron Archie's hideous ring stuck on her finger be-

cause no amount of urging it off—nor a really big can of Crisco—had been successful?

Mmmm, could be.

So much for the odd exhilaration, she thought. So much for starting her life all over again. So much for the clean slate, the no expectations, and the opportunity to do and be whatever she wanted to do or be. She was *doomed*.

Without allowing herself another troublesome thought, Lucy pushed her thumb against the button on the security gate and waited for a response. While she was waiting, she ran a hand over her new, light brown hair, marveling at how quickly the chin-length bob came to an end beneath her fingers. She had opted for the least funky of Phoebe's outfits this morning, hoping to make a good impression on her new employers: a paisley miniskirt in varying shades of pink and orange, along with a short-sleeved knit top the color of raspberry sherbet. Well, it *was* the least funky of Phoebe's outfits. Lucy couldn't help it if her best friend was a bit whimsical. Nor could she help it if Phoebe was a size smaller than she. Snugness was fashionable these days, she told herself. Of course, so was being a size negative two, which Lucy most certainly was *not*, but still . . .

At least the outfit was appropriate for the weather, seeing as how it was surprisingly hot in Kentucky this first day of September, a heavy, humid kind of heat with not even the merest wisp of a breeze to alleviate it. The lofty oaks lining the cobbled lane that wound up toward the Cove estate, and the wide maples that dotted the broad front yard, were all lush green, the sky beyond them a vivid blue that was streaked from west to east with gauzy white clouds. Amid the placid silence, a group of purple finches serenaded her with a cheerful tune, and somewhere deep down inside herself, Lucy felt a warm, wistful little bubble of hopefulness go *pop*. And somehow, she knew in that moment that everything was going to turn out all right.

Eventually.

She hoped.

She was about to push the button on the gate again when a garbled, static-laden voice came over the intercom. "Yes?" the feminine voice said. "May I help you?"

So startled was Lucy by the harmless query—or perhaps it was just that she was terrified of everything her life seemed to encompass of late—that she stammered out her response all in the inquisitive tense. "H-hello?" she said. "I believe I'm expected? I'm, um, Lucy? Lucy French? The new house-keeper? From Dust Bunnies? Mr. and Mrs. Cove are expect-ing me? This morning? I'm filling in for a few months? Did I mention I'm expected?"

She had to slap a hand over her mouth to keep herself from further babbling, "And please tell Mr. and Mrs. Cove that I'm *not* running from the Rhode Island State Police? Or the FBI, either? And I *didn't* murder anyone? Really? I just got in-volved with a moron? But he didn't murder anyone, either? 'Cause he's just a moron, not a murderer? And also, I believe I'm expected?"

The intercom crackled again, and the same voice said. "Oh. Yes. Just a moment, please."

The security gate began to hum then, and both halves of the black, scrolled wrought iron began to swing slowly away from her. But Lucy hesitated before passing through them, until she saw a woman striding down the long, cobbled drive toward her. Only then did she lift a suitcase in each hand and begin to make her way toward the huge, imposing house.

As she drew nearer and saw the woman more clearly, how-ever, Lucy realized it wasn't Mrs. Cove. Alexis Cove, Phoebe had told her, was a fortysomething socialite, and this woman appeared to be around Lucy's own age—her real age, not the one she was pretending to be. And in place of the expensive, conservatively tailored fashions one would expect of a woman in Alexis Cove's social stratum, this woman wore a loose-fitting, sleeveless, printed cotton dress in several shades of blue that fell to midcalf, coupled with plain flat sandals over white cotton anklets. Her only concession to jewelry was a delicate gold cross nestled just above the slightly scooped neck of her dress.

The word *wholesome* suddenly jumped into Lucy's mind as the woman came to a stop before her, even though that was normally a word she reserved for describing the ideal breakfast. The woman's light green eyes sparkled with mischief, at odds with her cautious hairstyle—the pale red tresses were braided around the crown of her head like a coronet. Her creamy complexion was flawless, save for a sparse scattering of freckles over the bridge of her nose and high cheekbones. All in all, the woman looked like a turn-of-the-century refugee.

The image was only enhanced when she smiled and extended her hand, and said with an accent that Lucy clearly recognized as Irish, "Hello. I'm Rosemary Shaugnessy. I'm the Coves' au pair. I care for their daughter, Abby."

"Lucin . . . ah . . . Lucy. Lucy French," Lucy quickly corrected herself. She set one of her bags down on the drive and extended her own hand, then was startled by the strength and confidence in the other woman's grip. Obviously she wasn't nearly as fragile as she appeared.

"It's nice to meet you, Lucy French," Rosemary Shaugnessy said, still smiling. "Welcome to Harborcourt."

"Harborcourt?" Lucy repeated, confused. She could have sworn Phoebe said this place was called Glenview.

Rosemary tilted her head back toward the imposing mansion behind her. "Harborcourt is what Mr. and Mrs. Cove call their house. They gave it a name when they bought it two years ago. A play on their own name, I suppose. They quite fell in love with the place. Pity they don't show the same affection for their only child that they show for their property," she added wryly. Then, obviously realizing she shouldn't have said what she did—at least not until she and Lucy knew each other well enough to bitch and moan about their employers, anyway—she quickly amended, "But that's not my place to say, is it? Me being the nanny and all. Abby's a trifle challenging at times, but she's a sweet child. The Coves are just a bit confused when it comes to their priorities. But then, that's the case of all people who have more dollars than sense, isn't it?"

Lucy bit her lip to keep in the comment she wanted to voice, deciding it would probably be best just to agree with Rosemary for now, even if she didn't really agree at all. Because in her own experience, economic privilege *didn't* necessarily equate to a lack of good sense, that moron Archie notwithstanding. Lucy French would doubtless agree with Rosemary Shaugnessy. They were, after all, both working-class.

So instead of replying, Lucy only nodded quickly, and said, "Is Mrs. Cove here? I'm supposed to meet with her this morning."

Rosemary shook her head. "I'm the only one at home right now. Well, me and Max. He takes care of the cars and does a bit of driving for the Coves now and then," she added. "Abby started back to school a week ago, and Mr. Cove is at work, as he always is. Mrs. Cove will be back shortly." In a tone that wasn't quite as wry as before, she added, "She had a terribly, terribly important meeting this morning with her manicurist. I'll take you up to the house and show you 'round, and get you settled. Mrs. Cove can go over your duties when she returns."

Without being asked—and with surprisingly little effort considering her seeming delicacy—Rosemary picked up the suitcase Lucy had placed on the ground and began to make her way back up the drive. Gripping her other bag with more determination, Lucy hurried her step to keep up. The nearer she drew to the house, however, the more her pace slowed. It was a massive place, in fact much larger than the house where she had grown up. The exuberant Tudor was a full four stories high, with numerous chimneys and dozens of mullioned windows that cast back the sunlight like crushed diamonds. The grounds, too, sparkled like gems, embellishing the front and sides of the house with vast, variegated landscaping.

Only the very, *very* rich claimed such accommodations, Lucy knew, and she couldn't help but feel intimidated by the place, even with her own socially advanced upbringing. The Coves obviously claimed at least three more zeroes on the bottom line of their personal wealth than the Hollanders did. And billionaires, ironically, tended to be even more rabidly possessive about their wealth than the average run-of-the-millionaires did. *Nobody* touched their bottom lines. Nobody touched *them*.

What must it feel like to live in a place like this for someone like Rosemary Shaugnessy? Lucy wondered. Or for someone like Lucy French? If Lucinda Hollander was anxious about entering the house, Lucy French would probably be terrified.

"It's not as scary as it looks," Rosemary said from a few steps ahead, evidently reading Lucy's mind. Again. "I thought the same thing, too, when I first saw the place. Halfway expected to hear some ghostly Heathcliff calling for Cathy that first night I spent here," she added with a laugh. After a while, you get used to it. Even if you never quite feel comfortable.

They had arrived at a point in front of the house by now where the cobbled drive divided to circle around a fanciful fountain depicting a trio of frolicking cupids. But Rosemary strode past the front door without a glance. "Servants' entrance is in the rear," she said. "Which is more convenient for us, anyway, because that's nearer where your quarters are. In the carriage house out back."

"Is my room close to yours?" Lucy asked hopefully.

Even having only met Rosemary a few moments ago, she already liked the woman—with her frank speech and kind smile, it was impossible not to. And it would be nice if Lucy had someone to talk to in her off hours, to help her make the adjustments she was going to have to make over the next few days. Weeks. Months.

Oh, she really didn't want to think about it.

"No, I live in the big house," Rosemary said. "My room is next to Abby's. The Coves travel frequently, and the child doesn't sleep well. Someone needs to be there when she calls out."

Meaning the parents evidently couldn't be bothered with that particular activity, Lucy translated, even when they were home.

"But you won't be alone out here," Rosemary continued. "Max also lives in the carriage house."

Max, Lucy recalled. The car guy. She formed a quick image of a wizened, little old man of German descent who knew auto mechanics and engineering backward and forward, who tinkered under the hoods and chassis of everything on wheels, murmuring things like, "Hmmm . . . hmmm . . . hmmm . . . ah hah! De problem, you see, iss viss da discombobulator intravector svitch, vich hass gone kablooey." Except that he would probably use real car words and not *discombobulator intravector svitch*. But Lucy didn't know any real car words. So sue her.

Then another, much more important, realization hit her: She'd be sharing her quarters with a strange little foreign man?

"The top of the carriage house is divided into two apartments," Rosemary told her, and Lucy wondered just how long it was going to take for the other woman's seemingly psychic abilities to start giving her the willies on a regular basis. "Max lives in one, and you'll be staying in the other as part of the package with Dust Bunnies."

"So the Coves have lots of servants, huh?" Lucy asked, feeling more and more uncomfortable by the minute. Just how many people was she going to have to deceive while she was here?

Rosemary nodded. "They have Mrs. Hill to cook for them every day, as well, and Mr. Cadogen, who cares for the stables."

Stables? Lucy thought, the estate growing larger in her mind with every new tidbit she learned about the Coves.

"And there's also Dimitri," Rosemary continued, "who comes a few days a week to see to the grounds. But it's only me and you and Max who actually live here on the estate."

A second building came into view then, which Lucy assumed was the carriage house, and she was immediately relieved. She'd be lucky if she ever met her neighbor at all, she thought, because like the Coves' primary house, the carriage house had, ah, exceeded its genetic potential in the area of size.

It, too, was Tudor in design, and had it not been for the low-slung, cherry red, vintage roadster parked in front with its hood up, Lucy could have easily believed the building was still intended for housing carriages. Nowadays, however, it was clearly used as a four-car garage—and, of course, servants' quarters. The doors spanning the lower level seemed to be original to the structure, claiming old-fashioned paned windows and filigreed handles to pull them open manually, instead of upward by machine. Windows lined the entire length of the second floor, too, where, presumably, her apartment and ol' Max's lay.

All in all, the carriage house was charming, Lucy couldn't help thinking. Like the big house, it was beautifully landscaped, bursting around the entire perimeter with fat fuchsia peonies and cascades of purple clematis, thanks, no doubt, to Dimitri. And it was shaded by sweeping, perhaps centuries-old maples that canopied the entire roof from each side of the building.

Really, she thought, a fugitive from justice could do a lot worse for a hideout.

"The apartment's quite charming, really," Rosemary continued as they approached the carriage house. "You should be very comfortable. So what is it you'll be studying at university this semester?" she asked, switching gears effortlessly. "I think Mrs. Cove mentioned you're working on your master's degree in—"

"John Donne," Lucy piped up without thinking, Phoebe's two words exploding in her brain. "I'm studying, uh, John Donne."

"Oh, the metaphysical poets?" Rosemary said, clearly delighted. "They're a favorite of mine. We'll have much to talk about."

Oh, *fabulous*, Lucy thought morosely. "Oh, *fabulous*," she said cheerfully.

"So what do you think about—"

A sudden *clank-clank-clank*ing from beneath the roadster cut short Rosemary's question—much to Lucy's relief—and the two women both turned their heads in that direction.

"Max!" Rosemary called out over the din, bringing it to a halt. "Come out and meet Lucy! She's to be taking Mrs. Lindstrom's place for a few months!"

Only then did Lucy notice that a pair of denim-clad legs and booted feet extended from beneath the chassis of the car on the side facing her and Rosemary. But instead of seeing a wizened little old German man push himself out from under the vehicle to say something about the discombobulator intravector svitch goink kablooey, the *clank-clank-clank*ing erupted again, as if the nanny had never spoken.

Poor old guy, Lucy thought. He must be hard of hearing, too. Or maybe he just didn't speak English very well.

Rosemary shook her head and set Lucy's suitcase down on the drive. Then she smiled and tilted her head toward the car. "He's playing hard to get," she said. "Let's go give him a nudge."

Lucy really didn't want to bother him, but Rosemary obviously had no qualms about it, because she was already making her way over to the little sports car. She halted next to the booted feet, then bent over at the waist to peer beneath the car. "Come on, Max," she said. "Don't be shy."

"I'm busy, Rosemary," came a deep, gruff voice in reply. Lucy wasn't sure, but it didn't sound particularly old or wizened or German.

Before she could ponder that realization further, however,

Rosemary was tapping one of the booted feet with the toe of her sandal and speaking again. "Come on," she repeated in the coaxing kind of tone one might use for an obstinate toddler who was turning up his nose at his mashed bananas. "You're going to have to come out sooner or later," she told the car guy. "And I want to take Lucy up to the big house to show her 'round. Come meet her now, so she doesn't frighten you later when you see her."

Oh, so he was shy, too, Lucy thought, in addition to being old and wizened and German. She made a mental note to be very polite and speak very softly and clearly and not make any sudden movements when he was around.

In response to Rosemary's cajoling, Lucy heard a muffled, uncomfortable expulsion of air issue from beneath the car—sounded like the poor old guy had a bit of a respiratory problem, too, she thought—followed by a heartfelt groan—maybe arthritis, as well, she thought further, or something else that made movement painful. She hoped the job of car guy wasn't too much for the old man. Then slowly, very slowly, the rest of his legs—surprisingly long for a little, wizened old man—began to appear from beneath the car as he pushed himself out from under it.

Without even realizing she was doing it, Lucy strode closer to the sleek vehicle, strangely drawn toward the emerging body. The denim-clad legs were attached to firm thighs and trim hips, and those, in turn, combined with a torso that was likewise covered in denim. No, wait, she realized as she drew nearer and Max pushed himself farther out from beneath the car—the torso wasn't exactly covered, because the denim work shirt hung open over a naked abdomen that looked way, way too sculpted to belong to a man of extended years. No, this abdomen was roped and corded with muscle and sinew, covered with a rich scattering of dark hair that spanned his upper torso before arrowing down over a flat belly to disappear into the waistband of his jeans.

Lucy's mouth went dry as she took in—so to speak—the

body that revealed itself. Not old. Not wizened. Not plagued
with respiratory problems. Not arthritic. *Next thing you
know*, she thought vaguely, *he'll be saying he's not German,
either.*

Two hands appeared next, gripping the bottom of the driver's side door to aid the body in its journey from beneath the
car. The fingers of those hands were long and blunt and
capable-looking, though smudged black with grease and car
grime. The denim shirt, too, was streaked with oily black, as
were the brawny arms, and the powerful chest, and the sturdy
neck, and the bold chin, and the intrepid jaw and the—

Whoa, baby.

The face. The incredibly handsome face. The face, when it
finally appeared, quite took Lucy by surprise. Not because it,
too, was streaked with grease. And not because it belonged to
a man far younger than she had guessed. But because it was,
without question, the most arresting face Lucy had ever seen.
Max's mouth was full and sculpted and very nearly pouty, as
if he were in a constant state of bad temper . . . or in a constant state of readiness to devour a woman alive. His jaws
were dark and uncivil with several days' growth of scraggly
beard, but that didn't hide the deep hollows beneath each
salient cheekbone. And his eyes . . .

Oh, his *eyes*.

His eyes were the smokiest, most turbulent shade of gray
she'd ever seen in her life, fringed by sooty lashes and looking menacing somehow beneath a shock of espresso-colored
hair that fell damply over his forehead. The moment her gaze
connected with his, a hot crackle of something reckless and
sharp bolted through Lucy's entire body, and every last scrap
of decent thought fled her brain. She was, she discovered, for
the first time in her life, speechless. Though not entirely
thoughtless. No, in fact the thoughts that began to dash
through her head just then were actually quite graphic indeed. Unfortunately, none of them was in any way appropriate for her to be entertaining in polite and mixed company.

Good thing she was speechless, she realized.

Rosemary, however, suffered from no such condition. "Lucy French," she said with a smile, "meet Max Hogan. Max, Lucy. Looks like you two are going to be roommates for a bit. I hope you can get along."

 Chapter 3

As Max Hogan shoved himself out from under Justin Cove's 1958 BMW 507 roadster and filled his gaze with the woman who stood over him, he did his absolute very best—honest, he did—not to look up her skirt. Her very short, very snug, very tempting little skirt. The short, snug skirt that—Whoa, momma—showcased some long, luscious gams. They were the kind of legs that he could envision—all too well—naked and sweaty and wrapped tightly around his equally naked and sweaty waist, as he gripped her naked, sweaty hips in both of his naked, sweaty hands, and lifted her off the bed to—

Dammit.

He should *not* be doing this, he reminded himself. It wasn't allowed. He bit back a growl of frustration, along with a few very ripe expletives, when he realized that, once again, his best efforts to be noble had failed. But then, he wasn't a noble guy, was he? Not by a long shot. And hell, how could he be expected not to look up the woman's skirt, when looking up her skirt was the closest thing he'd had to a sexual encounter in five years?

An attractive young woman on the estate, he thought dismally. Just what he needed. He forced his gaze upward, pulling his attention from her long, luscious gams, but doing that left him gazing at her full, rounded hips, the ones he'd just envisioned being naked and sweaty and filling his hands. So he propelled his gaze higher still, which—oh, hell—

meant his eyes rested on her breasts, and those, he decided, were her best feature yet, full and round, the scooped neck of her short, snug, tempting little shirt only hinting at their perfection. Those, too, he could easily envision naked and sweaty—not to mention filling his hands—as he lifted them toward his mouth so that he could—

Dammit.

He forced his gaze yet higher, until his focus fell on the woman's face, which he immediately decided was even better than the rest of her. And that was when he realized just how much trouble he was in. Because the last thing Max needed to have around him was a pretty woman. A pretty woman with soft, silky brown hair that just begged for a man's fingers to thread leisurely through it. A woman with eyes bluer and brighter than the summer sky overhead. A woman who, judging by her expression, obviously knew *exactly* what Max had been thinking about ever since he pushed himself out from under the car and started imagining her naked, sweaty thighs wrapped around his naked, sweaty waist as he—

Dammit.

Then he realized something else, something that pretty much sealed his doom. Because further judging by the woman's expression, he realized she might not necessarily take exception to such naked, sweaty behavior, and that, in fact, she might very well be entertaining a few naked, sweaty thoughts of her own about him. Because her pupils had expanded to nearly the edges of her bright blue irises, and her full, erotic—oh, man, was it erotic—mouth was open just the merest bit, as if she were having a little trouble breathing. Or else as if she had every intention of tasting him the moment she had a chance.

Oh, man . . .

This was *really* just what he needed. A pretty woman wandering around the estate who made him feel things he had absolutely no business feeling, because he wasn't allowed to have such feelings. Max had promised himself—he had *sworn an oath*—five years ago that he would never, *ever*, allow himself to feel such things again.

Still, he knew he shouldn't be surprised by the intensity and immediacy of his reaction to her, nor that she reached him on such a primal, sexual level. Any man who'd gone without sex for five years, especially when he'd been used to a steady—and quite varied—diet of sex before going cold turkey, would react the same way. But he had thought that living the way he had chosen to live since . . . well, the way he had chosen to live for the last five years—a quiet, secluded life, far away from the fast lanes of Europe, where he'd lived much too fast, for much too long—would keep him safe from encounters like this one.

Hell, it was bad enough that he had to bump into Rosemary Shaugnessy every day and be reminded of everything he was missing. Not that he'd ever even *consider* hitting on Rosemary, even under normal circumstances, even in his previous life. She was much too nice a girl for Max *ever* to try and make time with her, even if she was pretty. Hitting on Rosemary would be like hitting on the Flying Nun, so sweet and chaste and innocent and Catholic was she. Except that, you know, Rosemary didn't lift off in high winds.

This new one, however . . . She went beyond pretty. And in that short, snug, tempting little skirt, and that short, snug, tempting little shirt, garments that just made it all too easy to envision her naked and sweaty and—

Dammit.

Well, she just didn't much seem sweet or chaste or innocent, that was all. He supposed there was a possibility that she *could* be Catholic, though. Not that that was a problem, mind you, because Max Hogan had always been an equal opportunity womanizer. He had, however, always made it a point to steer clear of one type of woman. He'd always steered clear of Nice Girls. Nowadays, of course, he steered clear of All Girls. There was a reason for that, of course, one that he didn't much like to dwell on, mostly because it made his heart hurt—among other body parts. Still, he was determined to resist this woman, just as he resisted all others. Because, hey, why torture himself that way, right?

Then again, he goaded himself, wasn't torturing himself for the rest of his life the whole point?

"Max," Rosemary said, thankfully scattering his thoughts. She must have realized he'd barely heard her first introduction—he had been pretty busy looking up the newcomer's skirt, after all—because she repeated it again. "This is Lucy French. She's filling in for Mrs. Lindstrom while she's up in Columbus. Say hello."

"Hello," he replied dutifully.

"Hi," Lucy French with the long, luscious—potentially naked, sweaty—gams replied. Then, strangely, she added, "You're, um, you're not German, are you?"

Max narrowed his eyes. "Not last time I checked, no."

"Ah."

"Is that a problem?" he asked.

She shook her head quickly. Nervously, he couldn't help thinking. But what would she have to be nervous about? "No," she said. "Not a problem."

"Because if it is, I'm sure I could scare up someone of Teutonic origin from my family tree," he offered. "We Hogans are pretty much mongrels from way back. A family without a country, you might say."

Her beautiful blue eyes widened in surprise—or maybe nervousness, he couldn't help thinking again. "Mongrels?" she asked. "You mean like . . . Genghis Khan?"

Hoo-kay, Max thought, so maybe she wasn't so nervous as she was just . . . ah, not bright.

She must have realized immediately that he considered her remark to be kind of odd, because she hastily tried to recover herself by adding, "Or do I mean Kahlil Gibran? Or Chiang Kai-shek? Or Omar Khayyám? I always get all those guys mixed up," she finally finished lamely. "All those Ks and everything. It's not exactly the most commonly used letter of the alphabet, is it?" She squeezed her eyes shut tight as she concluded the observation, obviously as distressed by her rambling thoughts as Max was.

And then she tittered apprehensively. Which meant maybe she wouldn't be such a temptation after all, even if she did have great gams and a pretty face. Because tittering had always bugged the hell out of him.

"Didn't you say you were working on your master's degree in literature?" Rosemary asked Lucy. "One would think that Omar Khayyám and Kahlil Gibran wouldn't be so very confusing to you."

"Hey, they're not John Donne, are they?" Lucy pointed out.

"Well, no . . ." Rosemary agreed. Still, she threw Lucy a strange look.

All right, so maybe she wasn't in the running for lifetime Mensa membership, Max thought. Hey, who was? Except for lifetime Mensa members, he meant. "I think it's Genghis Khan you're looking for," he said as diplomatically as possible, "though he was actually a Mon*gol*, not a mon*grel*. Anyway, the Hogans are more like a pack of wild dogs than they are poets or warriors of the eastern hemisphere."

Lucy nodded once and murmured, "Ah," again. Then she bit her lip anxiously, and Max's entire body surged in response, because he couldn't help wondering what it might feel like to have her nibbling his own mouth. And he realized then that even tittering wasn't going to put him off this time.

Dammit.

He sighed heavily, resigned to his fate, and jackknifed into a sitting position, hooking his arms loosely over his bent knees. "Nice to meet you, Ms. French," he said, trying to be polite. Trying not to think about all the erotic images just the sound of her last name evoked. Trying to not look up her skirt again. He extended his right hand.

"Likewise, I'm sure," she replied automatically, extending her own hand gingerly to take his.

Funny, though, Max thought, but in spite of the heated looks she'd been throwing his way, she didn't sound any hap-

pier about meeting him than he was about meeting her. Not
that that was a problem. In fact, it would make things infinitely easier if she was as reluctant to be around him as he
was to be around her—for whatever reasons *she* might have.
Then maybe, just maybe, he could survive her stay here.

Still, as irrational as it was when he was trying so hard to
escape his old life, it galled Max that Lucy French wasn't eager to make his acquaintance. He wasn't used to women not
wanting to meet him. Even after five years of self-inflicted
exile and better—i.e., boring—living, he still expected to
have women drape themselves over him and shove their
tongues down his throat before they even mentioned their
names. He still expected to have women he'd never met in his
life knocking on the door of his hotel suite in the middle of
the night wearing nothing beneath their coats. He still expected to find panties with phone numbers inked inside them
dangling from the side view mirror of the Formula One Ferrari he didn't even drive anymore.

Certainly he still expected that a housekeeper might find
him attractive enough to at least smile at him. But Lucy
French wouldn't even do that. And it bothered Max—a lot—
that he wanted her to.

She gave his hand a quick shake, pulling his thoughts back
to the present, then withdrew hers to nervously twine the fingers of both hands together in front of her, at waist level.
Helplessly, Max followed the movement of those hands, then
was struck by what he saw on the left one. On the *ring* finger
of the left one, to be more specific: what appeared to be an
engagement ring.

So. Ms. Lucy French was intended for another man. Another man with exceedingly bad taste, judging by the ring
he'd given her, but another man nonetheless. No wonder she
wasn't—or at least didn't want to be—interested in Max.
Then the phrasing of his realization hit him—hard. Why
would he consider her fiancé to be "another man"? That
made it sound as if Max was in the running for her affections,
which he most certainly was not, seeing as how he had just

met the woman and had no intention of vying for her affections in the first place.

He shouldn't be irritated that she was engaged, he told himself. Now he could be sure she wouldn't offer him any encouragement to get all naked and sweaty with her. 'Cause there was one thing he knew for sure, even after having known Ms. Lucy French for only a few moments—he needed absolutely no encouragement there.

"So," he began again, nudging his thoughts away from Lucy French's bad-taste fiancé, "you're filling in for Mrs. Lindstrom for . . . how long did you say?"

"Through the end of the year," she told him.

Four months, Max calculated. Four months of being reminded of what he couldn't—wouldn't—have. Four months of working every day on the same estate as she. Four months of sleeping right across the hall from her. Four months of lying in bed at night, wondering what she looked like naked and sweaty and—

Dammit.

—and knowing she belonged to another man. Knowing he couldn't have her, even if she didn't belong to another man. He might as well just go throw himself off the Sherman Minton Bridge into the Ohio River right now, he thought, and save himself the trouble of a slow and painful death. Because there was no way he was going to survive four months of Luscious Lucy—*engaged* Luscious Lucy—right there under his nose, not to mention his other body parts.

Man, he was a goner.

An hour after meeting Max Hogan, mongrel—and non-German and *way*-nonwizened car guy—Lucy sat in the window seat of her temporary living room, gazing out her temporary window at her temporary surroundings, listening to the steady *clank-clank-clank*ing of her temporary neighbor in the driveway below, and wondering how long she was going to have to put up with it. Not the *clank-clank-clank*ing so much as the presence of Max Hogan. Because never in her life had she been more fiercely attracted to a man—and in only a matter of moments, too.

Oh, God, she thought as she dropped her head into her hands, recalling their initial encounter. Had she really said she got Genghis Khan and Kahlil Gibran and Omar Khayyám and Chiang Kai-shek mixed up? Even *she* knew the differences there. Sort of. She'd seen all of them profiled on *Biography*, after all, hadn't she? Kahlil and Omar had poetry in common, and Genghis and Chiang were historical figures, right? And here she was with her supposed 3.5 average in literature. Maybe she really should go back for her degree.

Or maybe she should just *go*.

She was nuts—and so was Phoebe—for ever thinking she could pull this off. But if she left the Cove estate, where could she go? She was completely unfamiliar with just about every place that wasn't Newport. Her sense of direction was deplorable, and she got lost easily.

Surely she wouldn't be here long enough to get into any further trouble, she told herself. Surely it would only take a few days for Phoebe to figure out what was going on with that moron Archie and straighten things out with the authorities. Surely they'd discover they'd made a terrible mistake, then Phoebe would call and tell Lucy it was all right for her to come home.

Surely.

Lucy could keep a low profile for a few days. Good heavens, considering the size of the house where she'd be working, she could probably go for weeks without meeting another human being if she put her mind to it. Of course, she'd have to return to her apartment at the end of her workday. Her apartment right across the hall from Max Hogan, mongrel—i.e., Max Hogan, wild dog.

And why did that analogy seem so appropriate? she wondered. He'd been perfectly polite to her. He hadn't been a wild dog at all. Of course, there had been those rabid looks he'd given her when he'd first emerged from beneath the car, looks that had made her feel all naked and sweaty for some reason. But those had only lasted a few moments. Until she'd brought up Khan, Kahlil, Khayyám, and Kai-shek, she reminded herself.

He must consider her a complete idiot. And here, she'd been thinking since her arrival that she might be able to start anew here at the Cove estate. Yeah, right. There were some things, Lucy thought, that a person just couldn't escape. Not when they were obviously an intrinsic part of that person's character.

But why should she care what Max Hogan thought about her? Not only was she misrepresenting herself to the man, but she'd only be here for a short time. It was pointless to think anything might arise between them. Anything more than a major physical lust, anyway.

Which was another thing. Just where had that physical lust come from? Lucy still couldn't understand why she'd had such a strong, immediate reaction to the man. Just because he was incredibly good-looking—in a sullen, swarthy, dangerous, furious, hard, wild, rabid, rowdy, overwhelming, sexy, hot, erotic, naked, sweaty . . .

Where was she? Oh, yes. Just because he was incredibly good-looking in an ah, intense kind of way didn't mean she had to go all hot and gooey every time she looked at him. But hot and gooey were good words to describe her reaction to him earlier. They were good words to describe her reaction to him now. Because even the passage of an hour had done nothing to diminish the man's impact.

An hour, she repeated to herself, frantic. Oh, dear. Rosemary had told her to come back up to the big house in an hour, because Mrs. Cove would be home by then and could go over Lucy's duties. Glancing down at her watch, she realized she had roughly two minutes to cover the roughly two hundred miles between the carriage house and the big house if she was going to arrive on time.

With a quick stop in front of the mirror that hung by her front door to check her makeup and hair—telling herself she was doing it to impress Mrs. Cove and *not* because she might have to run by Max—Lucy hastened down the stairs on the side of the carriage house and prepared to zoom by the red roadster. However, when she rounded the corner, she saw Max standing beside the car, wiping his greasy hands on a rag, and she stopped short. She couldn't help herself. The man just had a presence—or something—about him that made it impossible for her not to stop for a moment to notice it. Be distracted by it. Respond to it. Succumb to it.

What was it she had just been planning to do . . . ?

He glanced up just as she skidded to a halt, those smoky eyes of his raking over her from head to toe and back again. "Well, hello, Ms. French," he said in that whiskey-rough voice of his that could make even a simple greeting sound like a seduction attempt.

A very successful seduction attempt, too, seeing as how with those four little words and that one steamy look, he made her want to wrap herself around him and devour him in one big bite. "Hi," she said. "I—I have to go up to the big house to see Mrs. Cove."

Max continued to wipe his hands on the greasy rag, his expression bland, but his eyes alive with something sharp and watchful and hot that Lucy figured she'd be better off ignoring.

Yeah, right.

"She just got back," he said. "I'll walk up with you. Lunchtime," he added by way of an explanation. "I'm *really* hungry."

Oh, and why did that remark sound just *so* suggestive? Lucy wondered. Was it because *he* had intended for it to sound that way, or because *she* had wanted it to sound that way? And really, which would be more troubling?

She nodded in response to his suggestion, not so much because she thought it was wise, but because she simply found it impossible to say no to him.

Not a good sign.

He fell into step beside her as she strode past him, much too close for comfort. But then, he would be too close for comfort as long as he was in her zip code. Area code. The Western Hemisphere. Whatever.

She wished he would at least button up his shirt, because the gentle breeze kept blowing it open, displaying every distinct, solid—naked, sweaty—inch of his lean torso. She swallowed against the dryness that overtook her mouth—funny how her mouth went dry when other parts of her were getting, ah . . . not dry—and forced her eyes ahead. Not that she had any idea where they were going, because only now did she realize that it wasn't Max who was following her, but she who was following Max, and the route he had chosen wasn't the same one Rosemary had taken earlier. This one was a narrow dirt path overgrown by lush foliage, shaded from the sun and out of view of both the carriage house and the Cove mansion.

Maybe this was a shortcut, she thought. Or maybe Max was leading her into a secluded area so he could make a pass at her. Well, a girl could dream, couldn't she?

"So," Lucy began, hoping to end the awkward silence that was creeping over them. Because, after all, awkward conversation was always preferable. "How long have you worked for the Coves?"

"Five years," he said. But he offered nothing further.

"So," Lucy tried again, "are you from around here originally?"

"No." And nothing more to enlighten her.

"So," she tried once more, "where are you from originally?"

"Here and there," he said. And nothing more.

"So," she continued, "have you always worked around cars?"

"Pretty much," he replied. But said nothing more.

"So," Lucy began again, "what exactly is it you do for the Coves?"

"I take care of all of Justin's cars," he told her. And offered nothing more to elaborate.

"All of them?" she asked. "How many does he have?"

"This month?"

Lucy's eyebrows shot up in surprise. "I guess."

"Twelve."

"Oh," she said with some surprise.

"Of course, four of them are parked at his other residences."

"Oh?"

"In New York, Maine, London, and Aruba."

"Ah."

"He has other people to work on those, of course."

"I see."

Holy moly, Lucy thought. Who needed twelve cars? Or five residences, for that matter? Especially when one's primary residence had already set one back seven figures. Then again, if one could afford all those things, why not have them, right? Then again, if one could afford twelve cars and five residences, then one could probably afford to feed a small, sovereign nation, and that might be just a *tad* more worthy a cause than all that conspicuous consumption. But then, that was just Lucy. Always playing devil's advocate. It was a quirk.

She shook off the questions and observations and turned her attention back to Max. "So," she continued, "what all does working on Mr. Cove's cars—here, I mean—involve?"

He lifted a shoulder and let it drop in a way that she supposed was meant to be casual, but which was really incredibly sexy and arousing and stimulating and libido-charging and mouth-watering and . . . Well, it was just really noticeable, that was all.

"Maintenance mostly," he said. "But also keeping up with the paperwork on the vehicles and their registration and insurance and such. Washing them. Driving them occasionally to make sure they're running well. Making sure they're ready for Justin or Mrs. Cove when they need them. Occasionally I act as their driver when they go out to some formal function."

Wow, Lucy thought. That was actually an answer with

some information. Funny how he could talk easily about someone else's cars, but not about his own bad self.

Lucy stifled a sigh of frustration. "So—"

"Look, Lucy . . . Ms. French," he hastily corrected himself. He halted suddenly, circling her wrist with loose fingers to stop her, too. The second he touched her, however, he released her again, with such vigor and velocity that she almost thought he had been reviled by the feel of her. Then he took an equally quick, adamant step away from her and said, "I'm not much one for chitchat, okay?"

Well, not unless it was about cars, obviously, she thought. She opened her mouth to apologize, then realized she had nothing to apologize for. So she only said coolly, "Fine. No chitchat." No nothing, as far as she was concerned.

She spun around and hastened her step to put some distance between them, then remembered she had no idea where she was going. Still, as long as she stayed on the path, she should make it to the big house, shouldn't she? Unless, of course, her previous assumption that Max was luring her to a secluded rendezvous was right.

Well, a girl could dream, couldn't she?

And dream it would be, she was certain. The man obviously wanted nothing to do with her. As for those heated looks he'd been giving her, she must have imagined them. And a good thing, too, she told herself. Because the last thing she needed was heat of any kind from this man. She had enough trouble on her hands.

"Ms. French," she heard him call from behind her, his voice sounding apologetic, even if the rest of him hadn't seemed so.

Lucy stopped and turned around.

"I'm sorry," he told her, his voice now somehow sounding less apologetic as he offered the actual apology. "I didn't mean to be rude. I just—"

"What?" she asked when he didn't finish.

But he only shook his head and said nothing, and began to

stride forward again. When he reached her, he kept going, a silent indication, she supposed, that she should follow him. Follow him and not say another word.

Great, she thought. The strong, silent type. But then, she didn't need to be having conversations—or anything else— with him. So she only walked along behind him, saying noth- ing, focusing instead on the uneven path. It turned out to be a shortcut after all—damn her luck, anyway—emptying out in the garden at the back of the Coves' house. She noticed that there was a garage here, too, with four doors, and she as- sumed this was where the Coves kept the cars they actually drove around town for daily jaunts, the ones worth less than, oh, say a half a million dollars.

By the time Lucy reached the house, Max was already there, holding the back door open for her. He looked so in- congruous, an oily grease monkey making such a gentle- manly gesture. He'd even buttoned up his shirt as he'd walked along before her, she noted, and she discovered she had mixed feelings about that. On one hand, it made it im- possible for her to enjoy the sight of his naked torso. On the other hand, it did keep her from drooling all over herself.

"After you," he said, sweeping his hand in invitation.

"Thank you," Lucy replied as she passed him.

She entered what she decided was a mud room, even though it was the size of the living room in her carriage house apartment, and she sincerely doubted there had ever been a drop of mud on the floor. A heavy, antique deacon's bench was pushed against one wall, its high back hosting a series of hooks from which dangled a variety of outer wear. Two ladder-back chairs stood sentry against the wall opposite the bench, a variety of footwear stored beneath them. Beyond the mudless mud room was a large, sunny breakfast room, furnished with a wide pine table and a half dozen more ladder-back chairs. Floral chintz curtains hung from the wraparound windows, thrown open wide to welcome in the sunny day, and a hammered tin chandelier hung from the center of the ceiling.

Lucy started to continue on through there, toward the kitchen that lay beyond the breakfast room, then hesitated when she realized Max didn't seem ready to accompany her.

"Aren't you coming in?" she asked.

He shook his head. "Just tell Rosemary I'm out here. She'll bring me something."

Lucy narrowed her eyes curiously. Surely he was welcome past the breakfast room, she thought. Nobody, not even the very, *very* rich were so snobby these days that they didn't allow the outside help inside the house proper. Were they?

"But—" she began.

"It's not allowed," he said mildly, verifying her suspicions.

Wow, she thought. Evidently the Coves really were that snobby.

"I'll wait here," he told her, effectively ending whatever further objection she might have uttered.

Reluctantly, Lucy continued on to the kitchen that was probably larger than most suburban homes. But it was surprisingly cozy, in spite of its vast size. She guessed the house itself was probably about a hundred years old, and the Coves obviously had an eye for fine antiques and good reproductions, just as Lucy did herself. The cherrywood cabinets were almost certainly original to the house, so fine was the sheen of age upon them. The terra-cotta tiles on the floor, however, were much more recent additions. More windows with more chintz curtains spilled more sunlight into the room, enhancing the appearance of warmth and welcome. All in all, it was a wonderful room, one that put Lucy immediately at ease.

Until she realized she wasn't alone.

Rosemary was seated at an antique writing desk that somehow didn't look at all inappropriate nestled beside the double-door, state-of-the-art, Subzero refrigerator/freezer. Beside her stood a woman who could only be Alexis Cove. She looked to be in her forties, her platinum blond hair swept up in a French twist that was held in place with a sedate tortoiseshell comb tucked into one side. She wore tailored beige trousers and a short-sleeved, ivory blouse. A thin gold bracelet encircled one wrist, while an understated gold watch wrapped around the other, and rings sparkled from nearly every finger. Her engagement ring was especially striking. To Lucy's well-trained eye, even from a distance, it looked to be nearly four carats of exquisite gemstone—unlike the ugly meteorite she wore on her own left hand.

"Oh, here she is now," Rosemary said upon noting Lucy's arrival. She stood and turned to Mrs. Cove. "Lucy, this is Mrs. Cove. Mrs. Cove, this is Lucy French, from Dust Bunnies."

Alexis Cove smiled warmly, though Lucy could tell it was one of those smiles that only *looked* warm, but wasn't really. The very, *very* rich, she knew, tended to erect invisible borders around themselves when they were in the presence of those who were not so very, *very* rich. Alexis Cove, Lucy saw, was exceptionally good at putting her borders in place. Lucy *almost* didn't detect them. Alexis Cove must have been very, *very* rich for a very, *very* long time.

"Lovely to meet you, Lucy," she said with that same warmth that really wasn't. Instead of extending her hand in greeting, though, she lifted it to loop her gold necklace once around her finger. "I'm so glad Dust Bunnies was able to find a replacement for Mrs. Lindstrom on such short notice. You've arrived just in time. I'll be throwing a dinner party this Friday, as we have friends in town unexpectedly. Nothing huge, only twenty or thirty people. But I'm going to have to put you right to work organizing it. Still, I know you'll be up to the task. Won't you?"

 **Chapter 4**

"**B**ut, Phoebe, I don't know nothin' 'bout birthin' no parties!"

Lucy gripped the telephone receiver in her hand—*hard*, on account of her palm was so sweaty with nerves at the moment—and did her very, very best not to succumb to the panic that had been rocketing through her ever since Alexis Cove had uttered her fateful words about her "smallish" party fifty-six minutes and forty-two seconds earlier. Not that Lucy was counting or anything. Fifty-six minutes and forty-five seconds now. Forty-six. Forty-seven. Forty-eight . . .

"Calm down, Lucy," Phoebe said from the other end of the line.

Lucy heard ice shift in her friend's glass as she spoke, so she figured Phoebe was probably enjoying a Margarita out on the terrace of her condo, soaking up some afternoon rays and gazing off at the glassy, deep blue Atlantic. Oh, sure. Easy for Phoebe to stay calm. There was nothing like a Margarita and a view of the ocean—not to mention not having to plan a smallish party for thirty people or being a murder suspect—to make a person feel calm.

"Mrs. Cove must have a regular caterer she uses for her parties," Phoebe continued. "She doesn't expect you to do all the work, she expects you to *call* all the people who do all the work."

"Well, she did give me a list of people to call for food and rentals and stuff," Lucy conceded. "And she gave me the phone numbers of everyone on the guest list, too, so I can call them and follow up with invitations I have to send out. *This afternoon*," she added meaningfully.

"Then you just have to make some calls and address some envelopes," her friend told her. "What's the problem?"

The problem, of course, was that Lucy had to make some calls and address some envelopes. Not that she wanted to tell Phoebe that. Instead, she said, "I just don't think I can handle all the responsibility, that's all."

Back in Newport, Phoebe emitted a rude sound. "What responsibility? If the stuffed mushrooms are mushy and roomy, it's not going to reflect on you. Mrs. Cove will just never use the caterers again. You're temporary, Lucy," Phoebe reminded her. "If she fired you, she'd have to get another temporary housekeeper. Stop being so paranoid."

"Oh, yeah, right," Lucy said sarcastically. "Just 'cause I have the cops in at least one state *and* the FBI looking for me, that's no reason to be paranoid, is it?"

"Hey, I'd worry more about Mrs. Cove than the cops and the FBI," Phoebe said. "Those society matrons can be a hell of a lot more dangerous than overzealous, gun-wielding G-men any day. I mean, my God, would you want to meet Martha Stewart in a dark alley after she'd strapped on a couple of melon ballers? Think about it."

"Phoebe . . ."

"Come on, Lucy. WWDD?"

Lucy sighed. What *Would* Dino Do? "He'd probably fix a drink, call Sinatra and the boys, hire a caterer, and then sing 'Volare.' But—"

"Look," her friend interrupted her, "just think about the kind of food you've liked at the parties you've attended. Think about the most popular recipes in *In the Kitchen with Bitsy and Friends*."

"Oh, yeah," Lucy said, brightening. "I forgot about that. Pinky Mortonson's artichoke puffs would be perfect for appetizers. And I've always adored Georgie Thurston's coq au vin, even though everyone *knows* she stole that recipe from her personal chef, Raoul. She paid him off in exchange for his silence. It was all they were talking about at the club last winter."

"So then all you have left is to send out invitations and call the people on your list," Phoebe said, not commenting on the Raoul controversy. Though what could she say, really? Everyone *knew* Georgie stole that recipe.

Lucy glanced down at the handwritten list she clutched in her other—equally sweaty-palmed—hand, contemplating it as if it were a butcher knife with which someone had just tried to eviscerate her. The analogy wasn't that far off. They were both equally damaging to her peace of mind.

"I don't like my job," she said morosely.

"Yeah, you and 99 percent of the rest of the world," Phoebe replied.

Lucy said nothing for a moment, then, "When can I come home?" she asked plaintively.

This time she heard her friend sigh wearily at the other end of the line. "I don't know, Lucy. It doesn't look good at this end."

"What have you found out?"

"Well, first, that your family is frantic with worry."

Naturally, they were frantic, Lucy thought. A murder accusation was bound to be a blot on the Hollander name. Her mother and Antoinetta must be having a terrible time explaining *that* to the neighbors. "They don't honestly think I'm guilty, do they?" she asked.

"Of course not," Phoebe assured her. "They know what a moron Archie is. They're just worried."

"About how I'm embarrassing the family name?"

"Well, yeah, among other things," Phoebe admitted.

Those other things being about how Lucy was also defaming, dishonoring, and/or disgracing the family name, she thought.

"Should I call them, do you think?" she asked half-heartedly.

"Absolutely not," Phoebe said. "The police can check that

stuff, and I'm sure they'll keep tabs on your family's phone records."

"Have the police come to see you?" Lucy asked, feeling the panic creeping higher with every word Phoebe spoke.

"Yep," her friend replied succinctly.

Ooo, another notch for the panic. "How do you know they're not keeping tabs on your phone records?" she asked.

Phoebe emitted an indignant sound. "They wouldn't dare. Besides, I switched cell phones with my friend Dominic, remember him? The one who's into mild domination and submission? If the cops trace my calls now, all they're going to get are the numbers for some questionable after-hours establishments in three states, and my regular phone will be ringing off the hook with date offers. Life is good."

Lucy decided not to comment on that. Instead, she asked, "What did you tell the police when they came to see you?"

"I told them that Archie's a moron who couldn't execute an arabesque, let alone murder a guy, and that there was no way you could be involved in anything like that, either."

"And did they believe you and drop the charges against me and say it was all right for me to come home?" Lucy asked hopefully.

"Nope," Phoebe replied succinctly again.

"Damn."

"I told the cops I hadn't talked to you since before the Wemberleys' party," Phoebe added. "And that I had no idea where you might go, but that it wouldn't hurt to check your family's Maine retreat up in Bar Harbor. That ought to keep them busy for a while."

"You *lied* to the police?" Lucy asked, aghast that her friend would do that, even while feeling immensely grateful to her for it. "I mean, I thought you'd just withhold information. I didn't think you'd actively lie to them."

"Please, Lucy, you make it sound so sordid. I only bent the truth into a many-sided pretzel and danced all over it, that's all. Hell, it's not the worst sin I ever committed."

"And what would that be?"

"Ah, ah, ah. I don't kiss and tell."

"Phoebe!"

"Anyway, I'm reasonably certain they believed me about not having seen you. They didn't confiscate my computer records or try to lift prints from the bar glasses or anything like that, even though that would have been really cool to see."

"Phoebe . . ." Lucy cautioned again.

"I'm not telling!" her friend assured her. "No way would I rat you out. You know too many things about me that I don't want getting out."

"Have you heard anything more about Archie?"

"All I know is that he's still missing, and no one has a clue where he's gone. The newspapers say he's suspected of murdering a guy who was trading in government secrets and black-market Tupperware."

"Black-market Tupperware?" Lucy echoed, certain she must have misheard.

"Evidently, it's extremely hard to come by in some Eastern European countries, but they just can't get enough of that burp freshness feature on the lids," Phoebe said by way of explanation.

"Oh."

"And according to a homicide detective I used to date—"

"Dave?"

"That's the one."

"I always thought he was so nice, Phoebe. You really should have taken him more seriously."

"He has an extra toe on his left foot," her friend said. "It just creeped me out. Anyway, he said from what he's heard down at the station, the Russian mob is involved somehow, but that part is all hush-hush, and no one is talking about it."

"The Russian *mob*?" Lucy repeated incredulously. "Archie was mixed up with the *mob*?"

"Not just any mob," Phoebe said. "The Russian mob. And according to Dave, they make the Sicilians look like those singing ragamuffins from *Annie*."

"Holy moly."

"Well put."

Had Lucy thought she was panicked before? Gosh, had she been totally mistaken about that. What she felt at the moment went way, *way* beyond panic. *Fright* was a much more appropriate word. So were *menace*, *terror*, and *abject horror*.

"Phoebe, what have I gotten myself into?" she asked.

"*You* didn't get yourself into anything," Phoebe told her firmly. "That moron Archie did. And we're going to get you *out*, don't worry. It's just going to take a little time, that's all."

"But what if the mob is looking for me, too?"

"Sing a couple choruses of 'Tomorrow.' God knows that scared the hell outta me when I saw it. 'Course, it was the traveling production . . ."

"Ha-ha."

"Look, just sit tight," Phoebe instructed. "I'll keep up with things at this end. No one could possibly find you where you are. You're perfectly safe there."

Oh, except for rabid, wild dog Max living across the hall, Lucy couldn't help thinking. One bite from that animal, and heaven only knew where she'd be. And why on earth did the thought of being bitten by Max make her blood run all hot and shivery?

Naturally, she said nothing of that to Phoebe. Instead, she told her friend, "Hurry, Phoebe, okay? I'm not sure how long I can do this."

"You'll be fine," Phoebe said. "Just . . . don't . . . panic."

Lucy glanced down at Alexis Cove's list again, focusing intently on the collection of letters and numbers. Maybe if she just concentrated really hard this time, it would all make sense. But the harder she tried to understand it all, the less sense all of it made.

Different learning pattern, she told herself. That was why she had so much trouble with this kind of thing.

Don't panic, she repeated morosely to herself. *Yeah, right.*

* * *

Max was pondering what to do about the funny *cachunking* sound that had been coming from beneath the hood of Justin's 1937 Bugatti Type 57SC Atlantic-Electron coupé—man, did that guy know cars—when he decided to call it a day. After all, everyone else had called it a day hours ago, back when it still actually *was* day, so why shouldn't he knock off now that the sky was smudged lavender at its brightest edge in the west? Just because he hated to quit when there was something left undone? Just because when he wasn't working on cars, it left his mind open to think about other things he'd really rather not think about? Just because it meant he had to go upstairs and spend the rest of the night—the long, lonely night—in his apartment—his quiet, lonely apartment—knowing that right across the hall slept the lovely and talented Juicy—ah, Lucy—French?

Carefully, he lowered the black Bugatti's hood, stroking his hand over the slick metal surface when it clicked lovingly into place. He loved cars. More than anything else in the world. He loved their luscious curves, their well-toned figures, their elegant beauty. He loved the way they handled, the way they rode, the way they sounded, the way they smelled. He loved the pump of their pistons, the murmur of their motors, the tremor of their tires as they took an unexpected, precarious curve. He loved the volume, the vibration, the velocity. He'd been born with a carburetor for a heart and petrol flowing through his veins, and he never quite felt comfortable unless he was seated in the driver's side of a well-honed machine.

You could trust cars. The good ones, anyway. And you could always tell the good from the bad. They weren't like people at all. Even the worst lemons you could spot with one test drive.

Max wiped a clean rag over the hood of the Bugatti, rubbing away the scant evidence of his fingerprints upon it. Would that life could be cleaned up so easily, he thought, not for the first time. Unfortunately, there were stains there that weren't ever going to come out, no matter how hard he scoured. So he might as well just learn to live with them.

And he was learning to live with them. Pretty much. Or, at least, he had been. Until pretty Lucy French and her short, snug skirt had come along. And now she would be living mere feet away from him, for months no less. But there was something oddly appropriate about that, really. He'd accepted this job from Justin five years ago because he'd wanted to punish himself, surrounding himself with the beautiful cars that would never—could never—be his. Adding Lucy to the mix now only compounded that punishment. He ought to be overjoyed by her arrival.

After wiping off his hands as best he could, Max tossed the rag into a basket with the rest of his dirty laundry—well, the dirty laundry he could see, anyway—then reached up to switch off the bare bulb overhead. In the purple, day's end light that filtered through the carriage house windows, he almost felt as if he'd been carried back in time. Justin didn't keep any cars out here that had been built after World War II, and from where Max stood, he could see first the Bugatti, then, beside it, the 1933 Duesenberg SJ Arlington Torpedo sedan, then, beside it, the 1937 Mercedes-Benz 540K Special coupé, an exceptionally beautiful machine. And then came the 1930 Isotta-Fraschini 8A SS cabriolet, with its spectacular radiator mascot, an Art Deco angel with wings spread back and arms stretched forward, as if she were reaching for the sky itself.

And then, suddenly, Max was thinking about Lucy again.

He expelled a soft sound of frustration, raked a restless, oily hand through his hair, and tried to banish the thought. He remembered then that he'd never had any supper and wondered if he ccould catch Mrs. Hill or Rosemary up at the big house. He remembered, too, the way Lucy had looked at him earlier that afternoon, the clear curiosity etched on her face when he'd been reluctant to enter the kitchen. He hadn't known what to say to her then, so he hadn't said anything at all beyond his assurance that his entering the house wasn't allowed.

But that wasn't because Justin and Mrs. Cove didn't want Max in the house, as he was certain Lucy had concluded. It was because Max wasn't comfortable up there. The place reminded him of too many things he'd just as soon forget, of a life he'd never have again. A life he didn't *want* again, so what was the big deal? Still, he wondered if Mrs. Hill or Rosemary might still be up there, and if they'd bring him something to eat. If not . . . well, he probably had a box of crackers or something in the apartment.

Or maybe he could see if Lucy French—

No. He couldn't do that.

The clock hanging at the far end of the carriage house read nearly nine-thirty—boy, time flew when you were working on beautiful cars and thinking about pretty housekeepers—so he knew Mrs. Hill would be gone. Rosemary, too, would probably have turned in by now, because she never strayed far from Abby once the girl was in bed.

Max's stomach rumbled softly, and he knew he wouldn't be able to sleep unless he had something to eat. Ah, what the hell? he thought. Justin had made it clear when he hired him that Max had the run of the house. Of course, Alexis had quickly countered that that meant the public rooms only. Not that Max had ever considered any part of Harborcourt to be public, seeing as how the Coves restricted guests to only the cream of polite society. Still, he shouldn't feel uncomfortable in a house where he'd been told he was welcome, right? Especially since there had been a time when he'd been the cream of polite society himself. Well, society, anyway. He'd never much been considered polite back then. And maybe he'd been more of the spoiled cream. Still, he shouldn't feel uncomfortable. Even if he did.

But when he rang the bell at the back of the house, it wasn't one of the Coves who answered, anyway. It wasn't Rosemary, either. No, it was—of course—Lucy French who opened the back door to him. She still wore her clothes of earlier in the day, and Max's gaze went right to the scooped neck of her top, whereupon he found himself wanting to run his open mouth along first one delicate collarbone, then the other, to see if she tasted as sweet as she looked. Oh, yeah, he was getting hungrier by the minute. But not for the dinner he'd initially come for.

"Hi," Lucy said when she saw him.

And he told himself it must just be a trick of the light, the way her eyes seemed brighter and her cheeks looked rosier, and her lips appeared plumper than they had that afternoon. Then he remembered that it was nighttime and there was no light to be playing tricks. Then he wondered how that could be, when he suddenly felt so warm and sunny inside.

"Hiya," he replied automatically. "I, uh . . . I missed dinner," he said by way of explaining his appearance.

She nodded a little jerkily. "Rosemary told me you'd probably come by for something when you didn't show up earlier. She said you work late a lot."

Did he? He didn't feel like he worked that much later than other people, any more often than they did. Justin often came home from his own work long after Max had knocked off for the day. Just because Max was always exhausted at day's end, and just because it was usually dark when he finished, and just because it didn't get dark in the summer until after nine o'clock at night, that didn't mean anything. Did it?

"Looks like you're working late, too," he pointed out.

"I, ah, I have a party to plan," she told him.

"Mrs. Cove put you right to work, did she?"

Lucy gave that herky-jerky nod again. Funny, she seemed to be nervous about something. Then again, it *was* her first day on the job, Max reminded himself. And God knew Alexis Cove could scare the bejeezus out of anybody when she turned that Mrs. Freeze look on a person. Even after five years, Max didn't feel at all comfortable around Alexis. But then, she did remind him a lot of the women he'd known before, in his previous life—totally self-absorbed and terrified that no one else realized how important they were.

Lucy stepped aside to allow Max entry, and he tried not to notice as he strode by her how good she smelled, all sweet and soft and womanly. And he tried, too, not to notice how clean she was compared to his own scurvy, unctuous self. Even though he'd washed his hands before leaving the carriage house, he felt dirty and low-down next to her. But then, that really didn't have anything to do with Lucy French. It didn't have anything to do with the grease on his hands, either.

"There's some leftover chicken," she said, as he passed her.

And he tried not to notice how nice she sounded when she spoke, how her voice was breathy and melodic and touched with a gentleness that reached too deep down inside him.

"And rice, too," she added, as Max continued walking and trying not to notice all the things he couldn't help noticing about her. "And there's some salad and carrots and, I think, squash. But Abby may have finished that, I'm not sure."

He willed her not to follow him into the kitchen, but she was obviously much too nice to pick up on that vibe, and instead passed him, beating him to the refrigerator. In an effort to drive his gaze away from her, Max glanced over at the desk beside the big, double-doored appliance and saw papers fanned out, and a phone book open, and pieces of paper crumpled up, and a pencil broken in two, and he realized he was keeping her from her work.

"I'll get that," he said, as she started to reach into the refrigerator for the leftovers. He tilted his head toward the clutter on the desk. "Don't let me keep you from what you were doing."

In fact, he added to himself, *why don't you take it into the next room and finish it there? Or, better yet, the next state. Or, better still, the next planet. Or, best of all, an alternate universe.*

Yeah, that'd work.

Lucy followed his gaze to the desk and grimaced eloquently, and when she looked back at Max, he somehow got the impression that she very much wanted him to keep her from her work. "That's okay," she said, verifying his suspicion. "I could use a little break. Besides, Rosemary offered to help with most of it."

She started to pull a square covered dish from the refrigerator, so Max leaned forward, preparing to take it from her. His shoulder bumped hers in the process, and when it did, he fancied he could feel the heat of her bare arm seeping through his work shirt into his muscle beneath. And he couldn't quite quell the flinch that shook him when his hand closed over hers as he moved to take the dish from her. Her hand was definitely warm beneath his—nothing fanciful about that—just as, he was sure, the rest of her would be warm beneath him when they—

He heard her gasp at the negligible contact of their hands and knew she was thinking the same thing he was. And it was only because she was so easy to read that he was able to catch the dish effortlessly when it went tumbling from her fingers.

"I-I-I'm sorry," she apologized. "I-i-it slipped out of my hands."

"No problem," he told her, trying not to think about how the word slipped made him think about things he shouldn't be thinking about—like how it would be to slip in and out of her as she thrashed and groaned beneath him, commanding him in that breathy voice to go faster, deeper, harder, longer, and to never, ever, stop.

Jeez, Max, get a grip. "I've got it," he added, gripping the dish way more tightly than was actually necessary.

"You certainly do," she said so softly, he wondered if she had even intended for him to hear it.

He was going to ask her what she meant by the comment, but judging by the look on her face just then, he figured he was better off not knowing. So he only took the dish over to the counter and flipped off the plastic lid, finding Mrs. Hill's extremely delectable poached chicken on wild rice beneath. He was turning to collect the rest of the leftovers when he realized—too late—that Lucy French had already retrieved them and was bringing them his way. Once more, their bodies connected, this time front to front, and in addition to a frisson of electricity fairly baking him, a bowl of carrots and plate of salad went tumbling right to the floor at his feet.

And then he and Lucy were both stooping to clean up the spilled food, their arms and hands and fingers tangling as they went about it, both of them apologizing profusely at once, neither hearing the other, neither paying attention to anything except extricating themselves, succeeding only in making matters worse, until finally they bonked their heads hard enough together to send them both slamming backward to land on their fannies. For one brief moment, they only looked at each other blankly, both of them rubbing their foreheads, and neither quite seeming to understand what had just happened. Then, as one, they both began to laugh. Hard. And as they laughed, the tension and awkwardness that seemed to have settled over them evaporated.

For all of fifteen seconds.

Then Max made the mistake of letting his gaze drop to the spilled food. Except that, when he did, it wasn't the spilled food that captured his attention. Because Lucy had landed with her legs sprawled clumsily open, and before he could catch himself—without meaning to, honest—he caught a glimpse of black lacy panties beneath her hiked-up skirt. She must have noticed what he was noticing, because she hastily scrambled to her knees and yanked her skirt back down over her thighs. Then, without speaking a word, but blushing lavishly, she pushed herself to standing and raced to the other side of the kitchen, to wrestle a roll of paper towels from the holder over the sink.

Oh, damn. Max *really* wished he hadn't seen that feathery, black lace covering that silky, soft part of a woman every man fantasized explicitly about. Especially Max, since fantasizing was the only thing he was able to indulge in these days where women were concerned. It had been a long time since he'd enjoyed an actual glimpse of a woman's actual underthings, and he'd *almost* been able to make himself forget what a view like that could do to a man like him. A man who had a *very* healthy sexual appetite and a history of satisfying it whenever—and wherever—he wanted to. And now that he *had* enjoyed an actual glimpse of a woman's actual under-things, and now that he *did* remember what it could do to a man like him—oh, *boy* did he remember . . .

Well. It would probably be best if he just went back to fan-tasizing, he told himself. Unfortunately, he suspected that fantasizing was never going to be enough again.

"I don't think anything got broken," Lucy said as she has-tened back over to where Max still sat on the floor, his arms hooked loosely over his denim-clad knees.

"Just my heart," he said under his breath.

"What?" she asked as she stooped to clean up—keeping her legs clamped together and turned to the side, he couldn't help noticing.

"Nothing," Max said, more loudly this time. "It was noth-ing." He knelt and began to scoop up what he could of the mess, trying to nudge Lucy aside. "I'll do that," he told her. "It's my mess."

"That's all right," she assured him, nudging him back. "I'm the housekeeper, remember? This is my job."

"But you've got something else to—"

"It's okay," she interrupted him. "I'll take care of this. Go ahead and heat up what's left of dinner. I'm sure you're hungry."

Understatement of the century, Max thought. But he con-ceded to her wishes and, after discarding what little of the mess he had managed to clean up in the trash and washing his hands, he returned to the chicken and rice that still sat on the counter. Mostly, though, he'd only conceded to her wishes because he hadn't wanted to get into a nudging match with her. Two nudges and a collision with a woman were about all his deprived libido could stand these days. As it was, he probably wouldn't sleep a wink tonight, because he'd be too busy replaying those nudges and that collision over and over again. He was getting hot already just thinking about the replaying.

Oh, yeah. He had a full night ahead.

He watched Lucy surreptitiously as he prepared a plate and popped it into the microwave for a quick nuking. Always, he made sure he glanced away before she looked up and caught him observing her. Because she did look up while she was cleaning, though whether it was because she liked looking at him, or because she was afraid he might be looking at her, he couldn't exactly say. He did like looking at her, though. He liked it too much. And all Max could do was hope like hell she didn't like looking at him, too. Because if they both liked the *looking*, then there was way too much potential for *doing*. And doing was strictly forbidden. It was forbidden for Max, since he wasn't allowed such pleasures anymore, and it was forbidden for Lucy, since she had a rock on her finger the size of Alcatraz that signified she was meant for someone else.

And then, because he figured he needed reminding of that, Max forced his attention toward that very ring. It was still on her left hand, still ugly, and still representative of her intention to marry another man. It didn't matter if Lucy French looked at him, Max told himself. It didn't matter that she made him wish for things he'd sworn he'd never wish for again. She wasn't his to nudge. She wasn't his to collide with. She wasn't his to laugh with. She wasn't his to watch. She wasn't his to think about at all. She belonged to someone else, someone who obviously intended to keep her forever.

Of course, that someone else wasn't here now, Max couldn't help remembering as he watched her finish cleaning up, then washing up. And if that someone wasn't here now, then who was going to inform Lucy that, during her cleanup, she had somehow gotten a little smudge of butter on her face?

The timer on the microwave beeped for the second time, jolting Max out of his thoughts. But he couldn't bring himself to open the door and remove his dinner and hie himself back to his apartment, the way he knew he should. Because he couldn't bring himself to look away from that shiny little dab of butter on Lucy's upper lip.

"Hey," he said, as she strode by him, presumably to return to her paperwork at the desk. And without thinking, he extended a hand and circled her wrist loosely in his fingers to halt her forward motion.

Immediately, he regretted the action. And immediately, he rejoiced in it. She really was soft. Warm. Womanly. The silky caress of her skin against his bare palm was a sweet torture, one he couldn't resist. Just the feel of his fingers wrapped around her wrist made Max remember what it was like to lie with a woman, to be buried deep inside her as she clung to his back, bucking beneath him, groaning her need, her passion, her fulfillment—

Ah, hell.

No matter his discomfort, though, Max couldn't make himself release her. The contact was just too pleasurable for him to end it yet.

At first, she seemed not to feel quite as moved by the touch as he was himself. But when she glanced up at his face, her pupils dilated, and her cheeks darkened with color. She didn't pull away, though, and didn't comment on his touch. Max wasn't sure if that was good or bad. So he decided not to think about it. And he decided not to end it, either.

"You, ah . . ." He swallowed with some difficulty when he realized how rough his voice sounded, how ragged it felt. "You, um . . ." Still unwilling—unable?—to release her wrist, he pointed the index finger of his other hand toward her face. "You have butter on your lip," he said with a smile.

Her eyes widened in horror, as if he'd just accused her of the most heinous crime. "I do?" Immediately, she swiped at her upper lip with the back of her free hand, but she just missed hitting her target.

"No, here," he said.

And again, without thinking—or maybe he was thinking more than he wanted to admit—Max moved his free hand to her face and, with the pad of his thumb, gently brushed the smudge of butter away. But he pretended he missed it, pretended it was bigger than it really was, pretended he needed to touch her a second time, just to be sure he got it all. And then he realized he wasn't pretending about needing to touch her a second time. And then he was doing more than touching. Then he was cupping her jaw in his palm and gazing intently into her eyes, and wondering what she would do—wondering what he would do—if he leaned forward and covered her mouth with his. For one scant, scintillating heartbeat of a moment, he felt himself take a single step forward in preparation of doing just that. Then, thank God, sanity returned. He released her with much reluctance, and shoved himself away, back to the counter, where he scooped up his plate.

"Thanks for your help," he said without looking at her. "I'll just take it back to my apartment."

And without waiting for an answer, Max Hogan, a man who had once gleefully faced death and dismemberment at speeds nearing 200 miles an hour, ran away. Ran away from a beautiful woman who had the softest skin and the most expressive eyes and the nicest smile he had ever seen.

Only after he'd retreated to the safety of his apartment—safety, yeah, right—did he allow himself to replay the scene in his mind. In slow motion, because he didn't want to skip over a single frame. And as he recalled the way the two of them had laughed for that brief spell, so freely and without inhibition, he realized it was the first good, genuine laugh he'd enjoyed in more than five years. And when he remembered the way Lucy had felt when he'd held her—and he'd only held parts of her, too, and not the best parts of a woman, at that—he realized how badly he'd been kidding himself in thinking that he didn't miss the presence of women in his life these days.

In less than twelve hours, Lucy French had crawled inside him, had located places Max had sworn he'd closed off to the world forever. Worse than that, she had thrown them open wide. And all he could do then was wonder that if she'd done all that in a half day's time, then how much damage was she going to do being here for four months?

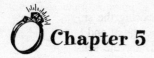 **Chapter 5**

As he leaned against the ornate, cherrywood mantelpiece in Justin Cove's cavernous, grandiose living room on Friday night, surrounded by fine antiques and artwork, sipping eighty-year-old Irish whiskey, gazing at a host of beautiful women, many of them women he'd known intimately in the past, Nathaniel Finn realized he was exceedingly and profoundly bored. Of course, that wasn't unusual. Lately, he'd been spending the better part of every day being bored, often exceedingly and profoundly. If he wasn't bored, he was irritable. And if he wasn't irritable, he was gloomy. And if he wasn't gloomy, he was surly. Which made no sense, really, seeing as how he was living exactly the kind of life he wanted to live, the kind of life that was the envy of every man. He was, after all, the Bad Boy of the Thoroughbred Racing Set—everybody said so. Strangely, though, for some time now, he hadn't been able to feel much satisfaction about that.

Still, his *was* a most excellent life, he once again reminded himself—mostly because he kept forgetting it—and it was only going to get better in a couple of months, once Keeneland held its annual November sale of fillies. Nathaniel had one particularly fine mare to sell this year, a dam to a Triple Crown champion who was in foal by a Derby winner, and he was certain she'd fetch him a cool two million, at least, expensive lady that she was. But the Keeneland sale was months away, and it was much too early to get excited about his prospects there. Not that even that prospect excited him as much as it probably should.

He sipped his drink again, savoring the smoky, mellow spirit as it warmed his mouth and throat and belly. And he smiled grimly when he realized that the sensation of the liquor kindling his insides was the most stimulation he'd enjoyed in months.

Sighing with something that felt vaguely like resentment, Nathaniel pushed himself away from the mantel and made his way across the room to where a trio of his friends—other horsemen—had gathered amid much avid discussion and cigar smoke. He raked his restless fingers through his straight, jet-black hair, then loosened the Valentino necktie he had knotted expertly at his throat. He had conceded to Alexis's edict that he wear a suit and dress shoes to this party to impress her out-of-town guests, but he'd be damned if he'd feel comfortable in them. Give him the solace of denim and boots any day—he was far more comfortable around horses than he was in polite society.

"Justin," he greeted his host and closest friend.

In his sartorial milieu, Justin was dressed in a charcoal-colored power suit and ultraconservative burgundy silk tie. His wavy auburn hair was thinner and a bit grayer these days than it had been when the two of them roomed together at Vanderbilt two decades ago, and his brown eyes were smudged with the perpetual circles caused by too much work and too little play. But then, he was a shrewd, business-minded man, one who had invested well enough and worked hard enough over the years to add a few more zeroes to his family's wealth. Justin was as sharp tonight as he always was, despite the straight two fingers of Bourbon in his cut-crystal glass.

"Nathaniel," Justin greeted him amiably. "Good to see you. Sorry we didn't get a chance to talk earlier when you arrived. Alexis always makes me greet everyone at the door, whether I like them or not. And since they're mostly her

friends . . ." He left the statement unfinished. Not that it necessarily needed finishing, especially when Justin punctuated
it with a theatrical rolling of his eyes. "How are things with
the Bad Boy of the Thoroughbred Racing Set?" he asked instead. "How was Belize?"

"Excellent, as always," Nathaniel replied perfunctorily. It
was a lie, of course. Belize had been exceedingly and profoundly boring, just like everything else. One could only tolerate so much unspoiled natural beauty and so many
nameless, sexually agreeable women, and so long on a lavish
luxury yacht, after all.

"Did you take Tracy with you?"

Nathaniel shook his head. "Candy."

"Oh, ho, back with the Red Zinger are we?"

Nathaniel smiled at Justin's nickname for the leggy redhead who had been his on-again-off-again companion for
years. But if there was one thing Candy did do to a man, it
was zing him. So to speak. And the man nearly went blind
when she did it. Not that Nathaniel minded that part. It was
everything *besides* the zinging that annoyed the hell out of
him where Candy was concerned.

"I was only with her temporarily," Nathaniel assured the
other man. "In fact, she stayed behind in Belize. Photo shoot
or something. Photographer, maybe. I can't remember what
she said."

Justin chuckled knowingly. "Must be hell being the Bad
Boy of the Thoroughbred Racing Set," he observed dryly.

Wasn't it just? Nathaniel thought.

Justin ran his gaze quickly around the room. "Gee, I'd
introduce you to someone new, but I think you know—
biblically, in fact—just about every woman here. Except
Alexis, of course."

Of course, Nathaniel agreed mentally. Not that Alexis
hadn't tried getting to know him biblically. On more than one
occasion.

His host shook his head. "Nope. Sorry. I honestly think
you've had just about every woman in this room, save two or

three, and if you wanted them, you'd have had them by now. You always get your woman. And other guys' women, too, come to think of it."

That last was said without malice, because Justin was confident his own wife would never stray. The sap. Still, he'd been right in saying that the handful of women in the room Nathaniel hadn't had were those whom he had no intention of having. One was way too young, one was way too skinny, and the third was way too married. Not that any of those qualities would normally be an impediment to his bedding a woman, provided she didn't indulge in any offputting behavior like attending *NSYNC concerts or practicing eating disorders or relying solely on the missionary position. But Suzanne Dormer had just barely started her freshman year at UofL and deserved a few drunken frat parties at least before hitting the big time, and Patrice Gordon could give the Grim Reaper a run for his money in the skin-and-bones department, and Sissy Donovan's husband often golfed in the same foursome Nathaniel did, something that would blow his concentration on the greens and therefore affect his game, and God knew he couldn't have that. So those women would just have to suffer without his sexual expertise.

Oh, well.

"So how's that mare coming along?" Justin asked, as he inevitably did every time he saw Nathaniel.

It was no secret to anyone, least of all Nathaniel, that Justin had his eye—both eyes, in fact—on the very mare he intended to sell for that cool two million, at least, in a couple of months. Justin had, in fact, already made an offer for the horse. Unfortunately his offer had been half what Nathaniel expected to make on the sale, the cheapskate.

"She's sassy as ever," Nathaniel said. "Taking nicely to her pregnancy. She ought to go in January."

"Excellent," Justin said. Then, not surprisingly, because it always came to this, he added, "I'll give you a million for her."

Nathaniel laughed. "Dollars American? I don't think so."

"There's no guarantee she'll go in January, or even until November," Justin pointed out. "Anything could happen between now and then. You might end up with a lot less than a cool million. You might end up with nothing at all."

Nathaniel met the other man's gaze levelly. "Is that a threat, Justin?" he asked calmly. Not that such a thing would be unlike his friend. Justin had even fewer scruples than Nathaniel did. And that was saying something, because Nathaniel had, at last count, zero scruples.

His friend smiled indulgently. "Of course it's not a threat. You know I could never allow a fine animal like that to be intentionally hurt."

Of course not, Nathaniel agreed to himself. Justin appreciated anything that was worth a lot of money. Monetary value was, in fact, just about the only thing Justin *did* appreciate.

"I'm just saying," the other man continued, "that a million now is guaranteed. More in November isn't."

"I'll take my chances," Nathaniel said.

"Yeah, you always do," Justin agreed with a chuckle.

What went unsaid—because it didn't need to be said—was that in taking his chances, Nathaniel would naturally win. He always did. Because in addition to being a horseman, a womanizer, and a cad, Nathaniel Finn was a gambler. A good one, too, seeing as how he hadn't come by his initial wealth the way Justin had—by inheriting it. No, though his beginnings were by no means meager, Nathaniel had damned well *earned* every penny he possessed—one way or another.

He was about to change the subject when he noticed that his host was eyeing him in a strangely speculative way. "What?" Nathaniel asked.

But Justin didn't respond right away, only continued to study Nathaniel with a hazy, hypothetical half smile.

"What?" Nathaniel asked again.

"Taking chances," Justin said. "You always do that, don't you?"

Well, what kind of Bad Boy of the Thoroughbred Racing

Set would he be if he didn't gamble relentlessly? Nathaniel wondered. Aloud, though, he only said, "Yeah. So?"

"So how about we make a little wager where that fine filly of yours is concerned?"

Warning bells immediately began to blare at the back of Nathaniel's brain, but thanks to his cockiness and curiosity— not to mention the whiskey and a half he'd already consumed that evening—he didn't listen to them right away. "What do you mean?" he asked.

"I mean a wager," Justin repeated. "You love those. I've never seen you turn one down."

"Not unless it's one I know I'll lose," Nathaniel pointed out.

"You never lose," Justin said.

"Because I'm not stupid," Nathaniel retorted.

"So how about taking me up on this one?" Justin asked.

"Probably because you're so eager to make it," Nathaniel told him.

Justin stopped just short of uttering a pshaw, but he did expel a sound of utter unconcern. Those mental warning bells began to erupt even louder in Nathaniel's head then, and they started hurtling forward, to the very front of his brain. But he still couldn't quite bring himself to heed them.

"What would be the object of this wager?" he asked, knowing it wasn't a good idea to provoke his friend, but curious to hear the terms nonetheless.

"If I win," Justin said, "I get that horse of yours at no charge. If you win, I'll give you *four* million for her."

"Either way, you get the horse," Nathaniel pointed out, not sure he liked those terms, in spite of the potential to double his money.

"And if you win, you'll make twice as much as you're hoping to make on her," Justin reminded him.

There was no way Nathaniel would make four million dollars on the sale of his mare, no matter how naive or uneducated the bidder. Still, it really was way too easy, and Justin really was way too eager. The only way he'd part with so much money would be if he was absolutely certain he would win this bet. Still . . .

"And what would be the terms of the wager?" Nathaniel asked.

"You'll love them, trust me."

Oh, Nathaniel didn't like the sound of that *at all*. "No thanks, Justin. I'd rather—"

"No, really," Justin interrupted. "This wager will be fun for you. It involves having sex."

"With a woman?" Nathaniel asked. He wouldn't put it past Justin to pull something of a questionable nature.

Justin laughed out loud. "Of course with a woman."

"A *human* woman?"

"Yes, a human woman," his host assured him, still laughing. "I'll bet you four million dollars against your mare that I can name a woman in this room you can't get into bed. For sex," he clarified. "You'd have to screw her."

And, oh, wasn't *that* just the most tasteless wager in the world? Nathaniel thought. He liked it. "For the first time? Hell, Justin, as you yourself just pointed out, there's hardly a woman in the room I haven't already had." And if his friend intended to name his wife, Nathaniel had that covered, too. Alexis had come on to him at least a half dozen times in the past. She'd be a pushover.

"Not necessarily for the first time," Justin said. "In fact, it would probably be a bigger challenge for you to get some of them in the sack for a second time. Some of these women, I know for a fact, don't want you in their beds ever again."

Nathaniel smiled. "Their mouths might say no, but their eyes . . ."

"Can it," Justin told him. "I know you don't always end things cleanly with women. I heard you broke up with Cornelia Portman with a fax, for God's sake."

"Hey, that's not true," Nathaniel said. "It was an e-mail, and she was in Bermuda at the time."

Justin made a face of mock concern. "Oh, excuse me for

not thinking you wouldn't take into account her tender sensibilities."

The other part of his friend's statement, however, was true, Nathaniel had to concede. He didn't always end things with women well, and some of them had, oh, taken exception over the years. Some of them wouldn't even attend parties if they knew he was going to be there. Still, it didn't take much to change a woman's mind. The right word, the right look, the right gesture . . . a really expensive piece of jewelry. They were all pushovers as far as he was concerned.

"So if I can bed any woman of my choosing in this room, you'll pay me four million dollars for my horse?" It really was way too easy. Those alarms were just about to deafen Nathaniel now. But for some reason, he couldn't quite bring himself to bail out yet. He didn't know if it was the four million dollars, the prospect of a wager, or the wager itself he found most attractive. There was something sordidly appealing about each of those in itself, but combined . . .

"Not any woman of your choosing," Justin corrected him. "I get to name the woman. And the woman I name, you have to screw her. Within one month's time. Or else I win the bet."

Ah-hah, Nathaniel thought. So there was a catch. Nevertheless, surveying the collection of women present again, he realized he really had already been intimate—so to speak—with the majority of them, and a few of the ones he hadn't been with had made it clear they were interested in him. And none of them was a totally unattractive prospect. The few he'd thought earlier he wasn't interested in suddenly looked more interesting. Hell, he could stand an *NSYNC concert for four million bucks. Probably. And there were a lot worse things to find on a woman than skin and bones. And his golf game probably wouldn't suffer that much.

Despite his realizations and rationalizations, though, the warning bells just wouldn't quiet. And even though Nathaniel knew better, he couldn't quite bring himself to listen to them.

"I don't know, Justin," he said, lifting his drink to his mouth to enjoy another sip. "It just doesn't seem right."

"What? You're morally opposed?" his friend asked incredulously. "When did this happen? Have you seen a doctor? They can fix moral uprightness now. With a debauchery implant or something."

Nathaniel made a face as he swallowed the smoky whiskey. "Hey, my debauchery is just fine, thanks. Of course I'm not morally opposed. What could be morally wrong about having sex? Just because there's a wager involved? Don't make me laugh. What I meant was that taking you for four million dollars doesn't seem right. It'd be like taking candy from a baby, this wager. Even if you are asking for it."

Justin smiled that knowing smile again. "I don't plan on giving you the four million, Nathaniel. I plan on taking that horse from you at no cost to myself."

It was Justin's absolute certainty and smug arrogance as much as anything else that spurred Nathaniel into saying what he did next, though, certainly, the whiskey may have had something to do with it, too. "All right," he told his host. "You're on. You name a woman in this room, and I'll have her in bed—for sex—before the month is out. Hell, I'll have her in bed for sex before the night is out. If I fail, you can have the horse free of charge. But when I win, I'll take that cool four million off your hands in exchange for her."

Justin's smile went supernova at that. "Please, take the whole month to bed her," he said. "I think you're going to need it. Because, Nathaniel, the woman I have in mind for you is right . . . over . . . there."

He pointed toward the far corner of the room, where two big potted palms flanked a baby grand piano. On the bench before the piano, seated nearest to Nathaniel, was Justin's eight-year-old daughter Abby, plinking out a tinny version of what sounded like "Alley Cat." But it wasn't her to whom his host was pointing. Otherwise, Nathaniel would be on the phone in a heartbeat, having his friend arrested for a variety of nauseating crimes—okay, so maybe, deep down, he had *one* scruple. No, it wasn't Justin's daughter to whom his host was directing his pointed finger. It was his daughter's nanny, a drab, colorless woman Nathaniel always overlooked whenever he came to Harborcourt—hence, his neglect in noticing her tonight. Dammit.

"Rosemary," Justin said. "Abby's au pair. Nathaniel, my friend, if you want that four million dollars and don't want to lose that valuable mare, then you're going to have to bed the nanny."

Rosemary hummed softly to herself as she stood at the kitchen sink, rinsing out the dishes from what Abby had called her "bednight snack" since the little girl was old enough to utter her first words. She'd come to work for the Coves right about that time, fresh off the boat from Ireland, a newly educated au pair of only nineteen pressed into service in the New World. Everything about her had felt new then, she recalled now. New life, new job, new outlook, new everything. She hadn't been able to wait to begin. And now, she almost felt as if her other life had happened to someone else entirely.

The hustle of the caterer's employees was beginning to ebb now that the party was past the food stage and well into the drinking stage. Knowing the Coves, though, the party would last long after the caterer had left. Mr. Cove would pour drinks at the bar himself, and Mrs. Cove would take to the piano and play Broadway tunes until she chased the last malingerers home in the wee, wee hours of the morning.

Beyond the window over the sink, Rosemary saw one of the caterer's employees on the patio, taking a cigarette break, and she smiled. How often had she snuck from a big house like this one when she was a teenager, to have a quick smoke? Or, more often, to do other things that she shouldn't have been doing? Ah, well. That was a decade and a lifetime ago. She didn't smoke anymore. And she didn't sneak around. And she didn't do things she shouldn't. She was a grown woman with a good job and a good life, and she wasn't going to do anything to bungle that. No one in this country had any idea about her past. They all thought she was decent and kind and good. And these days, of course, she was.

Even her reflection in the dark window glass threw back an image of a woman who was a proper lady. Well, proper and ladylike enough for a rowdy country like this one. Her hair was knotted atop her head in a discreet bun, and her rose-colored, cotton dress, with its terse row of covered buttons that ran from the hem at midcalf to the only slightly scooped neck, was the picture of conservatism. Oh, yes. These days, Rosemary Shaugnessy passed quite easily for a good girl. Only a fool would do anything to jeopardize such a reputation.

Once the last of the catering staff had left, Rosemary locked up behind them and began dimming the lights, leaving the recessed lighting on so that the Coves wouldn't kill themselves when they stumbled drunkenly in later to open another case of wine. As she stroked her fingertip over the last in a long row of light switches, someone did indeed enter the kitchen, though he wasn't stumbling drunkenly when he did so. Nor, she realized immediately, was that person either of the Coves.

No, it was one of the guests, a friend of Mr. Cove's named Nathaniel Finn. Not that Rosemary had ever paid much attention to the man beyond the casual introduction to him she had received some years ago. Oh, certainly she knew he was one of the area's foremost Thoroughbred breeders, and that he lived in a huge, sprawling estate out Highway 42 some miles—she drove past it occasionally when she had extra time to spend before picking up Abby at school—and that he never seemed to come to the Coves' house with the same woman twice—not that Rosemary cared a whit about that, of course—and that he was forty-two years old, a native of this very state, a graduate of Vanderbilt and had never been married. Oh, and also that he was the Bad Boy of the Thoroughbred Racing Set. Everyone said so.

Beyond that, though, she knew nothing of him. Except

that he was terribly handsome and had the loveliest green eyes she had ever seen.

"Hello," he said before she could say anything herself.

"Hello," she replied politely, telling herself she only imagined the way her stomach flip-flopped at the soft sound of his deep, velvety voice. Then, because she couldn't think of any reason for him to have wandered into the kitchen, other than it being a flagrant mistake, she added, "Can I help you with something? Were you looking for someone?"

He nodded slowly and took another step into the kitchen, his lovely green eyes focused on her face as if it were something worth focusing on. "I was looking for someone, as a matter of fact," he said. "And lucky me. I've found her."

Automatically, Rosemary turned the upper half of her body to look behind herself, to see who the woman in question might be. But behind her, she saw only the empty, sparsely lit, kitchen. She turned again to find Mr. Finn still gazing at her. And then she understood, and the flip-flop in her stomach turned into a full-out typhoon.

"*Me?*" she asked incredulously, stabbing her index finger to the middle of her chest to punctuate the question.

He chuckled a deep, velvety chuckle, his mouth opening into a wide grin over perfect white teeth. "Yes, you," he told her in a voice that was smoother and more intoxicating than good Irish whiskey.

Rosemary expelled a short, nervous laugh. "You must be joking."

He looked puzzled. "Why?"

"Because I'm Rosemary," she told him. "Rosemary Shaugnessy. I work for the Coves. I'm Abby's nanny."

His smile yielded some, but was still charming, and dazzling, and intoxicating. "I know who you are," he said. "Why do you find it so hard to believe that I'd be looking for you?"

She felt a bark of anxious laughter threatening, and slapped a hand over her mouth. "Because I'm Rosemary," she said again, this time from behind her fingers. "Rosemary Shaugnessy, I work for the Coves. I'm Abby's nanny."

"You're also a very beautiful woman," he told her.

And in that moment, Rosemary suddenly understood what was going on. Nathaniel Finn was trying to charm and dazzle and intoxicate her—and damned if he hadn't nearly succeeded—because the evening's festivities and his own overindulgence had made him feel randy. And the nanny was better for warming a man's bed—or the backseat of his car, or the kitchen pantry, or whatever was most convenient—than no one at all, right? It didn't happen often, but it did happen—on occasion, one of Mr. Cove's guests had overindulged and decided the nanny would be an easy target. Normally, Rosemary handled herself well in those situations. But normally, the guests who cornered her didn't have the loveliest green eyes she'd ever seen.

"Mr. Finn," she began.

"You know my name," he interrupted her, taking yet another step into the kitchen, another step closer to Rosemary.

"I know most of the Coves' friends," she told him. "I've been with them for years."

"Do you know some of their friends better than others?" he asked.

His tone of voice was all innocence, but there was something in the question that put Rosemary on even higher alert than before. "Perhaps," she said, taking a step in retreat for no reason she could name, other than that she just felt like she should.

In turn, Mr. Finn took another step forward. He appeared relaxed, his suit jacket open, his tie hanging unfettered from his open collar. He wasn't holding a drink, nor did he reek of liquor or carry himself as a man who was overly intoxicated might. Still, there could be no explanation for his behavior other than that he'd had too much to drink. And Rosemary was smart enough—and experienced enough in such matters—to know that men who were under the influence were in no way predictable.

"Maybe you'd like to get to know *me* better?" he asked as

he took another step forward, his smile and expression innocent, his manner in no way threatening.

In spite of that, Rosemary took another step in retreat.
Then she gracefully circled the cooking island in the center
of the room so that the appliance stood between her and the
unpredictable Mr. Finn.

"Not tonight," she told him, surprised at how very courteous she sounded in light of the less-than-courteous situation.

"Why not tonight?" he asked. To his credit, he halted his
forward motion on the other side of the island, and, clearly
detecting her alarm now, added softly, "You don't have to be
afraid of me, Rosemary."

She swallowed with some difficulty. "Who says I'm afraid
of you? And please. Call me Ms. Shaugnessy."

He smiled at that, and there was something almost appealing in the gesture. "All right. Ms. Shaugnessy," he said politely. "You don't have to be afraid of me. It's not my
intention to hurt you."

"Then what is your intention?"

He lifted one shoulder and let it drop in what she supposed was meant to be a shrug. Somehow, though, she detected nothing casual in the action. "I just want to talk to
you, that's all," he said agreeably. "Get to know you better."

"Some other time," she said. "Right now, I need to check
on Abby."

He eyed her with much speculation. "I thought Abby went
to bed a long time ago. I saw her say her good-nights to her
parents."

"She doesn't sleep well," Rosemary said. "It usually takes
her a while to get to sleep. And she doesn't always stay
asleep. Now, if you'll excuse me . . ."

But instead of catching her drift and leaving, Mr. Finn
said, "I'll wait for you to come back."

She shook her head. "I won't be coming back."

Nathaniel Finn's lovely green eyes narrowed at that. "Why
are you afraid of me?" he asked.

"Why are you here?" she countered.

"I told you. I want to get to know you better. You're an attractive woman."

"And you're an intoxicated man," she replied before she could stop herself.

"I'm not drunk," he said calmly.

Maybe he was, and maybe he wasn't, Rosemary thought. What she did know in that moment, though, was that she was in a dimly lit, deserted room with a man she didn't know well but who had the loveliest green eyes she'd ever seen, and that he was telling her he wanted to get to know her better, and that she was hoping against hope that he was serious but knew he really wasn't, and that she wasn't comfortable in the situation. Whether that was because of his actions or her own responses, she didn't want to consider right now. She only wanted the situation to end, so that she could go back to thinking clearly.

Still trying to hang on to her civility, Rosemary said, "Please excuse me, Mr. Finn. I have to go."

For one scant moment, she thought he was going to bolt around the island and make a grab for her. Something in him seemed to tighten, seemed to radiate, seemed ready to blow to bits. And Rosemary, God help her, found herself halfway wanting him to do it. She had no idea why, but there it was all the same. There was something about Nathaniel Finn that made her want to do things she shouldn't do, things she hadn't done for a very long time, things she had sworn she would never, ever do again.

And then, suddenly, he relaxed. He took a step backward, holding his arms out to his sides in an unmistakable gesture of surrender. "My apologies," he said. "I didn't meant to upset you."

"You didn't upset me," she told him.

"Didn't I?"

"No."

He smiled at that. "Then I must be losing my touch."

"Good night, Mr. Finn," Rosemary said firmly.

He dipped his head forward in clear concession. But Rosemary suspected that, although he might be conceding the battle now, he was by no means conceding the war. Whatever he had begun, and whyever he had begun it, he wasn't finished with it—wasn't finished with her—yet. That, if nothing else, Rosemary knew. She just wished she understood the *whyever*.

"Good night, Ms. Shaugnessy," he said in the same deep, velvety voice that had initially set her on edge. And with the uttering of those four words, he spun around and began to make his way out of the kitchen. But he halted at the door and pivoted one more time to look at her. "Until we meet again," he said levelly.

"We won't meet again," Rosemary assured him.

But Nathaniel Finn had already gone, and she was fairly certain he hadn't heard her.

It was going on four in the morning when Nathaniel finally untangled himself from Patrice Gordon's bony arms and said his good-nights to Justin and Alexis. He shuddered involuntarily at how distasteful it would have been to have sex with someone that gaunt and haggard. She could have put an eye out with one of those elbows. Give him a woman with curves any day. Thank God Justin had named Rosemary Shaugnessy instead.

Strangely, as the sentiment unrolled in his head, Nathaniel realized it felt genuine. Not that he was in any way happy about having been stupid enough to fall for Justin's wager, mind you. But since he *had* been stupid enough to fall for it, and had no choice now but to go through with it, at least he was oddly satisfied with Justin's selection of the nanny as part of the terms of that wager.

Of course, Nathaniel hadn't been satisfied with her as Justin's selection at first. No, his first thought had been something along the lines of how he was about to lose the best piece of horseflesh he'd ever owned. Because he'd figured there was no way—*no way*—he was going to warm up that icy little nun. Even Nathaniel Finn couldn't work miracles. But as he'd watched Rosemary Shaugnessy at the piano, as he'd noted her frequent smiles and more frequent laughter with Abby, as he'd realized that she was actually kind of pretty in a wholesome, go-to-church-every-Sunday, eat-all-your-vegetables, down-on-the-farm kind of way, he'd begun to think that it might be fun to try.

And then, when he'd cornered her in the kitchen, he'd felt much better about his prospects. He had known instantly that not only did he stand a chance with Miss Chaste Little Nun, but that she was ultimately going to be just as big a pushover as any other woman. Because there had been something in her eyes and demeanor that he had detected right off, something passionate and fiery and simmering just beneath her surface. She might try to fight it, and she might try to hide it, and she might even succeed in both for a while, but eventually, Rosemary Shaugnessy would succumb to the conflagration blazing inside her.

Eventually, Rosemary Shaugnessy would be his.

And once Nathaniel had realized that, suddenly, his life no longer felt exceedingly and profoundly boring. No, suddenly, he couldn't wait to wake up the next day. It might take a while—hell, it might take the entire month Justin had given him—but Nathaniel would have Rosemary. And it was going to be great fun getting her.

When he finally made it to his car, he hesitated before climbing into it. He'd been one of the first to arrive at the party and had, as always, parked in back of the house, near the garage. As he approached his midnight blue Jaguar roadster, however, a light went on in the kitchen behind him, and, reflexively, Nathaniel turned around to look. Inside the house, he saw Rosemary Shaugnessy carrying Abby Cove into the kitchen, hoisting her up onto the counter closest to the window. Abby's chestnut hair tumbled in a tangle around her shoulders, and she rubbed her nose with the short sleeve of her pink pajama top as Rosemary disappeared from view.

The open window allowed Nathaniel to hear the soft murmur of their voices, even though he couldn't understand a word of what either of them said. But there was something about the gentle lull of combined feminine sounds that was soothing and cheerful, as was the unexpected ring of Abby's sudden laughter. Coupled with the gentleness of the sight, Nathaniel felt a strange sense of well-being wash over him.

Not sure why he did it, he hesitated by his car, realizing he had an odd desire to observe the display a bit longer. Probably, he thought, it was only because in that one brief glimpse he'd enjoyed of Rosemary before she'd vanished from view, he'd seen that she was dressed in a white cotton nightgown, with thin, lacy straps, one of which had slipped low over her creamy shoulder. And also because her long, long hair hung down her back in a ponytail that had been gathered loosely at her nape with a length of pale blue ribbon. He hadn't seen the end of that ponytail from where he was standing, even though, from his viewpoint, he had been able to see the nanny nearly down to her waist.

Really, he told himself, there was nothing much in the scene to keep, or even draw, his attention. A wakeful, scrawny little girl, and a farm girl/nanny dressed in celibate white. Somehow, though, he couldn't tear his gaze away. Abby was swinging her spindly little legs as Rosemary reappeared to hand her a glass of milk, and Rosemary—

Good God. Nathaniel's heart nearly stopped beating when he saw what Rosemary was doing. Because what Rosemary was doing was so remarkable and so fantastic, he simply could not believe his eyes. What Rosemary was doing then was—

Smiling. Rosemary was smiling.

And not just any smile. No, as she handed the glass of milk to Abby, she smiled at the little girl in a way that Nathaniel had never seen a person smile before. In his experience, there was always something hiding behind a person's smile—a deception, a favor, a trade. The only reason people ever smiled at him was because they wanted something in return. But Rosemary's smile for Abby was natural, untainted, guileless. The only thing behind it was an obvious love for the child in her care. It was a smile that had come about simply because she must have felt happy in that moment. Happy about giving a little girl a glass of milk in the middle of the night. There was nothing more to it than that. And something about seeing that smile twisted something inside Nathaniel so hard, and with such a keen pain, that he actually felt his knees weaken beneath him.

Naturally, he caught himself before he crumpled to the ground, but he dropped his car keys. And the quiet crash they made as they hit the pavement carried loudly through the still night, right through the kitchen window. Rosemary obviously heard it, because she darted closer to Abby and glanced out the window. And her smile fell when she saw who stood beyond it.

She said nothing, but draped an arm protectively around Abby as if she feared for the girl's safety. Nathaniel had to smile himself at that, though it wasn't a smile of happiness. He just found it ironic that Rosemary would be so worried for her charge when in fact it was she herself she should be worried about. Her days as a chaste little nun were numbered, he thought as he bent to scoop up his keys and continue toward his car. She might try to hide behind that sweet and innocent veneer, but he'd discovered something inside her earlier that evening that he fully intended to exploit, guileless smile or no. She would be his. Soon. He only had to be patient.

He started his car and listened with contentment to the quiet, easy rumble of the engine, then began to plot just how he was going to win his wager with Justin. And he ignored the strange little prickle of what felt suspiciously like a scruple nibbling at the base of his brain. And as he threw the car into reverse and eased the sleek vehicle carefully back from where he had parked, the Bad Boy of the Thoroughbred Racing Set never, not even once, looked back at the peaceful scene in the kitchen.

He didn't dare.

 Chapter 6

In her first week of working as housekeeper for the Coves, Lucy had eight problems, averaging a little over one per day. But she figured the first one, "Meeting Max Hogan," was un-avoidable—how, after all, was she supposed to avoid the car guy when she'd be residing in the building where he lived and worked?—so maybe she shouldn't include that one, since it wasn't so much a problem as it was a great, hulking insur-mountable obstacle.

So that left her with only seven problems in that first week. Which, actually, was surprisingly few for her, once she thought about it.

Astonishingly, none of these problems had arisen with or during Alexis Cove's "smallish" party Friday. But that was only because Rosemary had volunteered her services, not the least of which had been calling the guests because Lucy hadn't known any of them and might therefore be uncom-fortable speaking with them. Then the nanny had taken Lucy aside on party night to point out each guest and give her a quick rundown on that person, so that the next time Lucy was obliged to call them, she wouldn't feel shy, thereby abolish-ing that little obstacle.

Naturally, Lucy hadn't wanted to tell Rosemary that knowing more about the people on the list wouldn't neces-sarily abolish that obstacle, since it was the list itself, and not its manifested contents, that gave her the most trouble. Still, it had been nice of Rosemary to help her out. And Rosemary had helped more than she knew.

Lucy had spent the rest of her week doing all the usual things one did when one was beginning a new career in a strange place: avoiding the car guy, avoiding the nanny, avoiding the little girl for whom the nanny cared, avoiding her employers, avoiding work, and, once, having a panic attack in the linen closet on the third floor. It helped enormously that Mrs. Lindstrom had given the house a good going-over before she left, because no matter what room Lucy checked at Harborcourt when she was busily avoiding everyone and everything, it was spotless. The Coves—except for Abby—were fanatically tidy people, but Rosemary had assured Lucy that she would tend to the little girl's room, along with the little girl. That tidiness was probably made possible by the fact that the Coves also were seldom home. The elder Coves, at least. Abby, except for school, seemed to go out very little.

So really, Lucy's first week working for the Coves was a remarkably uneventful one, something that one might conclude would lead to *no* problems, instead of seven—plus one great, hulking insurmountable obstacle. Still, even those seven problems probably wouldn't have been all that bad, except that, although she averaged one problem per day, all seven of them actually occurred in one day. The good news was, they came on her day off. The bad news was, they came on her day off. And the worst news was, on her day off from work, Lucy started her first day of school.

When Phoebe had hacked into the local university's enrollment records, she had signed Lucy up for three classes, the first of which was the inescapable Engl 628, Metaphysical Poets, a three-hour session on Monday nights taught by a Professor Besser, which was probably the last night of the week that you wanted to be studying metaphysical poets, coming off the weekend the way it was. Not that Tuesday would have been any better as far as Lucy was concerned. Or

Wednesday or Thursday, either. Especially since she had the equally inescapable Engl 542, John Donne, taught by a Dr. Proctor, for three hours on Wednesday evenings, and the probably also inescapable—if Lucy could just figure out what the hell it meant—Engl 609, Special Topics: Scholastical Quiddities, taught by a Mr. Lister, for three hours on Thursdays.

Really, she thought after she was *finally* able to decipher that last class on her schedule—though sometimes she had to wonder if she actually *had* deciphered it—she should have stopped Phoebe after that first green martini. Because between Mr. Lister, Dr. Proctor, and Professor Besser, she figured it was a good bet to conclude that her student advisor was going to be Dr. Seuss.

Monday was going to be the worst, she decided, since that was already her least favorite day of the week, anyway— problem number one—and, call her crazy, three hours of metaphysical poetry just didn't seem like something that would improve it—problem number two. As she stood outside Professor Besser's class, dressed in what she hoped was a student-appropriate combination of Phoebe's black mini-skirt and cherry red tank top sporting the command "Kiss Me, You Fool"—though, judging by the looks of the young men entering the classroom, she was dressed in a combination that was appropriate for something else entirely, if it were actually appropriate at all (*Note to self, Lucy: Shop for your own wardrobe pieces this week, before it's too late*)— and holding the massive tome she'd been required to purchase at the UofL bookstore that very afternoon—problem number three—she asked herself, not for the first time, what on earth she thought she was doing. Besides living a lie and kidding herself and thinking she would be able to pull off an impossible charade, she meant.

She had ridden to school with Dimitri—problem number four, though that wouldn't become evident until later—who had finished working on the roses and peonies at Harborcourt about the same time Lucy was ready to call a cab to take her to school. Though why she found it necessary to perpetuate that part of her deception, she still wasn't sure. She supposed she just didn't want to risk *anyone* becoming suspicious of her presence, not even university instructors who didn't know her from Adam—or Eve, as might be more appropriate in this case. At any rate, when Dimitri—who, incidentally was no more old, wizened, or foreign than Max was—discovered she was off to class and that he was, too, he immediately offered her a ride. And Lucy had been able to find no good reason to turn him down.

Surprisingly, once her metaphysical poetry class got going, it moved along nicely with fairly little incident. Well, okay, with only two incidents. The first was when Lucy got disoriented while trying to follow along in her massive tome and almost threw up—problem number five. But she remedied that by giving up on actually looking at the collection of letters and words on the page and only pretending to be interested in the lecture. The second incident was when Professor Besser called on her and asked her a question about Gongorism and/or the European baroque—problem number six—and Lucy had replied by saying that she had to go to the bathroom.

Thinking back, though, maybe that wasn't actually a problem after all, as Professor Besser—after gazing curiously at Lucy for a moment over the lenses of his big glasses—told Lucy she could be excused, and when she got back, the lecture had moved on to something else entirely. Still, Lucy made a mental note to look up Gorgonism and/or the European opera as soon as possible—which made *that* problem number six.

She managed to stay blissfully preoccupied for the remainder of the class by thinking about all the things she was going to do once she was cleared of her murder charge—starting with strangling that moron Archie, which would necessitate, she supposed, another murder charge, but at least that one would be justified, not to mention worth it. Then, finally, after three grueling hours, the class ended, and Lucy was free. So she gathered up her massive tome and her notebook and her pen, and packed them all up in her backpack—pretending all the while that they *weren't* the tools of Satan—grabbed the empty Diet Pepsi can that had been responsible for her trip to the bathroom in the first place—well, that and Goldyism and/or the Ugandan opera—and walked out of the classroom . . .

. . . to find Max Hogan leaning against the wall opposite the door. Problem number seven.

Which, now that she thought about it, was worth way more than all the other problems put together. The moment she saw Max standing there staring at her, one thought, and one alone, stampeded to the forefront of Lucy's brain: WWDD? Fortunately, an answer was right behind it. Well, Dino would probably fix a drink, then call up Sinatra and the boys, then say hello, and then sing "Mack the Knife." "Mack the Knife," though, Lucy thought, was pretty much out of the question, because she never could remember all the words. And the drink would have to wait until she got home. Sinatra and the boys, she was certain, were much too busy to take her calls. However . . .

"Hello," she said nervously. That much, at least, she could do in Dino's honor.

She really had done her best to avoid Max since their curious exchange in the Coves' kitchen. Oh, she'd seen him, but she'd made sure it was always from a distance—her apartment window, say, when he was working shirtless in the afternoon heat, his muscular torso streaked with perspiration and machine oil, his faded blue jeans hugging his tight butt with much fondness. Not that she'd paid that much attention to him, mind you. She was, after all, avoiding him.

Or else she'd seen him returning from the big house after dark carrying a plate of food, clearly reluctant to take his meals there at any time, the moonlight silvering his dark hair and handsome profile and giving him the appearance of a

brooding Heathcliff haunting the moors. And when she'd
seen him like that, all she'd been able to think about was how
it would be to sit beside him in the darkness and watch the
moonlight reflected in his dusky eyes, then trace the line of
his full lower lip before covering his mouth with her own, and
curving her hand over the taut muscles of his shoulder as she
urged him backward, down to the ground, so she could kiss
him and kiss him and kiss him. Not that she'd paid that much
attention to him, mind you. She was, after all, avoiding him.

And once she'd seen him, late at night, when she'd been
having trouble sleeping—she couldn't imagine why—and
was up late watching *Guys and Dolls* on cable. Right at the
point where Sky Masterson had no choice but to accept
Nathan Detroit's dastardly bet that he couldn't take Sister
Sara Brown to Havana—boy, good thing Marlon Brando re-
deemed himself at the end of that one—she'd heard Max
drive up and had gone to the window to see him returning
from having apparently driven Mr. and Mrs. Cove to a formal
event. Because on that occasion, he had been dressed in full
chauffeur livery, complete with dark gray, double-breasted
jacket, jodhpurs, and shiny black boots.

Lucy had never fancied herself to be the kind of quivering,
giggly society deb who lusted after the servants, but seeing
Max dressed in those boots and jodhpurs, all she'd been able
to think about was what it would be like to unfasten each of
those shiny brass buttons on his jacket, thrust it open, and
tumble him into the backseat of the Duesenberg for a quick
game of handle-the-stick-shift. And then, as she'd watched
him through the window, he himself had begun to unfasten
those shiny brass buttons, one by one, revealing nothing but
his naked, brawny chest beneath. He must have sensed her
watching him—all right, all right, *ogling* him—as he performed the action, because he'd glanced up at her window
and caught her staring, and Lucy, panicked, had quickly
moved away. Still, she hadn't slept much that night, thanks to
the tumble of strange visions—most of them featuring a

nearly naked Max Hogan and a wide, leather-upholstered backseat against her bare bottom—that had kept her staunchly awake.

Not that she'd paid that much attention to him, mind you. She was, after all, avoiding him.

It made no sense. She wasn't the kind of woman who normally indulged in such whimsy. Especially such *explicit* whimsy. Although she'd had a boyfriend or two over the years—she'd even been intimately involved with one of them for a time—Lucy had never considered herself to be a sexual animal. Neither had any of the boyfriends, as a matter of fact, something that had inevitably contributed to the dissolution of those involvements. Even the one with whom she'd been intimate had told her she wasn't adventurous enough for him. Not that he'd given her a chance to be adventurous, so quick on the, ah, outlet had he been.

But ever since her first glimpse of Max Hogan, Lucy had felt sexual—had felt *animal*—in the extreme. He was just that kind of man, the kind who immediately made clear, probably without even realizing it, that he knew things a woman wanted to learn. It was more than just how handsome he was. There was an air about him. An aura. An attitude of having gained more knowledge and enjoyed more experience and lived more life than anyone else ever could. Yet he worked as the car guy for the Coves of Kentucky. How, Lucy wondered, could he give the impression of someone so worldly, so sophisticated, so accomplished?

And try as she might, she hadn't been able to avoid replaying in her mind—over and over again, in fact—that little scene in the Coves' kitchen. She told herself she must have only imagined the way he had touched her that night when he'd gone to wipe the butter off her face, that the brush of his fingertips over her cheek couldn't possibly have been as intimate or as affectionate as it had felt. And she told herself she also must have only imagined the look in his eyes when he touched her, so peculiar and hungry and needful had it seemed. And she told herself, too, that she must have only imagined her own response to him, the quick, hot swelling in the pit of her stomach that had made her want to reach out and touch him back.

But now she was beginning to think that she hadn't imagined her response at all. Because tonight, just looking at him, leaning so insouciantly against the opposite wall, that hot, swollen feeling was back—with a vengeance. Max was no less appealing now than he had been every other time she'd seen him, wearing extremely snug, extremely faded Levi's, and a shrunken, likewise snug, heather gray T-shirt emblazoned with the sole, red word "Ferrari"—she recognized it not so much because of the word, but because of the prancing horse logo at the end; her brother Emory drove a Ferrari. And, somehow, even in that simple ensemble, Max exuded an allure, a fascination, a downright bewitchment. She supposed he did that simply by being alive.

"Hiya," he said in response to her greeting, just as he had that first night when he'd come up to the Coves' kitchen for dinner.

"Hi," she replied obediently again, mostly because she'd forgotten she'd already said hello, so drawn into his enchantment, so fairly drowning in it, was she by then. "What, ah . . . What are you doing here?"

"I came for you," he said.

His voice, she noted as she always did when he spoke, was dark and rich with sexuality and innuendo, even when he said nothing that could possibly be mistaken for anything other than the simple statement that it was.

"Why?" Lucy asked, thinking it a very good question.

"Dimitri's class ended an hour early, but he didn't want to leave you stranded," he said. "He knew I was out, so he called me on the cell phone and asked if I could swing by and pick you up. He had something else he wanted to do. There was a girl involved, I believe."

"Oh."

Lucy told herself to say something else, something along the lines of, "Help! Help! There's an overly sexy man offering to give me a ride home!" but no matter how hard she tried, she couldn't for the life of her manage to get any words out. Not that anyone would have probably come to her aid for yelling such a lame thing anyway. Lots of women probably would have liked to have an overly sexy man offer to give them a ride home. So would Lucy, come to think of it. Under other circumstances. Circumstances like, oh . . . she didn't know. Maybe like if she *wasn't* living a lie. Like if she *didn't* have the FBI breathing down her neck. Like if the Russian Mafia *wasn't* looking to make her food for the sturgeons. Like if that moron Archie *hadn't* stuck an ugly engagement ring on her finger.

Stuff like that.

Max nodded toward her outfit—at least the top half of it, the part with writing—and asked, "Am I supposed to take you at your word on that? Of course, if I did, I'd have to admit to being a fool, wouldn't I? Not that that's necessarily such a bad thing. There are some things that are worth being a fool for."

Oh, God, Lucy thought, her mouth going dry. He was doing it again. Saying things in a way that made her feel all hot and wobbly all over, looking totally earnest as he said them, as if she were the only one getting ideas she shouldn't be having.

"Ah . . ." she began eloquently, stringing the single syllable over several time zones. "No," she finally concluded. "It's, um . . . The shirt, I mean . . . It's . . . uh . . . A friend gave it to me," she finally managed to get out, amazed at not only being quick on her feet—even if it really wasn't all that quick, and even if it was in a decidedly monosyllabic way—but also at how she had been able to be honest while doing it. "A gag gift," she added—still monosyllabically, she couldn't help noting—so that he wouldn't get the wrong idea about her alleged friend. Even though she knew Phoebe wore this particular tank top with a straight face, and that any ideas he was getting about Phoebe as a result of this particular tank top were probably dead on target anyway.

He nodded, but, thankfully, refrained from comment. "So," he said when her silence dragged on. "Need a lift home?"

Lucy swallowed hard and nodded. "Uh-huh," she said, immensely proud of herself for being able to actually expel a sound when she noted again the way his hard, muscular torso filled out that tight T-shirt. And it was a sound that wasn't rude or socially unacceptable, either, by God. She didn't dare ruin that by dropping her gaze any lower—as much as she found herself wanting to. "I mean, if Dimitri's left, I do," she managed to add. Wow. She was really cookin' now. Last time she checked, the word Dimitri was *not* monosyllabic. "I'm not really positive how the buses work yet," she finally concluded, becoming even more polysyllabic in the process. Good for her.

"Buses don't run to Glenview, anyway," Max told her, pushing himself away from the wall. "I mean, they do, but not into Glenview proper. You'll have a walk ahead of you if you take the bus home."

"I don't mind walking," she said.

He shrugged. "Fine. I'll just head on back then."

As he started to turn away, Lucy fairly shouted, "No, I didn't mean that! Please don't go!"

When he turned back around, she saw that he was smiling. A devilish, teasing little smile that had the effect of making her feel as if she'd just been . . . Gosh. Swamped by a mighty, boiling-hot tidal wave that knocked her right off her feet and filled her entire body with a dangerous, languorous sort of warmth. Wow. That felt really . . . interesting.

He'd only been joking, she realized then. And now he knew how very badly she wanted him to stay and give her a lift home.

"I mean, I don't mind walking the next time," she said. "I'd really appreciate a ride home tonight. If it's not too much trouble."

"It's no trouble at all, Ms. French," he said. "I'll be glad to give you a ride anytime you want one."

And although that statement could most certainly have been taken as sexual innuendo, there was instead something in Max's voice when he said it that sounded almost . . . wistful? Oh, surely not, Lucy thought. Surely she was only imagining that. Surely it was only politeness that she detected. Men like him didn't get wistful. It wasn't manly.

He took a few steps toward her, and even that uncomplicated movement was filled with something rawly masculine, and purely carnal, and utterly irresistible. But Lucy honestly didn't think his obvious—and ample—sexuality was intentional, or even conscious; it was just the way Max Hogan was. She supposed he really couldn't help himself. The problem was, neither could she.

"Carry your books?" he asked as he came to a stop beside her.

Someone exited the classroom behind her without watching where he was going and bumped into her, pushing her over the scant foot of space that still separated her from Max. He caught her effortlessly and kept her at a safe distance when she would have slammed into him, and when her backpack went sliding down her arm, he caught that effortlessly, too, and, in the same fluid movement, swung it over his own shoulder.

"Jeez, how many books do you have for this class?" he asked.

She made a face. "Only one."

"Feels like a force to be reckoned with."

"Yes, well, Professor Besser's course *is* a force," Lucy told him. "But the woman sitting next to me said that Mr. Lister's class is a blast. And she said that Dr. Proctor really rocked her last semester."

Max eyed her warily. "Why do I feel like I just fell into a Danny Kaye movie? Is there going to be a chalice from the palace in this conversation?"

Lucy smiled, delighted to discover he was an old movie buff, too. "Maybe just a flagon with a dragon," she said.

He smiled back. "So you like old movies, huh?"

She nodded. "Yeah. A lot."

"Me too," he told her, sounding reluctant to reveal that for some reason. "They pretty much helped me survive my childhood."

There were three things about his statement that Lucy found amazing. First, that a man would confess to liking old movies to begin with. Second, that he would admit the pastime had gotten him through a rough time. And third, that the words he spoke could just as well have come out of her own mouth. Old movies had always been her salvation as a kid, too. Hers and Phoebe's both.

She smiled at Max again as she replied, "Yeah. Me too."

Neither seemed to know what to say after that, so, as if by mutual agreement, they both began walking toward the stairs. As they strode along in silence, Lucy tried not to feel too awkward. And she tried not to notice how much taller he was than she, or how much broader, or how much harder he was than she. And she also tried not to notice how he seemed to have shaved very recently, because the normal dark stubble that made him look so dangerous and overwhelming was gone, making him look . . . Well. He still looked dangerous and overwhelming, she thought. But he probably wouldn't abrade her skin while he was being dangerous and overwhelming with her. And then she thought about him being dangerous and overwhelming with her—not to mention abrading her skin—and she suddenly felt herself coloring, and made herself glance away so that he wouldn't see her blush.

And as they exited the Humanities Building into the dark, balmy summer evening, she was suddenly very happy that she didn't have to take the bus home.

"I parked in one of the faculty spaces," Max said, as they strode through the parking lot. "But this time of night, I don't think they much care."

"You rule breaker, you," she teased.

"Not really," he replied. "Not anymore."

Something in his tone kept her from responding to that, as much as she wanted to. So she only walked along with him in silence, then was surprised when he led her to a car she recognized as Justin Cove's. Not one of the rarer, older, more expensive models that the man collected, but the ah, less rare, less old, less expensive, Porsche Carrera, which was still a very nice—and costly—bit of machinery. Max seemed to detect her reaction, because as he pushed the keyless entry and the car responded with an elegant chirp, he smiled again—though a bit more grimly than before.

"Justin doesn't mind me driving one of his regular cars on occasion. He knows I appreciate exceptional craftsmanship."

"You don't have a car of your own?" Lucy asked.

Max shook his head. "It's not allowed."

She wanted to ask him about that curious reply, too—Why would the Coves forbid him from owning his own car, and more to the point, why would he go along with such a rule?—but he opened the passenger-side door for her to climb inside, tossing her backpack into the rear compartment. And by the time he'd rounded the front of the car and climbed in himself, she got the distinct impression that he didn't want to continue with that line of conversation *at all*. Actually, she got that impression when he immediately turned the key in the ignition, bringing the tiny black car into roaring life, something that pretty much prohibited her from commenting on anything, so noisy was the rumble of the engine.

She got the impression even more strongly when, after he thrust the gearshift into reverse, he said, "Let's talk about something else."

But the car bellowed even more loudly as he started backing it out, making Lucy think that maybe she should wait a bit before starting up the conversation about anything. Not that she could have said much at that point anyway, because when he extended his arm across the small confines of the car and braced it over the back of her seat—presumably to aid himself as he backed out of the parking space, because why else would he do it?—he brushed his forearm over the side of her neck. And although Lucy was certain it was an accident, that didn't keep a little explosion of heat from detonating on her skin where he made contact.

"Sorry," he said when he realized he'd touched her.

But there was nothing apologetic in his voice when he said it. No, mostly his voice was strained and irascible when he said it. But he immediately removed his arm when he turned his body forward again, to shift again and accelerate, making the car howl as loudly as ever as it leapt into drive.

They rode without speaking for some moments, then Max pressed his thumb over the buttons that lowered the car's windows. "Do you mind?" he asked. "It's a good night for it."

"I don't mind at all," she said. "I love it with the windows down."

He smiled, all grimness suddenly vanishing again. "Me too. Let's take the scenic route home, shall we?"

She nodded. Like she would have known differently if he hadn't?

But she realized quickly that she would indeed have known differently. Where Dimitri had driven to campus over suburban roads and an expressway, with Max, she found herself traveling from campus through an urban neighborhood filled with big, old brick Victorian homes that were interspersed with laundromats and liquor stores. Neon mixed with lamplight, and concrete sidewalks mingled with massive, sprawling oak trees. The night wind was muggy and mild as it hurried through the windows, whipping Lucy's hair wildly around her face. She wasn't used to having hair this short. Before, she'd always had it bound in some way, so that it couldn't fly free. The feel of it now, caressing her skin, her cheeks, her mouth, was an oddly erotic sensation.

"So are you from around here originally?" Max asked suddenly, loudly, to be heard over the rumble of the engine.

"No," Lucy said. "I grew up in Rho . . . Um . . ." Now what?

she wondered, her brain scrambling frantically for some birth-place other than Rhode Island. Rhodesia? Romania? Rome? Romulus? "Ah . . ." she tried again. Then, suddenly, "Roanoke," she said in a burst of inspiration, fairly shouting to be heard over the car's thundering. "Roanoke, Virginia."

"Is that where your fiancé lives, too?" he asked further, never taking his eyes from the street.

"My fiancé?" she asked, confused.

"Yeah," he said. "The guy who put that ring on your finger."

Oh, *that* fiancé, she thought. Funny, she kept forgetting she was supposed to have one. And not just in her phony life, either.

Automatically—and not a little anxiously—her right hand flew to her left and she tried to twist the gaudy ring from side to side. It was marginally looser now than it had been when that moron Archie first shoved it over her finger—not that that was saying much—but no amount of soap, butter, salad oil, Vaseline, ice, or any other material had aided her in its re-moval. It was almost as if the hideous thing had marked her, had branded her as the fiancée of a man who had very bad taste. So what did that say about her? she wondered. She sup-posed she really didn't want to know. Because whatever it was, that was what Max Hogan thought of her.

"Uh, yes, he still lives where I grew up," she said, congrat-ulating herself for not lying. Not on that one answer, anyway. That one answer among the scores of false ones she had given in the past week.

She also wanted to not lie and say that that moron Archie wasn't her fiancé, either, because technically, she hadn't told him she would marry him, but something kept her from doing so. Maybe it would be better if Max thought she was engaged, she thought. And maybe it would be better if she kept remind-ing herself that she was supposed to be engaged. Because there was obviously something burning up the air between the two of them—she only wished she could figure out what—and she didn't think it would be a good idea for either of them to do anything that might turn up the heat on whatever that something was. It was damned near explosive as it was now. She didn't want to think what would happen if it got any hotter.

Well, okay, maybe she did want to think about that. Maybe she already *had* thought about that. But it was only thinking. Perfectly safe. Except for it making her want to, you know, stop thinking and start exploding.

"So when's the big day?" Max asked, snapping her out of her troubling reverie and dropping her back into her troubling reality.

"Big day?" she echoed.

"The wedding," he said, enunciating the word carefully, his tone of voice indicating that he couldn't understand why she couldn't understand what he was talking about.

"Oh, that," she said. "Um, it's sort of up in the air right now."

At that, Max did take his eyes off the road and turn his head to look at her. She told herself he was only doing it because they'd stopped for a red light, and not because he was so interested in her answer to that last question. But he did look awfully interested in her answer to that last question. Too interested.

"Up in the air?" he said. With much interest.

She nodded. But all she could bring herself to say was, "Uh-huh."

"Up in the air, like, because you're having trouble finding a reception hall? That kind of up in the air?"

"Something like that, yes." Except that it was really, like, because they were having trouble eluding the police. Details, details. Sheesh.

He nodded slowly. Thoughtfully. Interestedly. "I see."

Well, she sincerely doubted that. But if it made him feel better . . .

"We just recently got engaged," she added, congratulating herself for yet again telling the truth. Except for the part about her not having technically said yes to the proposal, something that sort of negated the reply's essential truthfulness. So she quickly amended, "He just proposed a couple of weeks ago." There. That should take care of that.

Except that it didn't take care of anything, because Max seemed oddly uplifted by her qualification. "So then you must still have quite a bit of planning to do," he said. "You still have lots of time before the actual ceremony. I mean, especially if he's still in Virginia. Those long-distance relationships and all."

Actually, Lucy thought, long-distance had only improved her relationship with Archie. Of course, that wasn't what Max meant. Of course, she didn't have to tell him that.

"Is he a student, too?" he asked, as the light turned green. He shoved the stick shift into first gear again, and Lucy tried not to swoon at how capable and confident his hand was on the gearshift, and at how seeing him grip the handle with such affection made her wonder how it would be to have him gripping other things with such affection, other things that weren't on cars, for instance, other things that were on, say, a woman's body, other things that were on *her* body, and—

"No, he's a mor—" Thankfully, she caught herself before completing what she had been about to say, because she hadn't been thinking about what she was about to say, on account of she was too busy thinking about Max's hand gripping her—

"He's a what?" Max asked.

"He's a mor . . . ah . . . mortician," Lucy said off the top of her head. And damn the top of her head anyway. Though she supposed it could have been worse. She could have said, off the top of her head, that he was a Cobb salad.

"Really," Max stated. Stated, not asked, clearly having no trouble believing that Lucy would be engaged to someone who made a living out of pumping dead bodies full of noxious chemicals and then styling their hair. "That's a rather unusual occupation, isn't it?" he added.

"Not really," she hedged. "I think Archie must come from a long line of mor . . . ticians."

"Takes a special breed of man for that," Max said.

"Oh, Archie is definitely a breed unto himself," Lucy conceded. *Moronus Bozoclownus*, she added to herself. That would be the genus and species name for him, for sure.

"Archie, huh?" Max said.

And only then did Lucy realize she had used her faux fiancé's actual appellation. Not that there was only one Archie in the world for her to be engaged to, of course. But she probably shouldn't have said even that much. So, following Max's earlier example, she said, "Let's talk about something else."

She looked over at him when she said it, and saw his dark brows arch in surprise at her request as he kept his gaze trained on the street ahead. The wind rushed in through his window, lashing his long hair about his handsome face, and coupled with the fleetly flashing lights of the city beyond, he looked dangerous and edgy and very, very tempting. Her heart seemed to vibrate with the heat and harshness of the car's engine as she watched him, her blood racing through her veins with enough velocity to make her feel dizzy. Vaguely, she recalled that she was supposed to be breathing, and she sucked in a deep breath brimming with the scents of the city. Never in her life had she felt more aware of her surroundings than she did in that moment. And never had she realized just how deeply her feelings could run.

He was so handsome, she thought. So dynamic. So potent. She wondered why he closed himself off from the world the way he did. Because somehow she knew that was exactly what Max was doing, twenty-four hours a day, seven days a week. Keeping himself distant from the world and everything in it.

"Yeah, we can talk about something else," he told her, and only then did she remember they had been having a conversation. For a moment there, they seemed to have been communicating a different way entirely. "I just figured a woman newly engaged would be filled with talk about her upcoming wedding," he added. "What would you like to talk about instead?"

"You," she replied without thinking. But once uttered, she realized she had no desire to take the suggestion back.

"Me?" he repeated, sounding surprised.

"Yeah, you," she said. "You told me you've worked for the Coves for five years. What did you do before that?"

He was clearly uncomfortable in the change of subject. "I did car stuff," he said evasively.

"What kind of car stuff?"

"Pretty much the same kind of car stuff I do now. I just did it for someone different, that's all."

She narrowed her eyes at him. He was lying, she thought. Maybe not as blatantly as she was, but he was definitely hiding something. She wondered if he was on the lam from the Future Beauticians of Idaho, too.

"Where did you work? Here in Louisville?"

"No. Somewhere else."

"Where?" she asked, ravenous to find out more about him.

"I worked overseas," he said. And she could tell right away that he hadn't wanted to give even that vague answer, because he squeezed his eyes shut tight for a split second and muttered what sounded like . . . Well, like a word that Lucy only used when she smashed her finger really, really hard.

"Where overseas?" she asked. "I've never visited any country besides this one. I bet it was fun."

He made a strangled sound in reply to that, and his cheek—the one she could see—grew ruddy with emotion. "Yeah, well, all good things eventually come to an end, don't they?" he grumbled.

"I don't know. Do they?"

"Yeah," he replied tersely. "They do. Trust me."

Before she had a chance to comment further, he shifted gears again, urging the accelerator down toward the floor. She watched the speedometer needle dart upward, past forty-five . . . fifty . . . fifty-five, and feared they'd be stopped by the cops any minute, especially when he zipped through a just-turned-red light at a crowded intersection. But right when she was about to voice a warning, he removed his foot from the pedal completely, downshifting again, bringing their speed back into the legal range. By now they were nearly to the river, and he darted the little car expertly down a street that led them beneath a bridge and through a light, taking the last curve with a bit more speed than was necessary—or prudent.

There was something wild inside him, Lucy thought as he rocketed the car along the river. Something uncivilized and impetuous and quite possibly mad that he tried hard to keep a tight rein on, but which obviously refused to be restrained. She wondered about the origins of that something, wondered about how much of his life it spilled over into. And she found her gaze wandering again from his hard, uncompromising profile to the hand that manipulated the stick shift with such cool precision now.

Such a bundle of contradictions, she thought. Frantic and lawless one minute, composed and deliberate the next. Which was the real Max Hogan? she wondered.

And did she really want to know?

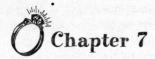 Chapter 7

Max was in the carriage house, bent under the hood of Justin's Gullwing Mercedes, just admiring the workmanship of the magnificent machine, when he heard the unmistakable sound of Power Puff Girl sneakers prowling around. More specifically, those sneakers—and the person they were attached to—were prowling around the desk where he did all the paperwork involved in the maintenance of Justin's vast car collection. Most specifically, they were prowling around the drawer in that desk where Max kept his stash of Lorna Doone cookies.

Without taking his attention off of his work, he said softly, though not quite softly enough to go unheard, "I think I hear a mouse eating my Lorna Doone cookies. I'd better tell the new housekeeper to call the exterminator right away. That'll take care of those nasty meeses."

"It's *mice*, Max, not *meeses*," said a tiny voice coming from the vicinity of the desk. "And they're not nasty, they're cute. And you better not let anybody exterminate them, or else." After only a moment's hesitation, the small voice added, "What's 'exterminate' mean?"

He turned the upper part of his body slowly around to find Abby Cove sitting on the wooden chair near his desk, shamelessly nibbling a pilfered Lorna Doone, and holding the box in her other hand, totally unconcerned that she'd been caught red-handed. Her bare, spindly legs swung in rabid, uneven circles, her huge brown eyes looked even more enormous than they already were behind the round wire rims of her glasses, and her chestnut hair was half in and half out of a ragged ponytail. Along with her smudged sneakers, she wore a pair of rumpled orange shorts and a rumpled lime green and yellow plaid sleeveless top.

Obviously, she'd chosen her own wardrobe before going to school that morning, Max thought, trying not to squint at the blinding color combination. And obviously, she'd made it out of the house without her mother seeing her. Rosemary always encouraged Abby to do her own thing and never hindered the little girl's, ah . . . self-expression. Abby's school, too, was firmly rooted in promoting individuality. Alexis, on the other hand, would never have allowed such an outfit to exist on her only child. Of course, Alexis didn't allow a lot of things with her only child. Sometimes Max wondered if she'd even allow the child herself if given a choice. Hopefully she would. But sometimes he did wonder.

He turned completely around now, leaning back against the chassis of the Gullwing, folding his arms over the oil-stained, faded navy blue T-shirt that stretched across his chest, and crossing his oil-stained, denim-clad ankles insouciantly. "Exterminate is what I'm going to do to you if you don't leave my Lorna Doones alone," Max said by way of a definition. He jutted his chin up toward the box she held in her hand. "That's private property you're munching there, kid."

"Property is theft," Abby replied succinctly before popping the last corner of the cookie into her mouth. She chewed vigorously to destroy the evidence, then stuffed her hand into the box to retrieve some more.

Max grinned. "Is it now?"

The little girl nodded as she pulled out another cookie and enjoyed a hefty bite. "Rosemary said so," she mumbled, shooting a few soggy crumbs out of her mouth as she did so.

"I think Rosemary might have heard it from someone else first," Max told her.

"Nuh-uh, she didn't. She made it up."

"Mm," Max said, giving up now, since it would be point-less to continue. He didn't like to argue with Abby. Mostly because she was usually right. And also because she could talk rings around a person when she got riled up. She was a smart little cookie. So to speak. Unfortunately, she didn't have that many people to talk to around Harborcourt, save Rosemary, who doted on her as much as Abby doted on the nanny. Nobody loved the Cove kid the way Rosemary Shaugnessy did. He didn't think anybody could.

"Rosemary also says I don't have to go to the reading place next week if I don't want to," Abby added out of the blue. And there was just an edge of defiance in her voice when she said it. Which really was remarkable, because, usu-ally, Abby's defiance was totally obvious. Not to mention completely boundless.

It was no secret in the Cove house—mostly because Alexis bitched relentlessly about it, though only when her daughter's name came up in conversation to remind her—that Abby was having trouble at school. Just starting third grade, she wasn't even able to manage kindergarten-level material. Experts who had observed her when she first started kindergarten had diagnosed her as having a reading disorder. Though they hadn't had a chance to pinpoint which one precisely, because Justin and Alexis—well, Alexis, any-way, since Justin hadn't seemed much concerned one way or another—had diagnosed their daughter as being lazy and re-bellious instead. Then they'd pulled her out of the study and refused to have her looked at again.

Max figured it was none of his business to agree or dis-agree with anyone about their own kid, especially since he didn't know that much about any of it—kids or reading dis-orders. Still, if forced into a corner, he'd probably have to side with the experts. Mainly because Justin and Alexis Cove tended to see only what they wanted to see—of the world and of each other.

"Well, kiddo, I'd say whether you go to the reading place

or not next week is up to you and your folks and your teachers," he finally said.

"And Rosemary," Abby quickly added.

"Yeah, I guess Rosemary, too," Max relented. She was, after all, Abby's primary caregiver. Not to mention the only
one who seemed to show any real concern for the girl. "Still,
if you need any help with—"

"I don't need help," Abby quickly cut him off. "I just don't
like reading, that's all."

"Fine," Max said. "I'm not that big a reader myself. But if
you're having trouble—"

"I'm not having trouble," she interrupted him again, more
tartly this time. Then, adamantly, she repeated, "I just . . .
don't . . . like . . . reading, that's all."

"Okay, whatever you say, Abby." Max blew out an errant
breath of air, then turned around again, to carefully lower the
hood on the silver Gullwing. It settled into place with a contented *thunk*, and he spun around to face the little girl fully.
"But if you do . . ."

"I *don't*."

"Fine."

Abby slammed the box of cookies down on the desk with
enough force to send crumbs flying high.

"Look, Abby . . ." Max tried again.

But before he could finish what he was going to say—not
that he really knew what he was going to say—the little girl
jumped down from the chair and went whizzing out the open
carriage house door, nearly knocking down Lucy French in
the process.

"Abby!" the housekeeper called after the retreating child.
"Rosemary is looking for you!"

"Don't worry," Max said, causing her to turn back around
to face him. "That's where she's headed now."

But it wasn't the fleeing Abby who was foremost in his
thoughts at that particular moment. No, it was lovely Lucy

French, who somehow managed to look prettier every time he saw her.

He'd about had a heart attack four nights ago when he'd gone to meet her after her class and got an eyeful of her in that black miniskirt and red, red top that had pretty much demanded he do something to her he'd been wanting to do since the day she arrived at Harborcourt, and making him feel even more like the epithet engraved below the demand than he already did. A gag gift from a friend, Lucy had said. Funny friend, Max thought. Real funny, in fact, giving him a heart attack like that. Not to mention the equivalent of a libido wedgie. Ha ha ha. Yeah, pretty damned funny.

He remembered how he'd sped through the city that night while driving her home, the first time he'd gone above the legal speed limit—hell, the first time he'd broken any rule—in five years. He just hadn't been able to help himself. Something inside him had just gone . . . wild . . . that night. Seeing Lucy looking as she had, knowing he could never have her, it had just roused something inside him that he'd thought he'd tamped down for good—a thirst for danger, a violent streak, an uncontrollable urge, an irresistible force, a death wish, whatever you wanted to call it. All those things the racing magazines had said about him before. All those things that had been a part of his previous life.

Until Monday night, he'd thought he had exorcised them all from his system, had thought he'd succeeded in making a new man of himself. But he'd realized in that brief moment of speeding through the city that he hadn't changed at all. Five years of starving himself and staving off the world, of asceticism and austerity, of denial and discipline, yet he was exactly the same man he'd been before. He was still no good. He was still way too dangerous to anybody who got too close to him

Lucy, though, she looked different today than she had before. At first Max couldn't put his finger on why. Her chin-length, caramel-colored hair still looked soft and silky, still beckoned for his touch, still offered a really nice view of her really nice neck. Her eyes were still wide and blue and candid, her mouth was still full and ripe and luscious, and succulent and sexy and arousing and . . . and . . . and . . .

Where was he? Oh, yeah. Her mouth was still really nice, too. But there was definitely something different about her today—he just couldn't quite say what. And then she took a step to her left, into a wide rectangle of sunlight that splashed through the window . . . and through her dress, too, outlining those gorgeous gams he usually saw in the flesh—literally. And that was when it hit him, while he was looking through Lucy's dress—instead of up it—what was different about her today. It was the dress itself. It concealed instead of revealed, covering her to midcalf and elbow in a flowing, loose-fitting, pastel floral instead of a skintight, blindingly bright, microscopic scrap of fabric. And oddly, Max considered her new look infinitely more appealing than the old one. Because the old one hadn't seemed real on her, hadn't looked genuine, hadn't felt right. This, however, this felt . . .

Oh, man. It felt really, really good. Too damned good.

"How do you know she's headed for Rosemary?" Lucy asked, obviously unaware of Max's slow perusal.

"She always runs to Rosemary when she's upset," Max said, forcing his gaze up to Lucy's face instead of letting it rove hungrily over her body, as it very much wanted to do.

Not that looking at her face didn't make him feel hungry, too. In fact, looking at her face made him want things even more urgently than what looking at her body made him want. Because her body promised untold sexual satisfaction, which, although certainly pleasant, wasn't by any means enough to get a man through life. Lucy's face, though, her expressions, her eyes, gave him a glimpse of the woman beneath the beautiful shell. And even with such a little peek, Max saw a lot of things he liked there. What he didn't see was starving or staving, asceticism or austerity, denial or discipline. And, strangely, he didn't see the same man he'd been five years ago, either. He saw someone . . .

He made himself look away, at anything other than pretty

Lucy French with her blue eyes filled with goodness and decency. Instead, he focused his attention on a table behind her, one filled with dirty, oily, broken auto parts that were much more in keeping with his character.

"What's she upset about?" he heard Lucy ask.

He swallowed all the weird emotions bubbling up inside him, but couldn't quite quell the irascible sound that escaped in response to her question. "School. Parents. Me. Life. Pick one," he said shortly.

"Why's she mad at you?" Lucy asked.

Funny how she didn't question Abby being mad at all those other things, Max thought, as if she could easily understand why a little girl would rage against all of those. Or maybe that wasn't so funny after all. Just what was Lucy French's story anyway? He didn't know that much about her. Of course, he hadn't told her anything about himself, either, so there hadn't been much encouragement for a give-and-take about their personal lives. Still, he did find her omissions interesting.

He shrugged. "I don't know. Abby gets mad a lot. She's eight. She's entitled."

Lucy nodded, as if she understood that, too. "Rosemary was looking for her because she has an overnight with a friend tonight. She figured Abby had wandered out here to visit you." She smiled, and the gesture had the same effect on Max that a good, solid blow to the back of the head would have had. "She says Abby has a crush on you."

Max laughed that off. "Nah. She just doesn't have that many people to talk to, and being an only child and all, she responds better to adults than other kids."

Lucy narrowed her eyes at him curiously. "You talk like you speak from experience," she said.

He shrugged again, told himself not to say anything, then heard himself reply, "Maybe I do."

"You don't have any brothers or sisters?"

He shook his head. "Always wished I did, though. You?"

"I have a brother *and* a sister." Her smile grew broader. "Interestingly, I always wished I was an only child."

He chuckled at that and felt some of the tension in his body ease. "You don't have class tonight?" he asked, because . . . Well, just because.

She shook her head. "No. Thank goodness."

"What?" he asked, feigning shock. "But school just started. You can't already be tired of it."

She shook her head again, but she didn't seem to be disagreeing with him so much as just clearing her head. "I just . . . I don't know what I was thinking to agree to go back to school, that's all."

Hmm, that was an interesting way to put it, Max thought. That she'd *agreed* to go back to school. "How long since you graduated?" he asked her.

She got kind of a strange look on her face when he asked the question, but recovered quickly. "A few years," she said.

"What have you been doing in the meantime?"

She glanced down at that, smoothing a hand over a nonexistent wrinkle on her dress. "Ah . . . I, um . . . I sort of worked in the publishing business."

He nodded. That was certainly appropriate for an English major. "Editing books?" he asked.

She continued to look down, now examining the nonexistent manicure on her hands and fingernails. "Actually . . . I, um . . . I wasn't so much editing books as I was, uh . . . driving them," she finally said.

Hey, how about that? Max thought. Something else that they had in common. Well, sort of. She'd probably never driven books at three-digit speeds. Not unless she was in a real hurry to deliver them to their destination.

Smiling, he said, "I didn't know you could drive books. Stick shift or automatic? What kind of speed can you get on one of those things?"

She glanced back up at that, smiling again, and something inside Max went *pop-fizz*. And damned if he didn't like the sensation a lot. He would have sworn pop-fizzing was something he would normally, manfully, avoid. But Lucy put pop-fizzing right up there with rugby in the mud.

"I didn't drive *them*," she said with mock impatience. "I drove them to where they needed to go."

"Ah. Gotcha. Well, there you go. Yet another thing the two of us could talk about. Our lives as drivers."

And dammit, why had he said that? Max wondered immediately. As far as Lucy was concerned, he'd only ever cared for cars. He didn't need her asking about his life driving them, too.

But she seemed in no way curious about his response, evidently concluding that he had been referring only to his position as the Coves' part-time chauffeur, the one aspect of his job that he really, really hated. It had been Alexis's idea that he should, as part of his employment, dress up from time to time in full livery and drive her and Justin to formal affairs. She really got off on the whole uniformed chauffeur thing, because so few Louisville families actually practiced such a—to Max's way of thinking—damned ludicrous indulgence. But Max had always figured it only added to his humiliation and disgrace, so it could only be a good thing—so to speak. He just hoped like hell Lucy never saw him dressed that way, because it would give new meaning to humiliation and disgrace, and he didn't think even *he* deserved that. Well, maybe not.

Her gaze skittered now over to the Duesenberg, and she eyed it with frank admiration. "Except that I've never driven anything like *that*." She sighed with much affection. "It's beautiful."

Max felt an odd sort of pride swell inside him when he realized she appreciated the grace and style of such machinery as much as he did. "You wanna sit in it?" he asked impulsively.

Her eyes went wide with surprise. "Oh, no," she said quickly. "I couldn't. I'd . . . break something. You don't want me to get close to that car, trust me."

"Oh, come on," he cajoled. "You won't break anything. This baby was put together back when cars were built like oil tankers. A wrecking ball would barely scratch this thing."

She eyed the vehicle again, obviously wanting very badly to take him up on his offer. So Max strode over to the dove gray car and opened the driver's side door. "Come on," he repeated. "You know you want to. It's just sitting, Lucy. You'll be fine. Trust me."

She bit her lip thoughtfully, then, with clear reluctance, shook her head. But she was smiling—and, he couldn't help noting with some confusion, blushing—when she said, very softly, "Not the front seat. Maybe the back?"

He thought it odd that she'd prefer the back to the front, but then, what did he know? He closed the driver's side door and reached for the one in back instead, drawing it open wide. Then he swept his hand toward the car's interior. "Your chariot awaits," he said.

For a moment, Lucy only stood silent and motionless, gazing first at Max, then at the Duesenberg, then at him, then at the car, then at him again, her expression now looking almost . . .

Uh-oh.

No. No way. For sure he had to be imagining what she seemed to be thinking, Max told himself. She couldn't possibly be looking at him as if she wanted him to *join* her in that car. On the broad backseat. Horizontal. Entwined. Naked.

But that sure as hell was the impression he got from her expression. He really had gone way too long without the basic release a woman could provide, he thought. Maybe he'd gone unnaturally long without it. Maybe he ought to modify that little part of his penance, he thought further. Maybe he'd been a little too hard on himself to make himself give up *every* little pleasure known to man. Maybe he could allow himself *one* little pleasure. It really wasn't natural, after all, to expect a man to give up *that* completely. Especially when he still had a good fifty years or so of that left in his body.

And it was that kind of thinking, Max reminded himself,

that kind of justification of unacceptable behavior, that had gotten him into this situation to begin with. Not that having sex with a beautiful woman in the backseat of a beautiful car was unacceptable, not normally. Not for most guys. But for Max, it just wasn't allowed. Not even some quick, shallow, meaningless coupling in an alley with a woman he'd never see again. And certainly not something leisurely and momentous and amazing with Lucy French in the backseat of a classic car. And it *would* be leisurely and momentous and amazing with her—and classic, too, for that matter—of that he was certain. Which was all the more reason he didn't deserve it, and therefore couldn't allow it.

She took a step forward, the glide of her dress skimming over her legs, whose silhouette he could still see in the sunlight. Then she took another step, and another, bringing her out of the light and into the shadows, and somehow she seemed more approachable then. A half dozen more steps brought her next to the Duesenberg, close enough for Max to touch her, and he tightened his grip on the car door so that he wouldn't act on that impulse. But then she placed her hand next to his on the door, brushing her fingers lightly against his own, and just that simple contact nearly undid him. But there was worse, far worse, to come, he soon realized, because Lucy settled her foot on the car's running board and gently pulled up the skirt of her dress to see what she was doing, and Max caught another glimpse of the creamy flesh beneath.

He had no idea why he should find the sight of her leg so erotic now, when before it had only been . . . Well, okay, it had been erotic then, too, but not like this. As he watched her tug the soft fabric of her dress up over her elegant calf, then her knee, something snapped inside him, and he found himself releasing the door and moving his hand to her shoulder. But he managed to stop himself just in time, just before he would have curled his fingers over that shoulder. Had he covered her shoulder with his hand just then, he knew he wouldn't have been able to stop there, knew he would have had to hold much more, and would have pulled her to him and held her, until neither of them would have been able to tell who was who.

Instead, he glided just the tips of his fingers down along her arm, over her short sleeve, stopping at the precise moment when his fingertips would have left smooth, cool fabric and gone to smooth, warm skin. But even then, he couldn't quite stop himself. Even then, he knew he had to touch her. So, with great indolence and even greater care, he moved his hand lower, cupping her elbow in his palm, and telling himself it was only because he wanted to do the gentlemanly thing and help her into the backseat of the car.

But when she glanced up to acknowledge the gesture, Max knew he was a big fat liar. He was nothing resembling a gentleman. He'd done what he had because he'd wanted to touch Lucy. Because he'd *had* to touch her. Somehow, he really had thought that that would be enough. But now that he *was* touching her, now that he felt the soft glide of her skin beneath his fingers, he wondered if he would ever have enough of Lucy French.

"Watch it," he said softly as she bent to enter the car. "Be careful."

But he knew it wasn't really the car's low ceiling that he was trying to warn her about. Hell, he wasn't even sure it was Lucy he was trying to warn when he'd said what he had. He may well have been talking to himself.

Just as she was bending her body to fold herself into the car—and just as Max was thinking that it was going to be inescapable that he follow her into it and lay her back across that wide backseat, and cover her mouth with his, and move a hand to the hem of her dress to lift it over her knees, her thighs, her hips, all of her, and then cover her breast with his hand the way he'd covered her mouth with his—just as he was thinking about all that, the scramble and squeak of Power Puff Girl sneakers erupted behind him, and he turned, as if in a dream, to find Abby and Rosemary both standing at the open carriage house door.

"Max, I hate to ask," Rosemary said, "but I promised a

friend of mine that I'd meet her for dinner. It is my night off,"
she added apologetically. "Could you please take Abby to
Hannah's house? I have her things all packed and ready to
go, but I really should have left twenty minutes ago if I'm to
be on time, so I'm already late, and—"

Max lifted a hand to stop her flow of words, and they
halted just as abruptly and completely as his errant, erotic
plans for Lucy did. "Go," he told Rosemary simply. "I'll be
glad to take Abby to Hannah's." Mostly because it would
keep him from taking Lucy . . . well, to a place they were
both probably better off not visiting. "You have a good time
with your friend tonight," he added. "You've earned it."

And she'd earned Max's undying gratitude, too, since her
appearance had kept him from making a colossal mistake
with Lucy.

Man, he would have done it. He would have climbed right
into the Duesenberg with her, and he would have kissed her,
and held her, and stripped her as naked as the car's close confines would have allowed, and he would have buried himself
deep, *deep*, inside her, and he would have savored every
breathless sound of pleasure she uttered in response. And she
would have responded breathlessly with pleasure, he knew.
She would have welcomed him inside her as enthusiastically
as he wanted to be there. He knew she would have. The way
she had been looking at him, the sizzle of heat that had ricocheted between the two of them, he knew she was thinking
the same thing he was. He *knew* it. And he would have done
it. And so would she. And he never would have forgiven himself when it was over.

"Go," he told Rosemary again. "I've got everything under
control here."

And, amazingly, he was able to say that without laughing.

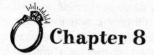 Chapter 8

The Wild Irish Rose was Rosemary's favorite place to be when she wasn't with Abby Cove. Formerly a cozy old Victorian house in the Highlands, the restaurant claimed three levels of comfortably furnished space, making her feel as if she were visiting friends instead of a commercial dining establishment. Tonight, as it was every Friday night, the place was packed with stout-drinking, cigarette-puffing, pub-grubbing regulars. Laughter rang out amid the wheeling smoke, the Clancy Brothers sang to her about a jug o' punch, bangers and mash was on the menu, and Harp's ale was on draft. It was as close to Ireland as Rosemary could come without leaving this country, and for that, she would love the place forever.

Tonight, however, she loved it a bit less than usual, though that was her own fault and no one else's. Thanks to her late start and the Friday night traffic, she was forty-five minutes late meeting her friend Charlotte, who worked as the nanny for one of Abby's friends. Now Charlotte was gone, and their dinner reservation had been given to someone else. So Rosemary squeezed in between two chatting couples at the bar and ordered a pint, then nursed the first half of it as she tried to reach Charlotte on her cell phone. But the other woman wasn't answering, just as she hadn't answered when Rosemary had tried to reach her before, to let her know that she would be late. And Charlotte didn't answer at her apartment, either.

Ah, well, Rosemary thought as she gave up, tucking her phone back into her purse. Perhaps Charlotte had met up with a better prospect and was enjoying herself without Rosemary. More luck to her then. Of course, now Rosemary would be left on her own on a rare night off—and looking quite spiffy, if she did say so herself, dressed in a straight, sleeveless dress of the softest, palest green cotton that fell nearly to her ankles, and flat sandals to go with. She'd woven her waist-length hair into a braid but had left it to swing free down the middle of her back, and had even given herself a manicure, so eager had she been to shed her workday self in favor of a more festive, night-off image. It was just a bad break that it would all be for nothing. Maybe, if she hurried, she still had time to catch a movie . . .

She was just curling her fingers around the cool, sweaty glass that held what was left of her pint when, amid the raucous din of the crowd, she thought she heard someone say her name, very close to her ear. And although it wasn't her first name the person used, the summons felt intimate and affectionate just the same, and sent a shudder of something earthy and elemental shimmying right down her spine.

"Miss Shaugnessy."

She spun around at the deep, masculine voice and found herself staring at a man's chest. A man's broad, nicely toned chest, clad in a navy blue polo that was tucked into a pair of faintly faded jeans, its collar unbuttoned to reveal a peek of rich, dark hair beneath. As Rosemary drove her gaze upward, she saw that the face above the chest was even more rugged and nicely formed than the rest of him was, but, alas, it belonged to a man she had steadfastly sworn she would avoid.

"Mr. Finn," she said with surprise, his name feeling awkward and uneasy on her tongue.

She had seen him only once in the week that had passed since he'd cornered her in the Coves' kitchen—the Monday night following that fiasco, when Mr. Cove had brought him home for dinner unannounced. Mr. Finn had said not a word to Rosemary that night about their exchange. Not that she had expected him to, of course—either because he didn't feel it necessary to apologize for his behavior, since he probably didn't think he had done anything wrong, or else because he didn't remember it, owing to having been too inebriated. And she'd certainly seen no reason to bring it up. She would just as soon pretend it never happened, and hoped eventually to forget about it. Though she sincerely doubted she would ever be able to completely banish the memory of the strange, heated sensations that had wound through her that night.

But even though he had said nothing to her Monday at the Coves', Nathaniel Finn had watched Rosemary whenever she and Abby had been in the same room. She had felt his eyes on her constantly, in fact, and every time she had glanced up, she had seen him gazing at her with frank consideration, and often speculation, though speculation about what, she didn't want to know. Once he had even smiled at her in a way that had made her think he remembered perfectly well what had happened in the kitchen and that he intended to repeat the incident at his earliest convenience, with a vastly different result this time. And even when Rosemary had frowned a response to indicate that no repetition of the event would *ever* occur, he had continued to observe her unapologetically, even when she caught him at it.

What was most troubling, though, was that as she'd watched him watching her, Rosemary had felt a slow, simmering heat ignite deep inside her, a heat that had gradually seeped throughout her body. It was the same unsettling sensation she had felt that night in the kitchen, something at once dangerous and intriguing, a mixture of aversion and fascination. And she had realized then that Nathaniel Finn was an infinitely more menacing man than she had first thought. Because in spite of everything, she wanted to know more about him.

And here, she thought now, was her chance. If she decided to take it. But, of course, she would not. Because no matter how fascinating she might find the man, he was trouble. And trouble was something she had left behind in Ireland. She *never* wanted trouble in her life again.

"I'm surprised to see you here," she said, blurting the first thing that came into her head. Well, all right, she supposed that wasn't the *first* thing that came into her head. But had she blurted out something about how sinfully handsome he was, and about how very much she wanted to know what it would be like to kiss him, it might have caused a problem or two.

He shrugged. "Well, with a name like Finn, it's kind of hard for me to escape a place like this, isn't it? My grandfather came over from Ireland seventy years ago. I heard too many stories before he died about County Cork not to feel like it's a part of me."

He wasn't lying, Rosemary knew. When she'd told him she was surprised to see him there, she had meant standing beside her, and not in the Rose proper. As a regular herself, she had seen him in the restaurant a time or two—or more— though naturally only from a distance, and naturally never to speak to. But she couldn't recall him ever seeing *her* here— certainly he'd never acknowledged her before. Still, she really shouldn't be suspicious of his appearance now. For some reason, though, she was. There was just something about his sudden arrival that didn't feel right. Or perhaps it was just the fact that he was speaking to her that didn't feel right. Why would he approach her this evening when he never had before?

"I, on the other hand," he said, "*am* surprised to see you here. At the bar, anyway," he hastily qualified. "Indulging," he qualified even further, dipping his head toward what was left of her pint. "Though, I suppose everyone who's Irish eventually finds their way to the Rose."

She wanted to tell him that she'd found her way here long before tonight, and ask him why he had only just now noticed that. Instead, she nodded toward the drink he held in his own hand, a short glass half-filled with something dark amber, straight up. "Is it only you who's allowed to imbibe then, Mr. Finn?" she asked.

He shook his head and smiled, and something inside her went fairly incendiary in response. Oh, dear. She really shouldn't encourage him. Not unless she wanted to spontaneously combust.

"Not at all," he told her. "I just didn't think you were the type."

She almost laughed out loud at that. "And why shouldn't I be the type?" she asked. "In fact, just what is the 'type'?"

Instead of answering her verbally, he lifted his free hand and began to guide it slowly toward her neck. Rosemary told herself to grab his wrist and halt him before he could touch her, but for some reason, she felt paralyzed and completely unable—or, perhaps unwilling—to react. He closed his fist loosely as his hand drew near her, all but his index finger, which pointed at the delicate gold cross she always wore, nestled just beneath the divot at the base of her throat. For a moment, she thought he was finished and would go no further, and she began to slowly release a breath she had been unaware of holding. But then he urged his finger forward some more, until he was tracing the tiny gold cross with the pad of his fingertip, first down, then across.

Problem was, the cross was so small and thin that his fingertip overshot it, and caressed the tender skin beneath it in the process. Problem was, that skin was so sensitized already that what should have been a completely innocent touch shot a quiver of electricity through Rosemary that made her gasp in shock. Problem was, Nathaniel Finn noticed her gasp. Problem was, he smiled knowingly when she uttered it.

And problem was, he didn't retreat when he heard it, but instead curled two of his fingers more completely beneath the cross, so that it lay against his fingertips and his knuckles lay against her, raking lightly over her skin now, before settling just beneath that delicate divot at the base of her throat where the cross had been before.

"It's just that *you* don't seem the type to imbibe, Miss Shaugnessy," he said softly, rubbing his thumb slowly over the cross, his bent knuckles still nestled against her breast-bone, her skin flaming where it made contact with his own. "I mean, you seem like such a nice girl."

"I am a nice girl," she replied quickly. Too quickly, really. Because her voice was rough and breathless and uncertain when she said it, and she didn't believe herself for a moment, and she figured Nathaniel Finn wouldn't, either.

Strangely, however, he did seem to believe her, because he abruptly dropped the cross and lowered his hand back to his side. She wasn't sure, but she thought his eyes suddenly seemed darker, and his cheeks a bit ruddier than they had been when he'd first addressed her. And she wasn't sure, but she thought the cross lying against her skin felt hot and alive.

"I know you are," he said. Then more softly, so softly she almost wondered if he meant for her to hear him, "That's the problem," he added.

For a moment, as Rosemary watched him, as she noted the way the black of his pupils nearly eclipsed his dark green irises, and the way his high cheekbones grew more promi-nent under the stain of his . . . what? Passion? Oh, surely not. Embarrassment? Even harder to believe. So why, exactly, had the man colored? she wondered. And as she wondered, as she observed the changes in him, Rosemary realized she had forgotten to breathe. She realized that, because she sud-denly felt dizzy and disoriented, and why else would she feel that way if not for a lack of air?

She fought the urge to snatch up her glass and drain it of its contents, and instead tried to think of a polite way to excuse herself from what was fast becoming an uncomfortable situ-ation. Here she was, in a crowded bar filled with loud conver-sation, and suddenly she felt as if she and Nathaniel Finn were the only people left in the world, enclosed by a silent sort of serenity that only the two of them shared. It was al-most as if she had slipped into another dimension, one where physical sensations were magnified and multiplied and made nearly impossible to bear. She needed to be somewhere else, outside, in the fresh air, where she could clear her mind of the odd unreality into which it had eloped.

"If you'll excuse me, Mr. Finn . . ." she said, letting her voice trail off, hoping he would take the hint. For some reason, she didn't want to flat out tell him good-bye.

And although he did seem to understand the hint—he smiled that knowing smile, after all—he didn't take it. "What's your hurry?" he said. "Have you had dinner?"

Yes, she told herself to say. "No," she heard instead. "I was supposed to meet a friend for dinner, but—" She halted herself before telling him that Charlotte had left before she got here. For some reason, she didn't think it would be a good idea to let him know she was here by herself. She didn't know why she thought that. Only that she did.

"I have a reservation for seven-thirty," he interjected. He twisted his wrist just enough to see the face of his wristwatch. "And what do you know, it's just that now." He turned his gaze to her again, fixing her with those green, green eyes. "Why don't you join me?"

"Oh, I couldn't—" Rosemary began.

"Of course you could," he objected.

"But you'll be meeting someone and—"

"I'm not meeting anyone," he told her. "I'm by myself tonight."

She gaped softly at that. How on earth could this man be out on his own on a Friday night? Now she was really suspicious. "Did she stand you up, or did you stand her up?" she asked, thinking the second possibility was the more likely.

He smiled again. "Who says there was a 'she' to begin with?"

Rosemary chuckled. "So it's like that, is it? I never would have taken you for a poofter."

He narrowed his eyes at that, but his smile never faltered. "No, it isn't like that," he said. "I like women. A lot," he added, his green, green eyes becoming hot, hot, hot. "But sometimes a man wants a little time to himself, that's all."

"Which means I should be on my way."

And then she managed to make herself move away from the spot where she had felt rooted ever since Nathaniel Finn had appeared. In fact, she completed one full step forward before he reached out his free hand again, this time curling his fingers lightly over her upper arm.

"Don't go," he said.

And there was something in his voice when he said it that was so soft and so solicitous that Rosemary melted a little inside. Only this time, it wasn't due to a quick, impetuous, explosive heat. No, this time it was due to a gentle radiance that seemed to meander through her body with the indolence of a summer's day.

"I didn't mean it like that," he added. "I may have come here tonight to be alone, but . . ." He hesitated for a moment before finishing. "But now that I've seen you, I . . . I discover that I don't want to be alone."

And, oh, there was something in the way he said that that made Rosemary want to come apart inside. She didn't dare meet his gaze when she responded, but kept her attention fixed on the restaurant's front door, the door that led to freedom. But freedom of what sort? she asked herself. And did she really want to be free just now?

"I really should go," she said. "I'm not sure it's a good idea to—"

"It's an excellent idea," he corrected her before she could even finish the thought. "We both came here for dinner. Your girlfriend never showed, and I never had one to begin with. It's worked out perfectly."

"How do you know it was a girlfriend I was meeting?" she asked.

He shrugged again, but there was something a trifle off in the gesture this time. "I guess I just assumed," he said. "I'm sorry. Was I wrong? Is there someone special? Some guy who might not appreciate your joining another guy for dinner?"

Rosemary shook her head, then immediately wished she hadn't. An imaginary boyfriend might have gotten her out of this situation without further ado. She really shouldn't be standing here, talking to the Bad Boy of the Thoroughbred Racing Set. It could only lead to trouble. Then again, maybe deep down, she really didn't want to get herself out of this situation. Maybe a part of her wanted trouble. Maybe a part of her had been missing it. Maybe a part of her still was.

"There's no guy," she said. "I was indeed meeting a girlfriend. But I was frightfully late getting here. She must have thought I wasn't coming and left."

"So then why not join me for dinner, Miss Shaugnessy?" Nathaniel Finn asked again. "It'll be my treat."

She immediately shook her head at that. "No. I'll pay for mine, thank you," she told him adamantly.

He opened his mouth to object, then stopped, a slow, happy smile curling his lips. Only then did Rosemary realize she had just consented to have dinner with him, without even realizing she had meant to.

"Fine," he said. "You can pay for yours. *This* time." A not-so-subtle implication, she concluded, that there would be a next time, and that on that occasion, he would be the one treating.

Well, not so fast, Mr. Finn, she thought further. The only reason she had agreed to this time was because she was hungry, having not eaten since noon, and even half a pint of ale on an empty stomach was making her feel a little too woozy to drive home just yet. So she would have dinner with the man. Tonight. And then she would drive herself home and get on with her life as if this evening had never happened.

Just, she was sure, as Mr. Finn would do.

By the time their server brought coffee for Nathaniel and tea for Rosemary after the conclusion of their meal, he had decided this wager of Justin's might not be such a bad thing after all. He hadn't been so sure initially, of course, and he had berated himself for the first few days for ever agreeing to such a heinous wager. Pride—and too much good Irish whiskey— definitely wenteth before a fall. Now, though, Nathaniel was resigned to what he and Justin had agreed upon. In fact, he was looking forward to completing the wager . . . in a strange, twisted sort of way. Hey, there *was* four million dollars at stake, after all. And he *was* the Bad Boy of the Thoroughbred Racing Set. The wager might have been heinous, but four million bucks was four million bucks, and bad boys would be bad boys. Plus, Nathaniel Finn was *not* a man to welch on a deal.

Still, he hadn't been relishing the prospect at first. From a distance, he'd considered Rosemary Shaugnessy to be plain and unremarkable, icy and unattainable. Up closer, but still in the dim lighting of the Coves' kitchen a week ago, he had found her to be a bit less plain and a bit more remarkable, a bit less icy and a bit more attainable. But she still hadn't seemed like anything special. Now, though, up very close and in good light, he saw that Rosemary Shaugnessy was actually quite lovely. Not the knock-down-drag-out, drop-dead gorgeous of the women he normally dated, certainly, but not off-putting, either.

No, not off-putting at all.

In fact, he thought, she might actually be gorgeous, if she put a little work into it. But she wore no makeup, had done little with her hair beyond braiding it, wore clothing worthy of no one but a minister's wife, and no jewelry other than the chaste little cross around her neck.

Still, he supposed, her plain clothing only directed that much more attention to her lovely face. And he had spun a number of fantasies over the course of the evening about how easy it would be to loose her hair from its simple arrangement and let it spill over his hands, his arms, his chest, his body, his . . .

Well, suffice it to say that he'd found there was something to be said for a simple hairstyle. And he supposed, too, that there was something to be said for the unadorned perfection of a creamy, flawless complexion. And a man could find worse eyes to gaze into than the clear, green depths of Rosemary's, which, on further consideration, he decided really needed no cosmetic enhancement, so large and beautiful and expressive were they already. In fact, he'd found himself drowning in those eyes more than once during the course of their meal, when he hadn't been spinning fantasies about her hair. And, truth be told, he hadn't been all that eager to come up for air.

It was the small, gold cross around her neck, however, that captivated him the most. He'd never spent any length of time with a woman who wore a cross. And he couldn't help thinking about all the things the tiny, holy icon represented—devotion to faith, purity of soul, conviction in morality. He held none of those things sacred himself, and could, in fact, be the poster boy for exactly the opposite lifestyle. He had faith in nothing—save himself, but there were times when even that faith wavered. He was pure in absolutely no way. He held no moral convictions whatsoever. And both of those last traits were perfectly well evidenced by his willingness to go along with Justin's reprehensible bet.

Nathaniel wondered briefly if Rosemary Shaugnessy was a virgin. And he was vaguely troubled to discover that, deep down, he hoped that she was.

"Sure you don't want any dessert?" he asked her now.

She shook her head. "Thank you, no. I'm much too full."

He was, too, for that matter. Oddly, though, he wanted to stretch the meal out for as long as he could.

She twisted the slim, leather-banded watch on her wrist toward herself. "Good heavens, it's nearly ten o'clock," she said. "We've been sitting here for more than two hours. I'm surprised they haven't booted us out by now."

Nathaniel knew nobody was going to boot them out tonight. Hell, he'd slipped the owner five hundred bucks to make a place for him on the reservation roster when he'd had no reservation at all, and another five hundred to make sure that he and Rosemary went unbothered for the entirety of their meal. He'd made sure of a lot of things this evening, in fact. Hell, he only had three weeks left to get Rosemary into bed. Though he was looking forward to that now a lot more than he had been a few hours ago. And not just because there was four million dollars at stake, either. He wasn't taking any chances on losing this bet.

"They're very accommodating here at the Rose," he said. "Besides, we're both regulars."

"You don't know that about me," she said.

"Oh, yes, I do," he replied.

And he did, too. Because Justin had told him so. Justin had also been the one to tell Nathaniel where he'd find Rosemary this evening, so confident was the other man that he would win the bet. He thought it a grand joke that he was helping Nathaniel in his quest to conquer the nanny, so certain was the other man of Miss Rosemary Shaugnessy's chastity. Justin was, in fact, already preparing a stall for Nathaniel's prized mare in his own stable. The big jerk.

"You've never seen me here before tonight," Rosemary said softly, lifting her cup to her lips. Her perfectly formed, very full, intensely beautiful lips, the ones that Nathaniel, even now, couldn't wait to taste, and couldn't wait to feel brushing over parts of his own body.

And then the gist of her remark struck him. How could she know he'd never seen her here before tonight? *Was* she a regular? Frankly, he'd never noticed her here. Maybe Justin had lied to him. Maybe she wasn't a regular. Maybe his friend had only told him that in an effort to scuttle Nathaniel's attempt to seduce her.

"How do you know I've never seen you here before tonight?" he asked, hoping his tone sounded teasing, and not wary.

She hesitated a moment before responding, but her gaze never left his when she finally did. "Because *I've* seen *you* here before tonight," she said softly. "And you never noticed me then."

A bubble of relief mushroomed inside him. "How do you know I never noticed you?" he asked.

"Oh, I know," she said.

Because she'd noticed *him*, Nathaniel realized. She'd watched *him* before when he was here, without him even knowing it. How very interesting. How very revealing. How very encouraging. How very easy it was going to be to maneuver Rosemary Shaugnessy right into his bed. That four million bucks was as good as his.

"Maybe I just never let you catch me noticing you," he said smoothly.

She said nothing in response to that, only sipped her tea slowly as she eyed him with what he could only identify as uneasy curiosity. He wasn't home yet, he knew. She still didn't trust him. But that was okay. Few people did. And it hadn't caused him any problems before.

The server brought their—separate—checks then, and after a halfhearted attempt to wrest Rosemary's from her, Nathaniel surrendered. There. That would show her he was trustworthy. He'd done exactly as he promised and was letting her pay her own way. This time. Yeah, he was a real prince of a guy. After they'd both paid their bills, Nathaniel extended his hand toward the exit, silently indicating that she should precede him out.

"I'll walk you to your car," he said.

She wanted to object, he could tell, but she seemed to think better of it when she looked outside to see that darkness had fallen. She wasn't stupid. It wasn't a bad neighborhood, of course, but then, one never really knew whom one could trust, did one?

"Thank you," she told him instead. "I appreciate it."

Outside, the September night was damp and warm with lingering remnants of summer and absolutely no hint of fall. The heavy Friday night traffic on Bardstown Road meandered past them as they began to make their way down the street, leaving behind the faint acrid scent of exhaust in its wake. That traffic meant that Rosemary had been forced to park a few blocks away from the restaurant, which, of course, Nathaniel already knew—he really had made sure of a lot of things tonight—so they had a bit of a walk ahead of them.

"Nice night," he said by way of nothing as they strode

leisurely along. And, surprisingly, he realized he spoke the truth. It was a nice night. Though the weather really had little to do with it.

"Mm," Rosemary agreed quietly from beside him. "I love this time of year. I love how summer hangs on for so long sometimes here."

What Nathaniel loved was the soft, mellow lilt of Rosemary's voice, and the way it sent a warm ripple of pleasure right through the center of him. Odd, that. It had never been a woman's *voice* that had brought him pleasure before.

"Just where in Ireland are you from, anyway?" he asked, suddenly curious to know more about her. They'd only made meaningless chitchat over dinner, about recently read books, or recently seen movies, or how Abby Cove was faring at school, as if they'd both been afraid of learning too much about each other. Now, though, Nathaniel was ready to learn more.

"I grew up in Derry," she said. "Rossville Flats," she then clarified. Then, just in case that hadn't rattled his political knowledge, she added, "In Northern Ireland."

Not the best place to be from, Nathaniel thought. He wasn't an expert on the troubles in Northern Ireland by any stretch of the imagination—his grandfather's stories of Ireland had been filled with the good times and great beauty and overriding joy he'd found in the south—but Nathaniel knew enough to realize that Rosemary had come from a very unhappy place. Derry had seen one of the most violent episodes of British oppression in recent history, and Rossville Flats was a notoriously poor Catholic neighborhood. But Bloody Sunday had happened more than thirty years ago, surely before Rosemary was born. Nevertheless, he supposed something like that cast a long-lasting shadow over a community.

"And what brought you to the States?" he asked, hoping he hadn't opened the door on memories she would have rather left locked away, and then wondering why he cared. It had never bothered him before to bring up unwelcome subject matter. Not that he went out of his way to make people feel bad, but, normally, it wasn't a concern if he did.

Rosemary smiled in response to the question, and deep down inside himself, Nathaniel felt a stirring of warmth, and something else, too, something he couldn't quite identify, wasn't sure he wanted to identify, where he'd sworn there was nothing to feel.

"Nanny school," she said.

For a moment, he couldn't remember what he had asked her to make her reply in such a way. Then he remembered, and shook off the odd sensation that had descended over him. Somehow he managed to chuckle, and hoped the action didn't sound as phony as it felt. "They actually have schools for nannies?" he asked

"Oh, yes," she told him. "When my aunt Brigid passed away, she left me a bit of money, and that, along with what I got when I sold everything that was left, gave me just enough to pay my way through a very good nanny school in Dublin. They placed me with the Coves when I was nineteen."

"And you've been with them how long now?"

"Since just before Abby's first birthday."

Making her about twenty-five now, Nathaniel deduced. She was actually older than he'd originally thought. Not by much, but it heartened him some to know he wasn't robbing a cradle. A bunk bed maybe, but not a cradle.

"I'm sorry about your aunt," he said in an uncharacteristic show of sympathy. What was even more uncharacteristic was that he uttered the sentiment honestly. "Do you still have family in Northern Ireland?"

She sobered again at that, but all she said in response was, "No."

"Your parents? Brothers or sisters?"

"Both of my parents are gone," she said simply. "I never had brothers or sisters."

"So then you never go back for visits?"

She shook her head. "I'll never go back."

There was a finality in the statement that indicated she was finished talking about Ireland now, thankyouverymuch, and could they please move on to another topic. So Nathaniel only made quiet conversation after that about nothing in particular—and he found it very strange that he would actually *enjoy* quiet conversation about nothing in particular—until they arrived alongside Rosemary's aged VW Beetle.

She pulled her keys from her purse and jingled them meaningfully. "Thank you for the escort," she said as she took a giant step away from Nathaniel. "And thank you for the dinner company, as well," she added, sounding reluctant, he thought.

"I should be the one thanking you," he said. "You saved me from a very boring evening."

"Well, I don't know about that," she said, smiling. "But I had a fine time, myself."

"Yeah, me too."

Neither of them made a move after that, as if they were each waiting for the other to do something. Finally, Rosemary stepped off the curb and rounded the front of her car, unlocking the driver's side. "Thanks again," she said as she tugged the door open with a very obvious *creeeaaak*. She winced when she heard it, and Nathaniel chuckled. "I'll have to ask Max if he can do something about that," she said. Then, "Thanks again," she added. "Good night, Mr. Finn."

In other words, he translated, *Beat it*. "Good night, Rosemary," he replied.

He lifted a hand in farewell, but didn't turn around, and instead began to walk backward as he waited for her to start her car. Deliberately, he kept his steps very slow, and, deliberately, he made sure he stayed within view. There was just enough light pouring from a nearby streetlight to allow him to watch her through the windshield as she inserted the key into the ignition and turned it . . . only to have absolutely nothing happen. Nathaniel's steps slowed even more, until he came to a halt. She turned the key again, and her effort was met by another ominous silence. Another turn. Another silence. Nathaniel smiled for just a moment, then schooled his features into a mask of concern as he made his way back to the little yellow car.

As he approached, she tried one more time to turn the key in the ignition, but, just as he knew would happen, nothing happened. He moved around the front of the car, into the street, pausing by the driver's side window, waiting for Rosemary to roll it down. For a long moment, though, she only sat in her car, staring straight ahead, as if she were hoping that if she ignored him, he would just go away. Fat chance. Finally, though, when Nathaniel made no move to disappear, she turned her head and gazed at him through the glass. She smiled half heartedly, but still didn't roll down the window.

"Problems?" he asked, raising his voice so that she could hear him.

She closed her eyes, blew out an exasperated breath, then, finally, cranked down the window. "Yes," she said shortly. "My car doesn't seem to want to start."

"I can take you home," he offered magnanimously.

Not much to his surprise, she shook her head. "That's all right. I'll call a tow truck. There's a gas station just a block or two up—maybe someone there can help me."

"I think they're closed," Nathaniel told her, hoping she wouldn't think about that too much, because what gas station owner in his right mind would close his business on one of the busiest roads in town on a Friday night?

Luck was with him, however. Because all Rosemary said was, "Oh." She quickly sabotaged his plans again, though, when she told him, "Then maybe I'll just call Max."

"What, and bring him all the way out here on a Friday night?" Nathaniel asked, hoping he wasn't pouring on the guilt too much too soon. "He probably won't even be home."

"Oh, he'll be home," she said. "He never goes out on the weekend."

This Nathaniel found hard to believe. If there was ever a guy who screamed self-centered, no-good, womanizing hound dog, it was Justin's car guy. Not that Nathaniel knew anything about Max beyond what Justin had said about him being a whiz with cars. But a man could always identify members of his own kind. Always. And Max Hogan was, without question, a charter member of Nathaniel's tribe.

"I don't suppose you know anything about cars, do you?" she asked hopefully.

"Not a thing," Nathaniel lied effortlessly. Except, of course, how to disconnect a battery wire to keep a car from starting. But other than that, he was pretty much at a loss. "Look, I practically have to drive right past your place on my way home," he pointed out. "It's no trouble to drop you off."

"But I'll still have to have my car towed," Rosemary pointed out.

"It's perfectly safe here until tomorrow," Nathaniel said. "You can bring Max back with you then. It's late, Rosemary," he added. "You don't want to drag anybody out if you don't have to."

Okay, that was just the right amount of guilt at just the right time. She had to go for it now. He could see that she wanted to decline again, and he wasn't sure he could press her any more without seeming desperate—or suspicious—if he tried to discourage her further. She had a good point about that towing business. Still, it was late. And she looked tired. He could tell she wanted to go home.

And, hey. He was just the guy to take her there.

"C'mon," he cajoled, injecting a lightheartedness into his voice that would make him sound less threatening. "Let me drive you home."

She blew out another errant puff of air, hesitated a fraction of a moment longer, then, much to Nathaniel's relief, she said, "All right. If you're sure it's not too much trouble."

Not too much trouble, Nathaniel echoed to himself. That was a good one. "Of course it's no trouble," he said. "Just the opposite. It means I get to spend a little more time in your company."

She tilted her head back to look at him when he said that, her expression still holding a certain vigilance. Jeez, what was it going to take to make her feel comfortable around him? Nathaniel wondered. He was being as sensitive and charming as he knew how. Still, she said nothing in response to his flattery, only jerked her keys out of the ignition and opened the car door with that lengthy *creeeaaak* again.

"I'll have Max take a look at that, as well," she muttered as she climbed out.

And then she was standing next to Nathaniel again, and for some reason, the entire evening seemed to go brighter and warmer as a result. He tipped his head in the direction from which they'd just come. "I'm parked over on the other side of the restaurant, I'm afraid," he said. "We'll have to retrace our steps and start over again."

And why, he wondered, did that sound like a very good idea?

She smiled at him, and something caught in his chest at seeing it. Because for the first time that evening, she smiled without wariness or suspicion, as if she had finally resigned herself to trust him. "That's all right," she said. "It's a lovely night for a walk."

Nathaniel nodded, but felt a little dizzy as he looked at her. "Yes," he agreed, "it is lovely."

They made more quiet conversation about nothing in particular—and once again, Nathaniel actually enjoyed it—until they arrived at his midnight blue Jaguar roadster. But when they halted by the lustrous, low-slung vehicle, Rosemary gazed at it as if it were something to be feared. He thumbed the keyless entry, then opened the passenger side for her. With great care and slowness, she ducked her head and settled herself inside, and Nathaniel closed the door behind her, rounded the front of the car, and joined her from the driver's side.

"Oh, my," she said softly as she buckled herself in. She ran a hand lovingly over the black leather upholstery. "This is . . . ah . . . a very nice car." She laughed as she concluded the observation, realizing, he supposed, what an understatement it was.

"Looks good on you," he said, smiling.

Upon further consideration, however, he realized that it wasn't the eighty-thousand-dollar car that improved Rosemary. No, it was Rosemary's presence that vastly improved the eighty-thousand-dollar car. Then, before she could respond or he could contemplate that oddity any further, he thrust his key into his ignition and started his car with absolutely no trouble at all. But then, no one had disconnected a wire on his battery, had they?

After maneuvering his way out of the parking space and into the city traffic, he thumbed a CD into the player—Paul Desmond, his favorite. Low, jazzy saxophone, *very* romantic. And he didn't know if it was because of the advent of the music or the mood that made Rosemary clam up like a . . . well, like a clam. For much of the drive, they rode in silence, and not a particularly comfortable one. And with every mile the rumbling Jag ate up, Nathaniel grew more aware of Rosemary. Of the way her heat seemed to creep across the small confines of the car and mingle with his own. Of the faint, clean scent of lavender that clung to her. Of the way the moonlight filtered through the window and gilded her hair. Of the way her breathing seemed uneven and edgy when she was with him.

Of the way she made him want things he'd never wanted, with a desperation he'd never felt before.

Eventually, she must have tired of the silence, because as they left the Highlands and drove down River Road, past rolling green fields turned black and silver in the moonlight, she said, "It's too bad it's dark. I love driving through here and seeing the horses when they're out."

Her admission surprised him, though why it should, he couldn't have said. "You like horses?"

"Oh, yes," she said enthusiastically.

"Do you ride?" he asked.

"Not since coming to America. But when I lived in Derry, I used to ride quite often."

"Really?"

He found this little snippet of information unusually interesting, and realized then that he wanted to know everything
she was willing to reveal about herself. Which was also interesting, because he also realized that what he wanted to know
about her were personal things. Intimate things. Things that
would define exactly who she was beneath the lovely shell.
And usually, he just didn't care that much about what made
people tick, particularly women. And he especially shouldn't
care about what made Rosemary Shaugnessy tick. He told
himself the only things he needed to know about her were her
weaknesses. Strangely, though, he wanted to know so much
more.

"So you had horses when you were growing up?" he asked

"No, not me," she said. "But my aunt Brigid worked for a
family who lived just outside Derry, and they kept horses.
When I was sixteen, the stable man offered me a job exercis-
ing them. They were beautiful animals," she added almost
dreamily. "I always thought when I came here I'd buy myself
a horse one day, but . . ." She sighed, and there was something melancholy in the sound. "Well, it's just not come
about. They can be very expensive and require great care.
And I don't have a lot of time to devote to one. Abby is my
first priority, of course."

Also interesting, Nathaniel thought, that she would consider someone else's child her first priority, a child she cared
for because she was being paid to do it. "What about on your
days off?" he asked.

She expelled a single, humorless chuckle. "I don't have
too many of those."

"Justin and Alexis don't give you days off?"

"Well, technically, yes," she conceded. "I have two days
off a week, and paid holidays. But it's not the kind of job
where you actually take those days, is it? Do you know what
I mean?"

No, frankly, Nathaniel didn't know what she meant. Oh,
he could have understood if her job had been like his—
breeding horses. That was pretty much a constant calling.

But baby-sitting? As long as Abby had someone around to make sure she didn't hurt herself or catch the house on fire, why wouldn't Rosemary take her days off?

"Abby needs me," she said quietly, as if she'd read his mind. "She doesn't really have anyone else."

"Except her parents," Nathaniel reminded her.

"That's what I meant," Rosemary said tersely.

Maybe that was what she meant, he thought, but it sure didn't make any sense. The horse topic, though, now there was something he understood. And could take advantage of.

"So when's your next day off?" he asked.

"Monday," she replied, sounding wary again. "Why?"

"I have to go to Woodford County to look at a horse a guy wants to sell. You want to come with me? Maybe we could get a little riding in."

"Oh, thank you, but no," she said quickly. "Abby has—"

"Abby has her mother to take care of her that day, obviously," Nathaniel interrupted. "Otherwise, you wouldn't have the day off."

"Yes, but you see, she's being tested that day for a reading problem, and I think I should—"

"You should let her mother handle it," he said.

For a long moment, Rosemary was silent, and in that moment, the temperature in the car seemed to drop sixty degrees. Nathaniel couldn't imagine what he'd said to generate such a chilly response.

Then, very softly, Rosemary replied, "I would if her mother *could* handle it. But if things don't go well, Mrs. Cove will make Abby feel like a broken piece of furniture she's going to haul out for the rubbish collectors in the morning."

Okay, so maybe Nathaniel could believe that. Maybe he wasn't all that crazy about Alexis Cove, either. But Alexis was still Abby's mother, and as such, she was the one who should be overseeing something like a reading test. "Maybe," he said, "things will go just fine. And maybe this will give Alexis an opportunity to practice her mothering skills."

Rosemary laughed outright at that. "Mothering skills?"

she echoed derisively. "That woman mothers about as well as a black widow spider."

Okay, so maybe Nathaniel had thought of Alexis as a black widow spider himself a time or two. But that was because black widows ate their spouses, right? Or was that praying mantises . . . mantisi . . . mantases . . . those ugly green bugs . . . who did that? In any case, he could easily see Alexis as one of those, too.

"I'm sorry," Rosemary hastily apologized. Though there was nothing apologetic in her tone of voice. "I spoke out of turn. I had no right to say such a thing about Mrs. Cove. Please. Forgive me."

Now it was Nathaniel's turn to laugh. "Why should I forgive you for saying something I've thought myself?"

Rosemary continued to gaze straight ahead through the windshield, but when he dared a quick glimpse in her direction, he saw that she was smiling. "She is . . . something, isn't she?" she said softly.

He nodded, returning his attention to the road. "She certainly is." He allowed another beat of silence to pass between them, then, "So how about it? Monday? Feel like driving to Woodford County with me? We could make a day of it."

He had thought she would either accept or decline outright, but instead, she turned fully in her seat to look at him. He, of course, had to keep his eyes on the road, but he felt her looking at him as clearly as if he had been watching her full on.

"Why are you inviting me?" she asked.

A tiny ripple of something he wasn't used to feeling purled through him, and Nathaniel was shocked when he finally realized it was guilt. "Why do you even ask such a thing?" he countered, evading her question for the moment.

"Because I can't imagine why you would want me along," she said.

"Why wouldn't I want you along?"

"Why do you answer all of my questions with another question?"

"Am I doing that?"

He heard her laugh, and the wariness was gone from it now. "Yes," she said. "You do. And you'll have to forgive me if I find it a bit odd that you're inviting me on a horse-buying trip."

By now, they had turned onto Glenview Avenue, so Nathaniel slowed the car as he focused on the winding, tree-dense, uphill road. "You think it's odd," he said, "that I'd want to spend the day with a beautiful woman?"

"No, I think it's odd that you'd want to spend the day with *me,*" she told him frankly. "I would think you'd have a host of other women who would love to come."

"And you wouldn't love to come?" he asked.

She said nothing for a moment, then, "Actually, I'd love to come," she conceded quietly. He waited for the *but* that he was sure would follow . . .

. . . and never heard it.

He turned left, into the quarter-mile-long, serpentine driveway that led up a hill to Harborcourt. "Then I'll pick you up Monday morning," he said, marveling at the nervousness that spilled into his belly at uttering the words. No, it wasn't speaking the words that had made him feel nervous. It was the realization that Rosemary Shaugnessy had just agreed to spend the day with him.

Oh, for God's sake, he thought derisively. You'd think he was fourteen years old again and had just asked Marilee Dewhurst to the ninth-grade mixer. Only this time, Marilee had said yes. Or, rather, Rosemary had said yes. Marilee, he recalled, had told Nathaniel to go jump in a lake. But who cared when he could have Rosemary Shaugnessy instead?

"Fine," she said, that wariness creeping back into her voice again. He really was going to have to work on that. "Monday morning."

And for the first time in a long time, Nathaniel found himself looking forward to next week.

Chapter 9

It was past ten-thirty when Lucy heard a car door slamming somewhere beyond the open window of her apartment. But it was so far away, she knew it was slamming at the big house and concluded that Rosemary must be home. She hoped the nanny had had fun tonight. Even in the short time Lucy had known her, the other woman didn't seem like she'd had too much of that. Rosemary was way too dedicated to her work. Lucy couldn't ever see applying herself to her own job the way Rosemary did to hers. Then again, nurturing a child was probably just a trifle more important than vacuuming up dead spiders and trying to sweep fossilized Froot Loops out from under the refrigerator. So maybe Rosemary had a good reason for being so dedicated.

Turning her attention back to the TV, Lucy thumbed the remote control with one hand and buried the other in a big bowl of microwaved popcorn. If she had to be in hiding, at least her accommodations were accommodating. She didn't know who was responsible for decorating the carriage house, but they'd had an eye for interiors. In keeping with the storybook look of the outside, the apartment's colors were all soft pastels with white trim inside—light yellow in the kitchen, faint blue in the living room, pale green in the bedroom. The furniture was mostly overstuffed solid chintz in contrasting pastels—greens and blues in the kitchen, yellows and greens in the living room, blues and yellows in the bedroom—with wool Dhurri rugs in the same soft colors scattered about the hardwood floors, and muslin café curtains on the windows. There had obviously been an attempt to make the decor gender-neutral, but somehow it still came across as feminine.

All in all, she almost felt as if she were living in a make-believe sort of gingerbread apartment. She could pretty well imagine someone nibbling-nibbling on her house, nibbling-nibbling like a mouse. Except that there was no wicked witch, or fiery oven, or caged little Bohemian children in *Lederhosen* to bother her.

She'd had her bath and dressed in a pair of Phoebe's pajamas—baggy boxer shorts and a short-sleeved, button-up top decorated with colorful images of breakfast foods. Now, she was passing the time until she was tired enough to go to bed by doing her favorite thing in the whole, wide world—flipping aimlessly through two hundred satellite stations and finding absolutely nothing to watch.

But if tonight was like every other night she'd spent since coming to Harborcourt, sleep was going to be elusive. Lucy had never been a good sleeper to begin with, and everything that had happened over the past two weeks had only compounded the problem. Virtually every night, she'd still been channel surfing at one or two o'clock in the morning, then she'd have to tumble out of bed at six-thirty to start work. She had wondered sometimes why the Coves didn't employ even more servants than they did—maids and such—but Rosemary had told her that wasn't customary in this part of the country, and that the Coves traveled so much, it hardly seemed necessary. Stolen naps in the afternoon, usually in the pantry or the linen closet—and once under the grand piano in the music room when she'd lain down to polish the pedals, but thank God no one had been home at the time—had helped Lucy get her through her days, but the exhaustion was beginning to catch up with her. She wouldn't be able to live this way much longer without losing her mind.

She eyed the coffee table, where a cordless telephone was sitting beside her glass of wine. She silently willed the phone to ring. She hadn't talked to Phoebe for nearly a week, and she knew that couldn't be a good sign. The last time they'd spoken, her friend had said that that moron Archie was still missing, that the police were still looking for Lucy, and that her family was still worried. It had been all Lucy could do not to call her mother to let her know she was all right. But who knew whether or not the police had the phone tapped at her parents' house? They did that on TV all the time, so naturally it must go on in real life, too. Besides, her mother was probably more worried about the blot on the Hollander name than she was about her daughter's well-being, and if nothing else, being a fugitive from justice had brought Lucy freedom from that.

She had just landed on a promo for *West Side Story*— "Next on Encore!"—when she heard the sound of another car, this one rolling to a stop in the turnaround in front of the carriage house below.

Max was back.

She had heard him leave about half an hour ago, and had assumed he must have a hot date with someone. Not that Lucy cared, of course—Max Hogan could date whomever he pleased, regardless of the woman's temperature. Still, that date—and that woman—must have ended up being on the tepid side if he was back already.

Gosh, she thought. What a shame. Not that she cared, of course.

Silently, Lucy crept into the bedroom, which also looked down on the turnaround below, where she would be in darkness and could peek through the curtains and not be seen. Below, she saw one of Justin Cove's newer sports cars—a red Ferrari this time—and Max leaning into the passenger side to retrieve what turned out to be a six-pack of something and a Blockbuster video bag.

Gee, *really* tepid date, she thought, unable to stop the smile that curled her lips when she realized. Not that she cared, of course. If Max chose to date a six-pack and a bag of rented movies, that was his prerogative. Lucy certainly wasn't one to talk. She'd dated a variety of six-packs and bags of rented movies in her day.

As he stepped away from the car, he must have sensed her watching him, because he started to glance up at the bedroom window. Just in time, Lucy jerked back her head, moving not a muscle until she heard the heavy tread of his feet moving over the gravel below, whereupon she wandered into the living room again. Then she heard the heavy tread of his feet moving down the hall toward his apartment. And then she heard . . . nothing. Curious, she made her way quietly to the front door and placed her head against it, listening for the jingle of Max's keys as he opened his. And she waited for the sound of his door clicking closed behind him. And waited. And waited. And waited. But none of those sounds ever came.

Very curious now, she moved her eye to the peephole, being extra mindful not to make a sound. And as she gazed through the peephole, she saw Max standing on the other side, in front of his own door, looking at hers, watching it with extraordinary intensity, as if he expected it to say, "Open Sesame."

Lucy swallowed hard, hoping he hadn't heard her moving around, praying he didn't know she was standing there at that very moment, watching every move he made, noting how his faded blue jeans hugged his muscular thighs and cupped his manhood with much affection, and how his white V-neck T-shirt was stretched out of shape enough that the *V* dipped low, revealing a generous scattering of rich, dark hair on his chest, and how his motorcycle boots were scuffed and worn and rebellious, and—

—and how she was gazing through a peephole and couldn't possibly detect that much detail, so her overactive imagination was obviously working overtime again, and it was really getting annoying how her overactive imagination kept doing that, and just this once, why couldn't her overactive imagination be an underachieving imagination instead? Honestly.

And then that thought evaporated, because instead of going into his own apartment and closing the door behind himself, Max was crossing the hall to Lucy's. And before she could prepare herself, he lifted a hand to knock, and the harsh rapping, sounding right next to her ear made her entire body jerk forward. Without thinking, she palmed the door handle and yanked the door open to see Max standing there looking more smug than she had ever seen him look. And that was saying something. Because over the course of the last two weeks, she'd seen the man looking *awfully* smug on a number of occasions. Usually when he caught her ogling him, which, she had to admit, she'd done a time or two. Or ten. Thousand. Whatever.

"Caught ya," was all he said. But he smiled when he said it, so she couldn't possibly be anything other than charmed.

Well, okay, maybe there were one or two things she could possibly be other than charmed, but those things weren't really fit to print in any kind of socially acceptable—or legal—medium. So charmed was what she decided to go with. For now, at least.

"Uh . . . hi," she said by way of a greeting.

His smile grew broader. "You were spying on me, weren't you?"

Oh, damn, Lucy thought. How was she supposed to get out of this one? *WWDD?* she asked herself immediately. Well, let's see . . . Dino would probably fix a drink—got that one covered—then call Sinatra and the boys—she made a mental note—then deny everything—*Good call, Dino*—then sing "Strangers in the Night." No, wait! Not "Strangers in the Night." He'd sing "The Lady Is a Tramp." No! Not that, either! He'd sing . . . he'd sing . . . "I've Got You Under My Skin."

Yeah, that's the ticket.

"Ah . . ." Lucy began articulately. *Deny everything*, she reminded herself. "Ah, no," she said. "No, of course I wasn't spying on you. Why would I be spying on you?"

"Good question," he said. "Got a good answer to go with?"

"But I wasn't spying on you," she insisted. A little too insistently, she couldn't help thinking. She gripped the door more firmly, knowing it was the most incriminating of the—admittedly abundant—evidence he had against her regarding the aforementioned espionage case. "I was just, um . . . I just, ah . . . I just so happened to be standing right by the door when you knocked, that's all."

He didn't look anywhere near convinced. "And why were you standing right next to the door, when there's nothing next to the door to be standing there for?" hc asked.

"How do you know there's nothing next to the door?" she retorted, sidestepping that question for now.

"Because I've been in this apartment."

"Oh, yeah?" she shot back wittily. Oh, she really wasn't presenting her case well *at all*.

He nodded, still grinning. "Yeah."

"Well . . ." she stalled. "Well, I was just thinking that . . . that since there's nothing here, maybe I should *put* something here. And I was measuring to see what would fit." Oh, yeah. That was totally convincing. Score another one for the prosecution.

"I see. So what are the dimensions?" he asked. Still grinning. Still looking charming. Damn him.

Lucy released her death grip on the door and spread her arms as wide as they could go. "About this long," she began, then shifted her hands a bit closer, "by this wide. Just right for, say . . . um . . . oh . . ."

"An area rug?" he supplied helpfully.

"Actually, I was thinking more along the lines of a coatrack. But an area rug would probably make more sense, now that you mention it, wouldn't it?"

"Probably. At least it wouldn't be something you had to

move every time you opened the door. A coatrack could get a little tricky there."

"I suppose you're right," she conceded reluctantly.

"Nice jammies," he said, changing the subject.

Changing it to one Lucy would just as soon not have had it changed to, quite frankly. She had forgotten she was in her— or, rather, Phoebe's—pajamas.

"Thanks," she said, crossing her arms over her midsection, hoping that might cover her a little, figuring the effort was probably pretty futile.

He opened his mouth to say something else, then halted, turning his head to the side. "Is that the overture for *West Side Story*?" he asked.

Lucy heard it, too, then, from behind her, the opening horns blaring *da-da-da-da-da . . . da-da-da-da-da-da-da . . . DA-DA*! signifying that da Jets were in da house. To put it in the modern-day urban vernacular.

"Yeah, it is," she said. "It's just coming on."

"On a commercial-free channel?"

She nodded.

"Were you planning to watch it?" he asked further, sounding as eager as an eight-year-old sandlot hero who had been offered the chance to attend the World Series.

Actually, what Lucy had been planning to do was go to bed and toss and turn for a few sleepless hours, wondering what Max Hogan looked like naked. But she supposed she could postpone her plans for a little while if it meant sitting beside him on the sofa, instead—even if he would have his clothes on. And even if it was a bad idea, she couldn't help thinking, seeing as how, not only would he have his clothes on, but she was supposed to be engaged to another mor . . . ah, another man. And even if she wasn't engaged to another mor . . . ah, another man, she still shouldn't do it, because she was living a lie, and that wasn't the best way to start a relationship with a man.

Not that Max had said anything about starting a relationship with her, she reminded herself. There were few men, in fact, who would equate watching a movie with a woman to starting a relationship, even though any rational woman knew that watching a movie with a man was a perfectly good prelude to marital bliss. One of those he said/she said things, Lucy supposed.

In spite of all her warnings and rationalizing to the contrary, however, she said, "Yeah, I was planning to watch it, as a matter of fact." Then, because she couldn't quite keep her curiosity about the matter in check, she asked, "You actually like *West Side Story*?"

He seemed to find the question unusual. "Sure. Why not?"

"Well, it is a musical," she told him.

Still, he seemed stumped by her response. "So?"

"So it's a musical," she repeated. "Men aren't supposed to like musicals. It isn't manly."

"But this is a musical about street gangs and switchblades," he said. "There's nothing more manly than switchblades."

"But it's still a musical."

"People die in this musical. They're murdered in cold blood. If that's not manly, I don't know what is."

"But it's still a musical."

"With a kick-ass Leonard Bernstein score."

"But still a musical."

Max growled something unintelligible under his breath. "Look, can I watch it with you or not? I can contribute to the evening," he offered, holding up the Blockbuster bag, and thrusting the six-pack toward her.

Automatically, Lucy took both from him and wasn't much surprised to find that the Blockbuster bag held three old film noire flicks: *Key Largo, The Big Sleep*, and *The Maltese Falcon*. She *was* surprised, however, to see that the six-pack consisted of a notoriously bad brand of beer. How odd, she thought. He seemed like the kind of man who would insist on only premium brews.

"So can I stay?" he asked again.

It was a bad idea, Lucy reminded herself. It was nighttime.

She was exhausted. She was in someone else's pajamas. She was drinking wine. It was nighttime. He was sexy. He was in tight jeans. He was bearing bad beer. It was nighttime. They were edgy. There was something intense burning up the air between them. And had she mentioned it was nighttime? Traditionally the time of beds in most modern cultures? There was no way of knowing what might happen if Max came in and joined her.

Bad idea, she told herself again. Really bad idea.

"Sure, come on in," she said. "I made popcorn. And thanks for the beer," she added, as he crossed the threshold and closed the door behind himself, "but I'll probably just stick with wine. I found a nice Australian Shiraz at the wine store today." She remembered the badness of the beer, and said meaningfully, "You're welcome to join me in a glass."

For a moment, an expression came over his face that seemed almost sentimental somehow. "Oh, man, I haven't had Shiraz in years, but I always loved it," he said. "Not that I'm a big connoisseur or anything, but I used to have a friend who was really into wine, and she introduced me to Shiraz and—"

He stopped speaking abruptly, and his expression went from nostalgic to glacial in less than a nanosecond. Lucy couldn't imagine what she'd said—or what he'd said, for that matter—to change his mood so utterly, so quickly. For heaven's sake, they'd been discussing wine. Good wine, at that. How could that put someone in a bad mood?

Then she rewound her brain a bit and recalled that he had used the pronoun *she* in his account, and, suddenly, it all made sense. There was a woman in his past who had once brought him great happiness—hence the sentimental expression— but now, thoughts of her made him feel cold—hence the glacial expression. And there was only one reason for something like that. The two of them must have parted under less-than-happy circumstances. And if Max was the one still feeling cold about it, then it made sense to conclude that he was the one who'd been most unhappy to see the relationship end. Ergo, Lucy thought further—even though *ergo* wasn't a word she normally used, much like *hence*, now that she thought about it, but sometimes you just couldn't get around them—he was still carrying a torch for this mysterious *she* who had enjoyed good wine.

And suddenly, lying alone in bed wondering what Max looked like naked sounded like a much better way to spend the evening. Because at least that way, it would just be her and Max, and not a third party wheedling into it.

"Anyway," he said, scattering her thoughts, "thanks, but I'll have the beer."

"You sure you don't want wine?"

He shook his head. "It's not allowed."

There it was again, Lucy noted. The *not allowed* business. It couldn't be the Coves disallowing it this time—even they wouldn't be so crass as to tell a man what he could and couldn't drink. Well, probably not, anyway. They were pretty crass. Still, she couldn't see Max as being the kind of man who would let someone push him around that way and tell him what he could and couldn't drink. So if his enjoyment of wine wasn't allowed, then he himself must be the one who was disallowing it. The question now was, Why?

"Okay, if you're sure," she said, considering the brand on the six-pack again. Ick. "Want a glass?"

He shook his head and propelled a hand forward, snagging a bottle from the corner of the cardboard pack, twisting off the cap with a flat hiss. Gee, she thought, even the hiss sounded icky. She crossed the small living room to the small kitchen and opened the refrigerator door, to put the beer inside, but Max stopped her, calling out from the living room, "That's okay, you can leave it out. I drink it warm."

The only thing, Lucy thought, that could turn bad beer into worse beer was drinking it warm. "You like warm beer?" she asked.

"I drink warm beer," he told her. As if there were some kind of distinction between the two verbs.

"Okay, if you're sure," she said again, not quite able to keep the tone of warning from her voice. She did, however, managed to bite back the *Eeewww* she had wanted to use to punctuate the comment. She didn't want to be a bad hostess, after all. And even though it wasn't mentioned specifically, the folks over at *In the Kitchen with Bitsy and Friends* would probably have frowned upon a hostess saying "*Eeewww*" to one of her guest's drink choices.

Lucy glanced down at Phoebe's silly pajamas, wondering if she should change her clothes. Really, there wasn't much revealing about what she had on—it was nothing a woman wouldn't wear outside on a warm day. A woman who was a bit peculiar, granted, considering the fact that the ensemble was decorated with illustrations of coffee, Danish, bagels, and doughnuts, but still. Plus, if she changed her clothes, Max would think she was only doing it because she felt uncomfortable around him in her pajamas. Of course, she *did* feel uncomfortable around him in her pajamas, but there was no reason he had to know that. Because if he knew she felt uncomfortable around him in her pajamas, then he would think it was because she was attracted to him. Of course, she *was* attracted to him, but there was no reason he had to know that. Because if he knew she was attracted to him, then he would think she would be easy to seduce tonight. Of course, she *would* be easy to seduce tonight, but there was no reason he had to know that. Because if he knew she would be easy to seduce tonight, then he would want to seduce her. Of course, she *did* want him to sed—

No, she didn't! she immediately reminded herself. She did not want Max Hogan or any other man to seduce her, tonight or any night. Well, not until she could get everything straightened out with that moron Archie and the murder charge against her and that ring on her finger and the Russian mob and—

Oh, God. Was she ever going to get her life back?

After placing Max's warm, bad beer on the counter, she

grabbed the bottle of Shiraz and took it back into the living room to top herself off. More wine sounded like a very good idea for some reason. And pajamas be damned—she wasn't going to change. They were just going to watch TV, for goodness' sake. Who cared if she was wearing her pajamas and Max was wearing tight faded blue jeans . . . that perfectly outlined every muscle in his strong thighs and hips and buttocks, she realized, seeing as how he was standing with his back to her, shuffling through the tapes he had brought from the video store. And who cared if he was wearing a taut white T-shirt that had been washed so many times it was very nearly translucent, sculpting each and every rope of brawny flesh and sinew in his back, and hugging the salient biceps of his upper arms, as if he were utterly naked.

And as Lucy noticed all that, her mouth went absolutely dry and, without even thinking, she lifted the entire bottle of wine to her mouth for a healthy swig. Max must have detected the motion, because he swung around at that moment and caught her doing it.

He smiled. "Good wine?" he asked.

She lowered the bottle with much care and dabbed her mouth daintily with the back of her hand. She didn't want to think about what the folks at *In the Kitchen with Bitsy and Friends* might have to say about *that*. And all she could manage in response was, "Yeah. Good."

By now the Jets were in full dance mode, cavorting through the schoolyard and across the television screen, and Lucy marveled, as she always did when she watched this movie, at how clean the New York ghettos and street gangs had been in the sixties. Gosh. Those were the days. She gestured toward the sofa, silently inviting Max to take a seat, and he did so, squinching his body *waaaaaaay* over on the far side, as if he wanted to keep as much distance between himself and Lucy as possible. Which was fine with her. The farther away from her he was, the less likely she was to be shocked senseless by the strange, electric current that seemed to arc between them whenever they were together. She moved the bowl of popcorn closer to the center of the couch, then took her own seat, *waaaaaaay* over on her own side. Gee, everything should be just fine now, she told herself.

Except, of course, that it wasn't.

Because every time Lucy reached into the popcorn bowl, Max's hand was there, too. And invariably, in an effort to be polite—or maybe because they were both terrified of touching each other—whenever their hands made contact, they immediately withdrew, usually with enough force to send popcorn flying everywhere. Which, in turn, necessitated picking up the spilled popcorn. Which, in turn, necessitated touching things. Things like furniture, sure, but also things like body parts. Body parts that were much better left untouched.

It was during just such an episode of this touch-don't-touch body part thing that Lucy decided it would probably be better if she popped a second batch of popcorn and divided it equally into two bowls. And then put on a robe—or a beekeeper suit, whatever it took to cover her. And then sat on the chair on the opposite side of the room. And then erected a brick wall between the two of them. And then moved to Abu Dhabi.

But popcorn first.

What she didn't count on, however, was that Max would follow her into the kitchen when she went to make the popcorn. But that was exactly what he did, ostensibly to grab himself another warm, bad beer—*eeewww*—his third—*eeewww*—which he then opened—*eeewww*. And he did it all without leaving the kitchen. And then he began to drink his bad warm beer—*eeewww*. Without leaving the kitchen. And all the while, he watched Lucy as she went about the motions of extracting another package of microwave popcorn from the cabinet and unwrapping it. Without leaving the kitchen.

"Need any help with that?" he asked.

She shook her head. "I'm fine. Go ahead. I think 'America' is coming up. It's a pretty kick-ass song, if memory serves."

"That's okay," Max said, smiling, "I'll stay in here. There aren't any switchblades in that number." He lifted the beer to his mouth for a lengthy swallow, then grimaced horribly after completing it.

In a word, Lucy translated to herself, *Eeewww*. Clearly he didn't like warm, bad beer. So why would he drink it?

"In fact," he continued, "I don't mind if I miss the rest of the movie, even the switchblades. It's been a long time since I saw it. I keep forgetting that, as good a movie as it is, I don't really like it."

"Why not?" she asked.

He took another swig of beer, grimaced once more with feeling, then told her, "It hits a little too close to home, I guess."

Lucy set the timer on the microwave and turned to face him. "What? You used to sing and dance on urban rooftops when you were a teenager?" she asked, hoping to make light of what somehow seemed to be a dark mood coming over him.

He shook his head. "No, no singing and dancing," he told her, leaning back against the counter. "But there were a lot of urban rooftops." He sighed heavily and enjoyed—though that probably wasn't the best word to use—yet another large swallow of beer. "Lots of ugly, decaying, urban rooftops," he added distastefully. Though she was pretty sure that the distastefulness this time wasn't due to the beer. Especially when he added, "And lots of ugly, decaying urban buildings. And ugly, decaying urban streets. And ugly, decaying urban people."

Finally, Lucy thought, she was getting an insight into the man. Funny, though, how now that she was getting what she'd wanted since meeting him that first day, she was reluctant to hear any more. In spite of that, she asked, "And what else was there?"

He snapped his gaze to hers at the question, and it occurred to her that he probably hadn't even realized he had been speaking aloud. He studied her in silence for a moment as he seemed to give careful thought to something, then looked like a man who had come to a reluctant conclusion. "There were a lot of stolen cars," he said in a low, level voice. "There was a lot of joyriding. And there were a couple of stays in juvenile detention centers."

Holy cow, Lucy thought. Although he'd certainly given her the impression of being a dangerous man, she hadn't really thought he was dangerous enough to be incarcerated. Even as a teenager. Her own youthful world and Max's couldn't have been further apart.

"So, is, ah . . . Is that where you learned about cars?" she asked, hoping her surprise didn't show.

But when he grinned—wryly, sarcastically, humorlessly—she knew he'd gauged her reaction perfectly. "Don't worry," he said. "It was a long time ago. A lifetime ago. Hell, *two* lifetimes ago," he added emphatically. "And I never did time for any violent crimes—only theft. And never as an adult. But, no, that's not where I learned about cars. Cars I've known since . . ." He expelled a restless sound. "Hell. Cars I've known for as long as I can remember. They just always sorta felt like they were a part of me, you know? I guess I just refined my skills when I was a teenager. But not by stealing cars so much. Eventually, I got a job working for a guy in the neighborhood who owned a garage and knew I had a way with them. More than just jacking them off the streets, I mean."

"Where did you grow up?" Lucy asked.

"Detroit," he said. "Motor City, appropriately enough."

"Why is that appropriate? Because of your car background?"

He lifted one shoulder and let it drop in what she supposed was meant to be a shrug. "Among other things."

"What other things?"

This time when Max looked at her, his grin was decidedly less edgy. "Christ, why am I telling you all this?"

Lucy offered him a halfhearted smile in return. "Maybe because you want to?" she said lightly.

He shook his head. "Or maybe because I should have stopped at two beers," he said. "I never *want* to tell anyone this stuff."

"You've only had two and a half beers," she reminded him, pointing at the half-empty bottle in his hand. "You can't be that far gone."

His gaze when it met hers this time was hot and steely. "Oh, yeah?" he said in a voice that was equally hot and equally steely. And somehow, she knew they weren't talking about the beers he'd had.

She swallowed with some difficulty and wondered why she suddenly felt like she was all sweaty and naked. All she was able to manage by way of a verbal response was a barely squeaked "Uh-huh?"

"Fine. Then turnabout's fair play," he said, the hot steeliness ebbing some. Not a lot. But some. Sort of. At least Lucy didn't feel naked anymore. Sweaty, yes, but not naked. Not quite. Sort of. "If I tell you about me," he said, "then you have to tell me about you."

Uh-oh, she thought. That wouldn't exactly be fair play, since he'd be telling her intimate details about his past, and she'd be lying to him about her own. Or maybe she could get around that. She could speak truthfully about herself without giving him specific details. Probably.

"So I know you're from Roanoke, Virginia," he began again, saving her from having to lie about that—since, hey, she'd already lied about it earlier in the week. "But just *how* did you grow up?" he asked. "Something tells me you didn't do any time in juvie."

She smiled at the thought of Lucinda Mirabella Hollander of Newport, Rhode Island, breaking the law in any way, then getting caught, then doing time for the infraction. What a laugh. Even if she had wanted to break the law—or at least the rules—on more than one occasion, she never would have had the nerve—or confidence—to do it.

"No, I never did any time in juvie," she agreed. Honestly,

too, by God. "My parents set pretty stringent rules for us to follow, and they made it clear we weren't allowed to even bend any of them. Or else."

"So where do you fall in the lineup of the French children?" he asked with much interest.

"My brother and sister are both older than me," Lucy said, sidestepping another lie by failing to specify the family name.

"The baby of the family," Max said, grinning again. "Why am I not surprised?"

"And you're an only," she said, remembering what he had told her during their conversation in the garage before.

He nodded. "Yep, it was just me."

"Parents?" she asked further.

His expression hardened some. "Just me."

Lucy bit her lip at having obviously brought up another unpleasant memory. "I'm sorry. How old were you when you lost them?"

He expelled another one of those errant, unpleasant sounds of restlessness. "Well, my dad I never knew. I don't think my mom knew him all that well, either, to be honest with you," he added confidentially, "and my mom took a powder when I was sixteen."

Mom took a powder, Lucy repeated sadly to herself. Such an indelicate, irreverent way to put a parent's passing. He must still hurt from the loss if he were still trying to distance himself from it by trivializing it. "How did she die?" she asked.

Max gazed at her blankly for a moment. "She didn't die," he said. "At least, I guess she's still around. Somewhere. She took a powder," he repeated. "She left, Lucy. I came home one night to discover we'd been evicted, but my mom hadn't bothered to tell me that when I left for school that morning. Not that I went to school that morning, mind you, since I spent most of my time dodging it, but when I came home that night, she was gone, and so was all our stuff." He took another matter-of-fact swig of his beer before adding, "That's when I decided to quit school and work full-time at the garage. Had to eat. Had to have a roof over my head. I lived in a room over the third bay as part of the arrangement."

He ended his account there, but Lucy scarcely noticed because she was too busy gaping at him in disbelief. She simply could not understand how a woman could abandon her sixteen-year-old son. And she couldn't believe Max would speak with such indifference about it. Certainly Lucy wasn't stupid—she knew there were neglected children in the world, had watched stories on the news, and had seen public service announcements on TV. But until now, she had never been faced with the hard evidence of such a thing.

"She abandoned you?" she asked softly. "Just took off and didn't tell you where she was going?"

"I wouldn't exactly call it abandonment," Max said with a remarkable lack of concern.

"What would you call it?"

He shrugged. "I was sixteen. She knew I could take care of myself."

"Yeah, and you ended up in a juvenile detention center," Lucy pointed out. "I wouldn't exactly call that taking care of yourself. You needed her, Max, and she let you down. I'd call that abandonment."

"Hey, I ended up doing just fine," he said, defensively now, and she wondered why he would want to defend a woman who had deserted him.

But there were too many questions swirling around in her head for her to be able to latch on to just one. So she only shook her head in disbelief and battled the urge to pull Max into her arms and hold him. And not because of that hot, sweaty feeling, either. No, at the moment, all she wanted to do was hold him to show him that she cared about what happened to him. Because she had the feeling he hadn't had much of that in his life.

"So then, judging by your reaction," he said, his voice a bit less clipped now, but still very cool, "I guess your folks stuck around while you were growing up. They were just like Ward and June Cleaver, I bet."

This time Lucy was the one to expel an uncivil sound. "Oh, they were around," she said. "They still are," she added. "But I'd hardly call them Ward and June Cleaver." For one thing, her mother wouldn't have been caught dead vacuuming in pearls. Francesca Hollander wouldn't have been caught dead vacuuming, period. And her father preferred illegally smuggled—and extremely expensive—Cuban cigars to a pipe.

"What?" Max asked, feigning the shock she had genuinely felt a moment ago. "You didn't do your growing up in the middle class in Middle America, with a father in middle management and a mother having a midlife crisis? They weren't both grappling to hold on to middle ground and railing against middle-of-the-road middle age when you went off to middle school?"

Lucy shook her head, but couldn't help chuckling at his assessment, albeit a bit sadly. "Not exactly," she said. In fact, her father was a bank president and her mother was a bank president's wife. Oh, there'd been the middle age and midlife crisis stuff, but not in the ways Max had interpreted them. Her father had faced both middle age and his midlife crisis by spending six figures on a red sports car. Her mother had faced hers by spending the exact same amount on cosmetic surgery. Nothing else in Lucy's background was mid- or middle-anything. No, all of the Hollanders were firmly perched in the upper class and on the right wing. All except Lucy, of course. She'd never really quite landed anywhere at all.

"No middle class, huh?" Max asked.

She shook her head again, but said nothing.

"Well, it's nothing to be ashamed of, coming from a working-class background," he said, obviously misinterpreting.

"It wasn't working-class, either," Lucy told him. Truthfully, too, though, honestly, she felt miserable about that, because she knew he would misinterpret further and save her from having to lie again. Well, to lie actively, anyway. Lies of omission, she supposed, were still lies.

"Gotcha," he said. "Well, speaking as a survivor of the lower class myself, it's no sin coming from poverty, either," he added. Then he eyed her a bit warily. "Unless you're going to tell me that it went the other way, and that your dad is Bill Gates and your mom is Liz Taylor and you grew up in a big country estate with dozens of servants to do your bidding. Maybe you even got to wear a white lace dress for your . . . your . . . your whattayacallit . . . ?"

"Debut?" she supplied helpfully, miserably.

"That's it. Maybe you wore white lace for your debut, and whizzed through some tony private school with flying colors, and your parents both doted on you on account of you were Little Miss Perfect."

Lucy shook her head again, dropping her gaze to the floor this time, mostly because she didn't want Max to see the truth in her expression. "No, I won't be telling you that," she said quietly. Honestly. Because that wasn't true, either. None of it was. "In a lot of ways," she said, just now realizing it was true, "my life was a lot like yours."

When she finally glanced up, it was to find Max eyeing her in that thoughtful way again, as if he didn't quite buy her assertion, in spite of her—admittedly misleading—assurances. "We had to buy all of our clothes at thrift stores," he said. "Somehow, I don't see you shopping at thrift stores. I was always having to wear T-shirts from places I never visited or sports I never played or schools I never attended. My mom got me one once from this tony private school that cost a fortune. She got a real kick out of dressing me in that. Thought it was pretty hysterical. I pretty much hated it myself. Not that that made any difference."

His expression when he looked at her this time held not a hint of what he might be feeling inside. Not that Lucy really needed a physical example of that, having heard what he just said.

"So," he added dispassionately, "did your mother make you wear shirts to tony private schools you didn't attend?"

Lucy hesitated for a moment before shaking her head. "No. We didn't shop in thrift stores. But she never noticed when I felt uncomfortable and embarrassed. Or else she didn't care."

He studied her in silence, then nodded. "Funny how mothers can be that way sometimes."

"Yeah," Lucy said quietly. "Funny."

So maybe she and Max didn't come from such different worlds after all, she thought when she further considered everything he'd told her. She'd never stolen cars or been evicted, of course, and she hadn't grown up in poverty. But, in a way, she'd never known her father, either, because he hadn't been around, and her mother, like Max's, had taken a powder of sorts early in Lucy's life. Certainly Francesca Hollander had never been there when Lucy had needed her. And there were other kinds of poverty besides lousy living conditions. And, too, like Max, Lucy had never been much of a student, either. Had she had the opportunity, she would have dropped out of school in a heartbeat. As for being homeless, well, home was a relative term sometimes, a word that stood for a place of warmth and welcome and family intimacy. And in that sense, at least, Lucy had known what it was like to be homeless, too.

"Life sucks sometimes, doesn't it?" Max finally said.

She nodded. "Yeah. It does. Sometimes."

"But it's no crime, Lucy," he told her with much conviction. "It is no crime to come from the place where we come from."

She squeezed her eyes shut tight at his wording, wishing she could tell him the truth. And not just one truth, either, but lots of them.

Chapter 10

If there was one thing Max couldn't abide in a person, it was stupidity. So why was he being so damned stupid? he asked himself as he watched Lucy take the popcorn out of the microwave. The last thing he'd intended to do tonight was tell her anything about his background. Oh, no, wait a minute, he immediately corrected himself. That wasn't the last thing he'd intended to do tonight. The last thing he'd intended to do tonight—or any night, for that matter—was come to her front door and knock. In fact, he'd promised himself the day Lucy arrived that he would never, ever, knock on her door, and he'd never, ever, have a personal conversation with her. So he'd actually done two things tonight that he'd sworn he wouldn't do, something that made him *really* stupid. And Max *really* couldn't abide *really* stupid people.

But how was he supposed to have helped himself? He'd known she was spying on him from her window, and he'd known she was lurking behind her front door, staring at him through the peephole. He'd known that because he'd felt it, as strongly as if she had reached out a hand and placed it on his shoulder. And he'd also known it because he'd been doing the same thing himself for the past two weeks, spying on her every time the opportunity had presented itself.

As much as Max had tried to deny it, he felt like he and Lucy were connected on some weird, cosmic wavelength that defied explanation, and they'd been plugged in that way from the moment their gazes had collided that first day they

met. No matter where they'd been, or what they'd been doing, every time they'd bumped into each other on the estate,
there had been an instantaneous click of some altered sort of
consciousness, where everything in the universe had just
seemed to fall into place in a harmonious planetary conver-
gence. Except that there was sex in the equation somewhere,
too—hot, naked, sweaty sex—and he just hadn't quite figured out where that part fit yet, which was why he'd made the
decision not to knock on her front door or have a personal
conversation with her.

And, hell, Lucy was partly to blame for his stupidity, too.
When he had knocked at her front door, she'd answered it,
hadn't she? She could have just ignored him, but noooooo.
And she was wearing her pajamas when she answered that
door. Granted, they were pajamas that any sane man would
have found off-putting, but Max, in his already agitated—
agitated for five years now—state had naturally found them
to be unbelievably, uh . . . on-putting. But hey, a man who'd
gone without the company of a woman for as long as he had
would be turned on by a woman dressed in a duck suit and
waders.

In spite of his lame rationalizing, though, Max knew he
had no one but himself to blame for his current predicament,
because he'd been the one to ask if he could come inside
Lucy's apartment and watch movies with her. *Come inside
and watch movies with her!* he repeated emphatically to himself. As if that was the most natural thing in the world for him
to do. As if he'd actually deserved to be in a room with her,
doing something enjoyable. And then the next thing he knew,
he was spewing out more information about his past than
he'd spewed in years, and he'd spewed it all over a nice
woman like her, who frankly didn't deserve to be sullied by
it. And *spew* was the right word for it, too. Because his past
was nothing more than a big splatter of— Well. Suffice it to
say that the past wasn't something Max wanted to step in. Yet
here he was, dancing all over the vomit of his life, without a
second thought.

What was it about Lucy that was chinking at the walls he had spent the last five years building? he wondered. How was it that she could be shaving away with such ease when he had been so certain he'd erected his self-contained prison with absolute invincibility? She must be a lot stronger than she looked.

Still, he had to concede that his spewing, however distasteful it had been, had given him an excuse to ask her about her own past, something he'd been curious about since day one, even though he'd constantly reminded himself that her past—and her present and her future and herself, too—was none of his business. And now that he knew more about her past, he was gratified to realize how much they had in common. He'd already known they shared a few interests, but learning that her roots were planted in the same kind of soil as his, and seeing that she was just as reluctant to talk about her childhood memories as he was, Max was strangely comforted. He felt a new bond with her now that hadn't been there before, a bond that went much deeper than a simple sexual attraction. And he liked Lucy even more because of it. Way more than he probably should.

But since neither of them wanted to talk about the past, then maybe they shouldn't talk about it, he thought. Maybe they should talk about something else instead. Something like the present, say. Because the present was a much nicer place than the past had ever been. And, funny, but it was getting nicer with every passing minute.

When Lucy was finished with the popcorn, she topped off her wine, and Max palmed his beer and followed her back into the living room. They took their seats at two opposite ends of the sofa again—or, more accurately, in two separate hemispheres again—then Lucy reached for the remote control and switched off the TV.

"You don't want to watch it?" he asked, surprised by the gesture.

"I didn't think you wanted to watch it," she told him.

"But if you want to . . ."

She shrugged. "I've seen it."

Yeah, he had, too. Too many times, in fact.

"We could watch one of the other movies you brought," she said.

"You've probably seen all of them, too."

"Yeah, I have," she conceded with a smile.

"So then . . . maybe we should . . . do something else," Max suggested.

And immediately regretted suggesting it, because he'd suggested it in a way that was much too suggestive. What the hell was he thinking? he asked himself. Well, he wasn't thinking, obviously. Or, more to the point, he was thinking too much. Thinking about things he had no business thinking about, let alone suggesting suggestively.

But Lucy seemed to be thinking about those things, too, he realized when he glanced over at her to see how she had re-acted to what should have been a perfectly innocent sugges-tion on his part, but had instead been an incredibly suggestive suggestion. Evidently, she hadn't interpreted it with any more innocence than he had spoken it. Evidently, she had thought it was suggestive, too. And judging by the hungry look in her eyes, she didn't find the idea so very off-putting.

Uh-oh . . .

"Uh, I mean . . ." Max quickly began backpedaling, scrambling to make the suggestion more innocent, because he couldn't tolerate her looking at him hungrily, since it made him feel hungry, too. "I mean we could, um . . . We could, ah . . . Um . . . Talk," he finally said. And immediately cursed himself. He had no more business talking to this woman than he did, well . . . Than he did doing that other thing he'd been thinking about doing with her.

But before he could backtrack and suggest a different something else—*Oh, like what, Einstein? Yahtzee?*—Lucy jumped on the less suggestive suggestion.

"Okay," she said enthusiastically. "Let's talk."

Max figured there was no way he'd be able to get around it, seeing as how he was the one who'd made the suggestion in the first place, so he decided that, if they were going to talk—*Dammit*—then at least they'd talk about *her*.

"So if you grew up the way I did," he said before she could get another word in, "then I guess Roanoke, Virginia, isn't a place you're all that keen to get back to." He stuffed his hand into the popcorn bowl as he completed the observation, then realized that it was a new one, and that now he and Lucy each had their own.

Well, hell, he thought. That was going to take all the fun out of the evening. Not that he'd been thinking it had been fun, necessarily, to constantly find his fingers twined with Lucy's and be forced to remember again how soft and sweet she was, and how lousy it was that he couldn't take advantage of that softness and sweetness and do what came naturally because he wasn't allowed such pleasures anymore. No, that had been more like torture. But it had been a damned enjoyable torture, and he hadn't had too many of those. Most of his tortures over the past five years had been pretty awful—like bad, warm beer, he thought with a disagreeable glance in that direction. And like not permitting himself to own a car. Oh, sure, it was okay for him to drive Justin's cars, but that had been the whole point. He was driving nice cars that belonged to someone else—which really was torture—and he never, ever, allowed himself to go over the speed limit—another truly intolerable punishment.

Then he remembered that he had driven over the speed limit the night he'd picked up Lucy at school, the first time in five years he'd broken the rules that way. And, damn, had it felt good. All of it. Driving a fast car, driving it faster than he was supposed to, and having Lucy in the seat beside him. For the first time in five years, Max had remembered just how pleasurable life could be. And it had been all he could do to rein himself in, all he could do to remind himself that he wasn't supposed to enjoy *anything*, not even his tortures. Because he didn't deserve to enjoy anything. Not after what he'd done.

Still, he tried to persuade himself now as he turned his attention back to Lucy, after five years of self-inflicted tortures, it wouldn't be such a terrible thing to allow himself to enjoy just one, would it? That was only fair. It would still be a torture.

"No, it's not," Lucy said. And it took Max a minute to realize she was talking about her reluctant desire to go home, and not the fairness or enjoyment of his various tortures and punishments. "I'm not especially anxious to go back," she said further. And he couldn't help thinking she sounded a little surprised by her admission.

"Not even to reunite yourself with that upright, forthright, do-right guy you're engaged to?" he asked.

"Well," she hedged, nervously thumbing the ugly ring on her finger, "well, I guess I'd just as soon he and I started our lives together somewhere different, that's all."

Yeah, Max thought. Like, say, with Lucy on the East Coast and her fiancé on the West Coast. That might work well.

"You know," he said, "every time you talk about your intended, you sound like you don't want to talk about him."

She tugged more nervously on the ring as he spoke, her gaze flying to everything in the room except Max. Another indication, he decided, that there was more to her engagement than she was letting on. Or could it be that there was *less* to her engagement than she was letting on? Hmm . . .

"I do?" she asked.

He nodded, smiling at how those two little words formed a question instead of a statement, the way they traditionally did when spoken together. It could only be a good omen. Then Max reminded himself he didn't need any good omens where Lucy was concerned. What he needed were bad reminders of how he shouldn't be with her, because she deserved a lot better, and because he deserved nothing at all.

"Yeah, you do," he said, nudging those reminders aside before they could take up too much room in his brain. Because, man, it was getting crowded in there, and he was getting tired of having those reminders rattling around. He needed a break from those reminders, even if only for a little while. "And I can't help wondering," he said further, "why you wouldn't want to talk about a man you're planning to spend the rest of your life with."

"I, ah . . ." she began again. "I just don't, um . . . I mean . . . Really . . . It's just that . . . I don't . . . I can't . . ."

By now, she was twisting and tugging so hard on her engagement ring, Max feared she was going to take off her finger. Not sure what possessed him to do it, telling himself he only wanted to help—*Oh, sure you do, Max, sure you do*—he scooted across the sofa and covered her hands with his, tugging her tangled fingers apart to halt their ceaseless, restless worrying. But in pulling her hands away from each other, he pulled her arms away from each other, too. And in pulling her arms away from each other, he left the rest of her wide-open to his gaze.

And when he saw her all wide-open like that, he drank in the sight with the thirst of a man who was too long parched for a lifesaving libation.

As he considered Lucy sitting there, in her funny pajamas, with her soft brown hair and softer blue eyes, time seemed somehow to grind to a halt. Suddenly, there was no past in his memory, only this present moment in his mind. No future to think about, only the here and now to feel. And here, now, Max let himself feel. He let himself think. Let himself dream. Let himself go. And he realized that here, now, he wanted Lucy. Better than that, here, now, Lucy wanted him, too.

Because she was gazing back at him with her eyes wide and unblinking, filled with emotions Max figured he probably shouldn't contemplate. And in that moment, she was so clear to him, so vividly detailed, so very beautiful, that he almost thought he was gazing upon a painting. But paintings didn't move, he reminded himself, not even infinitesimally, as Lucy did. Paintings didn't have delicate throats that worked over difficult swallows, as hers did just then. They didn't have pulses that leapt beneath their warm wrists, and Max definitely detected her pulse racing wildly under the pads of his

thumbs where he held her. And they didn't have breasts that
rose and fell with their rapid respiration, as hers did when she
looked at him. And paintings didn't have mouths that parted
on quick gasps, mouths that just begged a man to move forward and claim them.

And then, without thinking about what he was doing—
because somewhere at the very back of his brain he knew that
if he thought about it, he wouldn't do it, and he really, really
wanted to do it—Max was moving forward, across the
couch, pushing himself closer to Lucy and her throat and her
breasts and her mouth, and circling with more possession the
wrists he already held, and wondering what it would be like
to possess the rest of her, too.

And then he was possessing her, at least part of her, because still not thinking about what he was doing, and without
asking her permission first, he was covering her mouth with
his, and then he was kissing her and kissing her and kissing
her, and recalling vaguely how long it had been since he'd
kissed a woman—any woman—and how his memories of
kisses didn't do justice to this one. Because this one . . .

Oh, sweet Jesus . . .

This one was exquisite. Intoxicating. Narcotic. As Max
claimed Lucy's soft, warm, sweet—Oh, God, she was
sweet—mouth with his, he felt like a man possessed. Or,
more accurately, a man dispossessed. Because the moment
he felt her softness, sensed her warmth, tasted her sweetness,
he lost a part of himself forever.

But, oh, what a way to go . . .

For long moments, he only kissed her, still holding her
arms out to her sides, reveling in the leap and dance of her
pulse beneath the pads of his thumbs. Her breathing went
wild with every new caress of his mouth against hers, just
like his own savage respiration. She opened to him eagerly,
and he drove his tongue deep inside her, savoring every hot,
damp inch of her he could reach. She responded in kind, tangling her tongue with his, wanting to taste him as deeply as

he was relishing her. So he backed off some and let her, then nearly came undone at the sensation of her tongue venturing inside his own mouth.

Unable to stop himself, he released one of her wrists, drawing his fingers up along her bare arm, over her sleeve, her shoulder, her collar, finally curling his hand gently around her nape. He drove his fingers into her silky hair, loving the way the soft tresses tripped over his hand. Then he moved his hand lower, down the slender column of her throat, skimming his fingertips along the elegant divot at its base before moving lower still, to the top button of her pajama shirt.

Tentatively, fearful he might have forgotten how, Max slipped that button through its binding, certain he must have only imagined the puff of sweet-smelling ambrosia that filled his nostrils and weakened his senses when he did. Still kissing him, still driving him mad, Lucy moved her free hand now to his hair, tangling her fingers in the overly long tresses, cupping the crown of his head in her palm to urge him closer still, obviously mindless of the fact that they were already as close as they could possibly be without starting a fire. Max moved his hand to the second button of her shirt, freeing it, too, then on to the third, fourth and fifth, releasing each in its stead. Then he was able to push the garment open completely and flatten his palm against her naked torso.

So warm. So soft. He remembered now how good a woman could feel, how different her body was from his own. But his memories were nothing compared to the reality beneath his hand. Leisurely, methodically, he strummed his fingers up over each delicate, naked rib and back again, cupping his hand around the entirety of her rib cage before moving it back to the center of her torso again.

It had been so long, he thought, so long since he had touched a woman this way. And he wanted to discover every last inch of Lucy that he could, slowly, deliberately, completely, as if he were discovering a woman for the first time.

Because, in some ways, this was the first time for Max. The first time he had allowed himself to touch a woman because he simply couldn't resist the sheer, basic pleasure of it. The first time he touched one because he couldn't stand not to. The first time since he'd realized just how very much a woman's touch mattered in making him feel complete. And not just any woman, either, he realized then. There was only one who could do this to him now, only one woman who could make him feel this intensely about what he was doing, what he *had* to do. Only one who could make him forget, if only for a little while, all the things he'd promised himself he'd remember forever. Because until Lucy came into his life, he had been able to remember, much too well, all of those things. Now, though . . .

Now he just wanted to forget. He wanted to forget everything except Lucy.

As he continued to kiss her—deeply and relentlessly—he trailed his middle finger down the center line of her abdomen, dipping his fingertip into the tiny cleft of her navel and out again, then back up her rib cage on the opposite side. He knew he was denying himself the prize he truly wanted, but he needed to deny himself that for as long as he could tolerate it. Over and over again, he palmed her flat belly and tripped his fingertips over the ridges of her ribs, in front, then in back, until finally, finally, he could stand it no more, and moved his hand upward again, to the lower curve of her breast.

But even then, he couldn't quite bring himself to fully claim it. Instead, he turned his hand first one way, then another, letting the heavy weight of her flesh glide first over the heel of his palm and then over the back of his hand and then along each side. She was so soft, so round, so heavy, so perfect. And larger than he had realized initially. Had it been so long, he wondered, that he couldn't even accurately gauge a woman's curves anymore? Or had he just been trying to deny to himself how very luscious she was?

He still hadn't covered her breast with his hand, had only positioned his fingers so that he cradled the lower curve in the deep L created by his thumb and index finger. So soft, he thought again. So round. So perfect. He shouldn't claim such a thing for himself, he told himself, *couldn't* claim anything that was that beautiful or that he wanted so much. He was about to pull his hand away when he felt Lucy's hand upon it, urging it higher, up over the soft mound of her breast, until her nipple lay beneath the center of his palm.

"Please," she murmured against his ear. "Please, Max. Touch me. I need for you to touch me."

Immediately, he closed his fingers over her, nearly shattering inside. Not just because he held so heavenly a prize, but because she had offered it to him so generously. She sighed as he touched her, her damp breath warm against his neck. For a moment, he only held her in his hand, glorying in a sensation so long denied him, remembering how much he missed this sort of closeness with a woman—with another human being. Then, slowly, he began to move his hand, palming her breast, closing and opening his fingers over her, capturing the taut peak between thumb and middle finger, rolling it gently again and again, reveling in every soft gasp she uttered under his ministrations. He watched his fingers as they toyed with her, then moved his attention to her wildly expressive face, loving the way she responded to each caress. Then he lowered his head and, still fingering her delicately between thumb and middle finger, flicked the tip of his tongue over her nipple, once, twice, three times, tasting sweetness and promise and a forbidden sort of happiness he dared not imagine.

He felt her fingers tangle in his hair again as he tasted her, heard her not quite successfully trying to bite back a moan, sensed her pushing his head down more insistently against her breast. So what could he do but obey her? What could he do but move his fingers aside and grasp her breast at its base, then open his mouth wide and draw as much of her inside as he possibly could? With one long suck, and one lazy squeeze, he consumed her, laving her nipple with the flat of his tongue, tantalizing it further with the tip. Again and again he teased her with the pressure of both his mouth and his hand, pulling at her, gripping her more possessively, tasting her with a hunger whose depth he was only now beginning to realize.

She lay back completely against the side of the sofa now, one hand tangled in his hair, the other pushing up the fabric of his T-shirt to bare his back. He felt her legs parting beneath him, one foot dropping to the floor, the other bracing itself against the back of the couch. Deftly, Max positioned himself so that his thigh pressed against the juncture of hers, and immediately, she lifted her hips higher, to press herself even more intimately against him. She gasped at the contact, but instead of pulling away from him, as he feared she might, she lowered her hips back to the couch and then bucked them forward again.

Oh, God, Max thought. *Oh, sweet, heavenly God*.

He wanted to touch her there, too, *needed* to touch her there, too. Without thinking, acting only on instinct now, because thinking was just out of the question, he lifted his head from her breast and managed to shift their bodies so that they were lying side by side, with Lucy between him and the back of the couch. Helplessly, he gazed down at her torso when he did, and saw that her shirt was gaping open on one side, and that her breast was swollen and damp and pink from where he had so ruthlessly tried to consume her. He told himself he should apologize for manhandling her so, but she chose that moment to move her hand around his waist and cup it firmly over his buttock. And all he could do then was squeeze his eyes shut tight at the sensations that purled through him, one after another.

He waited for the ripples of pleasure to subside some, then thought, hell, what was good for the gander . . .

He urged his hand between Lucy and the couch, curling his fingers over the curve of her sweet ass, moving the fabric of her pajamas just enough to assure himself that she wore nothing else beneath them. Only one flimsy scrap of fabric separated him from her warm flesh, and he could feel her heat penetrating that scrap of fabric to mingle with the heat of his hand. He scooted his hand lower, to the hem of her loose shorts, then beneath those, too. And then he filled his hand with her soft, warm flesh, softer and warmer than he had imagined it could be.

She pressed her mouth to his neck when he touched her, dragging a long, openmouthed kiss along his throat, then retracing the motion with the tip of her tongue. Max bit back a groan at her action, then tightened his hold on her fanny, dipping his fingertips into the delicate cleft bisecting it. He moved his fingers along that elegant line, first up, then down, then lower still, until he felt the dampness of her response against his fingertips. She hooked her bent knee over his at the intimate contact, giving him better access to her, and Max took full advantage. From behind, he pushed a finger forward, into the damp heat between her legs. Lucy gasped at the scant penetration, then clipped him gently on the neck with her teeth.

He couldn't do this, Max realized. Not without going off like a bottle rocket. Hell, he was already halfway gone. One more touch, one more hint at how wet and ready she was to take him, and he was likely to empty himself before he even dropped his pants. Quickly, he jerked his hand backward, sliding his fingers one last time along the crease of her bottom before moving out of her shorts and up along her bare back. By now, his shaft had swelled hard and long against the fly of his jeans, and he felt certain it would burst right through the zipper, he was so fully-loaded.

Still recalling how damp and ready Lucy had been for him, and telling himself it was madness, he reached behind himself to where she still had her hand clamped over his ass, then pulled it back again, between their bodies, pushing it— hard—down over the denim that encased his erection. Without bothering to unfasten the garment, he shoved her hand down the length of himself, then back up again, then down once more. Together, they rubbed him, hard and slow and long, until Max felt as if he were damn near exploding.

Oh, God, he had forgotten how good this could be. He had forgotten what it was like to touch and be touched with such intimacy, to experience such a coupling of bodies and spirits and souls. He had forgotten how deeply he could simply *feel* things. And he had forgotten just how much he enjoyed the—

Oh, no. Oh, hell. He *was* enjoying it. Christ, he was enjoying it more than he had ever enjoyed anything in his life, even back when he had allowed himself such pleasures. But he didn't allow himself such pleasures anymore. He didn't allow himself to enjoy things. Because he didn't deserve to. Dammit, he had *promised* himself he would never do this again. He had taken a *vow*. He had *sworn a solemn oath*.

"Stop," he suddenly ground out, jerking himself away from Lucy with all the ferocity he would use to wrench himself free of a mauling lion. He leapt to his feet, and backed unsteadily away from her, holding his hands out before himself as if he were trying to ward off some evil spirit of doom, death, and destruction.

Then he looked at Lucy, saw her pulling herself gracelessly up from where he'd had her sprawled on the sofa, her shirt falling open over her naked breasts, her mouth full and ripe and red from where he had kissed her. Her hair was mussed from his own caresses, and her eyes were wide with innocence and uncertainty and something else vaguely reminiscent of fear.

Ah, hell . . . He never should have touched her.

She was no evil spirit, he told himself. She was an angel. An angel of sweetness, security, and salvation. She didn't deserve the likes of Max Hogan. And no way did he deserve her. If anyone was an evil spirit here, it was him. And he knew then that he had been right all along in telling himself to stay away from her. He *had* to stay away from her. From now until it was time for her to leave Harborcourt. Otherwise . . .

Well. There was no otherwise, that was all there was to it. He just plain had to leave her the hell alone. Because he just plain had to live in his hell alone.

"Max?" she said softly, her tone puzzled and worried and still very much aroused. "What's wrong? What happened? Why did you stop?"

She raked a hand nervously through her hair, grimacing when it caught on a snarl he had put there himself, with his own eager, amorous fingers. Then she seemed to recall that she was only half-clothed, and she dropped her hands to her pajama shirt, hastily jerking it closed.

"What did I do wrong?" she asked. "Whatever it was, I'm sorry. And I promise not to do it again."

He squeezed his eyes shut tight at the realization that she thought this was her fault. That she had done something wrong. Who could have possibly put such a ridiculous notion in her head? She was wonderful. She was perfect. She was everything . . .

Everything he could never have again.

"Nothing," he hastened to assure her. "Lucy, you didn't do anything wrong. You're . . ." Oh, God, she was so much, so many things. Gentle. Decent. Kind. "It's not you, it's me. I can't . . ."

But how was he supposed to explain it all to her when he could hardly make sense of it himself half the time? "It's not you," he said again. "It's me."

She studied him in silence for a moment, kneeling awkwardly on the couch, gripping her shirt closed tightly over herself, but not bothering to button it. Then, very slowly, she nodded. And in a very small voice, she said, "Right. It's you. Not me. I understand."

But clearly, she didn't understand. Clearly, she still thought she'd done something wrong. "Lucy," he began helplessly. He even took a halfhearted step forward before he stopped himself. He didn't want to be responsible for her desolation and despair. But he knew he was. And he knew there was nothing he could say or do to change it.

But then, hey, he was really good about introducing desolation and despair into a woman's life. He was even better at not doing or saying anything to change it.

"Lucy," he tried again anyway.

She met his gaze levelly and he could tell she was trying not to look hurt. "Are you leaving?" she asked in that very small voice.

He hesitated only a moment, then nodded.

"But it . . . it's not because of anything I did, right?" she asked flatly.

This time he shook his head. But he couldn't quite find the words to explain.

She nodded disconsolately, and he could tell she didn't believe a word he'd said. "Gotcha. Then I, um, I guess you should go."

Max told himself to get the hell out of there and leave her alone. He did manage to make himself turn around. And somehow, he forced his feet to move forward, toward the front door. He even managed to make himself grip the doorknob and turn it. But even after he'd opened the door, he couldn't quite get himself to go through it. Not until he'd tried one more time to make Lucy understand.

He pivoted slowly around again, only to find that she had turned her back on him and was buttoning up her shirt. Good, he thought. It would be easier if she wasn't looking at him. It was always easier that way for a yellow-bellied, chicken-hearted jerk like him.

"It wasn't you, Lucy," he said softly again.

She hesitated in her movements, then stopped buttoning herself up. She turned her head only slightly, so that he knew she had heard him, but she didn't turn around to look at him.

"You felt what you did to me just now," he added, still speaking in low tones. "You felt how I responded to you. You know I wanted you. You *know* it. I don't think I've ever wanted any woman the way I wanted you tonight." He swallowed hard. "But I can't have you, Lucy. It's not allowed. And wanting you like that, and knowing I can't have you . . ."

He expelled a restless sound, knowing he'd never be able to explain without telling her too many things he never wanted to tell anyone again. "Just try to understand," he concluded inadequately. "It's not you. It's me. I promise you, it's me."

And even though he hadn't come close to saying everything he wanted—everything he *needed*—to say, Max made himself walk forward, out the door, out of the apartment, out of Lucy's life.

He knew he couldn't avoid her for the rest of the time she'd be working at Harborcourt. But he'd be damned if he'd put himself in a position like this one again. Because after tonight, having touched her softness and tasted her sweetness and held her perfection, Max knew a new kind of torture. Before, he'd only been denying himself the presence of a woman in his life. Now, though, now he was denying himself the presence of Lucy.

And somehow, he wasn't sure that was a torture that he was going to be able to survive.

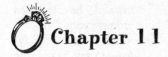 **Chapter 11**

"But, Rosemary, I don't want to go."

"Abby, you have to go."

"You told me I didn't have to go."

"I was wrong. You have to go. Your mother and father insist."

"But who cares what they say? I only care what you say."

"Abby, don't make this harder than it already is. You'll be fine, sweetheart. I promise you."

And as she made that promise, Rosemary sent a silent prayer heavenward that she wouldn't be a liar for uttering it. Poor Abby. Even though Rosemary had tried to argue against forcing the little girl to be tested for her lack of reading skills if she didn't want to be, deep down, she had known it would be for the best. Abby did have a problem, and she would only find help for it once that problem was identified.

Perhaps Alexis Cove's reasons for wanting her daughter's problem to be addressed differed from Rosemary's reasons—Alexis, of course, simply could not abide imperfection in anything that was present in her home, where Rosemary simply wanted Abby to be a happy, contented little girl—but at least both women wanted to find help for her. But Rosemary wished she could go with them today. And not just because she was having second thoughts about having agreed to spend the day with Nathaniel Finn, either.

What had she been thinking Friday night, to have said yes to this outing with him? And what had he been thinking, to ask her out in the first place? Rosemary still felt wary about his sudden interest in her. He'd been coming 'round to visit the Coves ever since she had started working for them, yet not once had he seemed to notice her. Granted, she had only been nineteen when she'd begun her employment, and he wouldn't have been interested in a teenager back then. Well, not unless he was a cradle robber, and, judging by the women he usually wore on his arm—thirtyish, overly made up, and full-breasted—he liked them very ripe indeed. Which made his interest in Rosemary all the more puzzling. Not only was she none of those things, but nothing in her had changed so recently to warrant his notice now. Nothing. So why, suddenly, was he noticing?

Oh, why question it, Rosemary? she asked herself as she ran a brush through her long hair in preparation of braiding it. *Why is it so hard for you to believe that a handsome, wealthy, successful man might find you attractive? It wouldn't be the first time, after all.*

Yes, but look what had happened then, she reminded herself right back. Handsome, wealthy, and successful Phillip Somerset might have been, but he hadn't loved her, had he? Certainly not enough to overcome the prejudices of his family—or his own prejudices, either. Certainly not enough to make her his wife.

"But can't you come to the testing, too?" Abby asked anxiously from her perch on Rosemary's bed. Though whether she was anxious about her upcoming test, or because her mother had insisted she wear a dress, Rosemary couldn't have said. It was a girly pink dress, too, and Abby hated all things girly.

"Your mother has asked me not to come, sweetheart," Rosemary said, hoping she succeeded in biting back any bitterness she felt about that. "She's afraid I might distract you."

"You won't distract me," Abby cried plaintively, her desperate tone tugging at something deep inside Rosemary that always got tugged whenever she was around the little girl. "I want you to be there. Can't Mom stay home and you go with me? Please?"

Rosemary turned back to the mirror of her dresser so that Abby wouldn't see her expression. Yes, Alexis would certainly be the greater distraction. Because she would be more anxious about this test than Abby was. And she would be constantly after the little girl to sit up straight and brush your hair and get that wrinkle out of your dress and oh, why did you have to have such poor eyesight, those glasses just aren't becoming at all, your father and I both have perfect vision, I can't imagine where you come by this.

"No, Abby," Rosemary said softly as she reached back to braid her hair. "Your mother should be with you." Hah. "And you'll do just fine."

"And besides," Abby added cheerlessly, "you're going out with Mr. Nathaniel today."

Rosemary's stomach roiled at the mere mention of the day ahead. But she tried to sound happy and excited when she replied, "Yes, sweetheart, I'm going out with Mr. Nathaniel today."

Instead of arguing any further, the little girl watched with much fascination as Rosemary effortlessly braided her long hair, then wound it around and around her head like a headband, and deftly fastened it in place. She hadn't been sure what to wear when the occasion was looking at a horse that someone else was considering buying. Back in Ireland, she would have worn something appropriate for riding in case an opportunity arose, but she'd only been a teenager then and hadn't known anything about social graces. Or life in general, for that matter.

So, today, she had opted to let the weather dictate her choice. Because it was hot and sunny with just a hint of a breeze, she had selected a casual, sleeveless, floral print dress that tied in back, coupling it with flat sandals. She knew she was no glamour-puss, but she was comfortable, and that was all that mattered.

"Will you bring me a present?" Abby said when Rosemary completed her preparations and stood.

Rosemary didn't bother to hide her smile. She strode forward and halted in front of the little girl, then bent to place a loud kiss at the crown of Abby's head. "Yes, Abby, I will. A very special present indeed."

Abby smiled back. "Then I'll pass my test. I'll pass it for you, Rosemary. Just you wait and see."

But there was more than a hint of apprehension in her tone when she spoke, and it tugged again at that place deep inside Rosemary. She should be with Abby today, she told herself. She had been there for every single one of Abby's milestones, both the good and the not so good. It had been Rosemary who heard the little girl's first spoken word because her parents had been in New York at the time, Rosemary who had witnessed Abby's first step when the Coves had been at a golf tournament. Rosemary had been the one who rushed to Abby's side at the hospital emergency room when she'd fallen off the monkey bars at preschool and required three stitches beneath her chin. And Rosemary had been the one, every night, who had come to the child's aid when bad dreams had kept her awake.

She should be with Abby today, too, she told herself again. But Mrs. Cove had made it clear that, this time, she would be the one there for Abby. Rosemary wished it was because the woman cared deeply about her daughter's welfare. But she feared, as she always did when Mrs. Cove took an interest in things, that the only reason Abby's mother wanted to be there was to dispute the findings. Mrs. Cove refused to accept that her child had a problem that called for professional help. She refused to accept that her child was imperfect. Bad enough that the little girl's eyesight was flawed. It was impossible that her brain might possibly be wired differently from the average brain, too. That simply didn't happen to the Coves.

So Rosemary wouldn't be welcomed at the testing, she knew. Because she would want what was best for Abby and not what was best for the Coves.

"Just do your best," she told Abby now. "That's all you can ever do." With another soft kiss to the little girl's head, she added quietly, "That's all any of us can ever do."

"I'll do good," Abby promised. "You'll see. I'll do good today."

Rosemary smiled again, but there was no happiness in the gesture this time. She had no doubt that Abby would do good today, regardless of how well she performed on her reading test. She only wished she could say the same about herself.

The drive to Woodford County was quite lovely, Rosemary had to admit, and once they arrived at Garamond Stables on US 60, she realized she'd been foolish to doubt Nathaniel's intentions when he had announced upon leaving Harborcourt that he thought it would be a good idea for them to take the scenic route. Why had she thought he was only doing that so that he might drive her to a secluded spot and make every effort to compromise her? Obviously he simply enjoyed a drive in the country as much as she did herself—provided she wasn't constantly questioning the designs of the man she was with when making that drive, she added dryly to herself.

But Garamond Stables itself was a beautiful thing to behold on a sunny day in September, its green hills rolling up and down beneath a bright blue sky as far as the eye could see. Wide, high-reaching maples dotted the countryside here and there, white slat fences striated the fields like stripes on an ice-cream vendor's shirt, and magnificent Thoroughbreds raced across the landscape for the sheer, abundant joy of it. Towering oaks lined the long drive to the main residence, a stately white house in the Federal style, with a chimney at each corner, and a cobbled walkway lined with pansies and peonies, and a wraparound porch, and a white wicker swing swaying laconically at one end.

Rosemary caught her breath as the house came into view, because it was the symbol of everything she had ever wanted in life—beauty, warmth, security, love. A home. That was what she truly would have loved to find for herself. A home of her own, and someone to share it with, a man who would love her to distraction and help her fill their house with children. Instead, she had found the Coves. And although their house was certainly beautiful and secure, and warm enough, she supposed, in a superficial sort of way, it wasn't Rosemary's home. Still, Harborcourt had Abby, didn't it? And Abby was as close to a family as anything she'd ever had in her life. Because Abby loved her. Abby needed her. And Rosemary loved and needed Abby, too. And nothing—nothing—would ever change that. Nothing—nothing—would ever separate her from that little girl.

So maybe Rosemary didn't have a home of her own. So what? The place she held in the world was just fine, thanks. Even if it lacked a certain something. A certain some*one*. She couldn't have everything, could she? No one could. So she'd be happy with what she had. Of course, she would.

Of course, she would.

Nathaniel rolled the midnight blue Jaguar to a halt just shy of the front steps, and immediately a man pushed open the screen door and strode through, lifting a hand in greeting. To Rosemary's way of thinking, he looked to be somewhere around 180 years old. He was dressed in faded denim overalls that were streaked with the morning's work, a checkered, short-sleeved shirt, muddy, muddy work boots, and a faded, battered ball cap.

"Silas Garamond," Nathaniel told Rosemary with a smile as he unhooked his seat belt and watched the man carefully make his way down the front steps. "He's a character. But he knows horses, and he and my grandfather were good friends. I've known him all my life."

"Nate!" Silas Garamond shouted, as Rosemary waited for Nathaniel to round the front of the car and open her door for her.

She smiled at the appellation. She could scarcely think of her companion as *Nathaniel*, let alone *Nate*, even though he had insisted that morning that he didn't want to hear any more of this "Mr. Finn stuff" from her. He seemed too sophisticated a man for "Nate." Yet somehow, "Nathaniel" seemed far too formal.

"Silas," he said as he opened the door for Rosemary and extended a hand to help her out.

He did it so naturally, too, she noted. He was very mannerly and attentive that way, very genuine in his social graces, as if he'd been bred for the good life. Of course, he probably had been bred for the good life, just as he himself bred horses for people who lived the good life. Still, he seemed to straddle two worlds in his choice of clothing for today, as he had opted for well-faded blue jeans and a forest green polo emblazoned with the logo of a popular Prospect restaurant. His shoes were sedate loafers worn without socks, but had, she was certain, set him back more than she earned in a week. And whether he was at one of Mrs. Cove's formal cocktail parties or a horse farm in the country, he moved as comfortably as if he had been born to them both.

Nathaniel's world was a far cry from the one amid which Rosemary had grown up, to be sure—with its three-room walk-up flat, and its meager, homemade wardrobe, and its public bus system. Nathaniel Finn had probably never ridden a bus in his life, and probably had no idea how much work went into the creation of a simple garment, and couldn't possibly imagine what it was like to have no privacy growing up. And he couldn't know what it was like to have no opportunities growing up, either, she thought. No family. No anything sometimes.

Of course he would be sophisticated, she told herself. Of course he would know how to be mannerly and attentive around a woman. Of course he would be completely wonderful.

Because he was completely wonderful—Rosemary could no longer deny that. Their drive to Garamond Stables had been filled with quiet conversation about the horse business and Nathaniel's grandfather, and Ireland. Strangely, though, he'd been the one to talk mostly about her homeland. Rosemary was a bit reluctant to cover that ground herself. But

Nathaniel wanted very much to visit Dublin and other south-
ern parts of the island someday, so really, it was two different
matters. Northern Ireland was a far cry from the rest of that
piece of land. And when Rosemary had asked Nathaniel why
he hadn't yet visited the country he so much wanted to see,
he'd seemed stumped for an answer.

"I don't know," he'd said. "I guess since I learned about it
from my grandfather, I just always thought I should visit it
with someone special."

Meaning there'd been no one special for him so far, Rosemary had deduced. And something about that realization had
sent a warm sensation wheeling about inside her.

He'd been a perfect gentleman over dinner Friday, too, she
recalled, and during the drive home that night. He'd walked
her to the door, made sure she got in all right, then had lifted
a hand in innocent farewell, said good night, and smiled at
her in a way that made her heart dance. She'd stood at the
Coves' back door and watched him walk back to his car. He'd
smiled at her again through the driver's side window, and
waved one final time before pulling out.

Even after he'd gone, she'd stood at the door, gazing out at
the nighttime, wanting to preserve it for a little while longer.
He'd been so handsome. So kind. So interesting to talk to.
And, then, Saturday morning, when a tow truck had shown
up at Harborcourt with her car, fully repaired, no charge necessary, thanks, Mr. Finn had taken care of it, Rosemary had
realized he'd been very sweet, too.

A loose wire on the battery, the mechanic had told her. She
chuckled now to think of it. No telling how that had happened. Max was kind enough to check her Volkswagen out
from time to time, but she supposed even he missed the occa-
sional loose wire.

Ah, well. No harm done. And now, thanks to that loose
wire, here she was, with a day to herself in the company of a
handsome, kind, interesting, sweet, completely wonderful
man. Sometimes, she thought, life worked out well. Not often. But sometimes. She wasn't sure what she had done to be

rewarded this way, but she decided not to question it. No, she decided she would simply enjoy the company of a nice man whom she liked very much.

"Silas," Nathaniel said again, this time in a tone of voice that indicated he was introducing the man instead of greeting him, "meet Rosemary Shaugnessy. Rosemary, this is Silas Garamond."

"Mr. Garamond," she said with a smile, extending her hand.

"Oh, none o' that now," the old man said, giving her hand a sturdy shake. "It's Silas. Pleasure to meet you, Rosemary." He turned to Nathaniel and winked. "Nice girl from the old country, eh, Nate? Your grandpa woulda been proud as punch to see it."

Rosemary felt her face warm with a blush. "Oh, no, I'm just a friend of Mr. . . . I mean," she hastily backpedaled when she saw Nathaniel's warning, though teasing, frown. "Nathaniel and I are just friends," she finally said.

But Nathaniel smiled in response, and asked, "Is that all we are?"

Rosemary opened her mouth to reply, realized she had no idea what to say, so closed it again and only gazed at Nathaniel with much curiosity. Of course they were just friends, she told herself. Weren't they? The point quickly became moot, however—as did the somewhat clumsy silence that lingered briefly between them—because Silas began speaking again.

"She's a real beauty, Nate," he said, and Rosemary felt herself coloring again. Until the old man added, "Ain't seen a horse like her for a looooong time."

Nathaniel laughed, though whether because of Silas's remark, or because he had observed her reaction to it, Rosemary couldn't have said.

"'Course, I'm only acting as the agent here, but I think she's got some real potential. You were the first person I thought about when I saw her. I think you'll be pleased."

The two men continued to chat as they strode toward the

house, but Nathaniel hung back with Rosemary instead of moving forward to walk with Silas. And when she realized what he was doing, a soft sort of warmth seeped into her body, going nearly incandescent when he slipped his hand beneath her elbow to help guide her up the stairs.

It was the first time he had touched her, she realized. Oh, no, wait, it wasn't. The first time had been Friday night, when he had lifted her cross to inspect it, and his knuckles had grazed her sensitive flesh. But that had been an accident. This was the first time he had touched her deliberately, and she relished the tenderness of that touch. For such a large man to be so gentle was truly a wondrous thing. It had been a long time since any man had treated Rosemary with such care and attention. A long time since any man had touched her with tenderness.

Too long a time.

The interior of the house when she entered it was as charming as the exterior, and Rosemary absorbed quick impressions of hardwood floors polished to a honeylike gleam, colorful hooked rugs scattered about, old furniture and photographs, and fat, pink roses climbing the wallpaper in the foyer and hall beyond. Immediately upon entering, she was besieged by the aroma of something sweet and heavy and high-calorie baking, and the soft strains of Bluegrass music, which she had come to love, since it reminded her of the music of her homeland in so many ways.

"Livvy!" Silas called out. "Nate's here! Come out and say hello!"

Before he finished speaking, a woman who was as tidy as Silas was, ah . . . not, came striding down the hall toward them. She, too, was of extended years, her hair short and curly and white, her blue jeans and red T-shirt crisp and unsullied. She had a sweet smile and crinkling brown eyes, and Rosemary liked her immediately.

"Nate," she said with undisguised delight, pulling him into a warm embrace that dwarfed her. She gave him a kiss on the cheek, and added, "We've missed you. It was Christmas when you were here last."

"I'm sorry, Livvy," Nathaniel said. "It's been a busy year."

She patted his cheek maternally. "Well, at least you call from time to time." Then she turned to Rosemary with another genuine smile of happiness. "And you brought your girl, too," she said by way of a greeting, extending both hands to Rosemary, who took them automatically.

"Actually, I'm not—" Rosemary began.

But Nathaniel cut her off with a simple introduction. "Livvy, this is Rosemary Shaugnessy. Rosemary, Livvy Garamond."

"Irish," Livvy said with clear delight. "Your grandpa would have been so happy."

"Actually—" Rosemary tried again.

And again, Nathaniel cut her off with a quickly uttered "So what's this I hear about a new yearling?" and then he and the Garamonds all fell into avid conversation. Clearly horses were a subject they all knew and loved well, and once the topic was introduced, everything else in the world dissolved.

For a good fifteen minutes, the three of them talked about horses in general, and this new yearling in particular, until Livvy suddenly remembered that she had fixed a snack for all of them, since Nathaniel and Rosemary were certain to be hungry about now and she knew how much Nathaniel liked her corn fritters and the boy just didn't eat right, which she could see for herself since he was all skin and bones.

This time it was Rosemary's turn to smile in response to his blush. Of course, he had nothing to be ashamed of. He wasn't anything closely resembling skin and bones. The man had quite a bit of meat to him, and every last inch of it was quite nicely arranged. Oh, yes. Quite nicely arranged, indeed.

"Not too much," Nathaniel cautioned Livvy. "Just a snack. Rosemary and I have something special planned for lunch later."

Did they? Rosemary wondered. This was the first she'd

heard about that. Of course, she had expected to eat at some point during the day she would be spending with him, but he hadn't specifically mentioned a "plan" until now. Or anything "special," either. She wondered what it was.

"Just a snack," Livvy promised. But she smiled at Nathaniel and winked at Rosemary when she added, "And then the two of you can have your *special* thing later."

Nathaniel was immediately unimpressed with the horse. Not that he'd had high hopes for it to begin with—the twenty thousand dollars her owner was asking for her was hardly the price tag of a champion. But he'd thought there might be a chance that he would spot some potential in the animal that the owner—and even Silas—had missed, and perhaps turn his twenty-thousand-dollar investment into a Triple Crown winner. After all, Real Quiet, who'd come *this close* to the Triple Crown in 1998, had gone for seventeen thousand dollars at auction. But this horse . . .

He considered the yearling first from a distance, watching from beyond the fence that surrounded the paddock. She had beautiful coloring, to be sure, a chestnut whose reds gleamed like fire in the sun, and her gait was steady and strong. She was on the small side, however, and her legs were a bit short to Nathaniel's way of thinking. Nothing more jumped out at him upon his initial inspection.

"Her name's Destinations South," Silas said. "Sire was Southernmost Comfort, and dam was Blue Destiny. She'll be fine for breedin'. You might even get a race or two out of her if you can find a good trainer."

Nathaniel nodded, and in spite of his tepid initial response, pushed the gate open and entered the paddock behind Silas, who whistled to the filly. She was alert and smart—Nathaniel would give her that—turning immediately at the summons and running to Silas, who caught her halter capably in one hand when she drew near. Nathaniel made a slow circle around the animal, inspecting her form and figure and height and weight, but, even up close, he couldn't find much that was compelling there. Certainly nothing that excited him. All in all, this horse was really nothing out of the ordinary. No more special than dozens of others he'd declined to purchase in the past.

"Oh, my, she's magnificent," Rosemary said from beside him, in a hushed voice that was laced with reverence. "I don't think I've ever seen a horse so beautiful."

When Nathaniel turned to look at her, her gaze was fastened on the filly, and her lips were parted in clear delight at what she saw there.

"That's right, you used to work with horses," he said, remembering their conversation of Friday night. "I guess you know a lot about them then, don't you?"

"Enough, I suppose," she told him, her attention still fixed on the filly. "Though, mind you, it's been a long time since I've been around any for any length of time. I don't even see much of Mr. and Mrs. Cove's horses, really. Abby's afraid of them, so there's no reason to visit the stables. This one, though . . ." Her voice trailed off into something reminiscent of a sigh. "I've never seen an animal like her before. She's very beautiful. And so gentle."

"How can you tell she's gentle by looking at her?" Nathaniel asked.

Rosemary turned to him, her expression puzzled. "Well, can't you?" she asked.

He shook his head. "No," he said honestly. "I'd have to ride her. Or at least watch someone else riding her. You can't just tell an animal has a gentle nature by looking at it."

She seemed to mull that over for a moment, then, "Oh," she said, offering him not a clue as to what she might be thinking.

"Wanna take her for a spin?" Silas asked suddenly. "Got the keys right here," he added with a wink, giving the halter a gentle tug.

Rosemary's eyes widened in surprise at the question, and

for just a brief moment, they shone with excitement like two bright emeralds. Then, "Oh, no, I couldn't," she told him. But there was clear reluctance in her voice when she said it.

"Sure you could," Nathaniel rejoined.

She shook her head quickly, looking now at him. "No, I can't. I'm not dressed for riding."

Silas uttered a sound of derision. "Don't let that stop ya. Livvy's 'bout your size. You can borrow somethin' of hers. Or one of the girls who works part-time—they leave blue jeans and stuff in the stables all the time."

"No, really," Rosemary said, shaking her head more vehemently now. Her gaze ricocheted from Nathaniel to Silas and back again. "I couldn't. Thank you. But no."

Nathaniel told himself her response wasn't unexpected or unreasonable. She really wasn't dressed for riding, and he could see why she'd be reluctant to borrow clothes from a stranger for that. Somehow, though, he suspected the reason she'd declined riding the horse had little to do with proper dress and more to do with something else. What that something else might be, however, he couldn't have said.

"You like her, though, yes?" he asked Rosemary.

When she turned her attention to him again, the breeze kicked up, tugging an errant wisp of pale red hair from her tidy braid and making it dance gracefully about her face. Nathaniel felt himself automatically reach toward it, though whether to restore it to its rightful place or hasten the undoing of that braid completely, he wasn't sure. Before he could make contact, though, Rosemary herself reached up to push it back into place, tucking it quite capably back where it belonged. And as she did, she laughed lightly, laughter that was so impartial and so intimate and so incredibly sweet that Nathaniel felt something inside him go warm and fluid and weak.

Never in his life had he felt weakened by a woman. Never. But Rosemary, by her simple presence, made him feel as nervous and unsteady as an adolescent boy. And never in his life had he been swayed by a woman's laughter, either. Or her smile. On the contrary, usually, when a woman smiled at him, Nathaniel was immediately on guard. Because he'd always been able to see what was really behind the smile, and nearly always, what was behind it was a matter of personal gain for the woman doing the smiling. Rosemary, however, didn't smile that way. Her smiles were generous and uninhibited and free of deception. Every time she smiled at him, something inside Nathaniel went upside down and inside out, until he could scarcely remember his own name. Hers was a smile of kindness, of gentleness, of happiness. It was a smile that was at odds with what he was used to receiving in life. When Rosemary smiled, she smiled so—

Good God, man, get ahold of yourself, he berated himself midsentence when he realized how sappy and simpering his thoughts had become. *Finn, you're getting maudlin in your old age. The last thing you need to be doing is getting weak-kneed over a woman and singing psalms about her smiles*.

"Oh, yes," she said softly from beside him, jerking him back into the present. Back into her smile. Back into his sappy simpering. "I like her very much indeed."

His gaze wandered from Rosemary to the horse, then back again. "You think I should take her then?" he asked.

She deliberated, considering the filly once more. "If you want her."

"I do want her," he said without hesitation. Without thinking.

She turned to look at him, too, and he told himself he couldn't possibly be seeing in her expression what he thought he saw in her expression. It was too soon. Too easy. And for some reason, he thought, Rosemary Shaugnessy shouldn't be easy. Couldn't be easy. Because if she was . . .

"Then you should take her," she said softly.

Nathaniel grinned, but something inside him went cold as he did.

Jackpot, he told himself grimly. Though there was nothing

triumphant in his feelings just then. Aloud, he only said, "Maybe I should take her." He nodded agreeably, feeling more than a little sick to his stomach. "Maybe I should."

Lunch, Rosemary discovered that afternoon, was indeed something special, and it had indeed been planned, right down to the red-checkered tablecloth that Nathaniel spread beneath a sweeping maple some hours after concluding business—and a long visit—with the Garamonds.

A picnic, she thought, smiling. She never would have guessed that the man would be capable of coming up with such a whimsical, romantic idea, but here they were, a mile from the Garamonds' house—though still on Garamond property, he had told her—and he was anchoring the tablecloth in place against the breeze with a willow basket. He had driven his car down US 60, then up a dirt road, then off the road and into a field, parking it on the other side of the tree. Rosemary thought they must look like a magazine ad for Jaguar, so unlikely and idyllic must the scene appear.

"Have a seat," he invited, kneeling on the tablecloth.

Rosemary chuckled. "I can't believe you did this," she said.

But she, too, knelt on the ground, curling her legs around her. Maybe a dress hadn't been such a good idea after all. She wished she had been more prepared. And not just for the picnic, either.

" 'A loaf of bread, a jug of wine,' " Nathaniel recited as he removed one of each from the basket, " 'and thou,' " he finished, smiling at Rosemary as he did.

"Oh, my, he spouts poetry," she said with another laugh. "I think I shall be quite overcome and swoon."

He laughed, too. "No swooning until after lunch," he said. "I worked hard on this."

"You mean some restaurant worked hard on this," she corrected him.

"Yeah, yeah, yeah," he conceded, still smiling. "Whatever. I'm the one who did the selecting and ordering."

And he'd selected and ordered enough to feed an army, Rosemary thought as he pulled what looked like a dozen containers from the basket, rearranging the chill packs he'd added to keep them cool as he went. "What have you got there?" she asked.

"I wasn't sure what you'd like," he said. "So I got a little bit of everything."

When he glanced up, his expression was that of an eager little boy, anxious to please. His green eyes rivaled the color of the maple trees behind him, and a thick lock of black hair had fallen over his forehead. He was so handsome, she marveled. So thoughtful. So kind. So everything. He could have any woman he wanted. Why was he with her?

She shook her head in mystification and decided not to think about that. Instead, she said, "You look as if you bought out the entire restaurant. You are a man of many surprises, Mr. Finn."

He met her gaze levelly at that. "Am I?" he asked. And somehow, he seemed as if he put great stock in whatever her answer might be.

Rosemary swallowed with some difficulty. "Yes," she said truthfully. "You are."

He smiled, and a tiny concussion of delight exploded in her belly, gradually spreading throughout her body. "Really?" he asked. "In what way am I surprising?"

Oh, where to begin, Rosemary thought. "You're just not the kind of man I thought you were, that's all," she told him.

He seemed to give great thought to that. "And what kind of man did you think I was?"

"I thought you were shallow and self-centered," she said. "The kind of man who would only do something for personal gain."

He eyed her in silence, and a slash of something dark and turbulent clouded his eyes for just the briefest moment. "And you don't think I'm like that now?" he asked, his voice laced with something she could only liken to caution.

She shook her head slowly. "No. I don't think you're like that. I can see that you're a good, decent man."

"But I'm the Bad Boy of the Thoroughbred Racing Set," he reminded her. "Everybody says so."

She shook her head and smiled. "No, you're a good, decent man," she said again.

"How can you know that?" he asked quietly.

She lifted one shoulder and let it drop. "I don't know," she said. "Just my feminine intuition, I suppose. That and the way you act. You're polite and attentive. You've been very kind to me. And you were wonderful with Mr. and Mrs. Garamond today."

He dropped his gaze at that, ostensibly to work the corkscrew out of the bottle of wine, but somehow, Rosemary got the impression it was because he didn't want her to see his face when he talked about the Garamonds. Either that, or he was uncomfortable with the other things she had said about him.

"Silas and Livvy are practically my grandparents," he said, dismissing everything else she had mentioned. "I've known them all my life. If it weren't for them, I wouldn't have anyone who—" But he halted abruptly, leaving the statement unfinished.

"Who what?" she asked.

But he only shook his head. "Nothing. Never mind."

"No, what?" Rosemary insisted, wanting very much to know what he had been about to say. "If it weren't for them, you wouldn't have anyone who what?"

He sighed heavily, and she could see that he was reluctant to reply. Nevertheless, he told her, "If it weren't for them, I wouldn't have anyone who . . . Well, I don't guess I'd have anything remotely resembling a family, that's all."

"Your parents are gone?" she asked.

He nodded. "In a manner of speaking. They split up when I was a kid. My mom went to California to live, and my dad stayed here. Well, his house—our house"—he then corrected himself significantly—"was here. My father was usually in

Europe. My grandfather lived with us, and he pretty much raised me. He passed away when I was seventeen."

"Has your family always been in the horse business?"

He nodded. "My father was a breeder, and my grandfather was a trainer. I learned things from both of them that helped enormously when I opened my own stables."

And turned what he had learned into a very successful business, Rosemary thought. "Is your father still in Europe then?" she asked.

This time, Nathaniel shook his head. "No, he died four years ago. My mother is still alive, still living in California, but I haven't seen or heard from her for years."

"I never knew my parents," Rosemary said. "They both died before I was three. Lost to the Troubles, both of them."

Nathaniel snapped his head up at that, and only then did Rosemary realize how matter-of-factly she had spoken about the tragedies of her childhood. But then, tragedy was a way of life for every family where she came from. People couldn't help but be matter-of-fact about it. If they weren't, they'd all go mad.

"The Troubles," he repeated. "That's another word for the animosity between the IRA and England, isn't it?"

"Animosity," she echoed mildly. "Trust me, Nathaniel, it goes well beyond animosity over there. But yes, I lost both parents as a result of the violence and the hatred and . . ." She let her voice trail off. Why spoil a beautiful day with talk of such an ugly topic?

"I'm sorry," he said.

"It was a long time ago," she told him. "My father died before I was even born, and I don't remember anything about my mother. And I had my aunt Brigid to care for me, after all."

For all the good that had done, she thought. Her aunt had been excellent at keeping Rosemary out of trouble. At least, until Rosemary was sixteen. But that had been about all Aunt Brigid was excellent at. Then again, where they came from, staying out of trouble was next to impossible, so she supposed she should be grateful to her aunt. Still, she wished her aunt had shown a little more affection. Or any at all. Then again, in Derry, whenever you loved something, it usually got taken away. Violently, at that. Maybe her aunt had only been anticipating another tragedy, and that was why she had kept her distance.

"Just like I had my grandfather," Nathaniel said softly, his voice softer now. "And then, after he died, the Garamonds."

"And yet you don't see them very often," Rosemary noted. "That's what Mrs. Garamond said."

He turned his attention back to opening the wine. "A lot of people don't see much of their families," he said.

"That's true," she conceded. "But that's usually because they and their families don't get on. You seem to get on very well with the Garamonds."

"That's because I care a lot about them."

"Then why don't you see more of them?"

"I don't know," he finally told her, sounding vaguely impatient, though she suspected that impatience was with himself and not her. He tugged the cork free of the wine, then looked at Rosemary again. "No time, I guess. Demanding job. Full life. All that. But I really don't know."

How odd. He really did seem to be confused as to why he didn't see more of these people he claimed to care very much about, people who obviously loved him very much in turn. Such a curious man. To act one way when he clearly felt another. To say one thing when he clearly meant another. Why was he afraid to act and say as he honestly felt? she wondered. And how could he be part of the Coves' social circle, a place Rosemary had seen for herself was populated by superficial, egocentric, I-got-mine hangers-on? He was none of those things, she realized now. So why did he pretend that he was?

"You ask a lot of questions, Miss Shaugnessy, you know that?" he said with a smile. But there was something in the expression that was in no way happy.

"Maybe it's because I'm curious," she told him.

"Or maybe it's because you're suspicious."

His remark surprised her. "Why would I be suspicious?"

"You were suspicious Friday night," he said. "Weren't you?"

She nodded. "Yes, I was suspicious. Friday night."

"Why?"

"Because I couldn't understand why you wanted to spend time with me," she said. "Truth be told, I still don't understand that."

"You're still suspicious then," he concluded.

"Perhaps I am still. A little."

"I wish you wouldn't be."

So did Rosemary. "Well, maybe you could say something that would make me not be suspicious," she told him, injecting a lightness into her voice that she didn't feel.

He grinned. "Like what?"

"Maybe you could explain to me exactly why you invited me to come with you today," she said.

Instead of answering her verbally, Nathaniel set the open bottle of wine back into the basket, then dropped back onto his haunches to study her. For one long moment, he gazed at her in silence, then, very slowly, he covered the scant distance between them and dropped to sit beside her. But still he said nothing. Instead, he lifted his hand to her face, cupping her jaw gently in his palm. Then, very slowly, so that she could have stopped him if she'd wanted to, he dipped his head to hers. He stopped before touching his lips to hers, as if he were still giving her time to push him away if she wanted to. His breath was warm against her mouth, and Rosemary held her own breath as she waited to see what he would do. Strangely, though, it was she who moved next, tilting her head to one side and urging the upper half of her body forward. When their lips finally met, it was because of her.

Nathaniel, however, was the one to take control of the kiss, the moment their mouths joined. As always, though, he was a perfect gentleman, touching her with tentativeness and tenderness, as if he wasn't quite sure how she would respond to him.

How could he not know? Rosemary wondered. How could he not know that this was exactly what she wanted him to do? Perhaps he just needed a bit of encouragement, she told herself. So she lifted a hand to his face, tracing her fingertips lightly along his throat and jaw before delving them slowly into his hair.

He deepened the kiss after that, but still didn't do any more than slant his mouth over hers, once, twice, three times, before pulling away. For a long moment, he only gazed into her eyes, as if he were waiting for her to say something. And Rosemary could only gaze back at him, completely uncertain what she should say.

"That," he finally said when she only continued to study him in silence. He pressed his forehead to hers, curling his fingers around the nape of her neck, dropping his other hand to curve it loosely over her hip. "That's why I invited you to come with me today, Rosemary. So that I could do that."

Her breath came in short, shallow gasps, but somehow, she managed to breathe the word, "Oh."

"And I'm hoping that maybe we can see each other again soon, so I can do that again." He pressed his mouth lightly to hers, then pulled away. "And again," he said. Then he kissed her once more. "And again."

Rosemary inhaled a deep breath and held it, hoping that by doing so, she might still the rapid, rabid beating of her heart. Then she released the breath slowly, curling her own fingers more possessively into his shoulders. "I think," she said, "that I'd very much like to . . . see you . . . again. Soon."

"Friday," he said. "I have to go out of town tomorrow, but I'll be back Friday. Have dinner with me. At my house."

"Oh, I—"

"Please, Rosemary."

He slanted his mouth over hers again, tasting her deeply, leisurely, profoundly. She told herself it wasn't a good idea to go to his house, not when he made her feel all the wild, tempestuous, forbidden things that he made her feel. Certainly, she could have dinner with him. But not at his house. Someplace public. Someplace crowded and loud. Someplace where she wouldn't get herself into trouble, as she had the last time she'd had dinner at the house of a handsome, charming, sexy man. Anyplace but there, she told herself. Anyplace but his place.

"Please, Rosemary," he said again.

And she felt herself nod her head against his. "All right," she told him. "I think I'd like that very much."

Chapter 12

The weekend that followed Lucy's little, ah . . . tête à tête, for lack of a better word, with Max—even though she wasn't entirely sure what *tête-à-tête* meant, it sure sounded a whole lot like what had happened between the two of them—she was surprisingly good at avoiding him. Though, on second thought, maybe that wasn't so surprising, seeing as how, shortly after their tête-à-tête—or whatever—Max had fled to his apartment, and then shortly after that, a cab had shown up in front of the carriage house, and then shortly after *that*, had taken off again with Max—and an overnight bag—in the backseat. Lucy had still managed to avoid him all weekend, and she congratulated herself for that. The fact that he wasn't on the premises at the time, she figured, was just incidental.

At any rate, he came back early Monday morning, and she was still able to avoid him—mostly because he fled to his apartment again, closed the door, locked it, did what sounded like pushing a big piece of furniture in front of it, and didn't come out once. And also because, since it was her day off, Lucy was able to flee to her own apartment, close the door, lock it, push a big piece of furniture in front of it, and not come out once.

Funny, but she and Max really did seem to have a lot in common . . .

What she couldn't avoid, unfortunately, especially since she was locked in her apartment with nothing to do, were her memories of their tête-à-tête, which assailed her at the most inopportune times—i.e., *constantly*—and which left her feeling all hot and bothered, and sweaty and naked, and wanting to relive the actual events over and over and over again. She still couldn't quite remember how things had progressed to the point that they had. One minute, she and Max had been eating popcorn and chatting like friends, and the next . . .

Well, the next they had been overcome by a sexual conflagration that had had them trying to consume each other. What exactly had been the bridge that led between the two states, however, Lucy honestly couldn't say.

Of course, she couldn't deny that she'd been physically attracted to Max since the moment she'd laid eyes on him. He was just too handsome, too masculine, too magnetic, for her not to be attracted to him. But she'd been physically attracted to men before, and never felt the kind of heat burning inside her that she'd felt for Max, virtually since day one. And then, on those occasions when they'd had a chance to talk, he'd been so sweet, and so kind, and so courteous, and so intriguing that her attraction had only multiplied. He was good-natured and friendly and self-deprecating, not at all the way she would have expected a man who looked like he did to be. Someone who looked like Max Hogan should be vain and shallow and self-absorbed. Yet he was none of those things. Instead he was . . .

Sweet. That was the only word Lucy could think of that properly described him. Sweet and sexy. What woman could resist such a combination?

Of course she had succumbed to him Friday night, she reassured herself. What woman wouldn't have? Had things continued the way they had seemed to be continuing, she would have woken beside Max on Saturday morning, naked and satisfied and pleasantly achy, and she wouldn't have felt one ounce of guilt because of it. Because as crazy as it sounded, she was halfway in love with the guy. She knew that, because her responses to Max, her *feelings* for Max, were completely unlike any responses or feelings she'd ever had for another man—even the one with whom she'd been intimately involved. What she'd thought was love with that man paled in comparison to what she felt now, this warm, gooey feeling of affection for him, and this blazing inferno of wanting and needing him and . . .

. . . and never wanting to let him go.

That was it, Lucy realized then. She never wanted to let Max go. She wanted to be where he was forever. The idea of not having him around was too intolerable to bear.

And not just because of the sexual thing, either. Even before their libidos had exploded Friday night, she had been feeling warm and mellow inside, happy just having him in the same room with her. Just talking with Max had felt good. She had shared things with him that she hadn't shared with anyone else, and had never once questioned the wisdom of that sharing. She had felt comfortable talking to him, where she normally felt uneasy conversing with people. Usually, she didn't speak much to others, because she was afraid no one cared about what she had to say. But Max had cared. He'd been genuinely interested in her. It had felt *good* talking to him.

He just . . . he spoke to something in her, that was all. And he touched something in her. Something that had never been spoken to or touched before. He liked her. She could tell that. He honestly, truly liked her. Yet as far as Max was concerned, she was just a housekeeper struggling to make it through school, a woman who came from meager beginnings and who'd experienced an unsatisfying life. As far as he was concerned, she had few prospects and little to offer. But he liked her in spite of those things. And that could only be because he appreciated her for what she *was*. Really was. As a person. He probably wouldn't even care if he found out that she was—That she had different learning patterns from other people.

Being with Max Friday night, before *and* during the time when things had heated up, had made Lucy feel things—good things, warm things, nice things—that she'd never felt before. And he'd seemed to be enjoying himself, too, before *and* during. He was right—she *had* felt his response to her. He *had* been turned on. And he had been as eager to make love with her that night as she had been to make love with him.

So why had he called a stop so suddenly, so completely, just when things were getting good? Why hadn't he made love to her, when it was obviously what both of them had wanted so much?

I can't have you, Lucy. It's not allowed.

His words echoed in her head like the rumble of a powerful engine. He'd said he couldn't make love to her because it wasn't allowed. He'd said that about a lot of things since she'd first met him, she recalled now. Going into the Coves' house wasn't allowed. Owning a car wasn't allowed. Good wine wasn't allowed. Having Lucy wasn't allowed. Surely, the Coves couldn't have made all those rules. Why would they? Besides, Max wasn't the kind of man who would stand for something like that. No, Max was the kind of man who made his own rules. So if none of those things was allowed him . . .

Then it was because he was denying them to himself.

But why? she wondered again. He didn't seem like the kind of man who would deny himself life's basic pleasures, either. So why was he doing it?

By midmorning on Monday, Lucy was actually wishing Monday wasn't her day off. Because she was feeling so restless and so edgy, she actually *wanted* to clean the Coves' house. From top to bottom, inside and out. She even wanted to do their windows. All seventy-eight of them. Maybe she'd go ahead and work today, she thought, and ask Mrs. Cove for Thursday off instead. She was just too het up to relax today, and she didn't have any mode of transportation to take her anyplace where she might work off all the excess energy— Dimitri had told her he'd be glad to make their nightly carpooling a regular thing in exchange for gas money, but he would be working until late afternoon today.

Of course, Lucy reminded herself, there were other ways to deal with excess energy besides housecleaning . . .

Oh, no, there weren't, she immediately contradicted herself. Not today there weren't. And not just because the house was already reasonably clean—Lucy really had amazed herself at how well she had been able to take care of things in that regard; she was surprisingly good at her job, provided there were no lists involved. Mrs. Hill probably didn't need any help with dinner preparation, either, since it didn't look like anyone was going to be home for dinner tonight. Rosemary was out with that nice Mr. Finn—something brewing there, for sure, Lucy thought with a grin—Mr. Cove was out of town on business, and Mrs. Cove and Abby—

Hey, Abby, Lucy thought, brightening. Abby's rooms were always a wreck—her being eight years old and all, it was their natural state. Still, Rosemary liked for them to be as neat as they could be. And following the weekend, they usually looked like a quick nuclear holocaust had blown through. And since Rosemary was gone for the day, she wouldn't be around to tidy them up. Lucy hoped the nanny wouldn't be home until late. She deserved to have some fun. Especially with a hottie like Mr. Finn.

Wearing faded jeans and a T-shirt emblazoned with the Dust Bunnies logo, Lucy was already dressed for work, so she might as well go up to the big house and do a little tidying up in Abby's rooms. That would take care of her excess sexual—er, she meant *restless*, of course—energy, and it would be a nice surprise for both Rosemary and Abby when they got home. Best of all, though, it would put some distance—literally, anyway—between her and Max. Because sitting here knowing he was right across the hall, even if there were two locked doors—and two big pieces of furniture—between them, was much too tempting for her to bear. Especially when what she wanted most *wasn't* to go over there and have her way with him sexually—as diverting as that sounded. No, what Lucy really wanted most was to just go over there and have her way with him verbally.

She wanted to talk to Max, that was all. Well, okay, maybe that wasn't *all* she wanted to do with him. But that was what she wanted most. Well, okay, maybe it wasn't what she wanted *most*, either. But it *was* what she wanted first. Sort of. And the first thing she would say to him was, Why? Why did he deny himself things that he fully deserved to have? That he obviously *wanted* to have? Especially when they were things Lucy very much wanted to give him?

They shouldn't be hard questions to answer. She was sure Max had his reasons. Unfortunately, though, he clearly had no intention of giving them to her. So all she had to do now was figure out a way that would bring him around to her way of thinking.

Abby Cove was the biggest pack rat Lucy had ever seen in her life, and she obviously liked to have everything out in the open where she could see it. There was stuff scattered all over her room, under furniture, over furniture, inside furniture, outside furniture, much of it reminiscent of Lucy's own childhood. She was surprised to find so many dolls and accessories for them—Abby, after all, was such a tomboy. Likewise, the pinks and lavenders of the rooms, not to mention all the white French provincial furniture, didn't suit the little girl at all. Still, most of the dolls didn't look especially played with, and all of them were in the playroom, on shelves, and not in Abby's bedroom proper, on the floor, where all her favorites obviously were.

Lucy suspected those dolls, like the color scheme, had been selected by Alexis Cove, for the perfect little girly girl she had always dreamed of having. Lucy remembered her own room as a child reflecting nothing of her real character, since her mother had been the one to choose such things for her, too.

What *didn't* surprise her about Abby's room was the clutter of sports paraphernalia—Abby, after all, was such a tomboy. There were balls and gloves and sticks for every sport, some Lucy didn't recognize, all *very* well played with, along with videos of every UofL basketball game that had been played last season. Many of these were in the bedroom, leading Lucy to believe they were Abby's most cherished objects. And amid all the game equipment, though half-hidden under the bed, was something else that vaguely surprised Lucy—a huge stack of car magazines and a handful of books about car racing.

Lucy eyed the pile of racing literature in the bedroom with a curious eye, then glanced around the rest of the room. The racing literature, she realized then, were the only reading matter in the bedroom. Oh, there were books in the playroom, all neatly arranged on the shelves—they and the dolls were the only things neatly arranged in that room, a clear indication that Abby never touched them. But the racing magazines, with their vivid photographs of cars and pit life, clearly this was something that fascinated little Abby. Though, with another sweep of the room, Lucy saw no other car apparatus— no toy cars, no racing sets, nothing to play with that had anything to do with cars. Only the magazines and books.

Still, Lucy smiled when she saw them. How cute, that such a little girl could be so swept up by auto racing. No wonder she had a crush on the Coves' car guy.

Lucy reached for the pile of magazines, fanned across the floor and under the bed, and began to stack them as neatly as she could in preparation of moving them to the shelves in the playroom. And as she stacked, she glanced idly at the photographs on the covers, pictures of blurrily speeding race cars and smiling, sweaty-haired men holding big trophies aloft. She was about to hoist up her first pile when her gaze fell to one of the magazines still fanned out on the floor. It shouldn't have caused her to glance twice at it, because, on the first glance, she saw that it was just another familiar pose of another smiling, sweaty-haired man holding another big trophy aloft. On second glance, however, she saw that the man was—

Max.

She closed her eyes and opened them again, sure she must have been hallucinating because her head was just so full of thoughts of him. But no, on looking at the photograph a second time, she saw that the man on the cover of the racing magazine did indeed look exactly like Max Hogan. His hair was shorter, and he looked a little younger, and his smile was ten times wider and brighter and happier than any she'd seen from Max, but the man could have easily been his twin.

No, not his twin, she thought, her stomach flaming at the realization. That was Max. She knew it was.

She screwed up her courage and forced herself to look at the words accompanying the photograph, swallowing back the nausea she felt rising as she did. Focusing very, very intently, and concentrating very, very hard, Lucy made out the letters M and X with fairly little difficulty. The H and O beneath them jumped around a bit and swam against the other letters there, but she was reasonably certain she made out a G and an N before they all began folding in on each other the way they always tended to do. Max Hogan. That had to be what the letters said when they were all arranged properly. Especially since it was Max Hogan that she saw in the photo.

She tried to decipher the name of the magazine, but all she could make out in her agitated state was a capital F and the number one. F1. Formula One, she thought. Her brother Emory loved Formula One racing. It was all he talked about sometimes. This was obviously a magazine devoted to Formula One racing. Lucy didn't know a lot about it, but she knew it was a big deal for its followers, especially in Europe.

I worked overseas.

I did car stuff.

Holy cow, she thought, remembering what Max had told her that first day she'd come to work, as they'd been walking up to the big house. She dropped down onto her fanny with a solid bump, clutching the magazine tightly in both hands. It really was Max in the photo. There was no mistaking that. He was on the cover of a racing magazine. And he was holding a trophy. And he was happy. Happy like she'd never seen him before.

"Miss Lucy?"

She turned at the sound of her name being uttered in a

small child's voice, and saw Abby Cove standing in the door-way of her bedroom, watching her. She was dressed in a tai-lored pink dress with a big green bow beneath its white collar—attire Lucy had never seen on the little girl before—and she was obviously uncomfortable about something. She straightened her round, wire-framed glasses, though they looked to be perfectly straight to Lucy already, then smiled a small, nervous little smile.

And Lucy realized then that she felt unaccountably guilty for some reason. She knew she shouldn't. She was the house-keeper, doing her job, and she hadn't been prying into Abby's personal things—she'd only been cleaning up the lit-tle girl's room, hoping it would help both Abby and Rose-mary in the long run. Then Lucy realized she didn't feel guilty because Abby had discovered her in her bedroom. She felt guilty because of Max. She'd discovered something about him he clearly hadn't wanted her to know. Had he wanted that, he would have told her. But he hadn't. And she couldn't help wondering why. This was obviously something that had been a huge part of his life at one time. This had *been* his life at one time. But when she'd flat out asked him about his past, he'd never mentioned anything about it. Why?

"Hi, Abby," Lucy said, smiling what she hoped was a reas-suring smile in response to the little girl's nervous one. "I was just doing some cleaning up in here. I hope you don't mind."

Abby shook her head. "No, I don't mind. Rosemary usu-ally does it, though."

"Well, I thought since she was out today, I'd give her a hand," Lucy said. "It is my job, after all."

Abby nodded but said nothing.

Lucy told herself she should ask the little girl how her test-ing went, show some interest in her, since so few people did that. And also because she genuinely wanted to know how it had gone. But Abby's eyes were red-rimmed behind her glasses—she had obviously been crying. Lucy remembered being tested when she was about Abby's age. She had cried, too, afterward. Both times. And she hadn't wanted to talk about either of them.

So instead, she nodded toward the pile of magazines and said, "I didn't know you liked car racing."

"I don't," Abby told her. "I just like the pictures of Max."

Understanding dawned on Lucy then. Dawned like a screaming freight train. Hurtling toward a stalled car. Full of nuns. And orphans. And kittens. Her mouth dropped open, and she pointed at the stack of magazines that stood nearly a foot high. "There are pictures of Max in all of these magazines?"

Abby nodded, but didn't seem to think the question in any way remarkable. "Yeah. And in the books, too," she added.

Lucy's eyebrows shot up beneath her bangs. "All of these?" she asked again, even though Abby had answered the question already.

Abby nodded and entered the room, collapsing onto the floor beside Lucy, crossing her bare legs pretzel-fashion, unconcerned about how unladylike it was to do so in a dress. She thumbed through the stack of magazines until she found one near the bottom. It, too, had Max's photo on the cover. This time he was wearing yellow coveralls decorated with a variety of patches and numbers and logos, and he was leaning with his arms and ankles crossed confidently, almost arrogantly, against a low-slung, bright yellow racing car. He was smiling in this photo, too, a huge grin that clearly indicated he thought he was sitting on top of the world.

Sitting on top of the world? Lucy thought further, biting back a distressed sound. Oh, he looked as if he *owned* the world.

"This is my favorite," Abby said.

But instead of showing Lucy the cover, she flipped the magazine open to an article inside. Through long practice, Lucy was able to ignore the printed parts and focus on the photographs instead, one after another of Max Hogan, Formula

One racer. One page in particular was filled with pictures—one with him standing between two other men in coveralls different from his own, all of them grinning as if they shared a private joke; one of him sitting in the yellow car on the front cover with a helmet half on and half off his head, yelling something at a man who stood beside it; one of him in soiled coveralls, wiping his dirty face and damp hair with a towel as he watched another car burn, an expression of grim resolution on his face.

And there, at the bottom, the photo Abby was pointing to, of Max in his coveralls again—he must have fairly lived in them back then, she thought—having obviously just won a race. Because his hair was matted with perspiration, and he held a bottle of wildly frothing champagne in one hand, and had his other arm looped around the neck of an exceptionally beautiful, dark-haired, dark-eyed woman. And he was smiling with yet another kind of happiness she'd never known him to show. As was the woman in the photo with him.

"This is the one I like," Abby said. "I like his smile in this one."

Lucy did, too. She just wished he hadn't been smiling about the other woman who was with him.

So focused on the photograph was she, that she spoke without thinking when she asked Abby, "Can you read what it says beneath the picture?"

Abby's head snapped up at that, the smile she had been wearing fleeing her face. She stared at Lucy with an expression that was at once hurt and defiant, but she said nothing in response.

"Oh," Lucy said when she realized what she'd done. "Oh. Oh, I'm sorry, Abby. I didn't mean . . . I mean . . . I forgot you can't . . ."

"I can, too, read," she immediately countered defensively. "I just don't like to, that's all. I could tell you what it says there if I wanted to."

Not if what Lucy had heard from Rosemary was true, she

thought. The nanny had voiced her concerns about Abby's inability to read since that first day Lucy arrived. But instead of challenging Abby, she said, "That's okay. I don't really want to know what it—"

"I can!" Abby insisted vehemently. "I can read! I can! I just don't like to! But I can, too, read!"

And as if she intended to prove it once and for all, she turned her attention to the magazine again, studying the picture of Max and the beautiful woman, and the tiny, tiny words beneath it. "It says," she began, "it says . . . it says . . ."

Lucy watched with much interest as Abby clenched her jaw tight and gripped the magazine hard in both fists. She was concentrating very, very hard, Lucy saw. She was very, very focused.

"It says," she began again, " 'Hogan.' It says, 'Hogan . . . Hogan a-and . . . S-s-s . . . I don't recognize that word," she said. "And the next one is too long. But after that, it says . . ." She continued to grip the magazine fiercely in both hands, her eyes never leaving the page. After a moment, her body began to sway back and forth a little, and her skin began to grow a bit pale.

"Abby?" Lucy asked cautiously. "Abby, are you okay?"

Abby continued to sway slightly back and forth for a moment, then, almost imperceptibly, she shook her head. "I think I'm going to throw up," she said miserably. "I feel sick."

"Look up," Lucy told her. Unable to wait for Abby to follow the instruction, however—knowing, deep down, that Abby would have trouble following it, because she may not have even heard it—Lucy took the girl's chin gently in her hand and urged her to glance up. "Look at me," she said. "Abby, look at my face."

Abby did as she asked, her dark brows arrowing downward as she focused on Lucy's face, her own face squinched up with much concentration. She looked pale and panicky and vaguely dazed, as if she'd fallen into some kind of strange trance. But after a minute of looking at Lucy, her expression began to clear. Eventually, the color returned to her face, and she blinked a few times in rapid succession.

"Miss Lucy," she said, as if she'd forgotten for a moment that Lucy was there.

"Do you feel okay now?" Lucy asked.

Abby nodded. "Yeah."

Lucy eyed the little girl with much interest. "Does that happen often?" she said. "Do you start to feel sick when you look at letters and numbers for too long?"

Abby's lips parted slightly, as if she couldn't quite believe what Lucy had just said. She nodded slowly. "Yeah. I do."

"And sometimes, when you're concentrating really hard, do you forget where you are?"

Abby nodded again.

"And then the letters start moving around on the page so you can't make out what order they're in, or even if they're right side up?"

Again, Abby nodded slowly.

"Oh, honey . . ." Lucy said.

"Lucy? What are you doing in here?" This time it was Rosemary's voice who summoned her, and when Lucy glanced up to look at her, she realized the nanny had been standing framed in the doorway throughout her entire exchange with Abby.

"I came in earlier to clean up Abby's rooms," Lucy said. "I had some sexu . . . ah, excess energy to work off," she quickly amended. "I figured I could surprise both of you."

"Well, you certainly surprised me," Rosemary said. But it clearly wasn't the room cleaning she was talking about. "What are you and Abby going on about?"

Lucy smiled halfheartedly. "Reading," she said.

"Reading," Rosemary repeated flatly.

Lucy nodded.

Although Rosemary continued to look at Lucy, she directed her next question to Abby. "How did your test go today, sweetheart?"

Abby, who had been gazing with fixed fascination at Lucy, dropped her gaze now to the ground. "It didn't," she said softly.

Rosemary strode quickly into the room and dropped to her knees on the carpet. She picked up one of Abby's hands and held it gently in her own. "What happened?"

For a moment, Abby said nothing, then, very quietly, she told Rosemary, "I didn't want to take it. So I didn't."

Rosemary's expression grew concerned, but her voice was totally calm as she asked, "You didn't answer the questions the reading lady asked you, the way you were supposed to?"

Abby shook her head, but said nothing, still staring at the ground. "I didn't do any of the things she told me I should do. I didn't want to."

"What did your mother do?" Rosemary asked, her voice still calm, but her expression hardening some.

Another brief silence from Abby, then, "She yelled. A lot."

Rosemary's cheeks went ruddy at that, but her voice was still deceptively mild as she continued, "And what did the reading lady do?"

"She told Mom to stop it."

"And then what happened?"

"Mom stopped yelling and took me out to the car," Abby said. "And then she started yelling again. She yelled all the way home. She told Mrs. Hill she was going out and won't be home for supper." Abby turned her face up to look at Rosemary. "She didn't say where she was going."

Rosemary dropped an arm around Abby's shoulder and pulled her close, hugging her for all she was worth, stroking her hair in a soothing gesture. Lucy wanted to mimic the action from her side of the little girl, but figured Abby needed Rosemary more. She wished she could have five minutes alone with Mrs. Cove. With Mrs. Cove and a blunt object. But since she couldn't have that, maybe she could do something else that would help Abby.

"Rosemary," Lucy said softly. "I think I might know the problem."

Rosemary turned to look at Lucy now, her expression confused. "What do you mean?"

"I mean, I think I know what Abby's problem is."

Rosemary looked skeptical, but she said, "Oh?"

Lucy nodded. "I think she might be . . ." She inhaled a deep breath and released it slowly. "I think she might be . . . dyslexic."

Rosemary's eyebrows arrowed downward as she continued to stroke Abby's hair. Abby herself snapped her head up again, this time to glare at Lucy, thrusting out her bottom lip as if in defiance. "I am not," she said. "I'm not . . . whatever that was you said. I'm not anything. I just don't like to read."

Lucy gave her the most reassuring look she could. "Actually, kiddo, I'm pretty sure you are dyslexic," she said softly.

"What makes you say that?" Rosemary asked.

"I say that because . . ." Lucy hesitated, then made herself continue. "Because Abby has the same reaction to the printed word that I do. And I'm . . ." She inhaled one more deep breath, then let it out on a shaky sigh. "I'm dyslexic, too."

Chapter 13

Lucy sipped carefully from the delicate china teacup Rosemary had placed before her, savoring the light flavor of the chamomile before swallowing. At Abby's request, they'd left the little girl alone to recuperate from the day's events on her own, then they'd retreated to Rosemary's rooms, which adjoined Abby's, for, as the nanny had offered, "A spot of tea."

Lucy immediately felt comfortable. The sitting room, where the two of them were enjoying their tea, was adjacent to a bedroom, and off of that was a private bath. The rooms themselves were smaller than most of the rooms at Harborcourt but, like those other rooms, were all furnished with fine antiques, and were very old-fashioned in their moods. In the sitting room, a hooked floral rug spanned much of the hardwood floor, complementing nicely the wallpaper decorated with tiny violets. The blues, lavenders, and greens of that room carried into the bedroom, where both the rug and the quilt on the bed picked up the violet design. All the trim was painted white, giving Lucy the impression of a coastal getaway cottage.

Cozy and old-fashioned. That was what the room was. And where Abby's rooms seemed to have nothing in common with the little girl, Rosemary's seemed to fit the nanny perfectly.

She had the added modern conveniences of a compact refrigerator tucked into one corner, with a small microwave sitting atop it. In the same corner hung an oversize bulletin board that was covered from top to bottom and then some with childish artwork—crayon and marker drawings of houses, dogs, rainbows, trees, and a little girl holding the hand of an orange-haired woman. Numerous—and very, ah, original—clay figures lined the bookshelves in front of the books, though Lucy was able to identify what few of them were. She had seen no such artwork displayed elsewhere in the Cove home. It was nice to know someone appreciated Abby's creative endeavors.

"I apologize for having heated the water in the microwave," Rosemary said as she poured herself a cup of tea. "One can only make proper tea by boiling the water, of course, but this is so much easier."

"It's fine," Lucy said. "Thank you again."

"Now you must tell me more about your dyslexia," Rosemary told her as she dropped two sugar cubes into her cup and stirred. "If that is indeed what Abby's problem is, we can seek treatment for it, yes? I mean, I don't know much about it, but it's my understanding that many dyslexics are able to read eventually, aren't they?"

Lucy set her teacup down carefully and wondered exactly what to say. "Actually," she began, "I've never been treated for my dyslexia. And I really don't know very much about it."

Rosemary looked up, clearly startled. "Why not?"

Lucy sighed. "It's kind of a long story."

The other woman gazed at her expectantly, obviously unbothered by the time investment.

"I was diagnosed, twice, as a child, as being dyslexic," she said. "But my mother always said the results of those tests were wrong, and insisted I *wasn't* dyslexic. That I *couldn't* be dyslexic. She said there was nothing wrong with me, except that I was lazy. That I just wasn't *willing* to learn to read. I couldn't possibly have a problem, because Hol—" She stopped herself just in time. "Because people in my family don't have problems. We're perfect, you see," she added derisively. "No one else had ever been dyslexic, so I couldn't possibly be, either. Things like that just don't happen to . . . to us."

Rosemary sat up straighter at that. "That's what Mrs. Cove says about Abby and about the Coves. She thinks her blood-line, like Mr. Cove's, is perfect. That they couldn't possibly have a 'flawed' child."

"Yeah, well, that doesn't exactly surprise me," Lucy said, trying to keep the bitterness out of her voice. "Mrs. Cove and my mother have a whole lot in common."

Rosemary eyed her with much consideration. "Really," she said, the word coming out as a statement, not a question.

Lucy nodded. "So I can't really help much with Abby, be-yond telling you that she's like me. Or, at least, she has the same reaction to reading that I have. But, as you said, there are people who can help dyslexics learn to read, or at least learn to read well enough to get by. Certainly she can do bet-ter than she is now, I would think. Provided Mrs. Cove looks for someone to help her."

"You don't read well enough to get by yourself, then," Rosemary said, another statement instead of a question.

"Sometimes I can get by," Lucy admitted. "But it's a struggle. I taught myself a few tricks over the years, and sometimes, if I concentrate very, very hard, I can eventually decipher enough words in something to get the gist of it. But, no, I can't sit down with a book or a newspaper, or"— she tilted her head toward the magazine with Max's photo on the cover—"or a magazine, and tell you what it says in any detail."

"But you're an English major," Rosemary pointed out. "A graduate student. You have a university degree."

Oh, damn, Lucy thought. She'd really been hoping Rose-mary would have neglected to make that connection. At least until after Lucy had left Harborcourt. Or at least until after she had gotten her life straightened out so that she could tell everyone the truth, she amended when she realized how the thought of leaving Harborcourt sent an unsettling sensation roiling through her. She decided to gloss over the first part of the other woman's observation and focused instead on the second, where she could be—sort of—truthful.

"I actually did my undergrad work in art," she said. "But I barely passed my classes. Don't get me wrong—I learned plenty, by listening closely to lectures and checking out as many books on tape as I could find and watching a lot of documentaries to get more information. And I could always hire someone to take dictation and transcribe my research papers for me. But I still did badly on every test I took. I could usually get by adequately with the multiple choice and true-false questions, but I couldn't answer the essay questions—not that there was time enough to answer them by the time I got to them anyway, because it took me so long to read the other questions."

"Well," Rosemary said, "that would explain the Omar Khayyám and Genghis Khan problem, wouldn't it?"

Lucy laughed nervously. "I actually do know the difference there," she said. "Like I said, I've always loved watching documentaries and biographies. I've learned more than a lot of people, in spite of not being able to read very well."

And only when she said that did she recognize the fact that it was true. All those years of hearing her mother say that she wasn't very bright, that she was lazy, had made Lucy think that it was true. Her mother had always equated "different learning pattern" with "not learning at all." But Lucy *did* have a different learning pattern. And she *had* learned. She *was* bright, she realized now. And she wasn't lazy. On the contrary, she'd probably worked twice as hard as most people to learn what she had. Only now was she beginning to understand that. Her mother had been wrong. About a lot of things.

"But my grades were never good," she continued, knowing that was true, even if there was a legitimate reason for it. "And I think, truly, that the only reason I lasted at college as long as I did was because my father endowed a chair at the university I attended."

At this, Rosemary's eyebrows shot up in surprise. "It costs a lot of money to do that, doesn't it?" she asked.

Lucy nodded. "Yes. It does."

"You come from a wealthy family then."

"Yes," Lucy replied honestly. "I do."

The nanny leveled another one of those long, considering looks on her, then nodded slowly, as if she understood. Wow, Lucy thought. That was pretty good, if Rosemary understood all that. Maybe, if Lucy asked nicely, she could explain it all to her, too.

"So then your studies now," Rosemary said. "Is your father footing the bills for those, as well?"

Lucy shook her head. "No. My parents don't even know where I am," she said. She tried to reassure herself that she was once again telling the truth, but she knew she was misleading Rosemary by doing so, so that kind of negated the honesty factor in her words. She supposed she would have to offer some excuse for her current enrollment to satisfy the other woman's curiosity, though. So, "Going back to college now," she began, "well, I guess it's been kind of a test for me."

And it was with much surprise that Lucy realized she was telling the truth when she said that, too. Attending her classes had certainly been testing. "And truth be told," she added, "I really did learn something, even after such a short time. Though I guess it's not what I thought I would learn."

"And what did you learn?" Rosemary asked.

Lucy smiled halfheartedly. "That I'm not lazy. And I'm not stupid. I'm dyslexic."

Rosemary smiled. "And now you can look for the proper help. We can look for someone who can help you and Abby both," she said.

"Oh, I—" Lucy started to object. Number one, she might be too old to be treated for her problem. Number two, she wasn't going to be here long enough to be helped by anyone who might help Abby. At least, she didn't think she would. Still, for some reason, she couldn't quite make herself complete the objection she'd been about to utter.

She glanced back down at the magazine sitting on the table between her and Rosemary and remembered the photos inside, one photo in particular screaming to the forefront of her brain. The one of Max and the beautiful dark-haired woman. And she decided it was as good a time as any to change the subject.

"Have you read the story?" she asked Rosemary, knowing the question would need no clarification.

Rosemary sipped her tea and nodded. "Yes, I have."

"So you know about Max's past."

"Yes. For about a year now."

"Abby's known about it, too."

"Yes."

"Does everyone at Harborcourt know?"

Rosemary shook her head. "Mr. Cove does, since Abby found those magazines down in the basement with some of his other reading material before claiming them for herself. He doesn't know she has them, but he hasn't mentioned them having gone missing, so I suppose he's not much interested in them anymore. I don't know if Mrs. Cove knows about Max, but I doubt it. She'd talk. None of the other employees knows. They'd talk, too, if they did. And no one talks about it. Not even me or Abby."

"So Max doesn't know you know?"

"No. I made Abby promise she would never bring it up with him, and she's very good about keeping promises."

"But why has no one asked him about it?" Lucy said.

Rosemary set her cup down in its saucer and met Lucy's gaze intently. "Those magazines are all more than five years old. Whatever happened to Max during that time, it was a long time ago. For whatever reason, he doesn't want to discuss it. Otherwise, he would." Her expression went almost grim as she added, "Everyone has something in the past that they want to keep in the past, Lucy. Everyone has a secret. And everyone is entitled to keep it, if they want to."

And, oh, boy, did that hit home. And not just with Lucy, either, she realized. Somehow, she knew Rosemary was talking about herself, too. Even though she couldn't imagine what kind of secret a nice person like Rosemary would have to keep.

But in spite of the nanny's admonition, she said, "If you've read the article, then will you tell me what it says?"

Rosemary studied her for a moment in silence. "You won't like it," she said. "It isn't about the Max we know. He was different then."

"I want to know what it says anyway," she told Rosemary. "I need to know. I need to understand him. He's . . ." She met the other woman's gaze evenly now. "He's become . . . important to me."

The other woman smiled at that, but there was something decidedly sad in the gesture. Before Lucy could question it, though, Rosemary reached for the magazine, and opened it up to the article about Max. And then she began to read.

Max was hiding out in his apartment—ah . . . actually . . . that is . . . he was taking a break from his work, which he had somehow totally neglected to start that day, and, gosh, look, it was already twilight outside, how had that happened?— when he heard a soft knock at his front door. He didn't want to answer it. Mostly because he knew it was Lucy coming to check on him. Or maybe not coming to check on him. Could be she was coming for something else, but he wasn't allowed to think about that. It was most definitely Lucy knocking at his front door, though. He knew that, because he'd heard her return from the big house a little while ago and go into her own apartment, and then he'd heard nothing at all until the soft, dual clicks of her own door opening and closing only seconds before the knock on his own door had sounded.

Another reason he didn't want to answer the door was because he was only half-dressed, seeing as how he'd somehow totally neglected to start work that day, and seeing as how the warm September air and lack of air-conditioning—not that he didn't have air-conditioning in his apartment, he just wasn't allowed to use it—meant that he had never gotten around to dressing that morning, so he was still sitting around in his boxer shorts. Drinking a warm, bad beer. Staring off into space. Fantasizing about making love to Lucy. Berating himself mercilessly for being such a jackass.

Hastily, because he knew the knocking would sound again—and it did—he scuttled to his bedroom and tugged on a pair of faded, ragged blue jeans and a plain, navy blue T-shirt. Then, because he knew the knocking would sound a third time—and it did—he went to answer the door. And gosh, what a surprise to find Lucy French standing on the other side.

"Hi," she said before he could get a word out. Though what that word might have been, anyway, besides *hubba-hubba,* Max really wasn't sure, so it was just as well she said that before he could get a word out, because *hubba-hubba* wasn't exactly the hippest comment in the modern world, and he would have sounded like a geek making it.

She looked, as always, incredibly pretty, her soft brown hair having been brushed to a honeyed sheen, her blue eyes clear and sweet and enormous. She had changed her clothes from what she'd had on when he'd spied on her earlier, and was now dressed in a skimpy little dress the color of late-afternoon sunshine, with a skimpy little hemline that fell to midthigh, and skimpy little straps to hold it up. Max had to stop himself from leaning forward and running the tip of his tongue leisurely along one of those bare shoulders. Especially since what he really wanted to do was hike up her dress, tug down her panties, and take her right there against the doorframe.

He squeezed his eyes shut tight to banish the image, then realized, too late, that closing his eyes only made the image of having her in such a way that much more graphic. So he forced his eyes open again, only to notice this time that Lucy was holding something behind her back. He frowned when he noticed that, because somehow, he knew—he just knew— that whatever she was hiding from him, he didn't want to find out what it was. He also knew that she was going to show it to him, anyway. And then she did show it to him, pulling the item gingerly from behind her back to hold it at waist level. And when Max saw what it was, a sick, ghastly feeling exploded in his belly, firing like a cannon blast to every cell in his body. Unfortunately, the explosion didn't shatter him or knock him dead on the spot. It really would have been so much better if it had.

More than five years had passed since Max had seen a copy of *Velocity, The Magazine of F1 Racing* upon which he had graced the cover. Hell, it had been more than five years since he'd seen a copy of the magazine at all—it wasn't allowed. But this copy in particular made him feel sick inside. Not just because of the photograph of himself on the cover, but because of the photograph of him and Sylvie Balzarantini on the inside.

"I, um, I found this today when I was cleaning at the big house," Lucy said softly.

Of course, Max thought. Of course, she would find something like that, somewhere, at some point. If she hadn't found it, then it would have miraculously materialized out of thin air and landed on her coffee table. The Fates would have seen to that. Hey, the Fates would go out of their way to make absolutely certain something went wrong to screw up any chance he might have with Lucy, since he wasn't doing enough to screw them up himself. Things with her had been going too well, in spite of his efforts to keep his distance from her. And he'd been feeling too good since her arrival at Harborcourt, in spite of his constant reminders to himself that he couldn't have her. Somehow, Lucy had effortlessly scaled the mile-high walls around him that it had taken him years to erect. Somehow, she had wheedled right under his skin and made herself comfortable—worse, she had made *him* comfortable—and no matter how hard he'd tried to make himself miserable, he hadn't felt miserable at all. No, he'd been feeling pretty damned good for the past couple of weeks. He'd actually started thinking positive thoughts. He'd even entertained a hope or two. Like maybe that he and Lucy might eventually—

Well. Just that maybe he'd finally paid his dues, and that maybe his penance was over, that was all. He'd started thinking that maybe Lucy French was his reward for living his ascetic life so dutifully for the past five years. But now, by her finding a remnant of his past, it pretty much killed off any chance he might have to find a future with her. Yep, the good ol' Fates—bitches and bastards the lot of them—had had to ensure somehow that Max would never be happy. Because he wasn't entitled to that.

Then he remembered that he had no one but himself to blame for his current state. The Fates were only doing their job. He had no right to be angry with them. He could only be angry with himself. How could he have even thought that he deserved a decent life with Lucy? he asked himself now. How could he have thought his penance would ever be over? Hell, after five years, it was just beginning. This new development was proof of that. How could he have thought he could keep his past a secret from her? He should have seen this coming from a mile away.

"I thought Monday was your day off," he said evasively, wearily, dispiritedly.

She scrunched up her—bare, luscious—shoulders and then relaxed them again. "Yeah, well, I was feeling a little restless today."

He expelled a rough sound at that. "Lotta that going around."

Neither of them said a word after that for a moment, and for that moment, Max allowed himself to hope wildly that Lucy would reconsider whatever she had come to say to him, would toss the magazine over her shoulder, and then walk away without a further word. Then he could go back to pretending that everything in his life was exactly as it should be.

"Can we talk about this?" she said instead.

Max uttered a single, ripe expletive in response.

Lucy didn't even flinch. "Please?" she asked. "I think it's important."

He shook his head vehemently. "Nothing about that time was ever important," he told her decisively. "Not one damned thing."

"I'd still like to talk about it," she told him.

"And I'd like to forget about it," he promptly replied. "The hell of it is, Lucy, we don't always get what we want, you know?" Then he smiled joylessly at his own wording. No, that wasn't the hell of it, he corrected himself. Hell was much worse than that.

"Then can I just come in?" she asked. "Can we talk about . . . what happened Friday?"

Max's first instinct was to tell her no, they couldn't talk about that, because he was trying to forget about that, too. Then he realized he was no more likely to forget about what happened Friday night than he had been able to forget what happened five years ago. So he took a couple of steps backward, pulled his door open wider, and allowed Lucy to step through. But he couldn't quite bring himself to close the door behind her. Probably, he thought, because she was going to need it open when she bolted from the room after finding out what a menace to society—and nice women—he was.

"Uh . . . nice place," she said as she entered, her gaze wandering around the living room, clearly absorbing the fact that there was nothing there to be absorbed.

With its sparse, unattractive, colorless furniture—he'd chosen it himself—and its complete lack of pictures, accessories, and warmth, his apartment, Max knew, left a lot to be desired. Which, of course, was the whole point. There was nothing inessential here. Nothing of a personal nature. Nothing luxurious. Nothing cozy. No creature comforts at all. Because, simply put, he wasn't supposed to be comfortable here. He wasn't supposed to be comfortable anywhere. He had eventually, grudgingly, bought himself a small black-and-white television and a cheap VCR to watch old movies. He'd done that because if he hadn't, he would have gone nuts. And going nuts would be too easy. Going nuts wasn't allowed. So in an effort to maintain his sanity—thereby maintaining his suffering, too, by God—he had allowed himself that one small concession. But that was it. Anything else that brought pleasure or distraction, Max wanted—deserved—none of it.

"Thanks," he said wryly in response to Lucy's comment. "It suits me well, I think."

She shook her head. "Not really," she told him. But she didn't elaborate.

"Can I get you anything?" he asked, striving to be a good host, since he couldn't be a good anything else. He held up the beer bottle in his hand. "Beer?"

She shook her head again and made a face. "It's bad beer, Max."

"Yes, it is," he agreed. "It's exceptionally bad beer."

"And you're drinking it warm again, aren't you?"

"You betcha."

"Why?"

"Because that enhances its badness."

"And you need exceptionally enhanced badness because . . . ?"

He lifted the bottle of beer to his mouth for a long, leisurely—exceptionally, enhancedly bad—taste, bit back a grimace as he swallowed it, and told her, "Because I'm an exceptionally, enhancedly bad person."

"No, you're not," she replied immediately.

He pointed to the publication she had let fall to her side. "Since you're holding the magazine," he said, "I'm assuming you read the article about me."

She glanced away as she told him, "I know what it says, yes."

"Then why do you say I'm not a bad person?" he asked.

Her gaze connected with his again and held firm. "Because the Max Hogan in this article isn't the Max Hogan I know."

He smiled humorlessly. "Same social security number, sweetheart. It's the same guy. Trust me."

"I do trust you," she said. "That's just the point."

She held up the magazine again, something that made him turn his back on her and make his way to the couch, where he slumped into a corner, wishing the world would swallow him whole.

"I wouldn't trust the guy in this article," she continued, following him. "This guy is vain, arrogant, and totally self-absorbed." She folded herself onto the sofa beside him, putting little more than a few inches between them. "You're none of those things, Max. You're not the same guy as him."

"I am the same guy," he insisted. "I just live differently, that's all."

"Which leads to my next question," she said quickly. "Why are you here? Why are you working as Justin Cove's car guy when you used to be so famous on the racing circuit that they put you on magazine covers? More than once? They even had a nickname for you. What was it they called you?" she asked.

She flipped open the magazine to the article in question. But she didn't read it herself, only held it up again for Max to look at it. But he didn't need to look at it. And God knew he didn't want to look at it. He remembered what they used to call him. They used to call him a lot of things, in fact, few of the terms polite, but all of them appropriate. The one Lucy was referring to, however . . .

"'Speed Demon,'" he said. That was what the press had labeled him, at any rate. Because he had pushed all the limits, velocitarily speaking, and he'd had the personal disposition of a creature from hell. Or had she happened upon one of the other nicknames? he wondered. "Motor Mouth," because of all of his incessant, arrogant, self-aggrandizing. Or maybe even "Lady Killer." Yeah, that had been a fitting one, too. Too fitting, in fact.

"That's it," she said. "'Speed Demon.' They said you

broke all kinds of speed records during your career, and that everyone else was afraid to go as fast as you did."

"Look, Lucy, I really don't want to—"

"Why, Max?" she interrupted. "Why are you here? What happened to change everything? According to this article—which, coincidentally is a little over five years old, which, co-incidentally is right around the time you said you came to work for the Coves—you used to have cars and homes and a lifestyle to rival the Coves'. But now you live alone in a tiny apartment in a carriage house and work on someone else's cars for a living. What happened between Europe and Glen-view? For that matter, what happened between the garage where you worked in the old neighborhood and the Coves' carriage house now?"

There was no way Lucy was going to be satisfied until he explained why he lived the way he did, why he *had* to live the way he did. He sure as hell didn't want to revisit all that, though. Mainly because he'd revisited it virtually every day for the past five years, and he still didn't understand any of it. Then he looked on the bright side. Maybe, by telling Lucy everything that had happened, she'd realize what a nasty, ter-rible guy he was and run screaming in horror in the opposite direction, and never let him come within a fifty-foot radius of her again.

Yeah, boy, that was a bright side, all right.

"You want to know what happened?" he asked.

She nodded silently.

"Fine," he bit off crisply. "I'll tell you. Long story short."

"No, I want the whole thing," she said.

"You're not getting it," he told her decisively. "Not today." Not ever, if he had his way. And once she heard the short ver-sion, he reassured himself, there was no way she'd want to hang around long enough to hear the rest of it.

Yeah, boy, that was reassuring, all right.

"I started racing when I was a teenager," he said. "My boss at the garage sponsored me. He'd done some racing when he was young. I started off small-time, then gradually got bigger time, because I was fast, and I was wild, and I didn't give a damn about anything. I thought I was immortal. And hell, if I wasn't, what did I have to lose, you know? Because of all that, I won. A lot. By my midtwenties, I was racing Formula One Grand Prix in Europe, and I had some of the biggest sponsors around. Because I was still winning. A lot. Because I was even faster by then, and I was even wilder, and I still didn't give a damn about anything. I still thought I was immortal, too. But I really, honestly thought that by then. Hell, I had plenty to lose by then, but I never thought I would lose any of it. Nobody and nothing could touch me. I was convinced of that."

"But something did touch you," Lucy guessed.

Max lifted a hand to his forehead and rubbed hard at a headache that seemed to have erupted out of nowhere. "Someone, actually," he said. "I met a woman."

"Sylvie Balzarantini," Lucy surmised.

Having read the article, she'd know about Sylvie, Max thought. So he didn't have to say anything more about the beautiful, gifted Italian ballet dancer with whom he'd been linked romantically. What he did have to say, though, was what wasn't in the article. "Sylvie and I weren't sexually involved the way everyone thought. We were just friends."

When he glanced over to gauge Lucy's reaction, he saw that she wasn't anywhere close to buying that.

"It's true," he insisted. "I mean, yeah, she was beautiful and glamorous and everything, but I respected her too much to get sexually involved with her. We were good friends. We had the same kind of upbringing, so we had a lot in common. But we never had anything sexual going on. She was too decent a person for me to subject her to something like that."

Too late, Max realized how Lucy would interpret what he'd said. He and Lucy had been friendly, too, and they had shared the same kind of upbringing, and they had a lot in common. Yet he *had* gotten romantically—and, boy howdy, sexually—involved with Lucy, however briefly, on Friday night. She might misconstrue that to mean he *didn't* respect her too much and *didn't* consider her a decent person. And judging by the way her expression fell just then, that was exactly how she'd interpreted his statement.

"Lucy, I didn't mean it like that," he said quickly. "I just meant that back then, I was no prize." Not that he was any prize now, he reminded himself. "Like you said, I was arrogant and selfish, and I went through women like most men go through breath mints, and showed them about as much consideration. That's not the case anymore. I'm not like that."

Her expression cleared immediately. "That's exactly what I mean, Max," she interjected quickly. "You're not like that. That's what I told you. Forget the social security number. You're a different person. You just said so yourself."

"But . . . but . . . but . . ." He expelled an impatient breath. "That's beside the point," he finally said. She opened her mouth to object again, but he forged on before she had a chance. He told himself it was because he wanted to get this over with. And it was. "Like I said, Sylvie and I were good friends because we had so much in common and had similar lifestyles. She was something of a celebrity, too, because she was a rising star in the ballet. At least she was until one night when—"

Max halted abruptly. He really didn't want to talk about this. He hadn't talked about it since it had happened, even though he thought about it virtually every day. Even Justin Cove, who knew the particulars of the events, had never once asked Max about it. For that, if nothing else, Max had to respect the guy.

"One night when what?" Lucy asked softly, dispelling his thoughts.

Max inhaled another deep breath and released it slowly. "There was an accident," he said quietly. "Sylvie and I were out driving . . . Well, I was driving," he qualified. "Neither of us was wearing a seat belt, even though I, at least, knew better, and should have insisted. I don't know why I didn't. If I had . . ." Hell, he couldn't say for sure it would have made a difference. But it might have. Not that dwelling on it now did any good. So, as he so often did, he pushed the thought away.

"It was one of the things we loved to do," he began again, "driving through the Italian countryside. Fast," he added. "Really fast. Because Sylvie liked going fast. She was always telling me to go faster."

And she had, too, Max recalled now. She'd gotten off on speed even more than he had, and that was saying something. Nearly every weekend, if he wasn't racing, they'd climb into his Ferrari—his Berlinetta, not the Ferrari F he drove for racing—and they'd leave Rome behind and head for the hills, and drive and drive and drive. *"Guidi velocemente, Max!"* Sylvie would shout over the roar of the engine. *Drive fast, Max.* Then, once they were out of town, *"Vada più velocemente, Max! Più velocemente!"* Go faster, Max! Faster! And no matter how far he pushed the accelerator to the floor, it was never fast enough for Sylvie.

Until that one night.

"It was a bad accident," he said with profound understatement. "I was in the hospital for a month afterward. And Sylvie . . ." He hesitated, as he always did when he thought about her, then, as always, he remembered too well. "Sylvie was in the hospital even longer than I was," he began again. "And where I eventually left with everything pretty much intact, Sylvie . . ." He inhaled another deep, calming breath—yeah, right, as if anything could calm him about this—and released it slowly again. "Sylvie lost a leg," he finally said, surprised at how clearly the words came out when the thought was never clear at all. "Before that night, she was a beautiful, vivacious, incredibly talented dancer, headed straight to the top. But that night I changed all that. That night I—"

He couldn't finish. He'd already said more than he wanted to say. So now he said nothing at all.

"Until that night when she told you to drive faster, and you did," Lucy finished for him. "Until that night that there was an accident. And that's what it was, Max. An accident. A terrible, terrible accident, but an accident all the same. You can't blame yourself for what happened."

He shook his head. "No, you don't understand. I should have—"

"You *both* should have been more careful," she interrupted him. "But neither of you was. And you can't dwell on the should haves and shouldn't haves," she added. "You'll make yourself crazy if you do that. Everybody has should haves and shouldn't haves in their past, Max. Everybody. But we have to leave them in the past. Because we can't change any of them."

Hell, Max thought, she didn't have to tell him that. He shook his head mutely again. She didn't understand. Hell, how could he expect her to, when he didn't really even understand it himself?

"That still doesn't explain why you live the way you do," Lucy said when he didn't respond. "Why you're living here, working the job you are. I mean, if you left the hospital intact, then why aren't you still racing?"

He expelled an impatient sound. "Well, that's obvious, isn't it?"

Lucy's eyes narrowed in confusion. "No."

He gaped at her. "There was no way I could go back to my career," he said. "Not after I ended Sylvie's the way I did."

Lucy gaped right back at him. "Max, you didn't—"

"And there was no way I could enjoy any of the things I had," he went on, this time interrupting Lucy, "not while Sylvie couldn't enjoy anything she had. I didn't deserve a good life after that, not when hers would be so miserable."

"Max, you don't know for sure that she—"

"So I gave everything away."

That, finally, seemed to stop Lucy cold. "You what?" she said.

He turned to look at her again, head-on. "I gave everything away."

She continued to eye him cautiously as she said, "By 'everything,' you mean . . ."

He shrugged. "Everything. The houses, the cars, the money . . . all of it. I gave all of it away."

"To whom?"

He shrugged again. "I deeded the houses over to whoever had a use for them, then sold everything else and donated the money to places that needed it for something."

She shook her head in disbelief, then smiled her soft, sweet smile. "Max, that's so . . . That's such a . . . I mean . . ." But she said nothing more, only continued to shake her head slowly and smile sweetly at him.

Until he said, "It didn't help Sylvie."

Lucy sobered at the reminder. "But I bet it helped a lot of other people who needed help."

"Not Sylvie," he repeated. "Nothing could help her."

Lucy studied him in silence for a moment longer, then asked, "How long has it been since you spoke to her?"

Max's eyes widened in panic, a splash of heat burning his belly. "I haven't spoken to her since it happened. I couldn't."

"You never talked to her afterward?" Lucy asked incredulously.

"I went to see her at her hospital after I got out," he admitted. "I got as far as the door to her room. She was sleeping. And then I saw the tent over her leg, and I . . . I . . ." This time Max was the one to shake his head slowly. "I couldn't go any farther. I just couldn't stand to see her that way, knowing I was responsible. I left Rome that day, and I didn't go back. I never saw or spoke to her again."

"Oh, Max . . ."

He lifted the bottle of warm, bad beer to his mouth and drained it, relishing the bitter, nasty taste and the burning sensation as it traveled down his throat and into his stomach. "So now you know why I drink exceptionally bad beer," he finished lamely, setting the empty bottle on the floor in front of the couch.

"And why you're not allowed in the Coves' house," she continued quietly. "And why you're not allowed to own a car, or allowed to drink good wine, or allowed to make love to me."

Oh, damn, he wished she hadn't said that. He closed his

eyes, hoping that might take away some of the pain. But that only increased it, because it made it too easy to remember what he was missing. What he had held briefly Friday night and would never have again.

"Because you're punishing yourself," he heard Lucy say further. "Punishing yourself for something that happened five years ago, something that wasn't even your fault."

"Lucy . . ." he began, his voice laced with warning.

But it did no good. She just kept on talking. "How much longer are you going to do this, Max?" she asked. "How much longer do you intend to deny yourself the things that would make your life enjoyable? The things that would make you happy?"

He opened his eyes and met her gaze steadily. "For as long as Sylvie can't enjoy her own life," he said decisively. "As long as she's living a life that's lacking in what she most wanted, that's how long I'm going to live a life that's lacking in what I most want." He paused for a moment, to let that sink in, then concluded, "So it's going to be a while, Lucy, before I can change my ways. Only in another lifetime will that ever happen."

It was after eleven when Lucy, clad in her pajamas, picked up the telephone in her kitchen and dialed Rosemary's number at the big house. She figured she'd be waking the nanny up, but Lucy—gosh, what surprise—couldn't sleep, and kept replaying her conversation with Max earlier that evening over and over in her head. At the moment, she doubted she'd ever be able to sleep again unless she got something straightened out, so she needed to straighten it out as soon as she could.

She'd noticed a computer in Abby's room earlier. She'd also noticed it was turned off. But she'd bet good money that Rosemary knew how to use it, even if Abby didn't. Phoebe had always told her you could find out anything you wanted on the Internet—anything. Lucy was about to put that to the test. She supposed she really should call Phoebe if she wanted the skinny on anything—or anyone—but she didn't dare risk calling her friend in Rhode Island, for fear that someone might be at Phoebe's apartment when she did, or that the police, or the Future Beauticians of Idaho, were screening her calls. Rosemary would have to be her first—perhaps her only—choice.

Rosemary picked up on the third ring, answering with a *very* sleepy, "'lo?"

"It's Lucy," she said quickly. "I'm sorry to wake you, but I need some help. Right away," she added urgently.

"Lucy?" Rosemary asked from the other end of the line. "What's happened? What's wrong?"

Hoo boy, was that a loaded question. "Long story," Lucy told her. "Look, do you know how to use Abby's computer?"

There was a moment of silence, followed by, "For some things."

"Would the Internet be one of those things?"

"Yes . . ." Rosemary said, her voice decidedly suspicious now.

"Then I need your help."

"With what?"

Lucy hesitated only a moment before asking the nanny, "Do you know what the time difference is between here and Italy?"

Chapter 14

The sun was coming up by the time Lucy and Rosemary finished their hunting and fishing expedition on the Internet, but, *boy*, what a haul they made that night. Once she'd gotten past Rosemary's objections that they shouldn't pry into Max's private life by convincing the other woman that it wouldn't be prying if what they found out was already public knowledge anyway—thank goodness Rosemary was addled by sleep—Lucy found out more about Max than she knew about herself. Then again, considering the fact that she had learned so much about herself so recently—since coming to Harborcourt, come to think of it—that wasn't exactly surprising.

Some of what she discovered about Max on-line she had already known—the meager beginnings in a depressed Detroit neighborhood, the stints in juvenile detention for stealing cars and joyriding, the fast rise in the racing circuit. Other things Rosemary read to her only confirmed what she had assumed from her conversation with Max about his life in the fast lane, to reduce it to a fitting cliché: the women, the money, the women, the cars, the women, the parties—and enough of the women, already, sheesh—all of the excesses that came with success like his. More of what Rosemary read to her, however, came as a complete surprise.

Many of the news and magazine articles had been on foreign web sites in languages that Rosemary couldn't read, but many had been carried by American and Canadian and British sites, so those were the ones where they found their information. Gradually, though, the articles about Max's career, his crash, and his convalescence dried up. A few ensued about "Speed Demon" Hogan's puzzling retreat from the racing circuit, but even those eventually dwindled off. One reporter for an American racing magazine, however, had written as recently as a year ago a follow-up to Max's amazing professional history and his mysterious disappearance, though he hadn't been able to find out—or had chosen not to report—where Max was now, or what he was doing.

There had, however, been other valuable information in the article.

Max had told Lucy he'd given away everything he'd owned, but he hadn't said who had benefited from his generosity, and she'd found the distribution of his real estate holdings in particular to be especially interesting. He had deeded over his huge, palatial main residence outside Rome, for example, to some local nuns who were about to lose their convent. His condo in Paris had gone to a woman who had been struggling for years to find funding for a building to house an art school for underprivileged children. He'd given his New York condo to a single mother who'd left her abusive husband and was trying to get back on her feet. His house outside London had gone to a veterinarian who wanted to open a much-needed animal hospital for the area.

Max, despite his gruff exterior, she realized then—though this discovery *wasn't* particularly surprising—had a very soft center. He'd given his things to people who really did deserve them and would use them to make the world a brighter place. Presumably because he thought he'd darkened it some himself.

But of all the things she and Rosemary found that night, what had captured Lucy's attention most of all was a story about Sylvie Balzarantini that had appeared in a British dance magazine three years after the accident. It was about how she had opened a dance studio in Rome for children with disabilities, and about the new man in her life, a widowed shipping tycoon whose daughter was one of her students, and about how happy she was with her new lease on life. In it, Sylvie herself spoke at length about how her old existence of endless partying and reckless extravagance seemed so meaningless now that she had purpose in her life. There were photographs accompanying the article, pictures of the beautiful, dark-haired Sylvie decked out in her dance attire, wearing a prosthesis she didn't bother to hide. Other pictures of her showed her dancing with little girls and boys who seemed to be having the times of their lives. And another photograph depicted her with her fiancé, Vincenzo Romero, sharing a quick smooch and a devilish grin.

And there was something very interesting that Lucy noticed about every photograph. In every last one, Sylvie Balzarantini had been smiling with sheer, unmistakable joy. Where Max had completely retreated from life after the accident, Sylvie had rebuilt hers. And in the rebuilding, she had found a much better life than the one she had lived before.

Max needed to know this, Lucy thought. But he needed to hear it from someone other than her. Not because she didn't want him to know she'd been snooping into his life, but because she knew he wouldn't believe her if she told him what she'd found. He'd only believe it if he learned it for himself. And he'd only learn it for himself if Sylvie Balzarantini told him about it.

"What did you say the time difference is between here and Italy?" Lucy asked Rosemary as she turned off the PC.

"I don't know," the nanny said. "It's five hours earlier here than in Ireland. So Italy can't be too far behind. Of course, we're on Daylight Savings Time right now, and I don't think they have that in Europe . . . Oh, Lucy, don't ask me to be doing math before I've even had my morning tea. I can't believe I let you keep me up all night."

Funny, but Lucy didn't feel a bit tired herself. She felt roaring and recharged and ready to take on the world. Or, at

least one little part of it. Europe, to be specific. Italy, to be
even more exact.

WWDD? she asked herself. Then she realized that was a
no-brainer. Dino would fix a drink, call up Sinatra and the
boys, leave for his homeland in a heartbeat, then sing "Night
and Day." Lucy didn't have the funds or the time to leave for
Dean Martin's homeland, but she could pick up a phone, and
if she concentrated very, very hard, she could probably push
the numbers in the right order. And, hey, if there was one
thing worth concentrating very, very hard for, it was Max
Hogan.

She glanced at the clock on Abby's desk and saw by the
placement of the hands that it was going on 7:00 A.M. That
would make it almost noon—or else 1:00 P.M., depending on
the Daylight Savings Time thing—in Ireland. No later than
2:00 or 3:00 P.M., she would think, in Rome.

She wondered if Sylvie Balzarantini—or, rather, Sylvie
Romero now—had a listed number. And then she said, "Just
one more favor, Rosemary, please. And then I promise you
I'll leave you alone for the rest of the day."

Tuesday evening found Max feeling cranky and uncomfortable for two reasons. Number one, he couldn't stop thinking
about Lucy and how much he wanted her and how there was
no way he could have her and still live with himself in the
morning. And number two, he'd been forced to wear his stupid chauffeur getup again, to drive Alexis Cove to a charity
fund-raiser in Lexington. Thankfully, he didn't see anyone
he knew, it being an out-of-town event, so he wasn't as
cranky or uncomfortable—or embarrassed—as he might
have been about that. There was nothing, though, that could
temper his irritation at missing Lucy so much, or at knowing
he couldn't have her and still live with himself in the morning, or at realizing things were going to be this way until she
left Harborcourt, a realization that only served to irritate the
hell out of him all over again.

It was a vicious cycle.

Luck was with him in other ways that night, however. Alexis, for once, decided not to stay late, so Max was driving west on I-64 by nine-thirty, pretending he didn't look like an idiot in the dark charcoal double-breasted jacket and jodhpurs, *or* the shiny black Gestapo boots, *or* the black-billed charcoal cap that topped off the ensemble. Damn Alexis anyway. Next she'd be asking him to change his name to Jeeves.

By the time he made his way up to his apartment, he was beat and angry and frustrated, and all he wanted was to have an exceedingly bad warm beer and go to bed, to escape into blissful unconsciousness for a while, because at least he could have Lucy in his dreams. But the minute he walked into his kitchen, his telephone began to ring, and he halted. The only people who ever called him were the Coves, and only because one of them needed for him to bring the car around. And seeing as how he'd just dropped Alexis off, and Justin was out of town until Friday, there was little chance it was one of them.

Warily, he reached for the phone and lifted the receiver to his ear. "Hello?" he said blandly, knowing the caller must be a wrong number.

"Max! Is that you? Is it really you?"

Heat flooded his belly and his knees buckled beneath him at the sound of the feminine voice tinted with an Italian accent. Gripping the countertop to keep himself standing, he replied incredulously, "Sylvie?"

"Oh, Max!" she cried happily. "It is so good to hear your voice! I have been trying to call you all night. Where have you been, you naughty boy?" And then she began to speak quickly in her native language, words that Max had trouble following, since it had been so long since he'd used Italian himself.

"Sylvie, stop," he said. "You're going too fast."

She laughed at the other end of the line. "That was never a problem for you before, Max."

Jesus, how could she joke about that? he wondered. "I'm

sorry," he said, the apology sounding so adequate, since it needed to cover so many things, he didn't even know where to begin. "It's just been a while since I've heard anything but English. You have to slow down."

He heard a soft *tsk*ing sound from the other end of the line. "You know me, Max. I can never slow down. I love to go fast."

There, she'd done it again. How could she speak so lightly about speed in light of what had happened? "Where are you?" he asked, fearful that she'd lost her mind on top of everything else.

"I am in Rome," she told him.

"How did you know where to find me? Why are you calling?"

"We have a mutual friend who telephoned me today, and it made me think of you, and so I wanted to call and see how you are."

"I'm okay," he lied, the reply automatic. "But how did you find me? And how about you?" he asked further, before she had a chance to reply. "How are you doing, Sylvie? Are you all right?"

Her laughter rang out again, from thousands of miles away, and it sounded so familiar, so intimate, that he almost felt as if she were standing right there in the room with him. He remembered her bright smile and her dark eyes, and the way she could laugh at just about anything. He wondered how much she had laughed in the last five years.

"Oh, Max," she said again. "I have so much to tell you. So many wonderful things have happened to me since I saw you."

Oh, yeah. He'd just bet.

"Are you busy?" she asked. "Do you have some time to talk?"

Max looked around at his empty apartment and thought about his empty life. And how it was all going to stay empty, since he wasn't allowed to fill it with anything other than emptiness. "I'm not busy, Sylvie," he said wearily as he opened a cabinet and reached for an exceedingly bad, warm beer. "I have all the time in the world."

And damn him for that, anyway, he thought morosely.

Lucy thumbed the remote control in her hand over and over again, then realized she wasn't paying a bit of attention to the images that flickered so rapidly across the television screen. So she switched it off, and wandered restlessly into her kitchen to see if anything in the refrigerator had changed since she'd checked it, oh, seven and a half minutes ago. She had tried to relax in a lavender-scented bath earlier, having heard somewhere that lavender was supposed to be a calming aroma. All it had done for Lucy, though, was stir her into a frenzy of needing and wanting. Or maybe the frenzy of needing and wanting had been caused by the fantasies she'd entertained about Max while soaking in that bath all naked and wet and hot. Much like her fantasies, now that she thought about it. In any case, at the moment, she felt anything but calm.

Max had left late that afternoon, driving the Duesenberg and dressed in his libido-scrambling chauffeur outfit. Lucy didn't know why she found the getup so sexy. Probably she wouldn't, if it hadn't been him wearing it. He'd returned about an hour ago, and now it was going on midnight, and all Lucy could think was that if she had to spend another night alone, recalling in vivid detail what it had been like to be half-naked and totally aroused with Max, she was going to have a nervous—or, at the very least, a sexual—breakdown.

She wondered if Sylvie Balzarantini had gotten ahold of him yet. And if she had, had it made any difference?

No sooner had the thought unrolled in her head than there was a soft tap-tap-tapping on her front door. Gosh, she wondered, a little flicker of heat igniting in her belly when she heard it, who on earth could *that* be? She swallowed hard, glanced at the bottle of exceptionally good Shiraz that she had opened a little while ago to let breathe, and tugged on the belt of Phoebe's ankle-length, pale pink velvet robe with the marabou collar—she did so feel like a Hollywood diva wearing it. Okay, an X-rated Hollywood diva, she amended, since she was wearing only a couple of scraps of pink lacy lingerie beneath it—she really did hope that Sylvie had gotten ahold of Max by now and that it had made a difference. Inhaling a deep breath for fortification, Lucy went to answer the door.

"Why, Max," she said lightly when she saw him standing on the other side. And then she couldn't say anything else, because she also saw that he was still wearing his chauffeur outfit.

But that was okay, because even though her mouth went dry and her vocabulary evaporated, every hormone she possessed leapt up to say "Howdy!" In fact, when she realized further that the jacket part of his chauffeur outfit was halfway unbuttoned, revealing a tantalizing glimpse of dark hair beneath, her hormones shouted a few more things, too, all of them much too indecent for her to repeat verbally. Not that she figured she needed to repeat them verbally when she saw how Max was looking at her. She was fairly certain then that his hormones had heard every word her hormones had said. And his hormones were responding very nicely, too, thanks.

"Ah . . . what a surprise," she added nervously, amazed she was able to manage even that small remark, and scarcely recognizing the deep timbre of her own voice. "What brings you out?" she ventured further.

He said nothing at first, only let his gaze travel hungrily from her face to her breasts—the top halves of which, oops, were revealed by her bra's demicups and the robe's gaping opening—then to her belly, and on to her legs—which, oops, were revealed to the thigh thanks to the robe's gaping opening—and then back up again.

"Hiya," he said in a very low, very sexy voice. He took in her attire again, then glanced down at his own. "I should probably go change, shouldn't I?" he said. "I'm kind of overdressed."

Lucy shook her head quickly. And just as quickly, she assured him, "No, you shouldn't. I, ah . . ." She battled a blush. "I kind of like you in that," she finally confessed.

He smiled, a devilish, playful smile. "Gee, you don't strike me as the type who'd like to play The Chauffeur and the Heiress."

Who said they'd be playing? she wondered. And then she shoved the thought quickly out of her head—not just because she was uncomfortable with how close Max had skated to the truth without realizing it, but because they were getting way ahead of themselves. The Chauffeur and the Heiress, she thought, would come later.

But not too much later.

She decided to ignore his quip for now, and instead said, "You want to come in?"

"Oh, yeah," he told her with much confidence, his tone indicating that he was talking about entering a lot more than just her apartment. Oh, goody.

Lucy's heart rate doubled at hearing the comment, sending her blood hurtling through her veins at a velocity that made a Formula One racer look like a Sit 'n' Spin. Though she did feel dizzy enough to have been going around in circles on the latter—at Formula One speeds.

She stepped aside and swept an arm toward the interior of her apartment, silently inviting him in. To her apartment. For starters.

"You look like you're getting ready to go to bed," he said as he strode past her. "Maybe I should come back tomorrow."

Or maybe you should stay *until tomorrow*, she thought. "No, no," she told him. "That's okay. I wasn't planning to go to bed until, ah . . ."

"When?" he asked, his gray eyes glowing like smoldering charcoal.

"Ah . . . later," she finished lamely, feeling weak in the knees when she contemplated all the possibilities in those glowing charcoal eyes.

He nodded. "Funny thing happened to me tonight," he said suddenly.

"Oh?" she asked innocently.

He nodded again, more thoughtfully this time. "I got a call, out of the blue, from Sylvie Balzarantini."

"Really?" Lucy asked even more innocently, hoping she wasn't pouring it on too thick. Then she got all hot and bothered again, just by thinking the phrase *pouring it on too thick*, because it conjured all sorts of things she probably shouldn't be contemplating with her clothes on—even if the clothes she had on currently numbered very few. As much as she wanted to hear about his conversation with Sylvie, she really hoped Max made a long story short. Real short. Like twenty-five words or less. Preferably less. In spite of her impatience, though, "How interesting," she added.

He nodded a third time, with yet more consideration. "Yeah. I thought it was kind of interesting, too, seeing as how you and I were just talking about her. And then, boom, she's calling me up from Rome, and she's telling me it's because she heard from a mutual friend of ours, and it made her think of me."

"Wow, what a coincidence," Lucy said, growing more impatient by the moment. She was pretty sure this was going to take more than twenty-five words. Dammit.

"It was a coincidence," Max agreed. "But you know, now that I think about it, she never did tell me who that mutual friend was she talked to, and she never answered my question about how she knew where to find me."

Lucy shrugged the comment off with a casually offered, "Women's intuition, I bet. Women know these things." Adopting her best noble savage voice, she added, "It is the way of the estrogen people."

"Mmm," he replied noncommittally. "We'll have to talk more about that," he said decisively. Then, even more decisively, he added, "Later."

"So did she tell you why she called?" Lucy asked with much interest, even though she already knew the answer. Even though she knew Max knew she already knew the answer. Even though she wanted it to be later *now*.

He hesitated before answering, giving Lucy another thorough once-over. This time, though, he didn't stop at the once-over. No, this time, he gave her a twice-over, then a three-times-over, as if he couldn't quite believe she was real. He took a few steps toward her, stopping when only a scant breath of air separated their bodies. Then he pushed the front door—which Lucy had been too busy lusting after Max to realize she had left open—closed. And then he took another tiny step forward, closing that last gasp of distance between them, and cupped his hands lightly over her shoulders.

"Yeah, she told me why she called," he finally said. He skimmed his fingertips along her shoulders, then down her arms to her elbows, then back again, lighting little fires on Lucy's skin beneath every spot where his fingers lingered on the robe. "She called to say she was happily married and joyfully expecting her first child with her wonderful husband. And she said she has an adorable stepdaughter she dotes on. And she said she has a thriving business that has brought her a meaning and a purpose she never thought she'd find. And she said . . ." He had been watching the movement of his hands along Lucy's arms and shoulders as he spoke, but his voice trailed off as he brought his gaze back to meet hers. "She said she's happier than she's ever been in her life. And she said . . . she said she hoped I was happy, too."

Lucy smiled, looping her arms around his neck. "And are you happy, Max?"

He lifted a hand to her hair, skimming his fingers lightly over her bangs. "I think you already know the answer to that," he said.

"You told me you weren't allowed to have things that make you happy," she reminded him.

"Yeah, funny thing that," he said, dropping his hand now to her cheek, strumming his fingertips over her cheekbone before turning his hand backward and tracing the line of her jaw, then her throat, with the backs of his knuckles. He touched her as if he wanted to get to know every inch of her—intimately. And Lucy found herself hoping he would never know her as well as he wanted to. Because she never wanted him to stop touching her the way he was touching her now. "Because, strangely enough," he continued quietly, "in spite of denying myself all those things that would make me happy, for the past couple of weeks, I *have* been strangely happy."

Lucy smiled, threading the fingers of one hand through his hair, cupping the other lightly over his nape. "Bet I could make you happier," she said softly.

He smiled back. "Bet you already have."

And, boy, if she hadn't been in love with the guy already, that would have done it right there.

And then she realized where her thoughts had traveled, and she knew that it was true. She was in love with Max. Truly, wonderfully, completely in love. Because he was sweet, and gentle, and kind, and decent. Because he had denied himself happiness when he thought he'd made another person unhappy. Because he'd given houses to nuns and children and single mothers and injured animals. Because he made Lucy feel beautiful and desirable and perfect, where she'd never felt any of those things before. Because he deserved to be loved, thoroughly and forever. Of course, she loved the guy.

Of course she did.

"So," she began, slowly pushing herself up on tiptoe in preparation for kissing him within an inch of his life, "does this mean you'll join me in having a glass of exceptionally good wine?"

"Maybe later," he told her as he slowly dipped his head toward hers, to meet her halfway. "There's something else I want to have first."

And then their mouths connected, in the sweetest, most delicious kiss Lucy had ever experienced. Max kissed her as if she were the secret to his happiness—which, she knew, she was, another reason she loved him. And he kissed her as if she had become a part of him that he never wanted to lose. He brushed his lips lightly over hers, once, twice, three times, then tenderly traced her lower lip with the tip of his tongue. As he kissed her, he skimmed his fingers down the length of her arm again, past the end of her sleeve, over her bare wrist, electrifying her when his bare skin made contact with hers. He tangled the fingers of his right hand with the fingers of her left, and when he did, he raked his thumb over the ring on her finger, making Lucy remember that it was there, and making himself jerk his mouth away from hers.

"What about this?" he said a little breathlessly, holding her hand up between the two of them, so that she could see the glaring, ugly piece of jewelry squatting there like a toad. "Your fiancé," he clarified, looking more hurt than anything else. "We both seem to have forgotten about the fact that you're supposed to be getting married soon."

Lucy had indeed completely forgotten about both the repulsive ring and her faux fiancé, and everything else wrapped up in the two things. For the last few days, she'd honestly forgotten about who she really was, where she really came from, and why she was really there. She'd been so focused on Max and what it would take to make him happy, and being happy because of his presence in her life, that she simply hadn't thought of anything that might make her *un*happy. And to be reminded of all of that now, of Archie, and the murder charge, and the police, and Newport, and the Hollanders, and everything else, just when she and Max were so close to finding what they had both been seeking for so long . . .

She untangled her hand from his, but couldn't make herself stop touching him, steepling each of her fingertips against his. "That," she said truthfully, staring at the ring, "is a mistake. All of it is a mistake." She turned her gaze to Max's, fixing her eyes on his. "It's not real. None of that is real. It's not like what I have here with you."

And she knew she spoke honestly when she said it. Her life back in Newport was nothing compared to the life she had here. It wasn't what she wanted. It wasn't what she needed. It wasn't what could make her happy. What she wanted and needed, what would make her happy, it was all right here, in this room. Because all she wanted and needed was Max. He made her happy. Nothing else mattered but him.

She never should have let Archie put the ring on her finger in the first place. And she'd certainly never told him she would marry him. She should have made it clear to him that she wouldn't. And had he not hurled himself out the window when he did, she was sure she could have done that. Now, though . . .

"I never loved Archie," she told Max. "And I never told him I would marry him. I never wanted to marry him. And I won't."

"Then take the ring off," Max said.

"I can't," she told him helplessly.

His expression went hard at her words. "Why not? If you don't love the guy, and you're not going to marry him . . ."

"It's stuck," she said. "The ring is stuck on my finger. Don't you see? That's the only reason I've been wearing it. Because I can't get it off. I've tried, Max. But it won't budge." And then, just to prove it to him, she gave the ring a good, hard tug . . .

. . . and then was amazed as she felt it budge. She tugged harder. It budged again. Harder. Again. Little by little, Lucy twisted and pulled the ring higher, ignoring the pain as it abraded her knuckle moving over it, until, astonishingly, she slid it from her finger completely.

She gaped first at the ring, then at Max. "I don't believe it," she said. "It was stuck. I couldn't get it off, no matter how hard I tried. I . . ."

She shook her head in mystification, having no idea how to explain what had just happened. She knew she'd lost weight in the two weeks since coming to Harborcourt, because she'd been too nervous to eat much of the time, and she'd been considerably more active than usual with her work and walking between the carriage house and the big house. Still, she wouldn't have thought she could have lost enough weight to make her finger smaller. Maybe she'd been retaining water the night Archie shoved the ring onto her finger—when she counted backward, she realized that would have been the right time for her to be midcycle, and she did usually retain water then. But even that seemed unlikely. Though it *was* convenient, she thought further, because it meant she was at the end of her cycle now, and wouldn't risk getting pregnant when she and Max . . . ah . . .

But she was getting ahead of herself again. Though not as far ahead as she had been before. She hoped.

Oh, what did it matter? she asked herself. The ring was off. And it *wasn't* going back on. For the first time in weeks, she felt free. For the first time in weeks, she *was* free. Free of so many things that had held her down for so long. So she only smiled at Max and let him pluck the ring from her fingers. He tossed it carelessly onto the coffee table, then pulled her toward him again. This time, when he kissed her, it was with greater passion and hunger than he had shown before. And this time, when he kissed her, he didn't stop.

Again and again, he slanted his mouth over hers, first one way, then the other, as if he couldn't quite decide which way he liked best. Lucy didn't quibble, though, because she was too busy enjoying his enthusiasm and responding with an eagerness to rival it. She battled with him for possession of the kiss, turning her own head to complement his actions, opening her mouth willingly to invite him inside. And then he was inside, tasting her deeply, his breathing growing raspier and more ragged every time his tongue penetrated her mouth. Lucy fisted the fabric of his chauffeur jacket in both hands, then spread her fingers wide over the broad expanse of his chest, then pressed her palms against him as she urged her hands up higher, over his shoulders and his neck, and into his hair.

Her actions caused her robe to slide off one shoulder and down over her arm, a development that did not escape Max's notice. He tore his mouth from hers and dragged it along her jaw, down her throat, along the creamy skin of that bare shoulder. Lucy threw back her head as he went, her own breathing coming in quick, rapid bursts. Never in her life had she felt such a need, such an urgency building inside her. Never in her life had she wanted anything the way she wanted Max.

He ran first his lips, then his tongue, along her collarbone, then dipped his head again, an action that sent the fabric of her robe lower still, until it opened completely over one pink-lace-covered breast. He hesitated for a moment when he realized what he had done, then, very gently, very slowly, he pressed his mouth to the bare flesh peeking out of the top of her bra. And when he did, it was with such aching tenderness, such reverent adoration, that Lucy felt herself go weak all over.

Not sure she would be able to keep standing much longer, she cupped her hands over his shoulders and took a step forward, silently suggesting that Max take a step back, which he instinctively did. When he straightened and gazed down at her face, Lucy smiled, and she thought he realized then what she intended to do. When she braved another step forward, he willingly took one back. Vaguely, she managed to direct them toward the sofa, and step by awkward step, kiss by lusty kiss, they made the trip, until Max bumped into it and lost his balance, landing on his fanny at its center, with Lucy standing before him, between his legs.

His hands landed on her waist, and he held her just firmly enough to make her think he feared she might somehow disappear. For a long moment, he did nothing but hold her that way. Then little by little, his hands moved lower, over the curves of her hips, and he began to slowly, methodically, trace his thumbs over her pelvic bones on each side. Lucy curved one hand over his shoulder and wound the fingers of the other through his hair, loving that simple moment of closeness and intimacy between them. Then Max moved one hand to the knot of her robe and tilted his head back to look at her, as if asking for her permission to loose it. Lucy smiled and nodded eagerly, and with one swift, deft gesture, he followed through. But that wasn't enough for her, and she shrugged her shoulders lightly, an effort that made the garment go slipping to the floor.

When it pooled around her feet like a frothy bit of pink cotton candy, she stepped out of it, kicking it carelessly aside. Then she moved back in front of Max, an action that made her knees collide with his. She faltered a bit at the contact, and he automatically lifted his hands to steady her, placing them gently on her hips once again. But when he realized what he had done this time, how he had touched the bare skin above the waistband of her pale pink panties, he closed his eyes tight, as if he almost couldn't bear the pleasure of touching her in so intimate a way. Lucy understood completely. She could hardly bear it herself.

She waited a moment for him to acclimate himself to the situation, loving the way he began to once again stroke the pads of his thumbs lightly, almost hesitantly, over her skin, as if even that small contact was overwhelming. The gentle friction generated a strange sort of heat on her flesh, a heat that spiraled gradually outward, seeping from her belly to her thighs, to her breasts, to that sensitive place between her legs, and everywhere else that could feel such an erotic warmth. Then he opened his eyes and tilted his head back again to look up at her face, his black pupils nearly eclipsing the dark gray irises.

Lucy smiled again, feeling a power unlike anything she had ever felt before. Max wanted her. He wanted *her*. Simply because she was who she was, and not for any other reason. She knew he didn't care that she had faults and imperfections. And somehow, she knew, too, that even if he discovered the truth about her, he wouldn't care that she wasn't a bright, shining beacon of society like her sister, or a rising star of academia, like her brother. He wouldn't care that she couldn't read well. He only cared that she was exactly as she was, exactly who she was: Lucy. And knowing that just made her love him all the more.

Her gaze never leaving his, Lucy reached behind herself to unhook the shell pink bra, then let the tiny scrap of lace glide slowly down over her shoulders and arms and hands, until she could discard it completely behind her. Max's gaze dropped immediately to her breasts, and his cheeks went ruddy with his desire. His grip on her hips went tighter, more possessive, more insistent, but he didn't remove his hands. So, thinking maybe he needed a little encouragement, and amazed by her own boldness, Lucy lifted her own hands to her breasts, cupping each lower curve gently, silently offering them to Max.

His lips parted in astonishment—or something—and she felt the fingers of one of his hands twitch against her flesh, as if he were battling the urge to claim what she so clearly wanted to give him. But still, he didn't move. So Lucy shifted one of her hands to her mouth, touching her middle finger to her tongue, wetting it, then dropped it back to her breast, slowly circling the rosy aureole as Max watched.

That, finally, seemed to do the trick. The hands on her hips went tighter still, but he jerked her forward, between his legs, and lifted his mouth to her breast. Lucy held it for him as he sucked her deep inside, cupping her other hand behind his head to hold him close as he covered the sensitive peak with his mouth and laved her wildly with his tongue. And as she continued to push her breast into his mouth, Max moved his hands to the waistband of her panties, hooking his thumbs inside, pushing the garment down, down, down, over her hips, her thighs, her knees, her calves, until Lucy stepped out of those, too.

And there was something so exquisitely erotic about being completely naked while he was completely dressed. She felt at once vulnerable and powerful, both fragile and strong. He pulled her toward him again, only this time he nudged his legs between hers, urging her down into his lap, so that she straddled him with her own legs spread wide. He continued to suck her breast as she held it for him, moving one of his hands to splay it open over the small of her back, holding her in place as he shifted his other hand to her thigh, close, so close, to where she lay open and vulnerable to him.

Lucy draped her free arm over his shoulder, curving her fingers over his nape to steady herself as she lifted her feet off of the floor. When she did, Max began to drag his fingers along the inside of her thigh, closer and closer to the part of her that was aching for his touch. And then he was touching her, and she gasped at the press of his long middle finger against the damp folds of her flesh, and writhed with anticipation when a second finger joined the first. She closed her eyes, reveling in the twin sensations of his mouth tugging relentlessly at her breast and his fingers rubbing insistently at the heart of her womanhood. Over and over he stroked her, back and forth, up and down, drawing erotic circles in the wet heat that drenched her. Lucy was just getting into the rhythm, was lifting and lowering her hips against his hand, when suddenly his fingers were parting her, and one was slipping deep inside.

"Oh, Max," she gasped as he penetrated her. "Oh, sweet Max . . ."

And then that finger was moving out of her again, then back in, then out, then in. Over and over he entered her that way, first with one finger, then with two. Lucy felt as if she were melting inside, turning to a hot velvet stream that spilled freely over and around him.

"Do you like that?" he whispered against her sensitive flesh. And only then did she realize he had moved his head away from her breast so that he might watch her instead.

"Oh, yes," she murmured, opening her eyes to meet his gaze.

"I like it, too," he said.

Their gazes held fast as he continued to penetrate her manually, until Lucy felt the stirrings of an oncoming orgasm beginning to swell inside her. She didn't want to be alone when it happened the first time with Max, so, reluctantly, she pulled his hand away. His expression reflected his bewilderment, but he didn't try to counter her action.

"I want you inside me," she told him breathlessly in explanation.

"I was inside you," he said with a wicked grin.

She shook her head weakly. "No, I want *you* inside me. Now, Max. Please. Please make love to me now."

His grin went broader at that, slow and sexy, a grin she hoped she would see a lot more often in the future. "I'm a little overdressed," he said again, as he had when he'd first arrived.

"Not for long," she told him, moving her hand now to the top button of his jacket that still remained fastened.

Her progress was hindered some, however, when Max took advantage of her preoccupation to cover both of her breasts with his hands. As she fumbled with the buttons on his jacket, he flicked the pads of his thumbs over her much-too-sensitized nipples, filling her with heat and an erotic sort of confusion that slowed her in completing the job she had set out to perform. But what was she supposed to do? Ask him to stop? Not when what he was doing was something she had fantasized about him doing for so long. Not when the reality of the pleasure she received from what he was doing was far better than it had been in those fantasies. Not when the feel of his hands on her naked body was just this side of euphoria.

Finally, though, the last button of his jacket did come free, and Lucy spread the fabric wide, burying her fingers in the rich scattering of dark hair on his broad chest. The skin beneath her fingertips was hot and alive, and she let her hands rove wildly over him, exploring every inch of him that she could see. And then she remembered that there was more of him she couldn't see, and that part was even more enticing. When she dropped her hand to the waistband of his jodhpurs, Max didn't flinch. But he moved one hand from her breast to her backside, curving his palm over the tender flesh of her bare bottom, giving it a gentle squeeze as she urged the zipper of his fly downward.

Lucy gasped at the liberty, then smiled a predatory smile. He'd gone after what he wanted, she thought, so now it was time for her to claim her own prize. Tucking her hand inside his jodhpurs, she did just that, dampening her palm with the moisture that had collected on the head of his solid shaft, then dipping lower to enclose him as fully as she could in her fist.

He uttered a rough, low sound in response, followed by what sounded like her name. So, holding him snug in her anointed hand, she ran her fingers deliberately down the length of him, then back up again, making him grimace and groan in a way that she knew meant he liked—very much—what she was doing. He moved his other hand away from her breast as she continued to stroke him that way, cupping it, too, over her fanny. But he only held her steady as she rubbed her hand over him, again and again, feeling more moisture accumulate between his hard, hot flesh and her feverish fingers with every move she made.

And then, before she realized what was happening, in one quick, fluid motion, Max was shifting both of their bodies until Lucy was lying on her back with the sofa beneath him, and he was kneeling between her legs.

"It's been a long time for me," he said, "and I don't think I can last much longer. I'm sorry," he apologized before she could say a word. "This first time between us won't be the best that it could be, because it's going to be over too soon." Then he smiled. "But the rest of the times, Lucy, it'll be phenomenal, I promise."

That, she thought, was good enough for her. Not the *phenomenal* part so much as the *rest of the times* part. Because in saying that, he made clear he intended for this to keep happening. And that was exactly what Lucy wanted, too.

"It's okay," she assured him. "It's been a long time for me, too. I already nearly, ah . . ." She blushed, amazed that she couldn't express herself with verbal explicitness in light of their physical explicitness. "I mean, I was practically there a few minutes ago, when you were touching me. I'm ready now. I want you inside me now. Now, Max, please. Make love to me *now*."

It was all the encouragement he needed, because the moment the words were out of her mouth, he jerked his pants down over his hips and reached for her. Then, without undressing any further, still wearing the gaping jacket and jodhpurs, still wearing the black shiny boots that had sent a thrill of excitement through Lucy when she'd first seen him in them, he cupped his hands beneath her bottom and pulled her up, toward himself. He pushed one of her legs over the back of the sofa and curled the other around his waist, then plummeted forward, plunging himself deep, *deep*, inside her.

Lucy felt the penetration all the way to her soul, so completely, so perfectly, did Max fill her. They both cried out at the joining, as if neither of them had ever felt anything quite so exquisite in their lives. For that first, crystalline moment, they remained perfectly still, allowing themselves to adjust to the coupling of their bodies. Then, his gaze never leaving hers, Max began to move, out and then in again, the friction of him inside her nearly more than Lucy could bear. Forward and backward he moved himself, gripping her hips hard in his hands to facilitate his entry. He lasted longer than she thought he would, evidently longer than he'd thought himself, because he looked almost surprised as he thrust in and out of her. And even though he held her firm in both hands, she bucked against him again and again, as if she couldn't get close enough to him in spite of their being united so utterly.

Just as she felt herself go spiraling out of control, he lunged against her one last time, and with a ragged moan, spilled himself hotly, completely, inside her. Again, they cried out as one at their culmination, and again, they remained perfectly still, as if frozen in time, as they peaked . . . and slowly began to ebb. Then, little by little, Max relaxed and released her. And little by little, Lucy felt herself uncoil. Before she lay fully back against the sofa, though, he was moving their bodies again, this time placing himself on his back and pulling Lucy atop him. He wrapped both arms fiercely around her to pull her close, covering her mouth with his in a kiss that was even more passionate than the ones they had shared before making love. Eventually, though, he pushed her away, but only far enough so that he could gaze into her eyes.

"I love you," he said plainly, his words lacking not one iota of conviction. Then, "I love you," he said again, in case she had missed it the first time.

But it was the second time she almost missed hearing, because the first time had nearly shattered her. She tried to tell herself he was only saying it because she was the first woman he'd made love to in so long. He would have loved any woman in that moment. But something in his voice made her realize he spoke the truth. Max loved her. He loved *her*. And somehow, that made her think that everything, eventually, was going to be all right.

"I love you, too," she replied breathlessly, her gaze never leaving his. "Oh, Max, I never thought I would find anyone who—" She halted abruptly when she realized there was no way she had time to enumerate all the empty places inside her that he had filled. So she only settled on repeating, "I love you, too."

He pulled her to him for another lengthy, lusty kiss, then tucked her head beneath his chin. "Next time we do this," he told her, "we're going to be in a bed, and we're *both* going to be naked."

Lucy nodded as she snuggled close against him. "Sounds good to me. So when is next time?"

"Depends," Max told her.

"On what?"

"On how long it takes to get to your bedroom and get me naked."

O Chapter 15

Normally, whenever Nathaniel drove down Highway 42, he was filled with a mellow sort of serenity that made him happy just to be alive. Supple green fields rolled out as far as the eye could see, checkered by white or black plank fencing, dotted by stately homes or quaint farmhouses, embellished with gleaming horses trotting along the landscape, or lush cornfields reaching toward the sky. Northern Oldham County was a peaceful little parcel of land, to be sure, and Nathaniel had spent the better part of his life living here. On his excursions to visit other parts of the world, whether to attend college or see to business, he'd always been filled with happiness to return home. Kentucky was in his blood as much as Ireland was—more even. He would always love this part of the world.

For the past two weeks, though, he'd been loving it even more than he had in the past, something he wouldn't have thought possible. The hills seemed greener, the sky bluer. The air felt balmier, smelled sweeter, felt cleaner. Life, in general, just seemed better. And there had been only one new development in Nathaniel's life that could have generated this newfound feeling of satisfaction. Of appreciation. Of happiness.

Rosemary Shaugnessy. The object of a heinous wager to which he never should have agreed.

Tonight, as Nathaniel drove down Highway 42 toward

Glenview to pick up Rosemary and bring her to his house for dinner, he was not filled with his normal mellow serenity, nor was he particularly happy to be alive. What he felt tonight was troubled. Conflicted. Confused.

He urged the accelerator toward the floor, propelling his Jaguar convertible faster, keeping his speed right around seventy on the two-lane country highway, as befitted the Bad Boy of the Thoroughbred Racing Set. And he was a bad boy, he reminded himself. The baddest of them all. He'd proved that time and again in the past, with behavior well suited to a man without a conscience. He was bad. His wager with Justin Cove illustrated that completely. Even if, lately, he hadn't much felt like he was living down to his reputation. Even if, lately, he hadn't much felt bad. No, lately—since that night he'd encountered Rosemary Shaugnessy in the Coves' kitchen, as a matter of fact—Nathaniel had felt surprisingly good. And with every additional encounter with the Coves' nanny, he'd felt better and better, until that kiss Monday afternoon . . .

That kiss Monday afternoon. He couldn't stop thinking about that kiss. And it hadn't even been one of his better efforts. Because as he'd lowered his head to Rosemary's that afternoon, he'd felt as uncertain and graceless as a thirteen-year-old boy, fearful that she might push him away. Only his fear hadn't stemmed from the fact that he might lose a two-million-dollar racehorse if she rejected him. No, his fear had stemmed from the simple fact that Rosemary might not like him well enough to let him kiss her. He hadn't given a thought to his horse that day. Because his head had been filled with thoughts of Rosemary.

And then he had kissed her. She had liked him well enough to let him. It had been a chaste, innocent kiss by many standards—certainly by his own standards—but it had set his heart racing, had made his blood simmer, had thrown his entire consciousness into a tailspin. He hadn't experienced such a staggering reaction when he'd had sex with a woman. Yet with one kiss, Rosemary had brought him to his knees.

It made no sense. Never in his life had Nathaniel been preoccupied by thoughts of a woman. But Rosemary had gone far beyond a preoccupation. She'd crawled right inside him, had taken up residence in a part of him he would have sworn was dark and empty. The crazy thing was, he *liked* her. And he couldn't remember ever *liking* a woman before. Oh, he'd been tempted by them, fascinated with them, bewitched, bothered, and bewildered by them. But he couldn't recall ever truly, genuinely *liking* a woman. But he did like Rosemary.

He liked her a lot.

And because he liked her so much, he'd been able to think about little else over the past couple of weeks. He thought about her smiles and her laughter. He thought about her irreverence and her wry sense of humor. He thought about her unqualified love for a little girl who wasn't even hers. He thought about how good he felt when he was with her and the way he'd caught fire when she kissed him back. He thought about the small gold cross she wore around her neck.

And he thought about how he had bet Justin Cove that he could bed her in exchange for a good deal on a horse.

Nathaniel had every intention of trying to seduce Rosemary tonight. But his reasons for wanting so badly to succeed had nothing to do with his wager with Justin. He *would* try to seduce her tonight, though. He would try with all his heart.

All he could do now was hope like hell that she told him no.

Although she knew her fears were groundless, the moment Rosemary set foot inside Nathaniel's house, she felt a bit edgy. She told herself it was only because she wasn't sure what to expect from the evening ahead. Even more worrisome, she wasn't sure what Nathaniel expected from the evening ahead. But really, what generated her response was the sense of déjà vu that wound through her upon entering the place. Even if, she tried to assure herself, there was no reason for her to feel such a thing.

The design of Nathaniel's house was, after all, very different from that of the Somersets' house, where she had worked back in Derry. Then again, the Somersets' house had been built before this state was even settled, so perhaps it wasn't a fair comparison to make. Their house had been a majestic estate nestled amid the rich, green hills of Northern Ireland, a three-story gothic mansion of obscene proportions that had originally been built for a British earl. There had been nights that Rosemary had spent there when she had expected ghosts to come drifting out of some of the rooms, and the entire place had been drafty and damp and cold, no matter the weather outside.

Nathaniel's house, though certainly large for one person, was modest by comparison. It was only one floor, for one thing, though that one floor probably covered at least an acre of land, so far did it sprawl in so many directions. And where the Somersets' furnishings had been passed down for generations—probably since Camelot, some of it, she'd thought back then—Nathaniel's tastes were obviously more contemporary and considerably less lavish.

He had driven to the Coves to pick her up, but, curiously, hadn't wanted to extend his greetings to her employers before they left. He'd seemed to be in a hurry—and also a bit tense—as he'd led her to his car and driven away. But as they'd pulled into the wide circular drive before his house, he'd relaxed noticeably. He'd turned to smile at her before climbing out of the car, a smile that had told her how happy he was to have her here. And then, as he'd led her through the house, as she'd taken in the hard, masculine surfaces, the dark, masculine furnishings and the sparse, masculine decor, she'd realized his home bore almost no similarity to the Somersets' at all.

And Nathaniel himself bore almost no similarity to Phillip Somerset, either. Phillip had been a boy of seventeen, not even a full year older than Rosemary, when they'd become involved. He'd been young and exuberant and full of romantic notions about turning his back on his family and his heritage and taking her to the New World, where they could be happy without a penny, since his family would surely disown him once he made his intentions known. He had laughed often, had been completely uninhibited in letting her know how much he loved her and wanted her and needed her.

Until the day his father had caught them together in Phillip's bed and fired both Rosemary and her aunt Brigid on the spot, and told Phillip if he ever dared consort with the Catholic whore again, he could leave his family and his home and never return. That was when both Phillip's exuberance and his idealism had cooled. That was when he had turned his back on her—quite literally, in fact—and left her lying naked and abandoned, forced to dress and leave under his father's watchful eye. Nathaniel, on the other hand . . .

Well. He wasn't exactly boyish or exuberant or full of romantic notions to begin with. And although she could tell that, like Phillip, he was no more likely to turn his back on his wealth or his heritage than he was to drop his pants and sing "Danny Boy" in front of his friends, she also sensed a decency in him that would prevent him from abandoning a woman naked and alone. Still, like Phillip, Nathaniel did indeed have a way of letting Rosemary know that he wanted her. But where Phillip had resorted to promises and vows that he ultimately didn't keep, Nathaniel did it just by leveling a certain look upon her.

And by kissing her with a quiet sort of desire that had reached deep down to her soul, a desire that could easily be stirred to a rousing passion with little provocation. The loving and needing part, however . . . Well, she supposed Phillip had never loved or needed her, either, not really. It was still too early for either of those things to be present with Nathaniel. Even if Rosemary had felt a few twinges of both herself where he was concerned.

He looked even more handsome than usual tonight, dressed in dark trousers and a lightweight, charcoal-colored mock turtleneck, in deference to a change in the weather from warm to cool. Rosemary, too, had dressed for the dip in temperature, opting for a ruby red dress of soft jersey knit, a fringed black shawl that had belonged to her aunt Brigid, and flat black skimmers to match.

And she couldn't help feeling anxious about the evening ahead.

After all, she didn't think she was presumptuous to assume that she and Nathaniel were now romantically involved. The kiss they had shared on Monday—only one kiss, but heavens, it had been a good one—had turned their association down an entirely new route, one that was unmistakable. She knew now that she hadn't been imagining the sexual charge that had arced between the two of them that night at the Wild Irish Rose. Or even in the Coves' kitchen that first night Nathaniel had sought her out.

And she knew now, too, that his response to her that first night hadn't come about because he'd had too much to drink. Had that been the case, he wouldn't have approached her a second time at the Rose. And he certainly wouldn't have invited her into his personal life the way he had. He must have felt a genuine attraction to her, to come looking for her in the first place. Where his feelings had come from, and why he was only now choosing to pursue them, she didn't know. Nor was she sure any of that was important anyway.

That was just the way it went sometimes, wasn't it? Who could say for sure what drew people to each other? Who knew why it sometimes took a while for something to materialize, or why that something materialized with such seeming suddenness? She told herself not to question Nathaniel's motives or his actions. She told herself to just enjoy them for what they were. And she told herself to stop worrying that history would only repeat itself. Nathaniel liked her. Rosemary knew that. And she liked him, too—perhaps more than she should this early in the game. Still, why not let things progress naturally? They were both adults, fully mature enough to handle whatever nature might have in mind for them, weren't they?

"Would you like something to drink before dinner?" he asked now as he led her into a room that appeared to be a den of sorts.

It was obviously a room he used frequently, because it was far more comfortable than the others she'd passed. The furnishings here weren't quite so sparse as they were elsewhere in the house, and the decor was more elegant and—surprise, surprise—horsy in theme. The walls were dark forest green, hung here and there with paintings of exquisite Thoroughbreds, and the furniture was fashioned of chestnut-colored, butter-soft, button-backed leather that gleamed from frequent use. A massive oriental rug splashed with rich jewel tones spanned much of the hardwood floor, and one wall was lined from floor to ceiling with shelves that were crammed with books. A quick inspection told Rosemary they dealt mostly with—surprise again—equine husbandry and the business of horse training and Thoroughbred racing. An ornate mantelpiece played host to a dozen or so trophies— some of them quite large—and a showcase nearby it was filled with more trophies, and a riot of colorful ribbons.

Opposite the entrance through which they had passed was a wall of windows that looked out through a frame of maple trees to an expanse of green pasture beyond. The sun hung fat and red and low over the trees in the distance, staining the sky with pink and orange and gold. Rosemary didn't know if it was the curvature of the earth here or what, but she'd never seen sunsets as spectacular as the ones she had witnessed since coming to Kentucky. This evening's was no exception. A dozen dark horses cantered across the scene just as she was about to turn away from it, and she smiled at the sight.

When she turned and saw Nathaniel's expectant expression, she recalled that he had asked her a question that required an answer. "Only if you're having something," she said.

"Good Irish whiskey, as usual," he told her with a smile as he moved to a bar tucked into the corner of the room. "What will you have?"

Rosemary wasn't much of a drinker, so she only said, "A little wine, I guess, if you have it."

"Red or white?"

"Red, please."

"Merlot or Beaujolais?"

She laughed. "I don't know. I don't know much about wine. Whatever you recommend."

"You seem more the Beaujolais type," he told her without hesitation and with much certainty.

"If you say so," she replied, battling a wave of anxiety that came out of nowhere to roll through her belly.

She watched as he ducked behind the bar and pulled out two glasses, filling one with ruby red and splashing two fingers of amber into the other. It was indeed good Irish whiskey, she noted from the label. Probably the same brand his grandfather had enjoyed.

"I thought we could eat dinner in about half an hour," he said as he crossed the room and handed her her wine. "Everything's ready. Just needs to be heated up." He grinned sheepishly. "At least, according to the restaurant."

She took the wine gratefully, thinking perhaps a sip or two might soothe her worries about the evening ahead. And, indeed, after a leisurely taste of the velvety wine, she felt a little better. "You have a lovely home," she said. Even if it was a bit lacking in, oh, say . . . warmth. At least, the other parts of the house were. This room, granted, did feel as if at least a little bit of living went on from time to time. She wondered what his bedroom was like.

No she didn't! she quickly reprimanded herself. That was the last room she needed to be visiting tonight.

"I guess it's all right," he said, giving the room a quick once-over, as if he hadn't done that for a while.

Rosemary chuckled at that. "All right," she echoed with good humor. "Very few people live this way, Nathaniel. Most would say it goes a bit beyond 'all right.'"

"I'll tell my decorator you said so," he replied good-naturedly. "Me, I really had little to do with it."

Which explained the lack of warmth, she supposed.

"Did you grow up in a house like this?" she asked.

He shook his head. "Not this large. My father's house was more like the one the Garamonds live in, an old farmhouse. But I grew up less than fifteen miles from where I live now."

"And I grew up two thousand miles from where I live now," Rosemary said with a sad smile. "So far away. And not just in geographic distance."

"Rossville Flats, I understand, is a pretty rough neighborhood," Nathaniel said.

"Oh, yes," Rosemary confirmed. "Not at all what you're used to."

"You said the other day that you lost your family to the Troubles," he added, his voice laced with an uncertainty that told her he wasn't sure if she was comfortable discussing her past.

So, to let him know she was okay with it—how were they supposed to get to know each other if they didn't discuss such things, after all?—Rosemary nodded and replied, "My father was an activist, a member of the IRA. My mother, too. According to my aunt Brigid, they were both quite passionate about the cause."

That seemed to astonish him. "You know, a lot of people would say your parents were terrorists, not activists."

His comment put Rosemary's back up, though she knew she shouldn't be surprised by his assessment. People who hadn't lived the life rarely understood it. "I suppose I can see where some people might form that opinion," she conceded coolly. "People who don't have all the facts. Or people who don't like to accept the facts that they hear. Or people who don't agree with the facts. Which one might you be?"

"I don't really have an opinion," he told her. "I don't know enough about any of that to have formed one."

"You have to have an opinion where I come from," she told him decisively. "If you don't have one, then you stand alone. And you don't want to stand alone where I come from."

"So who did you stand with?" he asked.

"I'm Catholic," she said without hesitation. "I stood with the Provos. You must understand, Nathaniel, there's a long history of terrible things there, a lot of reasons for why people feel the way they do, and for why they band together so resolutely. When I was a teenager, I fell in with a splinter faction, because I was so strong in my convictions. But I only stayed with my cell long enough to realize that I, personally, wasn't really cut out for bombing Saracens and ambushing soldiers, even though I didn't for a moment fault them for the things they did. Oh, my, he's shocked now," she said with a nervous laugh when she saw Nathaniel's expression change to one of clear alarm.

"Yeah, well, you'll have to forgive me," he said, his voice touched with more than a little sarcasm, "if I have trouble seeing you strapping on an M-16 and lobbing Molotov cocktails."

"We call them Armelites, and I was never comfortable strapping one on," she told him matter-of-factly. "And I only lobbed one Molotov cocktail, that missed its target—an empty police car—by a good fifteen feet. But I didn't leave my cell because I disagreed with them. I left because it seemed to me that they were more concerned with wreaking havoc than any sort of genuine political cause. I was afraid someone was going to get hurt. The way my father got hurt. And my mother. And I didn't want to see that when it happened. I just . . ."

She shook her head and expelled a long, weary sigh. "I guess I just got tired of the lot of them. The Provos and the Orangemen, the Republicans and the Unionists, Sinn Fein and the RUC . . . I suppose there are people on both sides who think their hatred is justified. But hatred is hatred, and I got tired of all of it. I just wanted out. And when Aunt Brigid died, there was no reason for me to stay."

Nathaniel shook his head in clear disbelief. "I just can't picture you in that setting at all," he said. "You're too . . ."

"What?" she asked.

He started to lift a hand toward her face, but halted at the tiny gold cross that hung from the delicate chain around her neck. As he had that first night at the restaurant, he dipped his index finger beneath it and lifted it up, skimming his knuckle lightly over the sensitive skin of her throat beneath. And just as it had that first night, Rosemary's heart kicked into a ragged rhythm that sent her blood racing through her body at such a frenzied pace, she fancied she was growing dizzy from its rush.

"I don't wear the cross because I'm a good, moral, innocent person," she told Nathaniel, because somehow, she knew that was what he was thinking. "And I don't wear it because I'm a staunch Catholic or anything else. If you must know the truth, there are times when I don't know for sure what I believe. You can't be innocent where I'm from. And I've done things in the past that aren't necessarily good, and aren't necessarily moral. I wear the cross because it belonged to my mother. My father gave it to her when they married. It's all I have left of either of them. But it doesn't mean anything more to me than that."

Nathaniel glanced up at her words, his eyes darkening, his cheeks going ruddy with what she knew must be his own heightened heart rate. She knew that, because her own was heightened, and in that moment, she felt as if she was a part of him somehow.

"You don't wear it because you're a good girl?" he asked roughly.

She shook her head slowly. "No. That's not why I wear it."

"Because you're not a good girl?"

She swallowed hard. "I am a good girl," she told him. "I just don't always do the right thing, that's all."

"I don't always do the right thing, either," he said, his voice low and coarse and very, very arousing.

"But are you a good boy?" she asked him, her own voice sounding a bit ragged to her ears.

"No," he said. "I'm not." He grinned, but there was no humor in his voice when he added, "Haven't you heard? I'm the Bad Boy of the Thoroughbred Racing Set. Everyone says so."

"Do they now?" she replied softly. "Where I come from, the bad boys lob bombs and shoot civilians. Trust me, Nathaniel. You're not a bad boy. You're not a bad man, either."

His brows arrowed downward as she said what she did, and his eyes went dark with confusion. He studied her in thoughtful silence for a moment longer, then, more quietly than before, he said, "Oh, I don't know. There's something I'd like to do right now, and it's something only a very bad boy would do."

Rosemary's heart very nearly stopped beating at that. "What?" she asked shallowly. "What is it you want to do?"

He released the cross he'd fingered so gently throughout their exchange and let it drop back against her breastbone, and Rosemary felt the impact of its descent all the way down to her soul. His pupils expanded as he held her gaze, until the deep green of his irises nearly disappeared. The temperature in the room seemed to skyrocket in that moment, and she felt as if she'd just stepped into the center of a fire raging wildly enough to consume every inch of her.

"What I want to do, Rosemary," he said very quietly and very hotly, "is carry you to my bedroom, and peel every scrap of clothing from your body, and stretch you out on my bed completely naked. And then I want to strip myself naked, too, and climb in beside you, and bury myself inside you, deep, *deep* inside you, again and again and again."

He dipped his head to hers, lowering his mouth to her ear, and whispered more erotic promises of things he wanted to do—very graphic promises of very explicit things. Rosemary closed her eyes and swallowed hard as she listened, then opened her mouth to inhale a deep breath, because she feared she might faint. But she couldn't do that. Not yet. Not until she'd done all those things to Nathaniel, too.

"I want to run my hands and mouth over every last inch of you," he concluded in a rough whisper. "And I want to feel your hands and mouth on every last inch of me, too. I want to take you in a dozen different ways. And then I want to start all over again."

"Oh, my," she managed to say quietly. "That's . . . that's very ambitious of you."

He smiled a smile that was full of seductive promise and sexual intent. "What can I say?" he murmured. "I'm an ambitious man. But I always get what I want, Rosemary. Eventually."

"Do you now?" she asked.

He nodded, but said nothing. Probably, she thought, because he knew he would get what he wanted tonight, too.

"You're not a virgin, are you?" he asked suddenly. And somehow, the question seemed perfectly normal.

She shook her head. "No. Does that make a difference to you?"

He shook his head, too. "No. It doesn't," he said. And she knew he was telling the truth. "I'm a not a virgin, either," he added. "Does that make a difference to you?"

She smiled. "Not a bit. Because everything that's in the past, Nathaniel, it—"

"—doesn't matter," he finished for her. And he sounded vaguely surprised by the realization.

"No, it doesn't," she agreed. "All that matters is what happens now. And maybe, to a lesser extent, what happens tomor—"

He stopped her with a kiss, one she felt in every cell she possessed. Where the kiss they had shared on Monday had been tentative and experimental, this one was commanding and sure. Looping one arm around her waist to pull her body flush against his, Nathaniel covered her mouth with his and gave her a taste of what was to come. Rosemary gasped at his intensity, and he took advantage of the action by thrusting his tongue into her mouth and tasting her thoroughly. Again and again, he savored her, until she felt an incendiary heat inside her threatening to explode. With no small effort, she tore her mouth from his, but only because she needed to voice an important question.

"What about dinner?" she asked breathlessly.

"Dinner can wait an hour or two," he said, his respiration

as rapid and ragged as hers. He ran his hand up and down the length of her arm, his touch setting off little fires in its wake. "Hell, as far as I'm concerned," he added, "dinner can wait until breakfast. I'd rather heat up something else instead."

Rosemary smiled, dipping her head to drag a few brief kisses along the column of his throat. "Well, then, Mr. Finn," she said against his warm skin, "if you've a mind to make love to me tonight, I guess we should get on with it."

It was dawn by the time Nathaniel drove Rosemary back to Harborcourt. She had told herself so many times over the last ten hours that she should be going, that she couldn't possibly spend the night at Nathaniel's house, that she really, truly, honestly had to get home. Then he would kiss her again, or run his hand along her naked body, or whisper some earthy, erotic promise into her ear, and she would succumb to him all over again. They had slept off and on for some of those hours, tangled in each other's arms, but for most of them . . .

She smiled as she grew warm inside. For most of them, they had enjoyed each other. Immensely.

He'd held her hand for the entirety of the drive home, but they'd barely spoken a dozen words since waking that last time. They had smiled a lot, and giggled once or twice, but words, somehow, seemed out of place after everything they had done during the night. Actions, after all, spoke louder than words. Rosemary felt better than she had felt for a very long time. She had already known Nathaniel Finn was a nice man. Now, though, she knew, too, that he was an attentive, affectionate lover. She couldn't wait until the two of them could be together again.

He pulled his frightfully expensive car—though, somehow, the frightful expense of it didn't bother Rosemary any longer, because she knew he valued other things more—to a stop behind Harborcourt, near the back door, so that she could enter without disturbing anyone. Mr. and Mrs. Cove were doubtless awake by now, but she didn't think either of them would have made it down to the kitchen yet. And Abby would certainly still be asleep. Rosemary wanted to be as quiet as possible when she entered, but not because she had anything to hide, or feel guilty about, or apologize for. She was a grown woman with a life of her own, and she was free to see anyone she pleased.

In spite of her reassurances to herself, however, she did feel a little guilty. She knew the Coves thought of her as a saint in nanny's clothing, chaste and moral and decent, someone who would never, ever, do anything like spend the night with a man. And although she was certainly moral and decent, she'd never laid claim to being a saint, or to being chaste. She was a normal, red-blooded woman who had wants and needs like anyone else. And last night . . .

Oh, last night.

Last night, Nathaniel had both satisfied those wants and needs, and stirred them into a new kind of frenzy. If the Coves wanted to judge her, then they'd judge her. But she hadn't done anything wrong.

"I'll walk you to the door," Nathaniel said softly.

"It isn't necessary," she replied just as softly.

He smiled one of his heated, sexy smiles. "Of course it's necessary. It'll shorten the time until I get to see you again. And by the way, when can I see you again?" he added hastily.

She laughed lightly. "When do you want to see me again?"

"Tonight," he stated unequivocally. "Have dinner at my house tonight. We never got to it last night."

"No, we didn't," she said softly, the heat of a blush warming her cheeks. They'd had other hungers to feed instead. "We got a bit sidetracked, didn't we?"

"Boy, did we," he agreed enthusiastically, giving her fingers a gentle squeeze. "But what a way to get sidetracked."

She felt the heat on her cheeks go nearly atomic as she remembered some of the things they'd said and done to each other, and she had to glance away before Nathaniel realized the intensity of her response. She still wasn't sure what to make of last night. In some ways, what had happened had felt totally unexpected. In other ways, it had felt like it was a long time in coming. And there was still a tiny part of her that couldn't believe Nathaniel's feelings for her were genuine, still a tiny part of her that couldn't understand why he had sought her out to begin with. She knew it was silly to feel that way, especially after last night, but there it was all the same. He was a handsome, charming, successful man who could have his pick of women. And a part of her still couldn't quite understand why he would pick her.

"C'mon," he said softly, tilting his head toward the back door that lay beyond the driver's side window. "Let's get you inside."

He released her hand long enough for her to exit the car, then captured it again the moment the two of them were close enough for him to do so. And as if that small contact wasn't enough for him, he pulled her hand up to his mouth and brushed his lips over her knuckles.

"I don't want to let you go," he said, as they climbed the stairs to the back door. "I can't stand the thought of not being with you today."

"I have to work today," Rosemary reminded him breathlessly. "And you told me that you have to be in Lexington today, remember?"

"Screw Lexington," he said carelessly. Then his voice went low and rough as he added, "Or better yet, I'd rather—"

"Don't," she said on a coarse whisper, pressing her fingertips to his lips. "Don't talk like that, please."

"You liked it when I talked like that last night." He nipped the pad of her thumb lightly with his teeth. "You liked it a lot."

"Too much," she agreed, heat swirling through her insides. "But when you talk like that, you make me want you all over again."

She felt him grin beneath her touch. "I'd like to be all over you again," he said with blatant masculine confidence.

"I have to go upstairs and get ready for work today," she said firmly, trying to ignore the wild heat shimmying throughout her body now. "Though how I'm going to work today when I won't be able to think about anything but you . . ."

By now they had passed through the back door and were standing inside the kitchen, and Nathaniel pulled her close to kiss her again, covering her mouth hungrily with his own. He dropped his hands to her hips and slowly walked her backward, until her fanny bumped into one of the countertops, then he lifted her up atop that counter and insinuated himself between her legs. Too caught up in the embrace to care about her surroundings, Rosemary hooked her legs easily around his waist, threading her fingers through his hair, and he spanned her back with both hands splayed wide. And all the while he kissed her, deeper and more thoroughly, a kiss that told her he was fully willing to take her again, right here, right now, right against the countertop, before anyone caught them, so that she'd still have time to get ready for work. And, oh, heavens, what a tempting little fantasy it was.

Until a stark fluorescent light bolted on above them, and a booming, angry voice cried, "What the hell is going on?"

Guiltily—because somehow, Justin Cove's witnessing her torrid embrace did indeed make Rosemary feel guilty now—she pushed Nathaniel away and leapt down from the counter. But Nathaniel immediately caught her and pulled her back toward himself, draping an arm across her shoulders, holding her close, as if he meant to protect her from some horrible monster.

How sweet, she thought, melting a little more inside at his reaction. It was dear of Nathaniel to appoint himself her champion, but she could manage Justin Cove. She'd been doing it for years now, after all. And truth be told, compared to his wife, Justin was a teddy bear.

"Mr. Cove," she began, ducking her head apologetically. "I was just about to come upstairs to see if Abby's awake yet."

His gaze flew from Rosemary to Nathaniel, then back to Rosemary again. "Looked to me like you were just about to do something else, Rosemary. And I must say, I'm a little surprised by your behavior."

She said nothing in response to that, mostly because she couldn't disagree with him. She was a little surprised by her behavior, too. But that was the way it was with Nathaniel. He could make her forget herself. Not that that was such a bad thing at times, but this, she knew, wasn't one of those times. Still, it was with great reluctance that she edged out from under his arm and turned to say good-bye to him.

But her employer prevented that when he said, with clear incredulity, "You're just now coming home, aren't you? You've been out all night with Nathaniel."

She bit her lip and, with a regretful look for Nathaniel—who suddenly looked a little pale for some reason—turned around. "Yes," she told Justin apologetically, though truly, she wasn't sure what she was apologizing for. "Nathaniel and I are seeing each other, and I was with him last night. I'm sorry to be coming in so late. It won't happen again."

But Justin Cove wasn't looking at her, she realized. He was looking at Nathaniel. Her employer expelled a single, humorless chuckle, and told the other man, "Christ, you actually did it, didn't you? I would have sworn even the Bad Boy of the Thoroughbred Racing Set wouldn't make it to first base with the ice nanny, but you hit a homer last night, didn't you?" Then he grinned grudgingly. "You old dog. I should have known better than to make a bet like that with you."

Something cold and hard settled in Rosemary's stomach at hearing her employer's words, even though she didn't quite understand what he was saying. She turned to Nathaniel, hoping for clarification, but he was gazing acidly at Justin.

"It wasn't like that," he told the other man.

"It doesn't matter what it was like," Justin said. "Hell, if it ended up being good, then that just made winning the bet even better for you, right? And you did win the bet, didn't you? You screwed the nanny. And in only half the time I allotted you. Way to go, Finn. You're my new hero. Even if you are costing me a fortune."

Oh, my, Rosemary thought, as she did indeed begin to get the gist of what was going on. She told herself there was a perfectly logical explanation for her employer's odd behavior and words. Unfortunately, she knew that "logical" didn't necessarily negate the possibility of "abominable."

"What's he talking about?" she asked Nathaniel, surprised at how calm her voice sounded. "What's this bet he's referring to?"

Nathaniel's face had gone rigid, and his eyes had gone dead, and something inside Rosemary began to unravel at seeing it. Where was the man who had held her so passionately only a moment ago? Where was the man who had pulled her close with a promise of protection? This man . . . This man looked ready to rip someone apart.

"It wasn't like that," he said again. Though whether he was speaking to Justin, or to Rosemary, she couldn't quite say.

Finally, though, he did turn to look at her, and when he did, his expression changed drastically again. But instead of returning to the warm, affectionate one he had shown in the car, now Nathaniel looked fearful and desperate. "It's not what you think," he told her.

And that, she thought, was a very bad sign. "How do you even know what I'm thinking?" she asked. "Could be I'm terribly confused."

Judging by the look on Nathaniel's face, she wasn't the only one. "I can explain," he said. "It's not what it was when Justin first proposed it."

Meaning there had indeed been a bet, Rosemary translated morosely. For some reason, her employer had bet his friend that he couldn't make love to her. Make love? she then echoed to herself derisively. Oh, love had had nothing to do with what had happened last night. Not for Nathaniel, anyway. For her . . .

Oh, God . . .

"Explain what? Proposed what?" she asked, even though she was fairly certain she already knew the answer, and was growing sicker with every passing minute because of it.

But it wasn't Nathaniel who ended up explaining it. It was Justin. More was the pity. "Your boyfriend there just got himself four million bucks for a horse that's only worth half that," her employer said. Then he smiled an oily, offensive little smile. "And all because he's such a stallion himself."

Rosemary took a step away from Nathaniel, and even though she told herself she didn't want to know the particulars of the wager, she heard herself ask her employer, "He what?"

Justin laughed, a careless, genuinely happy laugh, the kind of laugh that came out after one heard a truly funny joke. "At Alexis's last party, I bet Nathaniel he couldn't get you in bed," he said casually, as if that were the most normal thing in the world for a man to say to the woman who cared for his child. "I told him if he did—bed you, I mean—I'd buy a horse of his that I wanted for twice what it's worth. If he didn't, then I'd get the horse at no charge. He won. I lost."

Rosemary closed her eyes at that. Justin Cove had been the one to lose something, had he? Now that was a funny joke.

"Rosemary," she heard Nathaniel say, his voice pleading. "There's a lot more to it than that. You can't possibly think that I'd—"

She opened her eyes and leveled a gaze on him that stopped him cold. "You don't want to know what I think, Nathaniel. Truly, you don't."

It all made sense now, she thought, a cold, heavy feeling turning her entire body to ice. Why he had come looking for her in the kitchen the night of the party, why he had sought her out at the Rose, why he had pursued her so relentlessly. So he could seduce her according to the terms of a wager and sell his horse for a nice sum of money. There had been nothing more to it than that. She'd been right all along to be suspicious, she realized. That tiny part of her that hadn't been able to understand his motives had known what was what the whole time. If only she had trusted her instincts.

Finally, it seemed to dawn on Justin just what he'd said about the bet. In what Rosemary assumed was an effort to make her feel better, he said jovially, "Oh, don't get your feelings hurt, Rosemary. Hell, that horse is gonna cost me four million bucks. Not many women can say they're worth four mil."

Oh, my, yes, she could always be proud of that.

"Still," her employer continued, "I'm surprised Nathaniel nailed you as fast as he did. And I'm disappointed. Not just because of the money, but because I always thought you were such a nice girl, Rosemary."

That did it. Rosemary snapped. She glared first at Justin, then at Nathaniel, who seemed to have run out of words. Mostly, he just looked sick and scared. Well, that made two of them. However, Rosemary wasn't out of words. Oh, no. She still had plenty of those.

"Two men make a bargain that one can sleep with a woman in exchange for a horse," she said, "and *I'm* the one who's not nice? I have news for you two *gentlemen*," she added, fairly spitting the last word. "You're mean and thoughtless and horrible, the pair of you, and neither of you deserves the nice things you have."

She turned to Nathaniel, who had opened his mouth to protest, but seemed to be having trouble deciding what to say. "That's it, isn't it?" she asked him. "All those nice things of yours. That's why you are the way you are. You have *everything* you've always wanted, *everything* you've always thought it would take to make you happy. But it's *not enough*, is it? You're still not happy, are you? That's why you gamble so much, and so recklessly, isn't it? It's why you make bets like this one. Because you think having more will make you happy. And because you know that even if you *lost* everything, it wouldn't change the way you feel *having* everything. Because you *don't feel anything*. Not the things a decent human being feels, anyway."

"Rosemary, you don't understand," he said, finally finding his voice. But his expression was still fearful and unyielding when he spoke.

"Oh, don't I?" she retorted. "I think I understand quite well, even if that understanding comes too late. You're too blind to see that all the money in the world can't buy what you might have had for free, what could have made you happy. That's your curse. That you'll never, ever, be happy, no matter how much you have. And a fitting one it is, too."

He said nothing in response to that, only continued to gaze at her in stark, stoic silence.

"Well, you may have won your bet," she said. "But you lost more than you could possibly know." And then, because she just couldn't help herself, she hissed, "Bastard."

She felt tears prick her eyes at that, and the last thing she wanted was for either of these men to see her cry. So she turned her back on both of them and walked as calmly as she could out of the room. She heard Nathaniel call her name—twice—but she ignored the summons completely. And she told herself she was only imagining the panicky, desperate tone in his voice.

Oh, yes, she thought as she climbed the back stairs to her room, swiping her hands fiercely over the dampness on her cheeks as she went. She could take care of herself around Justin Cove just fine. When all was said and done, it wasn't the fact that he had made such an atrocious wager with Nathaniel that bothered her. That he would do such a thing didn't surprise her at all. It wasn't him from whom she needed protecting. Him she saw with perfectly clear vision.

What had surprised her, what she hadn't realized or seen, was that it would be Nathaniel—her protector—from whom she would need the greatest protection of all.

Chapter 16

At her oceanfront condo in Newport, Rhode Island, Phoebe Bloom was having a bit of trouble, and it wasn't even 7:00 A.M. Not so much because Dave, ex-boyfriend and current homicide detective, had shown up at her door before she'd even had her coffee—dammit, they'd dated long enough for him to know she couldn't function without at least two cups, which, now that she thought about it, was probably why he'd shown up when he did. And not so much because she was still in her sleepwear, either—which meant she was stark naked beneath her purple paisley silk robe, because she only wore pajamas for lounging and slept in the buff. And not even because Dave still had six toes on one foot—she'd already asked.

No, the reason she was having a bit of trouble was because Dave, shockingly enough, seemed to think she was lying about not knowing the whereabouts of her friend Lucinda Hollander.

Men. Who could figure them?

"Dave, I told you three weeks ago, I don't know where Lucy is," Phoebe insisted as she stood in her kitchen watching, with much gratitude, and even more impatience, the last few dribbles of coffee sputter into the pot beneath. And she wasn't lying when she said that, either, she reassured herself. Because she really had told him three weeks ago that she didn't know where Lucy was.

And when she'd told him that three weeks ago, she hadn't

been lying then, either. Because when she'd told him that, she *hadn't* known where Lucy was. Oh, she'd *assumed* that her friend was on a Greyhound bus headed for Louisville, Kentucky. And she'd *figured* it was probably headed down I-95 at the time. But she hadn't *known* that, not for *sure*. The bus could have been pulled over at a diner somewhere at the time Dave asked if she knew where Lucy was. Or it could have been at a gas station. Or it could have been on an interstate other than I-95, depending on whether or not it was making good time. Or Lucy could have gotten off at some point for some reason. There was just no telling. So Phoebe hadn't been lying when she'd told Dave she hadn't *known* where Lucy was. She hadn't. Not definitively.

"You know where she is, Phoebe," Dave said now from where he leaned against the doorway that connected her kitchen to her dining room. "And I'm not leaving until you tell me."

"You're nuts, you know that, Dave?" Phoebe said as she reached for the coffeepot, ignoring the hiss of the last few drops that hit the heat pad when she did so—she just couldn't wait any longer to pour herself a generous mugful.

Her response was, once again, honestly uttered, she reassured herself as she turned to look him in the eye. Because any man who would pair *that* tie, with *that* shirt, and wear *those* pants with a straight face, couldn't possibly be of sound mind. Honestly. What *had* she been thinking when she was dating him?

"And you're not even working Lucy's case," she reminded him, "so why are you here bothering me in the first place?"

"Aren't you going to offer me a cup?" he asked, nodding toward the coffee she cradled so lovingly in her hand.

"No," she said flatly. She enjoyed a long, careful sip of the hot, full-bodied brew. Then, "Mmmm," she added enthusiastically. "It's soooooo yummy, too. Jamaica Blue Mountain. Bet you can't afford that on your salary, can you?"

The dig struck home, because he frowned at her.

"I'll offer you a cup when you tell me why you're here," she said magnanimously.

He growled something unintelligible under his breath, then said, "I'm here because the department isn't getting anywhere finding Lucinda Hollander, that's why. Neither is the FBI, for that matter." He shoved a restless hand through his dark, overly long hair. Way overly long, Phoebe noted as he completed the gesture. And not the hippest style in the first place. Really. What *had* she been thinking? "And Archie Conlon claims he doesn't know where she is, either."

Well, now, that woke Phoebe up almost as much as a cup of coffee would. Almost. "You found Archie?" she asked.

Dave nodded. "Yesterday morning. Holed up in a crummy motel in Atlantic City. He's in jail down there for now, but we've started extradition proceedings. And we sent a coupla guys to talk to him." He eyed Phoebe thoughtfully for a moment, as if he were trying to decide if he should tell her any more. Then, obviously thinking it might sway her toward his way of thinking, he added, "Archie insists that Lucinda had nothing to do with the murder."

Holy moly, Phoebe thought. That certainly might sway her. *If* Dave was telling the truth. "Well, *duh*," she said eloquently. "Then why are you still looking for her?"

"Because Archie says she has evidence on her that will clear him."

Phoebe narrowed her eyes at him. "Evidence?" she asked suspiciously. "What kind of evidence?"

There was no way Lucy could have had any kind of evidence on her. She'd shown up the night of the Wemberleys' party with nothing but the clothes on her back—which Phoebe had carried out to the Dumpster the following morning—and had been carrying nothing but Phoebe's belongings when she left Newport. Oh, and, of course, she'd had the hideous ring that moron Archie had stuck on her finger. But she hadn't been carrying anything remotely resembling evidence.

"We don't know what kind of evidence," Dave said.

"Archie won't tell us. He just keeps insisting that if we can find Lucinda Hollander, he can clear everything up, once and for all. And I think *you* know where Lucinda is," he added meaningfully. "So I figured it might be a good idea if I came over and pumped you again."

Phoebe narrowed her eyes at him more, until they were mean little slits. "You never pumped me a first time, Dave," she said. "We only dated a month. What are you telling the boys down at the station?"

He grinned crookedly. "I meant I should come over and ask you questions again, that's all."

"Oh." She straightened, sipped her coffee, and looked at him normally again. "I knew that."

"And what I tell the boys down at the station is that you have a hell of a tongue," he added, his grin growing.

She gaped at him in outrage. "You *what*?"

He laughed outright at that. "I tell them you're witty, Phoebe."

Oh, right, she thought. Like she was supposed to believe *that*. Dave would never use the word *witty*. Not even in a desperate Scrabble strategy. "Have some coffee," she said tepidly. But she indicated he'd have to get it himself by striding past him, into the dining room, and then the living room beyond it.

She didn't need to tell him twice. Hey, he really couldn't afford Jamaica Blue Mountain on his salary. Not that his salary had been what had turned her off when they were dating. Truth be told, it wasn't his six toes or his dressing habits that had done it, either. Dave was actually a very sweet guy. But Phoebe wasn't much on romantic entanglements. They only led to trouble.

"So where is she?" Dave asked again when he returned to the living room. He sat in a chair opposite Phoebe, who had seated herself on the sofa. "You know where she is," he said confidently. "You and I may have only dated a month, Phoebe, but I know enough about you to know you and Lucinda Hollander are very tight. Too tight for her not to have contacted you at some point."

"And by 'contacted' you would mean . . . ?" Phoebe asked, stalling.

Dave rolled his eyes eloquently. "Phoned you?"

"No," Phoebe said honestly. "She hasn't phoned me." Because Phoebe had always been the one to call Lucy.

"E-mailed you?"

"No." Honest again. Hey, Lucy wouldn't go near a computer if it was spitting out thousand-dollar bills.

"Sent you a postcard?"

"Nope." Not likely, seeing as how Lucy was dyslexic, even if she wouldn't admit that herself on account of her mother—the old bat—had ignored specialists when Lucy was a kid and made damned sure everyone else did, too, including Lucy.

"Letter?" Dave asked.

"Nope." Ditto.

"Birthday card?"

"Nuh-uh." Although that was certainly something Lucy never forgot and no doubt would have remembered—and commemorated with a card, even as a fugitive from justice—thankfully, Phoebe's birthday wasn't until January.

"Carrier pigeon?" Dave asked halfheartedly.

"Uh-uh." PETA probably wouldn't have approved, and Lucy and Phoebe both were big on animal rights.

"You wouldn't tell me, even if you had heard from her, would you?"

"Oh, Dave," she said coyly. "You know me well enough to know the answer to that." Yes! Honest again! She hadn't lied to the police once, she congratulated herself smugly.

He nodded. "Yeah. I do know you well enough to know the answer to that. So then I guess it wouldn't make any difference to you if I told you that, after questioning Archie, we, and the FBI, really are fairly well convinced that Lucinda is an innocent party in all this?"

Ding ding ding ding ding! Warning bells went off all over

Phoebe's brain at his casually offered comment. This was just a trick, she told herself. Dave was trying to lull her into a false sense of security, that was all. He was hoping that by reassuring Phoebe—while she was still on her first cup of coffee—Lucy wasn't in any danger from the police anymore, then Phoebe might come clean with some info on her friend's whereabouts. Well, not . . . so . . . fast, Davy boy.

She drained her cup—scalding insides be damned—and jumped up and fled to the kitchen for her second.

"What do you mean?" she asked when she returned, sipping that second cup as quickly as she dared. *Come on, caffeine, do your worst.*

Dave hooked one leg over the other in a relaxed pose that was probably feigned. She'd need to finish this cup before she knew for sure. Hastily, she lifted her mug to her lips again.

"I just mean," Dave said, "that Archie was pretty convincing during interrogation, and it made our guys and the Feds think maybe Lucinda really was just an innocent bystander in all this." After another one of those thoughtful pauses, he added, "And earlier, we came across some evidence that pretty much backed up what Archie said, and indicated there was little chance Lucinda could have been in on it."

"What kind of evidence?" Phoebe asked, still suspicious. Still sipping.

"I can't tell you that," Dave replied.

"Then I can't help you out."

"Oh, come on, Phoebe."

"Sorry," she apologized without a bit of apology.

He blew out an exasperated breath. "All right, all right," he finally relented. "I don't guess I'll be telling you anything you don't already know. I'm just supposed to be keeping the particulars of this case under my hat. Like you said, it's not mine."

"Dave," Phoebe said mildly, "you're not wearing a hat."

He made a face at her. "Gee, I forgot how literal you are. Another reason why I don't believe a word you say about not knowing where your buddy Lucinda is." He hesitated for another moment, a moment that Phoebe spent sipping more of her coffee and gazing back at him expectantly. "Okay, here's what we know," he finally conceded, "We know that Lucinda Hollander is dyslexic."

Ding ding ding ding ding!

Phoebe eyed him warily. "Who told you that?"

Dave eyed her back in much the same way. "Her mother did."

Ding ding ding ding ding!

"Mrs. Hollander told you that Lucy is dyslexic?"

Dave nodded. "Yeah. And she showed us evaluations from a couple of experts who tested her when she was a kid. Her reading skills then were pretty much nonexistent, and both experts said there was almost no hope of improvement unless she got treatment, and there's no indication that she ever got treatment."

"Why would Mrs. Hollander tell you all that?" Phoebe asked cautiously.

Dave studied her over the rim of his coffee cup. "Because we told her that whoever was behind all this had to have a lot of sophisticated knowledge about computers and recent technology. A technological genius, if you will. Mrs. Hollander told us there was no way Lucinda could be that, because she was dyslexic and hadn't received treatment. And she had proof."

Ding ding ding . . .

Oh, hell.

Phoebe thought long and hard about what she should say next. She had to be very, very careful here. She knew Dave wasn't lying about Mrs. Hollander telling him Lucy was dyslexic, because no one outside Lucy's family—except for Phoebe, of course—knew about that. So if he knew about it now, it must be because Mrs. Hollander had told him about it. Though that *was* kind of hard to believe, since the old bat . . . er, Lucy's mother . . . had never once acknowledged—or accepted—it.

Then again, Phoebe thought, Mrs. Hollander had probably

had to weigh carefully what would be worse to have in the Hollander family, a dyslexic or a murderess. Boy. What a dilemma. That had probably kept the mean old broad . . . er, Lucy's mother . . . awake for nights on end. Still, ultimately, she'd done the right thing, telling the police the truth about Lucy's inability to read properly. The part about the police thinking Lucy might be innocent as a result of that knowledge, well . . .

"Archie Conlon, on the other hand," Dave said then, "is a technological genius."

Oh, now that really set off alarms. Deafening ones.

"What?" Phoebe demanded incredulously.

He seemed surprised by her surprise. "I said Archie Conlon is a technological genius."

Phoebe shook her head vehemently. "No, he's not. He's a moron."

Dave shook his head more vehemently. "No, he's not. He's a brainiac. He's been creating some of the most sophisticated technological equipment the U.S. military has in its arsenal."

"What?"

"You didn't know what he does for a living?" Dave asked carefully.

"He's got some boring government job," Phoebe said. "I figured he probably wrote reports and filed stuff all day. I mean, I guess I never really thought about it. I just assumed a moron like him . . ."

Dave studied her in silence for a moment, as if he were the one now who was weighing carefully what he should say. He uncrossed his legs, bent forward, placed his cup on the table. Then he propped his elbows on his knees, tented his hands over his mouth, and said, "A guy like him, Phoebe, has been creating sophisticated technology for our military and selling government secrets to foreign powers who aren't necessarily our friends."

"What?"

"And now he's got the Russian mob wanting to be a client."

"What?"

"And the Russian mob doesn't take *nyet* for an answer."

Phoebe stared at Dave openmouthed for a solid minute before she was able to respond. Finally, very quietly, she said, "I *told* you he was a moron." She blew out an incredulous breath. "So who's the stiff?" she asked. "And why does everyone think Archie killed him?"

"The stiff is George Jacobs," Dave said. "AKA Georgie Jakes. AKA Georgii Jakov. He's pretty much a lowlife scum, and the world is a better place without him, but we have to investigate it as a homicide because he had human DNA. Though I suspect he stole it, like he stole everything else," Dave added dryly. "And we think Archie Conlon killed him because Archie Conlon did kill him."

"What?"

"Probably in self-defense," Dave acknowledged quickly. "We've learned a lot more in the past few weeks than we knew that first night, and Archie's claiming self-defense. But we won't know everything for sure until we find this evidence he says Lucinda has. Even if he's innocent of murder, though," he added, "he still has to answer to charges of treason and some other things the government will probably want to put him away for, for a good long time."

Holy moly, Phoebe thought again. She'd known Archie was a moron, but he was like . . . like . . . like . . . *king* of morons.

"So how did Lucy get suspected of murder?" she asked. She needed to know as much as she could before making her decision on whether or not to turn her best friend over to the wolves . . . ah, authorities.

More coffee, she told herself, lifting the mug to her lips again.

"Lucinda Hollander was at Archie's place the day the murder took place," Dave said. "And we found the body at Archie's place."

"Ew," Phoebe said eloquently. "Lucy was in the same room as a dead body?"

"She didn't know it at the time," Dave said. "The body was

in Archie's closet. But that's another reason we need to talk to Lucy, to see if she can corroborate at least part of Archie's story of what happened that day, or add anything to it."

"She doesn't know anything," Phoebe said morosely. "She would have told me if she did. She was totally confused about everything that happened at the Wemberleys' that night."

Dave perked up at that. "So you *have* talked to her since the police tried to arrest her."

Oh, dammit, Phoebe thought, glancing down at her— unfinished—second cup of coffee. Four more swallows, tops, and she wouldn't have said that. She sighed heavily. "Yeah, I've talked to her."

"And you know where she's hiding out."

That, Phoebe decided, was a question she probably shouldn't answer yet. Because no amount of justifying it or fiddling with the facts would make it honest if she said no. She did know where Lucy was hiding out. She had the address, and she had directions on how to get there. So she only looked at Dave and said nothing.

"We just want to talk to her, Phoebe," he said. "We're reasonably certain that she's not involved in the murder of Georgii Jakov."

"Have you dropped the charges?" she asked.

"No," he conceded. "Not yet."

"Reasonably certain," Phoebe repeated. "That's misleading language, Dave."

He blew out another cautious breath. "I really don't think she's a suspect anymore, Phoebe. If she'll come back and tell us what she knows, then we can probably drop the charges against her."

"Why should I believe you?"

"I'll take you down to the station and let you talk to the detectives who are on the case," he said. "They just need to talk to Lucinda, to hear from her what happened."

"And then what happens?" Phoebe asked.

Dave lifted a shoulder and let it drop. "And then she'll probably be off the hook."

"Probably?" Phoebe echoed meaningfully.

"I can't make any guarantees, Phoebe," he said. "It's not my case. But this is her best chance of being fully exonerated. She can't stay in hiding forever."

That, Phoebe thought, was certainly true. Lucy wasn't the kind of person who could make herself over and start life anew and never return to the only life and family she'd ever known—even if that life and that family did leave a lot to be desired sometimes. She just didn't have it in her. For nearly three weeks now, she'd been pretending to be someone she wasn't, living a lifestyle totally unlike her own. She'd been completely alone, living away from all that was familiar to her, for longer than she'd ever been away. She must be going through hell, Phoebe thought. She must be lonely and miserable. By now, she would be desperate to come home, to return to life as she normally lived it, to be the person she would normally be. There was no way Lucy could be happy living the way she'd been living since going to work for the Coves of Glenview. No way.

No way.

Phoebe owed it to her friend to bring her home, where she belonged. But how to make sure Lucy was safe once she got here?

"So, Dave," she finally said, "how about another cup of coffee?"

Chapter 17

Lucy had never been happier in her entire life than she was in the week that followed her, ah . . . Gee, she wondered. What to call that night with Max? It certainly went beyond the *tête-à-tête* they'd shared that first time. Hoo, boy, had it gone beyond that. It had been more like a . . . like a . . . Hmmm . . . Well, keeping in line with the foreign language thing, the phrase *coitus maximus* came to mind. Translating to English, though, the closest she could come was *raging conflagration of sexual combustion*. Because Lucy very nearly burst into flames all over again just thinking about it.

And about the nights that had followed, too. She and Max had spent every free moment together since that first time, either at her apartment or his. Mostly hers, since his wasn't the most accommodating place in the world, though they had plans to rectify that. Lucy had made him promise to go shopping with her on their Sunday off this weekend, to buy him a few minor luxuries, one or two things that might make him happy. Even if she already knew what *really* made him happy.

She did.

And Max made her happy, too. Since meeting him, Lucy felt renewed, refreshed, rebuilt, revamped, re-everything. She felt like a completely different person from the one who had left Newport—had it only been three weeks ago?—and it was a person she actually liked. She had a good life here, a life with purpose and meaning. She'd found love with a wonderful man, and friends who felt more like a family than her own family did, friends who cared about her and didn't mind that she wasn't perfect. And she had a job she performed well. Okay, so maybe housekeeping wasn't the same as cancer research. But it was honest work, and she did it well. *She did it well*, she repeated emphatically to herself. Never in her life had Lucy felt like she'd done anything well.

What was different here than in Newport, she realized during that week, was that here she felt meaningful. She felt important. She felt as if she were making a contribution. Best of all, she felt loved. It was almost heaven, so ideal was her life. People needed her here. The Coves needed her to care for their home. Abby needed her for comfort and guidance. Rosemary needed her for friendship. And Max . . .

Well, Max just plain needed her, Lucy reflected with a smile. The same way she needed him.

Life here was better than she had ever believed life could be. Who would have thought that getting involved with that moron Archie, and being accused of a crime she didn't commit, and being a fugitive from justice, would have landed her in the exact place she needed to be? Lucy knew there would come a time—in the very near future, too—when she would have to go back to Newport to straighten everything out. But part of her hoped that time would never come. Part of her thought she could live quite happily for the rest of her life being a fugitive from justice. Because the way she felt during that week after making love with Max for the first time, she never wanted to leave Glenview again.

It all fell apart, though, the day two plain, black, government-issue sedans and a gray-and-blue Jefferson County police car drove up to the front door of Harborcourt. It was Saturday, the day before she and Max were to go shopping together for things that would make him happy. And the moment Lucy saw those cars, she knew happiness was the last thing that Max—or she—was going to find that weekend.

She was cleaning in one of the front bedrooms when she looked out the window and saw the cars roll to a stop in the

Coves' wide, circular driveway. For a moment, she was
nearly overcome by the strangest sensation, that she was still
standing in Babs and Barclay Wemberley's house, and that
the previous three weeks had been nothing but a dream, and
that she had a chance now to start all over from the beginning
of this bizarre chapter of her life, and make it all come out
differently. But then she realized where she was, and boy,
was she thankful, because she didn't want the last three
weeks to have been a dream, and she didn't want to start all
over, and she didn't want to make it come out any differently
than it had.

There were, however, she thought as she watched the cars'
doors open and their occupants begin spilling out, a few
things she wouldn't have minded altering a bit. The murder
charge against her, for one thing. That was going to be a trifle
hard to explain to Max. In fact, there were going to be quite a
few things that would be a trifle hard to explain to Max. In
many ways, the murder charge was the least of her worries.
Because at least that one was a mistake. The others,
however . . .

Max! she thought then, frantically. Her mind jolted into
action at the single word. She needed to get to Max before
the authorities did! She needed to give him her version of
things before he heard the more incriminating side. Then she
saw someone climbing out of one of the black sedans who
was infinitely more dangerous and troubling and scary than
any police officer or Future Beautician of Idaho could ever
hope to be. Because as Lucy watched in stark-staring terror,
Francesca Hollander, her mother, emerged from one of the
cars.

And that was when Lucy realized all hope was lost.

How had they found her? she wondered. They must have
tortured poor Phoebe relentlessly, with unspeakable horrors.
They must have strung her up by her thumbs, and then
slipped bamboo shoots under her fingernails, and then
dripped water on her forehead drop by maddening drop. And
then they must have gotten *really* ugly, and forced her to

dress in polyester. And then made her eat tofu. And then made Dave the homicide investigator take off his shoe and show her his six toes. And then made her listen while they told her the Republican party only had the best interests of the American people at heart.

Poor Phoebe, Lucy thought dismally.

Until Phoebe climbed out of the car behind Francesca Hollander, her hair dry and her manicure perfectly intact, a breathable cotton batik shift covering her perfectly untortured body.

Not a good sign.

Max, Lucy thought again. She had to get to Max. She had to try to explain things to him before the authorities—and, worse, her mother—got to him.

She dropped her cleaning equipment and swiped her hands down the front of her worn jeans and Max's gray Ferrari T-shirt—it had been convenient when she'd stepped out of the shower, and it had smelled like him, so she'd slipped it on—then raced through the house at what felt like F1 speeds, out the back door and down the path toward the carriage house. Max was polishing the Gullwing with much affection when she burst through the greenery, his own blue jeans hugging his lean hips, a snug black T-shirt molded to his muscular back. Even though she was frantic and in a hurry, she had to pause for a second to admire him. He was just so . . .

She sighed in spite of herself and marveled again that she had found such a man, and that he could love her the way he did. Then she remembered she might lose him if she didn't try to explain things to him before the cops and beauticians and—gulp—her mother did.

"Max!" she called as she sprinted toward him.

He spun around at the sound of his name and smiled when he saw her, that slow, sexy, secretive smile that made little fires erupt all over her body. "Hiya," he said by way of a greeting. "Couldn't stay away from me for even a whole morning, huh?"

She couldn't help but smile back. "Why should today be

any different? But then, I seem to recall that *you* were the one who came looking for *me* yesterday."

His smile went even sexier and more secretive at that, and he took a few deliberate steps toward her. "Yeah, and who would've thought a linen closet would turn out to be a great place to make love, huh?"

All the panic and terror flowed right out of her when he looked at her the way he did then. Everything would be fine, she assured herself. He couldn't possibly look at her that way unless he truly loved her. And if he truly loved her, he would also forgive her, once she explained it and made him understand why she had been forced to do what she had done. He had to forgive her.

He just had to.

She took a few deliberate steps forward of her own, until the two of them met halfway, standing toe to toe between the Gullwing and the garden path. "It was all those pillows," she said softly, lifting her hands to settle them on his shoulders.

"And the feathers that came out of the pillows," he added as he dropped his own hands to her hips. "We probably shouldn't have been so rough with them."

"Probably not," she agreed a little breathlessly. "But then we never would have found out what an extrasensory sensation feathers provide."

Max dipped his head and captured her mouth with his, treating her to a brief, soft kiss that promised of many more to come. Later. After they'd both quit work for the day and could retire to her apartment, and then fix dinner together, and then drink good wine together and eat good food together, and then watch old movies together, and then make love together. It was the perfect life, Lucy thought again as she returned his kiss. As long as they were together. And she would do whatever she had to do to make sure they stayed that way.

"We have to talk," she said as she pulled reluctantly away. "There's something I need to tell you."

"We can talk about it over dinner tonight," he said. "I can't take a break right now. Justin needs—"

"No, now," Lucy interrupted him. "We need to talk about this *now*. It's really important."

He looked vaguely alarmed at that. "Why? What is it?"

"There's something you need to know about me, Max."

He shook his head, but his worried expression didn't change. "I already know everything I need to know about you."

"No, you don't. There's something else," she said urgently.

He shook his head again, looking more panicked now, and somehow, she knew it was because he believed her about there being something important he needed to know, but he didn't *want* to know whatever it was. "I know you're perfect for me," he said decisively. "And I know you make me happy, and I know I love you. That's all I need to know, Lucy," he added adamantly.

"No, you have to know this, too," she said. She looped both arms around his neck now, suddenly fearful that he would try to pull away from her once he heard the truth. "It's something that will surprise you, and that you're not going to like, but even if you're surprised and you don't like it, you have to let me explain, and after I explain, you have to think about what I said, and after you think about what I said, you have to think some more, and after you think some more, you have to cut me some slack, and after you cut me some slack, you have to remember that I love you and that I would never, ever, do anything to hurt you." She knew she sounded more hysterical with every word she spoke, but she felt hysterical, too, and more scared than she'd ever been in her life.

Then she noticed that Max looked scared, too, and it only compounded her fear.

"Max?" she said. "Do you promise to do that?"

"Lucy . . ." he began.

"Promise me," she demanded.

"But . . ."

"Promise me!"

"I promise," he replied obediently, his eyes widening in clear alarm at her vehemence. "But why . . ."

His voice trailed off before he completed whatever he'd been about to ask, and Lucy realized he wasn't looking at her anymore, but at something over her shoulder. And she knew then that they weren't alone anymore, that someone must have seen her leave the house and followed her, and now any explanation she had planned to give Max was going to be polluted by interpretations other than her own. On the upside, she tried to tell herself optimistically, she wouldn't be a fugitive from justice anymore. On the downside, though, she knew she was going to be a fugitive from something far more important.

But then, how many ways could a woman tell the man she loved that she had a murder charge hanging over her head and that she'd been lying to him since virtually the moment they'd met? It wouldn't be the others polluting interpretations, she told herself. No, she'd done a pretty good job of polluting things all by herself.

"Lucinda Hollander?" a flat, emotionless male voice asked from behind her.

She squeezed her eyes shut tight, thinking that maybe, if she concentrated very, very hard, she could make all of this go away. Hey, concentrating very, very hard worked sometimes when she was trying to read things. Of course, she always ended up getting nauseous and discouraged and miserable when she did that. Then again, she was already nauseous and discouraged and miserable. It was worth a shot.

"Lucinda!" This time it was her mother's voice she heard, something that jacked up the nausea, discouragement, and misery to the next level. There was no way she could concentrate hard enough to make her mother go away. "Lucinda, is that you?" Francesca Hollander asked further. Then, sounding even more panicky than Lucy felt, she added, "What on *earth* have you done to your hair? And why on *earth* are you dressed that way? And who on *earth* is that man? And why on *earth* are you letting him touch you that way?"

Leave it to her mother, Lucy thought, to put it all in perspective. It was one thing for her daughter to be arrested for murder. But it was a far worse thing for her daughter not to be dressed appropriately or properly escorted for the occasion.

Lucy tried to meet Max's gaze, but he was still staring at what she realized now must be an entire group of people behind her. She found some solace in the fact that he hadn't released her, and had in fact, tightened his hold on her hips more possessively. But he still didn't look at her. And that, she thought, couldn't possibly be good.

"Lucy." This time the voice was Phoebe's, and it came from much closer than the others. It came closer still as her friend continued talking, until she was standing by Lucy's side. "It's okay," Phoebe said. "They're not going to arrest you. They promised."

Oh, fine, Lucy thought. *Now* Max returned his attention to her.

"Arrest you?" he echoed in disbelief. "For what? Who the hell are these people? And why are they calling you Lucin . . . ?" His voice trailed off again as he gradually must have digested the fact that he was currently holding on to a liar.

But before Lucy could utter a single word of explanation, she heard more stirrings of movement behind her, and, after a few seconds, felt a large hand clamp down on her shoulder on the side of her that Phoebe hadn't commanded. Even that, though, couldn't make her tear her gaze away from Max's.

Nor could the man's blandly offered, "Lucinda Hollander, you're under arrest for the murder of Georgii Jakov."

"What?" But it wasn't Lucy who uttered the outraged exclamation. It was Phoebe. "You said you *weren't* going to arrest her!"

And without thinking, Lucy said, "I thought his name was George Jacobs."

And that, she knew by the shutters that fell over Max's eyes, was the exact moment she lost him. Because he realized then that, even though he didn't know what the hell was going on, *Lucy* did. And even if he was surprised by the development, *Lucy* wasn't. Therefore, he must have concluded, she knew lots of things he didn't, things she had neglected to—or chosen not to—tell him. Therefore, he must have further concluded, everything between the two of them was just a big, fat lie.

He was wrong, of course. Yes, she had misled him about some things, and yes, she had lied to him. But her love for him was honest, and it was real. In many ways, her love for Max was the only thing she'd ever had in her life that had felt honest or real. How to make him understand that, though . . .

She went wooden as the man standing behind her—whom she still hadn't looked at, and didn't care to—tugged her hands from around Max's neck and pulled them behind her back. She heard the soft click of handcuffs, felt the cool steel wrapped around her wrists, but none of it seemed real. What did feel real, unfortunately, was the vast darkness that spilled through her when Max released her and dropped his own hands to his sides.

"I can explain," she told him miserably. And then, speaking over her shoulder, but still looking at Max, she said, "Please. Give me a chance to explain. Just a few minutes. That's all."

Surprisingly, the man who had handcuffed her released her, but he didn't move away. And as Lucy scrambled for words that might somehow make sense of everything, Phoebe moved closer, and her mother strode forward, until both women flanked her. Lucy waited for her mother to start berating her, then was astonished when, instead, Francesca pulled her awkwardly into her arms. She stroked her hand gently over her daughter's hair, as if Lucy were a small child, and sobbed uncontrollably against her shoulder.

A strange heat splashed through her belly at witnessing her mother's reaction. She told herself her mother was only crying because she was ashamed of the condition in which she'd found her daughter, and was worried about what she would have to say to explain it to all their friends. But then Francesca Hollander said the strangest thing.

"I was so worried about you, Lucinda," she mumbled between sobs. "I was so scared that something terrible had happened to you. And I couldn't bear it if I lost you. Not my baby girl."

Her mother's roughly uttered declaration was the only thing in the world that could have torn Lucy's attention away from Max. She turned her head toward her mother's, saw what appeared to be genuine fear and regret and so much more in the other woman's expression, but had no idea how to react to any of it. Never in her life had her mother said such a thing to her. And only now did she begin to realize that maybe, perhaps, possibly, her mother might honestly care about more than Lucy's performance on a social level. Maybe, perhaps, possibly, her mother might care about *her*. And maybe, perhaps, possibly, she just hadn't ever known how to show it.

"Lucy?" Max said softly, pulling her back to the matter at hand. By now, though, she felt so confused by everything, she was getting a little dizzy. "What's going on?" he asked again.

Lucy turned back to him, but before she could respond to his question, Phoebe started off on one of her indignant tirades.

"What's going on?" she repeated. "I'll tell you what's going on. Dave's going to lose every one of his eleven frigging toes when I get ahold of him." She turned to the man who had slipped the cuffs on Lucy. "Who the hell do you think you are, Efrem Frigging Zimbalist, Jr.? You can't put cuffs on her. She's a frigging Hollander. She comes from one of the oldest, most honorable, *wealthiest*," she added meaningfully, because if there was one thing Phoebe knew, it was that money talked, "families in Rhode Island. Her father could buy the entire frigging FBI. Her ancestors came over on the frigging *Mayflower*. Now are you going to take those frigging cuffs off of her, or will I have to resort to stronger language than 'frigging,' you frigger?"

Lucy heard nothing from the man in response, so assumed he wasn't swayed by her friend's, ah, passionate plea.

So, with a much-put-upon sigh, Phoebe turned back to Lucy. "Are you okay?" she asked. "Man, I can't believe you've been stuck here for three weeks, working as a *housekeeper*. I'm sorry I put you here. I honestly didn't think it would take this long to work things out. Not that they've worked out," she added meaningfully, looking at the man behind Lucy. But then she continued, "Yeesh, I don't know what's worse—being suspected of murder or having to work as a housekeeper. How could you stand it? I mean, I know I run the company and everything, and, hey, some of my best friends are housekeepers—my own mother included—but, really, it amazes me sometimes what my employees—not to mention my own mother—will actually do for a living. It must have been hell for you, living the way you have."

She expelled an unmistakable sound of disgust and gave a visible shudder of distaste. "But it's okay now, Lucy," she added. "Dave promised that all you have to do is talk to these goons, and everything will be fine. They found that moron Archie, and he says you're innocent, but you need to come back so he can prove that. Oh, and God knows why, but he said to be sure and bring that hideous ring he gave you. Actually, he didn't use the word *hideous*, but I mean, how can anyone talk about that hideous ring without using the word *hideous*, you know? It would be like mentioning the word *Archie* without the word *moron*, and that's just not doable, you know?"

When Lucy still said nothing—mostly because she was too busy sending pleading looks to Max, who only continued to gaze at her in silence—Phoebe added, "Where is the hideous ring, anyway? I see you were finally able to remove it. That must have been a load off. Literally."

"It's in my apartment," Lucy answered automatically. "In the carriage house. On the dresser in the bedroom." At her admission, one of the other men headed in that direction.

She was about to say more, but Phoebe continued relentlessly, "So now you can come home, and once all this is settled—and it *will* be settled," she added adamantly, with another meaningful look at the man who still stood behind Lucy, "—then you can return to your normal life. You don't have to live like . . . like . . . like *this*," she said with much repugnance, "anymore. We'll have you back just in time for Sissy Devane's housewarming. Well, mansion-warming, I think is what she's calling it. Not that her house is any bigger than yours, mind you. I know you're not usually up for that stuff, but it'll be a good way to chase away all the bad memories of the last three weeks. I know you can't wait to get back to Newport and forget you ever set foot in this place."

Lucy listened helplessly as Phoebe prattled on, telling herself to stop her friend, but knowing that nothing stopped Phoebe once she got going. Well, nothing short of a good, solid blow to the back of the head, which Lucy couldn't manage with her hands cuffed the way they were, much as she might like to. And knowing, too, that this was all inevitable anyway. Max was bound to find out what kind of life she had lived before this. Maybe he could have learned it with a little more tact, she thought morosely, but he would have drawn the same conclusions if Lucy had explained things her way that he must be drawing after hearing Phoebe's version of things—none of those conclusions being good. Or accurate, for that matter.

He was still gazing at her in silence, but when Phoebe—finally—stopped talking, he said, very softly, "You, uh . . . you don't usually make your living as a housekeeper?"

Lucy shook her head.

"Oh, stop," Phoebe said. "She doesn't have to work to make a living. Her family is worth millions. She does volunteer work for the Junior League to fill her time."

"Phoebe, please," Lucy said.

She threw her friend an entreating look, and only then did Phoebe—finally—seem to understand that Lucy was worried about a lot more than the handcuffs circling her wrists. Phoebe gave Lucy a puzzled look, then turned her attention to Max, who she seemed to—finally—notice was an incredibly handsome man. She looked at Lucy again, then at Max. And when she turned back to Lucy again, she was gaping softly and blushing. Oh, yeah. Phoebe—finally—understood. And that, if nothing else, left her—finally—blissfully silent.

"Your name isn't really Lucy French?" Max asked, pulling her attention back to him again.

"No," she said. "It's Lucy . . . Lucinda . . . Hollander."

"And you're not from Roanoke?"

"No. Rhode Island."

"And you obviously didn't grow up the same way I did." This time, it was a statement, not a question.

"No," she said miserably. "Not in the economic sense, anyway."

He eyed her in thoughtful silence for a moment. Then, very quietly, he said, "You told me you didn't wear white lace for your debut."

"I didn't," she replied just as quietly, feeling sick to her stomach. "I wore white silk."

He nodded at that, but his eyes went bleak. "Good to know there was something you didn't lie about."

"Max, I never meant to lie to you," she said. "I had no choice. Things just got really—"

"So I guess then we really were just playing the Chauffeur and the Heiress all along, weren't we?" he interjected before she had a chance to even begin explaining.

"Oh, Max," she said.

"Or was it the Murderess and the Chauffeur?" he asked coolly.

She managed to scrape up a little indignance at that. Not much. But some. "You know better," she said. "We weren't playing either of those things. It wasn't like what you're thinking at all."

He nodded dispassionately. "Yeah, I guess you're right. I guess what we were really playing was the Fugitive from Justice and the Schmuck Who Loved Her."

Lucy closed her eyes at hearing him use the past tense so easily where his feelings for her were concerned. Did love really dry up that quickly? It didn't seem possible. Because her love for Max, she was sure, would never go away, no matter how he might feel about her.

"When did you plan to tell me the truth?" he asked, his voice harsh now. "Hell, did you *ever* plan to tell me the truth?"

"I was trying to just now," she said.

"Yeah, because the cops were hot on your trail."

"I would have told you."

"Would you?" he demanded. "And even if you had, and even if you weren't wanted on a *murder charge*, for God's sake—" Here, he punctuated the comment with a strangled chuckle. "—how long would it have been before you got tired of all this and wanted to go home?"

"I am home," she responded immediately.

He shut his eyes tight. "No. You're not," he said. "You're not home, and you're not . . ." He opened his eyes again and fixed his gaze on hers. "You're not who I thought you were."

"Yes, I am," she countered, tears stinging her eyes. "Max, I—"

"No," he countered right back. "You're not."

"Max, please . . ." she tried again.

"Go," he said, taking a step backward. Then he laughed miserably at his own remark. "As if you have a choice," he added.

He lifted a hand and covered his eyes, rubbing his forehead hard. And then, without another word, without another glance, he spun around and began to walk back toward the carriage house.

"Max?" Lucy said, as two men approached her now and took her mother's and Phoebe's places on each side of her. One gripped her left arm and one gripped her right, and together, they began to walk her backward, in the opposite direction. "Max!" she called again.

But he only continued on his way, not looking back once.

WWDD? Lucy asked herself as she watched him go. Oh, well, that was another easy one. First, Dino would fix a drink. Then he'd fix another. And another. And another and another and another. Then he'd call Sinatra and the boys, but she was sure they wouldn't be home to answer. Then he'd be carted off to jail. And then he'd slur out a rousing rendition of "Please Don't Talk About Me When I'm Gone."

Oh, God, Max . . .

"I'll call you," she called out lamely. "We really do need to talk."

But she was pretty sure Max didn't hear what she said. He was much too busy walking out of her life.

Boy, he really was a schmuck.

As Max lay on his bed, staring at the ceiling, balancing an exceptionally bad, warm beer on his belly, he called himself every version of fool he could think of. Imbecile. Ignoramus. Blockhead. Bonehead. Nitwit. Dimwit. Half-wit. Twit. Oh, yeah. He could be here all night telling himself how stupid he'd been. And hey, since talking to Sylvie a week ago, he'd remembered a lot of his Italian, and some French, too. He could call himself an idiot in three languages now. Ignorant dolt. *Sciocco ignaro. Cancre idiot.* He was just getting warmed up.

Of course things would turn out this way, he thought as he watched the setting sun stretch long rays of orange and yellow and pink over the whitewashed walls of his bedroom. How could he have been foolish enough to think that things with Lucy would go well? How could he have begun to think that maybe he'd done enough penance for all his past sins, and that maybe he'd finally earned a shot at happiness, and that maybe Lucy French was his reward for having lived so long with so little? How could he have been stupid enough to think she was his salvation, when all she really was was just a new kind of torture for him to endure? And this time, *this* time, his life really would be unbearable to live. Because this time, *this* time, he would know what his life was missing. He would know what it took to make him happy. And he'd know what it felt like to have that ripped from him for good.

He'd know that, because he had, in fact, been happy this past week with Lucy, however briefly. This past week with her had been the greatest week of his life. Hell, even the two weeks before that, when he'd been so certain he couldn't have her, had been better than anything he'd known before, just by having her around, torturing him. But now . . .

Now he knew the sweet, pretty little housekeeper he'd come to love wasn't who he thought she was at all. At worst, she was a cold-hearted murderess. At best, she was a wealthy, glamorous heiress who came from a world Max had sworn he would never visit again, a world in which he absolutely did not belong. Either way, she wasn't the woman he thought she was. Either way, she wasn't a woman for him.

Obviously, he *hadn't* completed his penance for all his past sins. Obviously, his penance had just begun. Obviously, he didn't deserve to be happy after all. Because no matter how things worked out, whether Lucy was guilty of the crime she'd been charged with or not—though, truly, Max knew she couldn't possibly have murdered anyone—there was no way Lucinda Hollander could ever be a part of his life, or he a part of hers. And Lucy French didn't exist at all.

Yep, he was a schmuck all right. A schmuck who loved a fugitive from justice. He wondered if maybe Jerry Springer had a place for him on his freak show. Because, at the moment, Max sure didn't feel like he belonged anywhere else.

Chapter 18

"**O**h, my, you are a lovely creature, aren't you?"

Still dressed in the denim jumper and white T-shirt and sandals she'd donned to take Abby to the park that morning, Rosemary stroked the muzzle of the newest member of Justin Cove's stables. And every time she ran her fingertips over the animal's soft nose, she battled—without much success—the wave of turmoil that washed through her. Mr. Cove's new mare was indeed a beauty. The horse towered over her, its chestnut coat gleaming, its black mane glossy, its dark eyes bright and intelligent. She could certainly understand why he had made a wager to win the beast, whatever the cost. She just wished he had been decent enough to have wagered something besides his daughter's nanny.

Rosemary had thought about quitting her job without notice last Saturday, after the terms of that wager had been brought to light. But she had dismissed the idea outright. She could no more abandon Abby than she could her own child. So stay, she would, even with the awkwardness of the situation. The elder Coves weren't exactly lovable people to begin with, so it wasn't like she would be losing anything with regard to her relationship to them. They had never commanded her respect or loyalty—that was all given over to Abby. So Rosemary had decided to continue on as she had since coming to work for them and simply do her best to avoid them when she could.

She wished she could avoid thoughts of Nathaniel as easily. Unfortunately, the last week had been filled with memories of him and the time they had spent together. And of her feelings for him. As much as she had tried, she'd found it impossible to hate him. Certainly she was disappointed that he had turned out to be the way he was, but deep inside, she had been suspicious all along, so perhaps she wasn't quite so devastated as she might have been.

She expelled a sound of derision at that and fought back the sting of tears that erupted. Oh, she was devastated all right, she knew. And *disappointed* didn't begin to cover the way she felt. She had trusted him. She had admired him. She had halfway fallen in love with him. More than halfway, she made herself admit. And she had thought he cared for her, too. Never in her life had she been so wrong about so many things.

The horse had been delivered early that morning, on a crisp, blue Saturday, exactly one week to the day after Justin Cove had lost his bet with Nathaniel, and Rosemary had lost so much more. Now it was late afternoon, and surprisingly quiet at the house. Alexis had taken Abby to see a specialist in dyslexia, and for the first time in her life, the little girl hadn't balked at going. Discovering that Miss Lucy suffered from the same condition she did herself—and knowing she wasn't alone in the way she had difficulty learning to read—had brought a huge change in Abby's behavior. She had spent hours tagging after the housekeeper, asking her questions about her own childhood, and learning more about herself. Lucy had forged a bond with the child like none anyone else had managed to make. She reached Abby on a level even Rosemary hadn't been able to reach. And Rosemary loved Lucy even more for it.

And speaking of Lucy, Rosemary wondered where she was. Normally, she worked on Saturdays. But Rosemary hadn't seen a sign of her since returning from the park with Abby just as Alexis was returning from the hairdresser. Abby had literally climbed from one car to the other, and Alexis had driven off again, with barely enough time to make their appointment. Max, too, Rosemary thought, seemed to be making himself scarce today.

She smiled. Well, of course they'd be making themselves scarce, she thought, with both of their employers gone. She knew then exactly where the two lovebirds were. They were where they'd been every time they'd had a free moment together this week. Rosemary just hoped they'd found a place more accommodating than the linen closet this time. She was still finding stray feathers in the hallway.

Then she remembered how she might have had the opportunity to scatter some feathers of her own with Nathaniel, and her smile fell. How long would it take, she wondered, before every thought that entered her head stopped leading to memories of him? She sighed with much feeling when she realized she was still standing in Mr. Cove's stable, still stroking his new horse's velvety muzzle, still thinking about Nathaniel and how she wished things—he—had turned out differently.

"She's gorgeous, isn't she?"

When she first heard his voice, Rosemary was sure she must have imagined it, since she had just been thinking about him, and missing him, and wishing . . . Well. Wishing for what could never be. But when she heard the soft rustle of straw behind her, she turned slowly around, only to find that, no, she hadn't imagined his voice at all. Nathaniel Finn was standing right there, in a slice of dusty, late-afternoon sunlight that slashed through the door behind him.

Somehow, he looked even more handsome than she recalled, dressed for the warm Saturday afternoon in a pair of faded Levi's and a navy blue polo that hugged his biceps in a most loving fashion. Before she could halt the memory, Rosemary recalled pressing her fingers hard into those biceps as he entered her with such commanding depth, and it was all she could do not to squeeze her eyes shut in an effort to banish the image completely. Because part of her didn't want to banish the image. Part of her knew images like that would probably carry her through for some time. Until she met another man who could send her heart racing the way Nathaniel Finn had.

And that would surely happen sometime within this millennium, she told herself. She must just be patient for a few hundred years or so.

She opened her mouth to tell him he wasn't welcome here, then remembered that "here" didn't belong to her, so she really had no right to ask him to leave. All she could do was turn her back on him, and say softly, "Mr. Cove was called out of town yesterday and won't be back until Tuesday. You might want to try back then."

"I'd rather try right now," Nathaniel countered immediately. "Especially since it's not Justin I came to see."

A spray of heat lashed her belly at his statement, and she cursed herself for being so eager to think the best of him. "Why would you want to see me?" she asked without turning to look at him.

He emitted a single, unhappy chuckle in response. "What a question," he said morosely. "There are so many reasons, I don't know where to begin." But then, as if he knew exactly where to begin, he said, "Because I miss you." And when he said it, that spray of heat that had splashed through Rosemary's midsection became a stream of indolent warmth that wound through her entire body. "And because I owe you an apology," he continued. "Not that an apology will ever make up for what I did to you," he hastened to add. "And because I've felt empty inside all week without you. And because I want to try and explain. And because I can't stop thinking about you. And because my life suddenly feels pointless. And because there's nothing that means more to me than you. And because . . . because I love you, Rosemary."

She whipped around at that, fixing him with an incredulous look.

"Any of those sound like reasons you might want to hear?" he asked. He was smiling when he said it, but she could see he was completely uncertain about what his reception might be.

Good, she thought. He had no right to feel certain about anything. Especially when she felt anything but certain herself.

"Maybe," she conceded reluctantly. "I suppose I might listen to an explanation or an apology. Not that I'll necessarily accept either," she quickly tacked on when she saw him start to look hopeful. Why should he feel hopeful after dashing every last one of hers?

He took a few indecisive steps forward, halting when he was just within arm's length of her. To be on the safe side— and maybe to show him he was nowhere near forgiven— Rosemary took a step backward. Doing so made her bump her fanny into the stall door of the big horse she'd just been admiring, something that must have startled the mare a bit, because she whinnied softly and moved away. Rosemary didn't blame her. She felt like whinnying and moving away, too. Someplace she could try and work out what her feelings for Nathaniel were.

But he clearly had no intention of allowing her such a luxury, because he claimed another step forward, bringing himself within arm's length again. This time, Rosemary had nowhere to go to escape him. Strangely, though, she realized escape wasn't really on her mind.

"I'm sorry," he said simply. Up close this way, she saw that his green eyes were troubled, and smudged beneath by faint purple crescents. Obviously she wasn't the only one who'd been having difficulty sleeping. "I know that's hardly an apology for what I did, but, Rosemary, I am sorry," he added, his voice pleading.

She dipped her head forward imperiously. "All right. That's the apology," she said. "Now let's hear the explanation."

He expelled another one of those joyless chuckles and shook his head. "I wish I could give you one that made sense," he said. "I've spent the last week trying to figure it out myself, and I just . . ."

He sighed heavily, took another experimental step forward, but didn't reach for her. Somehow, Rosemary got the impression that his reason for doing so was simply because he wanted to be close to her, and not because he was trying to prevent her from leaving. So she didn't withdraw from him, only waited to see what he would say next.

"I never should have gone along with Justin's wager," he said.

"No," she agreed, "you shouldn't. A gentleman . . . any *decent* man," she hastily corrected herself, "never would have."

"I wasn't a decent man then," he told her readily. Then he smiled sadly. "I was the Bad Boy of the Thoroughbred Racing Set. Anybody would have said so. Anybody but you," he added softly.

And then, because he couldn't seem to tolerate not being able to touch her, he lifted a hand gingerly toward her face. He paused to see if she would pull away, and when she didn't, he moved his hand forward again, tracing his fingertips lightly along her cheek. Rosemary closed her eyes when he did it, and tried not to think about the night she had told him he wasn't a bad man. But the memories tumbled through her head one by one, and she remembered all too well.

"You told me I wasn't bad," he reminded her quietly. "And you know, that night, I actually believed you. Because that night, I wasn't. The whole time I was with you, Rosemary, I wasn't a bad man. I couldn't be. Not if a woman like you could care for me."

She opened her eyes at that, wanting to believe him, too wary, though, to give herself over. She'd been wrong about him once, she reminded herself. Hadn't she? She couldn't risk being wrong again.

"You did care about me, didn't you?" he asked, his voice sounding uncertain again.

Unable to help herself, she nodded, something that made his fingers go tripping along her cheek again, stirring hot little fires in their wake. He released a long, unsteady breath when she confirmed his suspicions, as if he hadn't, until that moment, been sure of them.

"And do you still?" he asked. "Care about me, I mean?"

Once more, Rosemary couldn't make herself lie. She nodded silently again.

"I care about you, too," he said.

He started to add more, and she feared he would tell her he loved her again, and she wasn't ready to hear it. Hearing it before she believed it would only make it that much harder for her to accept. He seemed to realize that, so he went back to trying to explain.

"I wasn't thinking the night I made the bet with Justin. And, truth be told, even if I had thought about it, I wouldn't have cared about how it affected anyone but me. Hell, I never did any thinking or caring back then." Then he laughed nervously. "It sounds like I'm talking about a long time ago, when it was really only a few weeks."

He turned his hand now, feeling bolder, she supposed, and grazed her cheekbone with the backs of his knuckles. Her eyes fluttered closed as a sweet sensation of wanting pooled in her belly.

"But that's just the point, Rosemary," he continued, his voice softer now, gentler. "It *was* a long time ago. It was before I met you. And meeting you changed everything."

She opened her eyes now, meeting his gaze, noting how his eyes were filled at once with both fear and yearning. "How could meeting me change anything?" she asked skeptically.

"Because meeting you changed me," he said. "The way I started to feel about you . . . I'd never felt that way about anyone before. And once I started feeling that way . . ." He lifted one shoulder and let it drop. "I felt different about myself. Before you came along, nothing seemed important to me. After you came along . . ."

"After that?" she prodded when his voice trailed off.

He smiled, and for the first time, he honestly seemed to feel a bit of happiness. "After you," he said, "nothing still seemed important. Nothing except you. And you . . . You became everything to me."

She told herself not to hope, not to believe a word he said. Somehow, though, she knew he was telling the truth. And maybe she knew that, because, in a way, meeting him had changed her, too.

"You were right last week when you said I don't value anything I have. I can't think of a single thing in my life that, if I lost it, I would feel badly about. Except you. The thought of losing you, Rosemary . . ." He took another step forward, lifting his other hand, framing her face in both hands. "I just can't imagine my life without you, that's all," he told her. "I can imagine it without anything else. But not you."

She felt herself swaying toward him, and quickly jerked herself back, far enough to escape his touch, because it was muzzying up her thinking, and keeping her from being as outraged and angry as she knew she should be.

"That's easy for a man to say when he's just pocketed four million dollars the easy way," she told him.

He shook his head adamantly. "There was nothing easy about that four million dollars," he said. "It's caused me more suffering than I ever thought I could know. And I didn't pocket it," he told her.

She narrowed her eyes at him suspiciously. "You let Mr. Cove keep the money and the horse?" she asked dubiously.

"Hell, no, I didn't let him keep the money," Nathaniel said. "I took the winnings that were due me."

Her heart began to sink again. "If you didn't pocket it," she said, "then what did you do with it?"

At first, she didn't think he was going to tell her, and that made her feel sadder still. Then, seeming embarrassed by what he had done, he said, "I divvied it up among all the Catholic churches in Derry."

Rosemary's mouth dropped open at that. "You gave away four million dollars?" she asked incredulously. "To churches?"

He nodded, still looking a bit self-conscious, as if he were uncomfortable about having been so big-hearted. "The money had no value to me," he said matter-of-factly. "On the contrary, it resulted in the biggest loss of my life, and the most terrible feeling of emptiness I've ever known. But I figured it would probably have a lot of value to some of the people where you come from, you know? That maybe it could help ease some of their losses or something."

She shook her head mutely, having no idea what to say. Obviously having no qualms now about taking advantage of her current state of confusion, Nathaniel took another step forward. This time, he seemed a bit less uncertain about what he was doing when he cupped his hands over her shoulders. But he still didn't have enough confidence to pull her close.

"There is nothing . . . and no one . . . I care about more than you, Rosemary," he said. "I'd give away everything I own if it would win you back. Because no matter how much I have, without you, it's worthless. I'm going to feel destitute without you. I love you," he said again, more adamantly this time, tightening his hold on her shoulders as if he needed a physical illustration to punctuate his avowal. "I've never loved any woman, but I do love you. And I'll do whatever I have to do to get you back. Whatever you tell me to do, I'll do it. I just . . ." He sounded almost desperate now when he added, "You have to believe me when I tell you I love you. That my life means nothing if you're not in it. That I want to be with you. Forever."

That sweep of heat went crashing through Rosemary again, and she met his gaze levelly with her own. "Did you really give all that money to the Catholic churches in Derry?" she asked.

He nodded, then moved a hand slowly to the back of her neck, halting his fingers at the hair she had coiled at her nape.

"If I call your accountant, he'll verify that?" she asked further.

"She can show you the cancelled checks when they come

back," he said, moving his other hand down her arm, around her shoulders, daring to pull her close.

"And you really love me?" she asked further still.

"I really do," he confirmed in the softest, gentlest voice she had ever heard him use, splaying his hand open over the small of her back, cupping his other hand lightly over her nape.

"And you really can't imagine your life without me?" she said.

"I really can't."

"You want to be with me forever?"

"I do."

She smiled at the words. "Why, Mr. Finn," she said, "that almost sounds like a marriage proposal."

"Almost?" he echoed. "Then I must not be doing it right." He dipped his head to hers, brushing a soft kiss over her cheek, then pulled back enough to meet her gaze. "Rosemary Shaugnessy," he said, "will you marry me?"

Her eyes went wide at the question. She honestly hadn't thought he would ask her. Not yet. Not until they'd worked everything out. Clearly, he had every intention of working them out, whatever it took. So now the question was, Did she?

Well, that was one question. The other one was, "Will I . . . what?"

He smiled with great assurance, his confidence seeming to have suddenly returned. "Marry me," he said again, this time making it a mandate instead of a question.

Rosemary narrowed her eyes playfully. "Don't be thinking you can order me around now, Mr. High-and-Mighty Finn, just because I'm to be Mrs. High-and-Mighty Finn."

Only when she said that did she realize he hadn't been confident of her reply at all. Because when he heard what she said, his smile went brilliant enough to make the sun look dark and to warm all the places inside her that had been so cold. Oh, yes, she thought. The High-and-Mighty Finns definitely had a bright future ahead of them. Provided Mr. Finn got a few things straight right now.

"And just because I'm to be Mrs. High-and-Mighty Finn," she said imperiously, "don't think I'll be quitting my job, because I won't. Abby needs me, and I intend to be there for her as long as she does. I love her like my own, you know."

"So that doesn't mean you're opposed to having a few of your own?" he asked hopefully.

She smiled, blushing a bit. "No. I'm not opposed to that."

"So then," he said, "I can assume that means I'll at least have you on the weekends?"

Her smile grew broader as her blush deepened. "When you can *have* me, Mr. Finn, depends," she said.

He narrowed his eyes suspiciously. "On what?"

Rosemary lifted her head confidently. "Just remember that you still have a lot to answer for, man," she told him. "It's going to be a good, long while before I've forgiven you for what you did. I see much groveling in your future."

"I'll start right away," he vowed. "Just as soon as I've kissed you within an inch of your life."

And before she could sputter a response to that, he did.

It wasn't until suppertime that Rosemary discovered what had happened at Harborcourt earlier in the day, and heard about how Lucy French, housekeeper, had turned out to be Lucinda Hollander, heiress. Or, perhaps, Lucinda Hollander, murderess, as Alexis Cove had insisted just before voicing her horror that they had housed a killer in their home. Rosemary, of course, took exception, even if she kept it to herself. For one thing, Lucy hadn't stayed in the house proper, so Alexis hadn't exactly housed her there. For another thing, Alexis Cove ought to worry more about the morals and convictions of other people she had housed at Harborcourt, starting with herself and Mr. Cove. For yet another thing, there was no way Rosemary would ever believe that Lucy could have killed anyone. She was much too kind and caring.

The heiress part, however, well . . . That part, of course,

Rosemary believed. There had, after all, been that conversation the two women had shared where Lucy herself had revealed that her family was wealthy. Rosemary had assumed she had simply estranged herself from her loved ones, for whatever reason she might have. And recalling some of the wealthy families Rosemary had known in her time, and the way they had behaved toward one another, she could think of a few reasons why one might want to estrange oneself from them. She had understood why Lucy might want to embark upon a new life, and she had known that Lucy was happy enough at Harborcourt not to want to return home.

However.

Now that Rosemary understood that Lucy's reason for embarking on her new life was because she had been wanted for murder, well . . .

Actually, that changed nothing as far as Rosemary was concerned. The murder charge was ridiculous. And she was confident Lucy would be proven innocent of any such malarkey. And once Lucy was proven innocent of such malarkey, then she would return to Harborcourt. This, Rosemary knew. Lucy had friends here. In a way, Lucy even had family here. She had Max, and she had Rosemary, and she had bonded with Abby in a way that would never allow her to abandon the little girl. Lucy French might be many things—not the least of which was Lucinda Hollander, a totally different person from the one she had claimed to be—but she wasn't one to turn her back on those who cared about her. Lucy would come back to Harborcourt. Rosemary had no doubt of that.

Still, Abby and Max probably wouldn't be quite so philosophical about this new development as Rosemary was. Abby would have trouble because she was only an eight-year-old, and Max would have trouble because he was a man, and therefore the equivalent of an eight-year-old. Abby, however, would eventually come around, once Rosemary explained things to her and promised that Lucy would be back. Max, though, wouldn't be quite so easily convinced. Men, fragile creatures that they were, could never be philosophical when it came to things like murder charges and lies and abandonment. So, after supper, Rosemary put together a plate of food and made her way to the carriage house.

She wasn't surprised when Max didn't answer her first knock. Or her second. Or her third. Or her fourth, fifth, or sixth. Which was why she then began to kick at the door after that, and shout out, "Max, you idiot, answer the damned door!" until he complied with her request. And when he did finally answer the door, he looked wretched and unhappy, which surprised Rosemary not at all.

"Whattayawant?" he growled when he saw her.

"I've brought you your supper," she told him calmly.

"Don't want it," he said, and began to close the door again.

"Don't be daft," she replied, sticking her foot easily between the door and the jamb. "Of course you don't want it, you silly git. It was only an excuse for me to come up here, anyway. I want to talk to you."

He narrowed his eyes at her, gave the door another half-hearted shove against her foot, then sighed with a much-put-upon effect and pulled it open. Rosemary smiled benevolently as she strode past him, heading straight for his kitchen, where she put his supper into the fridge. Then she returned to the living room, where Max had slumped into a blob on the sofa. He still wore the blue jeans and black T-shirt she had seen him in earlier that day, but both looked exceedingly rumpled and the worse for wear. Much like Max, she couldn't help thinking.

"I'm only going to say this once," she told him, positioning herself before him, crossing her arms over her midsection in a way that she hoped indicated she would brook no nonsense from him. "Are you listening, Max?" she asked further. "It's very important that you hear what I'm going to say to you."

He glanced up at her begrudgingly. "What?" he asked petulantly. "Are you going to stand there and tell me I've got it all wrong? That I've misunderstood everything? That should give Lucy a chance to explain? That I should forgive her for lying to me since the first second I met her? That I'm being unfair to her?"

Rosemary shook her head. "No. I'm not going to tell you that. I'm going to tell you something else. Are you listening?"

"Yeah," he muttered.

"Fine," she said. "Then here it is. A week ago, I found out that a man I fell in love with had sex with me because someone else wagered with him, on a horse, no less, that he couldn't. A horse, Max. Someone bet this man that I loved *a horse* that he couldn't bed me within a month's time. And the man did. Bed me, I mean. For a horse. A horse, Max," she said again, just in case he missed that part.

His mouth dropped open, as if he couldn't quite believe what she was saying. "Some guy seduced you in exchange for a horse?"

"Essentially, yes. It was actually for a good deal on a horse, but it was a horse, nonetheless."

"A horse?" he repeated again, more incredulously.

"A horse," she confirmed.

"Well, that sucks," he said with much understatement.

"Yes, it was appalling," Rosemary agreed.

"You must want to kill the guy."

"I did when I first found out what he had done," she told him. "Yes, of course, I did."

"So . . . what did you really do?" he asked when she didn't elaborate.

She expelled a philosophical sigh, met Max's gaze levelly, and said, "Well, to make a long story short, when I saw him this morning, I told him I'd marry him."

Max blinked several times in rapid succession, then said, "Huh?"

"I told this man who bedded me in exchange for a good deal on a horse—a horse, Max—that I loved him and would be his wife."

He was still gaping as he responded, "Uh . . ."

"I told him that, Max," Rosemary continued matter-of-factly, "because, after I talked to him this morning, I realized that I had it all wrong. That I'd misunderstood everything. That I should have given him a chance to explain things last week, before I concluded for myself that he was a despicable human being." She let those observations sink in for a moment before continuing, "And I realized that I should forgive him for lying to me since the first second I met him, since everything—*everything*—changed between him and me from that first moment to the last."

She dropped her hands to her sides and took a few steps forward, seating herself on the sofa beside Max. He was still pretty much a blob at that point, but he seemed to be listening to her, which was all Rosemary could ask of him for the moment. So, knowing she had his attention, however befuddled he might be, she continued.

"I realized this morning that, even though this man I love had done a terrible thing, he deserved my forgiveness, and that I would have been unfair to him by not giving it." She paused for another moment before concluding, "And I realized something else, too. That I should have known from the outset, that he was a decent man all along. Otherwise, I never would have responded to him in the first place."

Max turned to look at her, as if only now considering the possibility and significance of such a thing. His expression didn't seem quite as hard as it had before, and there was something in his eyes that made her think he was mulling over what she said. What conclusions he might draw, however, remained to be seen.

"Sometimes, Max," she continued a little more softly, "people do things they know they shouldn't, and then realize what they're doing is wrong. But they don't know how to go back and start over again, or they don't have the opportunity. Sometimes, they need—and deserve—a second chance. And sometimes they need a little help getting it."

His expression changed again at that, to one she couldn't decipher. But she told herself not to be troubled. Max was a decent man, too.

"Lucy will come back to Harborcourt," she said. "She'll come back for a lot of reasons, but mostly she'll come back because she loves you. She told me herself that you were important to her, and I got the feeling from my conversations with her that there hasn't been much in her life that she's considered important. She spent two days trying to find Sylvie for you, Max, because she knew you deserved to be happy. But she needs to know she's important to you, too. She needs to know she is a part of that happiness, or she won't even try."

At this, his expression went slack, something Rosemary took to be a very good sign.

"Don't blow this, Max," she said softly. "Yes, you made a mistake once, and a bad thing happened as a result. But something good came out of that bad thing, at least for Sylvie. Now it's your turn to find something good. It's been five years," she added. "It's time to get on with your life. Don't let your stupid self-pity get in the way of what you know, deep down, you deserve. Don't be such a coward."

At her last words, Max's eyes narrowed, sparking with something akin to anger. Good, Rosemary thought. Anger was better than self-pity and cowardice. It was more active. Max needed to be active now. He needed to take charge. It was long past due.

So, having said her piece, and feeling confident of his response, even if he hadn't said a word in reply to anything she'd said, Rosemary stood and made her way out of his apartment. She'd done what she'd come to do, had said what she'd needed to say. Max was smart enough to connect the rest of the dots by himself. She only hoped he would also be brave enough to do the right thing.

Max sputtered inwardly as he watched Rosemary leave, a good, self-righteous anger brewing just beneath his surface. He told himself to demand that she march right back into his apartment, so he could counter every eloquent word she had just spoken. Because as eloquent as her words had been, he thought, they were also complete hooey. All that stuff about a bet on a horse and having sex with some guy and getting married—what the hell was that all about? Had she been drinking? And who the hell did she think she was, calling him a coward? Telling him he should give Lucy an opportunity to explain? That Lucy deserved a second chance? Hell, none of that made any sense. Rosemary didn't know what the hell she was talking about.

Ah, hell.

As the door clicked shut behind her and he didn't do any of those things, Max pushed himself off the sofa and began to pace the room. He needed another bad, warm beer, to dull the edges of the cold misery that was still seeping into him— deep. But a bad, warm beer wouldn't come close to keeping the misery at bay. What he needed was something *really* bad. Something that would make him feel *really* miserable. Something that would *really* punish him. Something that would *really* allow him to . . . to . . . to . . .

. . . to wallow in his self-pity and cowardice for the rest of his life.

He stopped short as the thought unfolded in his head, then fell back against the sofa with a heartfelt "Oof." Was that really what he was doing? he asked himself, Rosemary's final words still circling in his head. Yeah, he'd known he'd been punishing himself and making himself miserable for the last five years—that was exactly what he had set out to do, because he'd felt like he needed to make himself pay for what he had done to Sylvie. But had there maybe been more to it than that? he wondered now. Had he really been driven as much by self-pity as anything else? By a fear of moving on with his life? In which case he really was a lame excuse for a human being, because his loss had been far less than Sylvie's had, and look how she'd turned her life around. She'd had to overcome infinitely more obstacles than Max had, and she'd done it with tremendous success.

Oh, man . . .

He replayed in his brain everything Rosemary had said to

him and was forced to admit that much of it—well, some of it, anyway . . . a little—made sense. Maybe his efforts to punish himself for what had happened to Sylvie had been mixed with a fear of racing—of living—again. Maybe that had played at least a small part in why he hadn't wanted to return to that lifestyle again. And maybe giving away everything he owned, in addition to being a penance, had been a reluctance to be responsible for anything, or anyone, again. Maybe while trying to castigate himself for his former excessive lifestyle, he had swung too far the other way and had become just as excessive at living an ascetic lifestyle. Maybe in trying to make restitution for the way he had lived his past life and the way he had hurt Sylvie, he had been hiding from life and trying to hurt himself instead.

And maybe by giving up on Lucy so quickly, he had been ensuring that he stayed hidden and hurt forever. His twisted subconscious had somehow reached the twisted conclusion that by pushing her away, he wouldn't have to risk losing her. Because before, losing someone he cared about had been unbearable to Max. Maybe, deep down, he was just too scared to face a risk like that again. So, he'd sabotaged his relationship with Lucy before it became too important to him.

Which was nuts, he told himself, because Lucy became important to him the moment he met her, and now he'd lost her because he'd been too stupid to realize what was going on.

Ultimately, though, ironically, it wasn't Rosemary's long, compelling speech that made Max rethink his convictions about his relationship with Lucy. No, ultimately, it was two little words he had spoken himself that made him do that. At one point, he recalled, Lucy had said what she needed to tell him would surprise him, and that he wouldn't like it, but that he had to let her explain. She had said he would have to think about what she told him, and then he would have to think some more, and then he would have to cut her some slack. And she had said he would have to remember that she loved him and she would never, ever do anything to hurt him. And after she said all that, she had told him to promise her he would do all those things. And what was it that Max had said in response?

I promise.

He had promised to think about what she said and cut her some slack and remember she loved him. And really, he did remember how much she loved him. It was probably one of the reasons he'd had so much trouble dealing with everything that had happened. Because he knew she loved him. And he couldn't understand why she would love him and still find it necessary to keep secrets from him, especially since she knew he loved her, too.

Didn't she? Didn't she know that he loved her, too?

His thoughts halted right there. Lucy must know he loved her. He had told her often enough. It had been easy to tell her he loved her, because he knew she loved him, too. And he knew that because . . .

Because she had shown him how much she loved him, he realized now. She had shown it by hunting down Sylvie and urging her to call Max and tell him how she'd rebuilt her life. In doing that, Lucy had shown him how much she cared for him. How much she loved him. And he, in turn, had shown her how much he loved her by . . . by . . . by . . .

Okay, so maybe he hadn't done anything to *show* her how much he loved her, but she must know, right? He had *told* her. Several times. Then he remembered that first night when the two of them had almost made love. He recalled what she had said about her mother. About how her mother had never noticed or cared when she was embarrassed or uncomfortable. He remembered other things she had told him over the course of the past week, as they spent more time together. About her dyslexia and how her family had refused to acknowledge it, instead preferring to think she was slow and lazy. About how her mother and father both placed more importance on superficialities than they did on what was inside a person.

And after learning what he had of Lucy's family today, it didn't take a genius to conclude that they would never show much affection to a child they considered an imperfection. Although Lucy had never spelled it out, Max had definitely gotten the impression over the last few weeks that her family had never much placed a great deal of importance on her, or shown her a great deal of love.

Maybe, he thought now, no one in Lucy's life had ever really shown her how much they cared for her. So maybe she had a little trouble believing it when someone *said* they loved her.

Man, bad, warm beer sure did make a person philosophical.

Maybe he had been too quick to make assumptions about Lucy—and himself—that afternoon, he thought as he wandered mindlessly toward his bedroom. Maybe he should have remembered a few things about her—and himself—before jumping to conclusions the way he had. Maybe he had been, you know, unfair to her. Maybe he should have given her a better chance to explain. Though, handcuffed and surrounded by G-men and her family as she had been, her explanation probably wouldn't have been the best one she could offer anyway.

So maybe he should *do* something, he told himself. Maybe he shouldn't wait for her to come back to Harborcourt. Maybe he should go find her instead. Show her how much he cared about her. How much he loved her.

He had opened his closet door, pulled down his tattered weekender, and unzipped it before he even realized what he was planning to do. The good thing about living the life of an ascetic, he thought as he went to his dresser and tugged open the top drawer, was that it was really easy for one to pack for a trip. The bad thing about living the life of an ascetic was having absolutely no money, even if one knew the nuns in Rome always found a good use for one's paychecks.

As Max stuffed the only three pairs of socks he owned into

his bag and reached back into the drawer for his other two pairs of briefs, he congratulated himself for having done all of his laundry the day before—it did, after all, require only one load. And he wondered if maybe Rosemary would float him a loan for a plane ticket to Rhode Island . . .

Chapter 19

By the Tuesday evening following her arrest, Lucy had been restored to the bosom of her loving family, reinstated to her rightful place at the Hollander homestead, returned to her job driving copies of *In the Kitchen with Bitsy and Friends* to various viable receptacles, and relieved of all charges against her. In other words, her life had reverted to exactly what it had been before the Archie fiasco.

In other words, Lucy was miserable. Funny how the whole time she had been living a lie, her life had felt more honest and genuine than it had ever felt when she'd been living the truth. Or maybe, she thought, that wasn't so funny after all. Maybe that just, you know, sucked.

Still, she had to concede, for the first time in weeks, she was free to do as she pleased and not worry about being found out. As luck—or some other strange and mysterious force with absolutely no sense of humor—would have it, Archie had turned out to be a genius at designing miniature technology. He was still a moron, though, as evidenced by his decision to sell said miniature technology to the highest bidder, instead of turning it over to his employers—the United States government—as he had sworn an oath to do when hired to design it. In fact, he had exceeded his moronic potential by deciding to sell it not just to the highest bidder, but to *any*one who made a halfway decent offer, even though he told all bidders that he was giving them an exclusive, and even though he sold the technology to some bidders for less than he sold it to others. Not surprisingly, in the long run, he had sold it to the wrong people—lots of them—and they had all taken exception when the exclusive arrangement he'd promised them turned out to be not so exclusive after all.

One group that had been particularly offended had sent a man to, oh, hammer home a message to Archie—quite literally, seeing as how the man had been a hired assassin who came armed with a ball peen hammer he had planned to use on Archie's moronic head. Just in case the hammer failed, however, the assassin—street name: Georgie Jakes—had also brought along a Saturday night special. And a boning knife. And arsenic. And a brick. Archie, however, illustrating a surprising lack of moronity for such a moron, had somehow sensed danger—probably because of all the death threats he'd been receiving on a regular basis—and had armed himself with a MAC-10 pistol. Which, it turned out, had come in handy when Georgie showed up at his house.

Long story short, Archie hadn't been killed, Georgie had, though at the time of Georgie's discovery, the police hadn't known the particulars of the situation. Upon arresting that moron Archie, and hearing his version of things, and checking them out, they had been forced to conclude that his biggest crime might very well be Failure to Have a Functioning Brain. It had helped considerably that Archie had kept tapes of the death threats against him, as well as a video of the altercation at his home—in addition to being an exceptional moron and a technological genius, he was also a colossal paranoid who had long ago installed security cameras in his apartment.

He hadn't kept the evidence on himself, however—he had turned it over to Lucy for safekeeping because, at that point, he hadn't trusted anyone, not even the cops. But Archie, through his technological genius—if not his exceptional moronity—had created a way to "shrink" such information onto a tiny computer microchip. So he had "shrunk" the evidence he had to exonerate himself and had ingeniously hidden it inside the most hideous engagement ring known to mankind. And then he had stuck the ring—literally—on Lucy's finger.

Without realizing it, she had been wearing the evidence that would have proved her innocence all along. Or at least she had been wearing that evidence up until the night she had made love with Max.

Which brought her thoughts full circle, something that wasn't exactly surprising, seeing as how she couldn't seem to think about anything without her thoughts eventually returning to memories of Max. And, inevitably, whenever her thoughts returned to memories of Max, she began to rehearse what she would say to him when she saw him again. Because she would see him again—that was something she had promised herself. She just wasn't sure when that meeting would take place, or under what circumstances, or whether or not Max would listen to her when she tried again to explain, or whether he would accept her explanation once he heard it, or whether he would still care about her even if he accepted that explanation.

Not that any of that mattered at the moment—well, not to anyone but Lucy—because she had other things to worry her right now. For some reason, her mother had thought it would be a good idea to throw an impromptu cocktail party to celebrate Lucy's safe return—not to mention the dropping of all charges against her—and had invited virtually everyone in Newport to attend the festivities. At the moment, the Hollander estate was overflowing with all the people Lucy least wanted to see, so she had done the only thing she could do. She had dressed in a sleeveless, petal pink silk sheath that would have done Jackie Kennedy proud, and had accessorized it with elbow-length white gloves and her grandmother's pearl necklace and earrings. Then she had made her way to the sweeping staircase that led down to the massive Hollander foyer and onward to the massive Hollander ballroom . . .

. . . and then she had immediately spun back around and

retreated to her bedroom, had locked the door, and had hidden herself away in the big walk-in closet that, when she was a child, she used to pretend was a spaceship that was carrying her to the farthest reaches of the universe, away from her family, her house, her school, her teachers, and her classmates, and all the other places she felt unwelcome.

When she was a child, this closet had been the only place Lucy felt safe and untroubled. Now, though, even hiding in her closet didn't bring her peace of mind. There was only one place in the universe now where she would feel safe and untroubled—wherever Max Hogan happened to be. And since there was little chance he'd turn up in Newport, it was a good bet she wouldn't ever feel as if she belonged here again. Not that she'd ever really felt as if she'd belonged here before anyway. The only place she'd ever felt she belonged was . . . sigh . . . with Max.

No sooner had the thought materialized than she heard a strange sound erupt on the other side of the closet door. She listened intently, to see if the sound would come again, and after a few seconds, it did. But she still couldn't discern what it was. So she exited the closet, moving to the center of her room, and waited for the sound to happen again.

There. From the window. A quick, rasping rattle.

She turned in that direction and saw that it was now dark outside. But the stately lighting amid the stately landscaping of the stately Hollander estate gave the impression of a stately aura of twilight. Lucy strode to the window to look outside, halting when she remembered that the last two times she'd looked out of windows that way, her life had taken a sudden, jolting side route. Then again, maybe another sudden, jolting side route was exactly what she needed. Because she certainly didn't want to stay on this road any longer than she had to.

Besides, she reminded herself, her bedroom overlooked her mother's prize rosebushes, and not the front drive, so there was little chance she'd see any vehicles of the law enforcement or Future Beautician persuasion pulling up to threaten her lifestyle.

More was the pity.

With a resolved sigh and a final step forward, she braved a look into the garden below. It took a moment for her eyes to adjust to the darkness, even with the stately lighting in the stately landscaping shining stately up at her, but she saw right away that there were no cars down there, thank goodness. Sort of. But what could have made the rasping sound? she wondered. Because the only thing she saw down in the garden that was out of the ordinary was—

Oh. Max.

Max Hogan was standing down there, right in the middle of her mother's American Beauties, which, of course, had faded for the season. Max, however, wasn't faded at all. Somehow, he seemed even more stately than the lighting that bathed him. He had one hand rubbing his opposite elbow where, evidently, he had been jabbed by a thorn, and the other hand fisted around something that she soon learned was handful of pebbles. She learned that because, before he saw her gazing down at him, Max straightened and hurled them at her window.

Lucy started at the spray of stones hitting glass, instinctively taking a step back from the window when they made contact. But she immediately moved back into place, throwing open the window to allow in the cool night breeze, the heavy, luscious scent of late-blooming peonies and the warmth of Max's smile.

"Hiya," he said when he saw her gazing down at him, in that sweet, seductive way he had of saying it.

Although he could be saying it in a completely different way, and she only heard it as sweet and seductive because she loved him so much. He could probably speak to her in a Mickey Mouse voice and it would make her melt into a puddle of ruined womanhood at his feet.

"Hi," she called softly down to him.

For a moment, neither of them said anything more, as if it were enough simply to be looking at each other again. And for Lucy, for now, that was almost enough. Just seeing Max here meant a wealth of things she wasn't quite ready to consider. She only wanted to look at him for a few moments, marveling at how well he filled out a pair of faded blue jeans and a black T-shirt. She had, of course, kept the Ferrari T-shirt of his that she had been wearing when she was arrested, and, like a lovesick fool—because she *was* a lovesick fool—had slept embracing it every night. It was soft and warm like Max, and it smelled like Max, and it was the closest thing to having Max with her. But now he was with her, or would be, as soon as she got him inside.

And suddenly, even though he was closer to her than he had been in days—though, truly, it felt like years had passed since she'd last seen him—he seemed much too far away.

"Don't you want to come in?" she asked.

"I got stopped at the door by a tiny woman with white hair and a mean disposition. She told me I wasn't dressed for the occasion, then closed the door in my face."

Lucy smiled. "That's Mrs. Bloom, our housekeeper. She's pretty hard-core about dress codes."

"Tell me about it," Max said. Then, out of nowhere, he added, "You look pretty, Lucy."

She felt heat creep into her cheeks at both the words he spoke and the way he spoke them. And also at the warm look that came over his face when he did. "Thanks," she said softly. Then, "Hang on a sec."

She raced from her room and up the hall, to her parents' bedroom, jerking open their closet and pulling out the first suit and shirt she came to on her father's side. Then she tugged a tie from the rack and grabbed a pair of shoes and went hurtling back down to her own room.

"Think fast," she said as she tossed the garments out the window.

But Max didn't think as fast as she thought he would, and

the clothes cascaded down over him. She wasn't sure, but she thought he got beaned by a Gucci loafer in the process.

"Sorry about that," she said.

"No problem," he assured her, rubbing his forehead. Oops.

He changed his clothes right there in the garden, his gaze leaving Lucy's only when he had to pull his T-shirt over his head. He didn't even look down to button his shirt or knot his tie, which meant that, all in all, once he finished dressing, he looked . . . well . . . like a man who had no idea how to wear a suit, quite frankly. Her father was two sizes larger than Max, and she hadn't exactly matched up tie to shirt to jacket color. She'd been in a hurry—so sue her. Nevertheless, she smiled as she absorbed the sight of him. And she hoped he never changed.

"You look wonderful," she said. "Go around to the front door and try again. If Mrs. Bloom won't let you in, I'll fire her."

Without awaiting a response, Lucy raced from her room again. This time, though, she ran in the opposite direction, toward the stairs and down to the front door. She arrived just as Mrs. Bloom did, then had to wrestle the housekeeper for possession, but eventually won—she did, after all, have love on her side . . . well, love and youth and a mean half nelson she'd learned from Emory when they were kids. Then she tugged open the door to find Max on the other side. He looked even more rumpled and mismatched—and wonderful—up close, and immediately, she reached for him, pulling him inside. Then, holding tightly to his hand, she began leading him quickly through the house.

She had planned to usher him up the stairs to her bedroom—well, duh, where else would she take him?—but saw her sister Antoinetta coming down, so hastily sidetracked to the music room. Unfortunately, it was occupied by a trio of music lovers who had congregated around the baby grand piano, so Lucy continued onward, still pulling Max behind her, through the conservatory—it had attracted a group from her mother's African Violet Club—and into the library, which, she was delighted to discover, was empty.

It was a room Lucy had always avoided while growing up, as it had filled her with discomfort. The books had never been friendly to her, and she, in turn, had felt nothing but animosity toward them. With Max, though, the room didn't feel quite so menacing. No, in fact, the room suddenly felt full of wonderful possibilities.

She closed the door behind them, leaning back against it as if that would keep out whatever marauding hordes were after them. The only light in the room spilled from a milk glass torchière in the far corner, an arcane, ethereal sort of glow that warmed and softened all the crooks and crannies and corners of the room. All around them, from floor to ceiling, were row upon row of books, a collection generations in the making. The furniture was fashioned of leather and studs and hulking mahogany, all of it sturdy and masculine and fine. Max fit right in.

"So," Lucy began nervously. She was out of breath, but she figured that had less to do with their harried hike through the house than it did Max's simple presence there. And then she realized exactly what was going on. For the first time in days, they were alone together, but there was so much cluttering up things between them that she didn't know where to begin. Although she had rehearsed in her head a million times what she would say and do when she returned to Glenview, she had no idea what to say or do now that Max had come looking for her.

He, however, didn't seem to have the same problem, because the moment she spoke, he did something. And what he did was something only a man who knew exactly what he wanted, by golly, would do. With a single step forward, he closed what little distance lay between them, bracing his forearms against the door on each side of her and leaning in close.

Then, very softly, he said once again, "Hiya."

Lucy flattened her palms against his chest, savoring the warmth and hardness of his body beneath the fabric of the garments that hindered her touch. More than anything in the world, she wanted to push from his body the clothes he had just donned and have her way with him on the library sofa. Although the sofa was a good ten feet away from them, she realized. So maybe she would just have her way with him right here against the door.

For now, however, she only replied, as softly as he had, "Hi."

"You look beautiful," he told her, moving his body closer still, until it was flush with hers and her heart was pounding against his, pushing heat throughout her body. "Real classy," he murmured before dipping his head to hers for a much too quick, much too light, kiss.

She wasn't sure if that was a good thing or not—the comment or the too-quick kiss—and all she could manage in response was an anxiously offered "Oh?"

He seemed to sense her misgivings, because he hastened to clarify, "I didn't mean it like that. I didn't mean you looked . . . you know . . . like you're out of my league."

"I'm not out of your league," she said quickly.

"I know that," he replied just as promptly. "It's just . . ." He inhaled a deep breath and released it slowly, letting his gaze wander now over their surroundings. "I mean, look at this place, Lucy. Look at the house where you grew up. The apartments I lived in with my mom weren't even as big as this room, and that couch over there alone probably cost more than she made in any given year."

Lucy couldn't deny it. That couch over there was over two hundred years old and its detail work had been carved by one of the finest craftsmen in Austria at the time.

"You and I couldn't have grown up in more different worlds," he said, returning his attention to her. "On the outside, we probably don't have a single thing in common."

Oh, Lucy really wasn't liking the route he was taking with this conversation. But she was helpless to say a word in contradiction.

"But," he began again, and a little flicker of something

warm and hopeful sputtered to life inside her, "there's something about you, Lucy, something on your inside, that makes me feel like we're two of a kind. No, more than that," he amended, his voice softening even more. He moved one hand to her hair, weaving his fingers through the chin-length tresses. "It's like we're two halves of one whole that got separated somewhere and then found ourselves again, against all odds."

Her heart hammered hard to hear him say what she had felt herself since the moment they'd met. Somehow, on some level, she had connected with Max that day, though she didn't think she'd ever be able to describe exactly what it was that had passed between the two of them. Not love at first sight, because she did believe you had to know something of a person before you could truly love them, but . . . connection at first sight. She couldn't think of any other way to describe it. Something in her *had* connected to something in him that day, and a flow of something undefinable and irresistible had been switched on in the process. And whatever it was, it was strong enough, and infinite enough, to light the entire world—their world—for the rest of eternity.

"This is a beautiful house," she agreed, skimming her fingertips lightly over his rough jaw. "And it has everything most people would ever need or want to be happy. But I've never been comfortable here, Max. Never. Not until this moment. And that's only because you're here."

He smiled in response to her confession, lifting his other hand now to thread his fingers through her hair.

"But if we left right now," she added, tracing his mouth with the pad of her index finger and marveling at the way his eyes went hot and insistent at her touch, "if we went someplace else, I'd be contented there, too. As long as you're with me. You're all I need to be happy, Max."

He studied her face for a long time in silence, then, very slowly, he nodded. "Yeah, me, too," he finally said. "I guess maybe it just took me longer to realize that than you did. It's been a long time, Lucy, since I let myself be happy. And even though I did my best not to let you get to me, you made me happy anyway. I figured you were my reward, you know? For living the way I had for so long."

"You *figured* that?" she said, apprehension inching its way up her spine. "Past tense?"

"No, present tense," he quickly corrected himself. Then he smiled again. "And better yet, future tense. You made me happy the last three weeks, Lucy. You make me happy in this moment. And I can't see there ever being a time when you're not still making me happy, as long as you're right there with me."

"I'll be right there with you," she vowed.

"I'm sorry about what happened Saturday," he said soberly.

"Yeah, me, too. It's no fun getting arrested. Especially for something you didn't do."

He shook his head. "No, I . . . I mean, I'm sorry you got arrested, yes, but I'm mostly sorry for the way I acted. I shouldn't have jumped to conclusions the way I did. I should have let you explain."

"What made you change your mind?" she asked.

He grinned a little sheepishly. "A certain redhead of the Irish persuasion who is named after a spice gave me a real talking-to."

"Actually," Lucy said, "I think rosemary is an herb."

"Not this Rosemary," Max assured her.

She chuckled at that. "Yeah, I guess I see what you mean."

He hesitated a moment, gazing into her eyes as if he couldn't quite believe she was real, then asked, "Did you know she's getting married?"

"Rosemary?" Lucy asked, surprised. "To whom? That nice Mr. Finn?"

"Hey, that nice Mr. Finn wasn't so nice to her," Max said.

"What did he do?"

Max shook his head. "I'm still not sure. Something about a horse. But it sounded pretty terrible. Appalling," he quickly corrected himself. "Rosemary said it was 'appalling.' "

"But she's still going to marry him?" Lucy asked, puzzled.

Max nodded. "She said he deserved a second chance. Seems Rosemary is big on second chances." He moved his hand to Lucy's face, brushing the backs of his knuckles lightly over her cheekbone, stirring little fires throughout her body as he did. "Sounds like a good idea to me, so whattaya say?" he asked. "You up for a second chance?"

She nodded enthusiastically. "Oh, yes. I'd love a second chance with you, Max."

He looked confused for a moment, then shook his head. "No, I meant would *you* give *me* a second chance with you?"

She smiled, a slow, thoughtful smile. Now they were getting somewhere. They could both do with a second chance.

"Only on one condition," she said.

He looked vaguely concerned. "What condition?"

"That you give yourself a second chance, too."

His concern vanished at that, to be replaced by what looked very much like contentment. "Deal," he said.

But Lucy knew it wasn't going to be quite as easy as it sounded. Both of them had some work to do when it came to "repairing" themselves. But that was okay. They had a long time to do that. A lifetime, in fact, if things were progressing the way she thought they were progressing. And she was pretty sure they were.

"So," she said, "do you want to meet my parents before or after you ravish me on that sofa over there that cost more than your mother made in probably ten given years?"

He arched his eyebrows in astonishment at that. But it wasn't the value of the sofa, she learned, that surprised him. "Am I going to ravish you on that sofa over there?" he asked.

"Oh, come on," she said, "don't tell me you haven't been thinking about it since the minute you noticed it."

"Hell, yes, I've been thinking about it," he said. "But I didn't think you were."

She rolled her eyes. "Well, what *else* was I supposed to be thinking about?"

He leaned in closer, arcing one arm over her head, crowd

ing her back against the door, and the heat and press of his body against hers sent a barrage of excitement rushing through her. "You were supposed to be thinking about how much you love me," he said, the roughness of his voice telling her he was no less affected by their closeness than she was. "The way I've been thinking about how much I love you."

"Oh, I've been thinking about that, too," she assured him, looping her arms around his neck, burying the fingers of one hand in the silky hair at his nape. "And not just since seeing the sofa over there, either."

He brushed his lips lightly over her cheek, her jaw, and along her throat, making her murmur with agitated delight before he pulled back again. "Oh, since seeing me outside your window, huh?"

She opened her mouth to tell him that she'd been thinking about it long before that, too, but instead asked, "How did you know that was my window, by the way?"

He grinned. "Easy. It was by far the cleanest one on the whole house. You always did a bang-up job on the windows at Harborcourt. I'm sure Alexis hasn't found anyone who could come close."

"Meaning my job is still open?" Lucy asked.

He looked surprised. "Do you still want it?"

She thought about that for a moment. "Well . . . maybe not that job exactly. Though I do have one or two things I intend to tell Alexis Cove when I go back."

Which was true. Max wasn't the only person Lucy had thought about since returning to Newport. She'd also thought a lot about little Abby Cove. And her mother. And how Lucy still wanted five minutes alone with Alexis. But instead of a blunt object this time—the last thing she needed was another murder charge against her, after all—Lucy would use some blunt talk. Although she'd never quite figured out over the past few days what she would say to Max upon her return to Glenview, she knew *exactly* what she intended to tell Mrs. Cove:

*You know, Mrs. Cove, I can't stop you from being the way
you are with Abby. But I can tell you this. I grew up with a
mother who was just like you. She was selfish and mean, and
she never showed an ounce of concern for my feelings. I
hated my mother when I was a little girl, Mrs. Cove. And I
hardly spoke to her when I became an adult. I would have
rather been with anyone—anyone—than be with my own
mother. And I hope when I have kids, I'm nothing like she
was when I was a child. But someday, she's going to be old
and tired and sick and lonely, and she's going to want me to
be there for her. And you know what? I haven't decided yet if
I'm going to be.*

Though, in truth, the strained relationship Lucy had always had with her mother hadn't felt quite so strained in the
days since her return. There had been moments when she'd
actually caught her mother gazing at her with a sad sort of
longing, as if there were things she wanted to say to her
daughter, but just didn't know how to go about it. Lucy understood the feeling. She knew she had a long way to go with
her mother, too, before things would be agreeable between
them, but for the first time in her life, she also felt as if maybe
the gap between her and Francesca might not be quite so un-
bridgeable as she'd always thought.

There was no reason to tell that part to Alexis Cove, however, Lucy thought. Let the other woman sweat for a while,
wondering if her behavior toward her daughter might leave
the elder Coves miserable and alone in their dotage.

"So you're gonna take on ol' Alexis, huh?" Max asked,
bringing Lucy's attention back to the present.

She nodded. "Oh, yeah. Which is another reason I
shouldn't pin my hopes on getting my job back there."

"But you are coming back?" he asked. And somehow, in
spite of everything they'd said, he still sounded fearful of her
response.

"Of course I'm coming back," she said.

"Even without a job?"

She smiled. "Who needs a job when I have you?"

Although that certainly seemed to please him, he replied a little nervously. "Ah. Well. You know. I don't, um . . . I don't have any, uh . . . What I mean is . . ." He inhaled a deep breath and released it slowly. "I'm not exactly coming to you with a dowry," he finally said.

Lucy chuckled. As if a dowry, even for trillions of dollars, would make him any more valuable than he already was. "That's okay," she told him. "I have a trust fund."

He sighed again, though this time it was with more contentment. "And why did I not see this coming from a mile away?" he asked.

Lucy shrugged and wove her fingers behind his neck. "Between the two of us," she said, "I'm sure we could find *some* use for the money."

"You sound like you already have an idea."

"Oh, I have lots of ideas," she said.

He looked vaguely concerned again. "So then . . . what do you plan to do exactly?" he asked.

"Exactly?" she echoed.

He nodded.

She grinned. Then she pulled his head down to hers and placed her mouth next to his ear, and began to whisper all the things she intended to do—exactly—the vast majority of them erotic in nature. By the time she finished, she could see quite plainly that Max was thinking the sofa over there was looking pretty good. And also the desk. And the oriental rug before the fireplace. And the coffee table. And the statue of *The Thinker*.

"You know, most of those things you just mentioned," he said as she concluded her list, "don't have anything to do with spending money."

"Well, not in a loving, respectful, ongoing, monogamous, legal relationship," she agreed.

"Like, say, marriage?" he asked.

"That would be a good one, yes," she told him. "Why? You know someone who might be interested?"

"In marriage, or in all those things you just said?"

"Both."

He smiled again, though this time it was with a significant amount of lasciviousness and intent, something that made Lucy feel all warm and gooey and naked and sweaty inside.

"Yeah, maybe," he said.

"What a coincidence," she told him, tightening her hold around his neck. "I know someone who might be interested in both of them, too."

Max dropped his hands to her hips and pulled her close, moving his hands to her backside, and curving his fingers possessively over her bottom to press her more intimately against him. A rush of heat raced through her when she felt him ripen against her belly, and she palmed the back of his head in preparation of kissing him for a good, long time.

Before she had the chance to begin, though, he said, "So you, uh . . . you say you wouldn't mind if I met your parents *after* I ravish you on the sofa?"

She shook her head.

"You don't think your dad might be put off when he sees how I'm dressed? Once I get dressed again, I mean."

"On the contrary," Lucy assured him, "he'll marvel at the fact that your taste is identical to his own." She just wouldn't comment, she decided, on the fact that her father never wore those clothes in that particular combination. Different strokes for different folks, that was all.

"Well, then," Max decided, "I see no reason for us not to . . . you know . . . get on with it."

Lucy grinned in response to that. "No," she said, "there's no reason at all why we can't get on with it."

And as she pushed herself up on tiptoe, he lowered his mouth to hers, meeting her halfway at getting on with the rest of their lives.

 **Epilogue**

The only thing Lucy hated more than Mondays were *cold* Mondays, and January in Kentucky, she had learned many years ago, was often even colder than January in Rhode Island. And the only thing that could make a cold Monday worse than it already was was when the minivan was making a funny clunking noise, and it was full of screaming kids who were already late to school.

Oh, yeah, she thought then. She also hated Monday because it was her car pool day. And even if all the currently screaming kids in the minivan were her own, she still didn't like it.

"Max," she called as she pushed open the back door of the big Victorian they had bought in the Highlands seven years ago, three years after marrying, and right before the birth of Sophie, their first, "the van is making a funny noise again." Their twins, Tucker and Tanner, were making a funny noise, too, but she figured that was nothing to be alarmed about. Five-year-olds were always doing that kind of thing.

Max was draining the last of his coffee as she entered, and he settled the empty cup in the sink before striding toward her. He was wearing the oil-stained coveralls he wore to work every day—Hogan's Import Service was *the* place for foreign car owners to bring their cars for maintenance, and he always made sure to go in early, because he never wanted to stay late, family man that he was—and he shrugged his winter coat on over them as he bent to give Lucy a kiss on the cheek.

"Look, Monday is your day off, so why don't you let me drive the kids to school today, and you go back to bed, all right?"

Lucy smiled. She wondered if he ever thought about the fact that he had once made his living driving a Ferrari race car at triple-digit speeds and now he cruised around town in a Chevy minivan? Probably a day didn't go by when he didn't think about that. What was so nice, though, was that he enjoyed driving the minivan more than he ever had the race car. Well, she conceded, he enjoyed the lifestyle personified by the minivan more than he ever had the lifestyle personified by the race car. Besides, he still tooled around town in his little Spyder on the weekends when he needed time to himself.

"You promise to keep it under a hundred?" she asked as she held out her keys to the minivan.

"Yes, dear."

"Okay," she said as she dropped the keys into his palm.

"As long as the kids are in the car," he immediately amended.

"Hah," she said, unconcerned. "As if the van would even *go* a hundred. Even if it wasn't eighteen degrees outside. And even if it wasn't making a clunking sound."

He smiled a knowing smile. "I forgot to tell you. I've been doing some tinkering under the hood."

She narrowed her eyes at him. "Max . . ."

"Just a little engine rebuilding, that's all."

"What did you do?"

"I added a few more horsepower."

"How many horses?"

He shrugged negligently. "Two or three hundred. Hence the clunking sound. It'll calm down soon, I promise. It's just acclimating."

"Max!"

"I'm kidding," he said, chuckling before bending forward to give her a quick kiss. "The clunking noise is nothing. It's weather-related, perfectly safe to drive. I'll take care of it today, and it'll be fine for when you go back to work tomorrow. I promise."

That was good enough for Lucy. One thing about Max. He always kept his promises.

"What's for dinner tonight?" he asked as he made his way to the back door.

"Oh, the usual," she said. "Good food. Good wine."

"Good conversation," he added with a smile, "good company."

"That, too," she agreed. Then she smiled seductively and strode toward him, pulling him close because that one little kiss, although delightful, hadn't been nearly enough to send either of them off on their day. "And then, later," she promised after laying a couple of really good ones on him, "we'll have some good fun."

"I hope it's not good, *clean* fun," he said.

She shook her head. "Nope. What I have planned couldn't even be remotely described as clean."

"Excellent."

Even if keeping things clean was what Lucy did for a living. She was, after all, the regional representative for the southeastern division of Dust Bunnies, Inc. The tutor the Coves had hired for Abby had helped Lucy enormously, too. Although she still wasn't a champion reader by any stretch of the imagination, she functioned very well with her job.

"Don't forget, though," she said, "this weekend, we're keeping all the little Finns. Rosemary and Nathaniel and the Coves are driving to Nashville with Abby to check out Vanderbilt."

"I haven't forgotten," Max said. "But, man, I can't believe she's starting college next year. It doesn't seem like any time since she was a little kid having trouble at school."

"Luckily," Lucy said with a smile, "she got help."

"Just like you," he replied, smiling back.

"Yeah, I'm lucky, too," Lucy agreed with much feeling. But not just because of the reading help, she knew.

Max tugged her close again, for a long, soulful kiss, pulling away only when the horn of a minivan began honking incessantly. Sophie, Lucy thought, was just way too knowledgeable about—and interested in—automotive machinery for a seven-year-old. She was going to be hell on wheels someday, just like her old man. Lucy frequently envisioned the headlines on *Velocity* magazine that were going to appear twenty years from now: *Sophie Hogan, First Female Winner of the European Grand Prix, a Chip Off the Old Block!*

"Happy?" she asked Max, pushing the thought away for now.

"Very happy," he told her.

"Yeah, me too."

And that, Lucy knew, was the only thing that mattered.

Who needs Buffy?

We've got adventurous women right here at Avon Books!

Yes, here at Avon we have heroines who would make Buffy think twice before going out at night . . . women who make Scarlett O'Hara look like someone who'd faint dead away at the sight of Rhett Butler. But, unlike Scarlett, Avon heroines know a good man when they see one . . . and they know how to treat him right. And, unlike Buffy, the guys they meet are *extremely* hot-blooded!

Meet the heroines of the Avon Romance Superleaders . . . and the men who are their matches!

Following are sneak peeks from four upcoming Avon Romance Superleaders. Some of these women are modern-day heroines . . . others face a world outwardly different, but actually much the same, as our own. For it doesn't matter if you're a Regency miss on the run from a bad match . . . or a contemporary woman looking for a happy life . . . these are gals who face life head-on—and who find love when they least expect it!

In January you'll get to gaze at. . . .

The Ring on Her Finger
by Elizabeth Bevarly

Lucinda Hollander was attending a big society blast with a dull-but-good-enough man one minute—the next, she's jumping out a ballroom window. Suddenly, this heiress is on the lam from the cops for a crime she didn't commit. So she "hides out" on a country estate, masquerading as a housekeeper . . . and finding herself attracted to a mysterious man named Max who everyone calls "the car guy . . ."

'I don't think anything got broken," Lucy said as she hastened back over to where Max still sat on the floor, his arms hooked loosely over his denim-clad knees.

"Just my heart," he said under his breath.

"What?" she asked as she stooped to clean up—keeping her legs clamped together and turned to the side, he couldn't help noticing.

"Nothing," Max said, more loudly this time. "It was nothing." He knelt and began to scoop up what he could of the mess, trying to nudge Lucy aside. "I'll do that," he told her. "It's my mess."

"That's all right," she assured him, nudging him back. "I'm the housekeeper, remember? This is my job."

"But you've got something else to—"

"It's okay," she interrupted him. "I'll take care of this. Go ahead and heat up what's left of dinner. I'm sure you're hungry."

Understatement of the century, Max thought. But he conceded to her wishes. Mostly, though, he'd only conceded to her wishes because he hadn't wanted to get into a nudging match with her. Two nudges and a collision with a woman were about all his deprived libido could stand these days. As it was, he probably wouldn't sleep a wink tonight, because he'd be too busy replaying those nudges and that collision over and over again. He was getting hot already just thinking about the replaying.

Oh, yeah. He had a full night ahead.

In February . . .

See Jane Score
by Rachel Gibson

Jane Alcott has no hesitations when she's assigned to cover the Seattle Chinooks hockey team—and tail their ace player Luc Martineau in particular. After all, she knows she's good for more than just writing a Single in the City column—and entering a men's locker room shouldn't be any problem for a fearless gal like her. But while she might not be intimidated by lockerroom antics, she's a little taken aback by Luc's definite . . . attributes.

"Are you escorting me to my room?"

"Yep."

She thought of the first morning when he'd carried her briefcase, then told her that he wasn't trying to be nice. "Are you trying to be nice this time?"

"No, I'm meeting the guys in a few and I don't want to have to wonder if you made it to your room without passing out on the way."

"And that would ruin your fun?"

"No, but for a few seconds it might take my attention off Candy Peeks and her naughty cheerleader routine. Candy's worked real hard on her pom-poms, and it would a shame if I couldn't give her my undivided attention."

"A stripper?"

"They prefer to be called dancers."

"Ahh."

He squeezed her arm. "Are you going to print that in the paper?"

"No, I don't care about your personal life." She pulled her plastic room key from her pocket. Luc took it from her and opened the door before she could object.

"Good, because I'm yanking your chain. I'm really meeting the guys at a sports bar that's not too far away."

She looked up into the shadows of his face created by her darkened room. She didn't know which story to believe. "Why the BS?"

"To see that little wrinkle between your brows."

She shook her head as he handed her the key.

"See ya, Ace," he said and turned away.

Jane watched the back of his head and his wide shoulders as he walked down the hall. "See ya tomorrow night, Martineau."

He stopped and looked back over his shoulder. "Are you planning on going into the locker room?"

"Of course. I'm a sports reporter and it's part of my job. Just as if I were a man."

"But you're not a man."

"I expect to be treated like a man."

"Then take my advice and keep your gaze up," he said as he turned once more and walked away. "That way you won't blush and your jaw won't hit the floor like a woman."

In March you'll be . . .

Getting Lucky
by Susan Andersen

Lily Morrisette felt anything but lucky when Zach came striding into her life—she wants respect . . . and Zach's not giving any to her. But amid a dangerous nest of secrets, Zach and Lily are pulled closer together than either thought possible, making them wonder if their meeting was better luck than either had ever dreamed.

"Who are you?" he demanded, swinging an olive-drab duffle bag off his shoulder and down to the tiled floor. "And what are you doing in my kitchen? Where's my sister?"

His eyes were a clear, pale gray, the irises ringed in charcoal. Intense and unflinching, they narrowed between thick, dark lashes to rake over her, taking in her thin cotton, peppermint ice cream–colored drawstring pajama bottoms and tank top. The scrutiny served to remind Lily of every one of the extra ten pounds she could never seem to shed, no matter what. She set her glass down on the countertop with a sharp click, but refrained from responding in kind to his rudeness.

"You must be Zach." She stepped forward, extending her hand to Glynnis's brother. "She's away right now, but I'm Lily—Lily Morrisette. I've heard a lot about you since I started renting a room here."

"The hell you say," he growled, ignoring her proffered hand. His voice was so deep she could practically feel its vibration through the soles of her feet, the way she always registered the bass thumping from the car of the teenage boy who lived down the block whenever he drove past. It was also nearly as frigid as those iceberg eyes of his when he continued, "Glynnis has always been a sucker for every con artist with a sad story to tell, but I didn't think she'd go so far as to actually install one in our house while I was gone."

"Excuse me?"

"I hope you got whatever you were angling for while the opportunity was ripe, lady." His gaze was so scornful it took all Lily's starch not to recoil. "But don't let that shapely little ass get too comfortable, because the free ride is officially over. Go pack your bags."

He thought her bottom was shapely? And *little*? Then she gave herself a sharp mental shake. Good God, what was the *matter* with her? His opinion of her butt was hardly the point. Straightening her shoulders, she tipped up her chin. "No," she said firmly, and crossed her arms over her breasts.

"What?" He went very still, as if no one ever contradicted him.

Perhaps no one ever did, Lily surmised, recalling that he was some hotshot Marine who specialized in reconnaissance missions. Then his mouth went hard, and part of her attention got distracted by the thin white scar that bisected his upper lip.

Funny the difference a few minutes and an insulting attitude could make. What she undoubtedly would have considered sexy as all get-out a moment ago struck her now as vaguely sinister. *Pretty is as pretty does*, Grandma Nell would've said, and for the first time Lily understood on a bone-deep, fundamental level exactly what her grandmother had meant. This guy's behavior wasn't pretty at all, and she refused to be the first to flinch in the strange game of chicken they played.

"What part of the word don't you understand?" she inquired sweetly.

In April experience . . .

Love With the Proper Husband
by Victoria Alexander

When Gwendolyn Townsend is left penniless and without prospects, she takes matters into her own hands and sets off to be a governess. So imagine her shock when this independent lady is told she has an inheritance after all . . . if she agrees to marry Marcus Holcroft, Earl of Pennington. Gwendolyn's not so certain she wants to marry at all—until Marcus manages to persuade her otherwise . . .

"Good Lord, it's you!" Gwen stared in disbelief. This was Lord Pennington? The arrogant, sarcastic and admittedly somewhat handsome man on the stairs was Lord Pennington? Her Lord Pennington?

Not that she had given him a second thought, of course.

Besides, at the moment, he appeared more insane than attractive.

"Why are you looking at me like that?" she said cautiously, wondering if it was too late to retreat to the corridor. "And why are you grinning like a lunatic?"

"It is only that I feel quite mad with relief." He strode to her, took her hand and raised it to his lips. His gaze never left hers. It was most disconcerting. "It is a true pleasure to meet you at last, Miss Townsend."

"Is it?" She pulled her hand away. "Why?"

"Why?" He raised a brow. "I should think that would be obvious."

She shook her head. "Apparently not."

"Forgive me." The earl's forehead furrowed. "I assumed Mr. Whiting had informed you as to our connection."

"He told me of an arrangement between our fathers," she said slowly.

"Excellent." He nodded and the grin returned to his face. It was somewhat crooked and if his dark hair were a bit ruffled instead of perfectly in place, he would look more like a mischievous schoolboy than a gentleman of nearly thirty. She suspected it could be quite engaging under other circumstances. This, however, was not one of them.

"Then we can proceed with the arrangements at once. I will secure a special license and we can be wed by the end of the week."

Shock stole her voice and for a moment she could do nothing but stare. The man was indeed every bit as arrogant as she'd thought at their first meeting and far more high-handed than she'd ever expected. She had no intention of marrying any man, let alone this one. And even if she were interested in marriage, she would much prefer to be asked rather than issued a command.

"Miss Townsend?"

"I fear you have me at a disadvantage, my lord." She fixed him with a steady stare, the kind she'd perfected to intimidate children even if it had never especially worked. "I cannot be certain from your words, but is this a proposal of marriage?"

"A proposal?" Confusion colored his face, then his expression cleared. "Of course. How could I have been so thoughtless? You would expect that. Any woman would, regardless of the circumstances. I simply assumed . . . Well, it scarcely matters now, I suppose, but I do apologize. Allow me to start over."

He took her hands in his and looked slightly ill at ease. "I suppose I didn't think of it because, well, I am not especially polished at this sort of thing. I have never been in this position before. This is my first offer of marriage."

"How delightful to know you do not suggest marriage to every stranger you bump into."

"Indeed I do not." His eyes twinkled with amusement. "My dear, Miss Townsend," he cleared his throat and met her gaze. "Would you do me the great honor of becoming my wife?"

His eyes were the darkest shade of green, cool and inviting like the depths of an endless garden pool and for the briefest fraction of a moment, Gwen wanted nothing more than to fall into the promise they offered. Nothing more than to stare into those eyes forever. An odd fluttering settled in her stomach, as unsettling as the feel of his warm fingers wrapped around hers.

"Thank you." She drew a deep breath and pulled her hands from his. "But I must regretfully decline."

Don't Miss Any of the Fun and Sexy Novels from Avon Trade Paperback

Listen to
New York Times Bestselling Author
SUSAN ELIZABETH PHILLIPS

Breathing Room
ISBN: 0-06-009259-9
$25.95/$38.95 Can.
6 hours/4 cassettes
Performed by Kate Forbes

Also available in a LargePrint edition
ISBN: 0-06-009391-9
$24.95/$37.95 Can.

This Heart of Mine
ISBN: 0-694-52493-X
$25.00/$37.50 Can.
6 hours/4 cassettes
Performed by Jennifer Van Dyck

Also available in a LargePrint edition
ISBN: 0-06-018803-0
$24.00/$36.50 Can.

Available wherever books are sold or call 1-800-331-3761 to order.

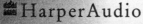

HarperAudio
An Imprint of HarperCollins*Publishers*
www.harpercollins.com

Harper
LARGE
PRINT
Edition

SPA 1002